"Why'd you kiss me?"

The simple question took him by surprise. In all his life, he didn't think a woman had ever asked him that question.

He had to think. He knew he could give her the glib answer, say something like "Because I wanted to." Which he had. But he figured he owed it to Ellie to give her the truth.

"When I saw him knock you to the ground, my heart stopped," he answered quietly. "I jumped him. If not for my damn injuries, I would have had him. You would have been safe and that piece of trash wouldn't have bothered you ever again. My blood was pumping, he got away and I let you down. When I saw you watching me, you looked scared and disappointed and..."

He dragged his hand through his too-short hair. "I wish I was better with words. I'm not saying it right."

A SECRET COLTON BABY & HER COLTON P.I.

KAREN WHIDDON
AMELIA AUTIN

HARLEQUIN® ROMANTIC SUSPENSE

ISBN-13: 978-1-335-08160-5

A Secret Colton Baby & Her Colton P.I.

Recycling programs for this product may not exist in your area.

Special thanks and acknowledgment are given to Karen Whiddon for her contribution to the Coltons: Return to Wyoming miniseries.

Special thanks and acknowledgment are given to Amelia Autin Lam for her contribution to the Coltons of Texas miniseries.

This edition published by arrangement with Harlequin Books S.A.

For questions and comments about the quality of this book, please contact us at CustomerService@Harlequin.com.

Printed in U.S.A.

CONTENTS

Karen Whiddon started weaving fanciful tales for her younger brothers at the age of eleven. Amid the gorgeous Catskill Mountains, then the majestic Rocky Mountains, she fueled her imagination with the natural beauty surrounding her. Karen now lives in north Texas, writes full-time and volunteers for a boxer dog rescue. She shares her life with her hero of a husband and four to five dogs, depending on if she is fostering. You can email Karen at kwhiddon1@aol.com. Fans can also check out her website, karenwhiddon.com.

Books by Karen Whiddon

Harlequin Romantic Suspense

The Rancher's Return
The Texan's Return
Wyoming Undercover
The Texas Soldier's Son
Texas Ranch Justice

The Coltons of Red Ridge

Colton's Christmas Cop

The Coltons of Texas

Runaway Colton

The Coltons of Oklahoma

The Temptation of Dr. Colton

The Coltons: Return to Wyoming

A Secret Colton Baby

Visit the Author Profile page at Harlequin.com for more titles.

A SECRET COLTON BABY

Karen Whiddon

As always, to my supportive husband.
He reads every book once it comes out
and has been wonderful about letting me
live my dream of being a full-time writer.

Chapter 1

A whisper of sound, so fragile it might have been only a fragment left over from a dream. Another woman might have burrowed back under the blankets, refusing to open her eyes as she willed herself back to sleep. Not Ellie Parker. Not only had the infant recently entrusted to her care awakened every protective instinct she possessed, but her past had made her overly wary.

The noise came again, an echo of a ghost. Heart pounding, she held herself utterly still while waiting for her eyes to adjust to the darkness. Luckily, the full moon brought traces of silver to light the room.

There. Near Amelia's antique crib that had been hastily brought down from the attic. A figure in black, wearing a hoody and a ski mask, reaching for the baby.

Leaping to her feet, Ellie screamed. Loud and shrill. The intruder froze, then ran for the window, yanking it open and racing away.

Baby Amelia began to wail, and Ellie rushed to her on shaky legs, trying to catch her breath.

"What is it? What's going on?" Theo Colton's deep voice, throaty from sleep and full of concern. He flicked on the light switch.

"A man," Ellie gasped, pointing past where he stood, his broad-shouldered body filling the doorway. "Dressed in black, wearing a ski mask. He was trying to take Amelia."

And then the trembling started. She couldn't help it, despite the tiny infant she clutched close to her chest. Somehow Theo seemed to sense this, as he gently took her arm and steered her toward her bed.

"Sit," he ordered, taking the baby from her.

Reluctantly releasing Amelia, Ellie covered her face with her hands. It had been a strange day, ever since the baby's mother—a beautiful, elegant woman named Mimi Rand—had shown up that morning insisting Theo was the father and then collapsing. Mimi had been taken to the Dead River Clinic with a high fever and flu-like symptoms. Theo had Ellie looking after Amelia until everything could be sorted out.

But Theo had no way of knowing about Ellie's past, or the danger that seemed to follow her like a malicious shadow. "I need to leave," she said to him. "Right now, for Amelia's sake."

Theo stared at her, holding Amelia to his shoulder and bouncing her gently, so that her sobs died away to whimpers and then silence. The sight of the big cowboy and the tiny baby struck a kernel of warmth in Ellie's frozen heart.

"Leave?" Theo asked. "You just started work here a week ago. If it's because I asked you to take care of this baby until her mama recovers, I'll double your pay."

"It's not about the money." Though she could certainly use every penny she could earn. "I...I thought I was safe here. Clearly, that's not the case."

He frowned. "I can assure you..." Stopping, he handed her back the baby, holding her as gingerly as fragile china. Once Ellie had the now-sleeping Amelia, Theo began walking around her room. "How about I check everything out? Is anything missing?"

Helpless to answer, since he obviously didn't understand, she managed a shaky shrug, gently patting Amelia's back. "I don't think he was here for possessions, which I have very few of anyway. He was definitely after Amelia."

"He?" Theo swung around to face her, his stance emphasizing the force of his muscular body. "Are you sure the intruder was a man?"

"Yes." Despite the baby's heat, she couldn't seem to get warm. "Who would try to kidnap a baby, especially with her mother gravely ill?"

"Maybe it just looked that way." He continued checking the room. "Nothing appears disturbed. Any idea how he got in?"

"No. He ran out the doorway into the hall when I screamed." For the first time she realized Theo was nearly naked, wearing only some sort of pajama bottoms low on his narrow hips. His bare chest gleamed. Trying not to stare and failing miserably, she felt her mouth going dry. For one brief second, she allowed the sight of him—so big, so masculine—to make her feel safe.

And then Theo went into her bathroom. He cursed, and she knew. Her stalker had somehow found her.

Pushing to her feet, she placed the sleeping baby carefully back in her crib and hurried over. Theo appeared tense, a muscle working in his jaw. "This seems to be directed to you," he said, pointing. *The only baby you'll be taking care of is OURS* had been written on the mirror with black marker.

Her knees again nearly gave out. She felt as if she'd been punched in the stomach. "That settles it. I have to go."

"No." He reached out and steadied her. "No, you don't. You're safe here, Ellie. I can help you, protect you. But you need to tell me what's going on."

Despite the fact that she knew sexy Theo Colton couldn't be her knight in shining armor, she took a deep breath. "A couple of weeks ago, I left my home in Boulder, Colorado, because I had a stalker. He seemed to find me everywhere I went, leaving me black roses."

"*Black* roses?"

She nodded. "I don't know why. He also left notes that said things like *No one will ever love you like I do* and *One day you'll be mine forever.*"

"Did you go to the police?"

"Yes, but they said they couldn't do anything unless he threatened me. None of the notes said anything about him wanting to harm me. I couldn't get a restraining order or anything."

He gave her a long look, his green eyes unfathomable. "Yet you felt threatened."

"Yes. Wouldn't you?"

"Do you have any idea who he is?"

"No." She blinked. "And believe me, I tried to find out. I had friends hide and watch me to see if I was followed. No one ever saw him. The note and the roses would appear. So finally I couldn't take it anymore. I left everything in my apartment, packed a small bag and took off. I didn't tell anyone anything, just got in my car and drove."

"You must have been followed."

"I don't know how," she cried. "Honestly, I was very, very careful. When I left Boulder, I drove to Fort Collins, then Laramie, before I headed to Cheyenne. I stayed in Cheyenne for a couple of days before I saw your ad for a live-in cook. My car barely made it here before it died." And as soon as she had the money, she planned to get it fixed.

He nodded. "Don't worry. I'll take care of this." Picking up the phone on her nightstand, he punched in some numbers. "Hey, Flint," he drawled. "Sorry to wake you so early on a Sunday morning, but I need you to come over." Briefly he relayed what had happened before replacing the phone in its cradle.

"You've probably heard that my brother is the police chief in Dead River. He's on his way."

Heart in her throat, she nodded. Despite the fact that police apparently didn't take this kind of thing seriously, maybe the fact that the police chief was a relative of Theo's would help.

If he couldn't, then she was out of here come sunrise, even if she had to take a bus. No way did she want to bring her personal dark cloud down on this family, who'd taken a chance on an out-of-towner with few references. Though Theo hadn't known it, giving Ellie this job had likely saved her life. No way did she want any of them hurt because of her, especially not such a sweet and innocent baby.

Theo stayed with her while they waited for his brother to arrive, leaving her only long enough to go put on a shirt.

Flint arrived a few minutes later. Like Theo, he was tall and muscular, with the same dark hair and striking green eyes. He appeared drained, but that might only have been due to Theo's call waking him in the middle of the night.

"I was on my way over here anyway," he said, a shadow crossing his face. "I just got word from Gemma at the clinic. Mimi Rand passed away a little while ago."

Both Theo and Ellie gaped at him. Theo was the first to speak. "What was wrong with her?"

"Cause of death hasn't been determined yet." Flint shrugged, his expression weary. "She had a high fever and flu-like symptoms. That's all I know."

Ellie glanced at Theo, watching for signs of grief. After all, if the ranch gossip was to be believed and Amelia was his daughter, then that meant the mother of his child had just died.

While he appeared a bit disconcerted, nothing more, she realized that might be because he wasn't the type of man to show his emotions on his sleeve. She then looked at Amelia, still sleeping soundly, her heart squeezing in her chest. "That poor motherless baby. What's going to become of her now?"

For the first time, Theo seemed uncomfortable. He shifted his weight and tugged at the collar of his shirt, before clearing his throat. "We need to get her checked out to make sure she's not sick like her mother. Mimi's ex-husband is a doctor at the clinic. Our sister, Gemma, works with him. I need to talk to him about all this. We'll work something out."

"Yes," Flint said grimly. "We certainly will."

Ellie got the distinct impression from the way the two brothers exchanged glances that they were saying without words that family stuck together, no matter what. A sharp pang of longing ripped through her, which she quickly pushed away. She'd realized years ago what her parents were and weren't capable of, and being a family wasn't one of those things.

"Now, what occurred here?" Flint asked. "Theo says you had some kind of break-in?"

She nodded. "Yes. I'm pretty sure the intruder was here because of me. For some reason, he wanted to take or hurt the baby to get at me."

Cocking his head, Flint frowned. "Why would you think that?"

Pointing with a shaky finger toward the bathroom, she swallowed hard. "Because he left me a message."

Flint hurried off to check it out. She and Theo waited. A second later, she heard the click and whirr of a camera. When he returned, his expression had gone grim. "What exactly is going on?"

Theo filled him in on Ellie's past, as well as details about what had just happened. Ellie tried like heck not to squirm as both men studied her with identical sharp gazes.

"Tell me exactly what you saw," Flint told her, his serious voice stern but compassionate.

"I'm afraid I can't help much." She wished she could stop shaking or at least get warm. The chill seemed to have snaked into the marrow of her bones. "Even back in Colorado, I've never known my stalker's identity. I've never even seen him."

"You did tonight," Theo reminded her, his gruff voice gentle.

"Not really. It was dark and I couldn't get a good look at his face. Even if I'd managed to turn on a light before he fled, I'm pretty sure he wore a ski mask."

Flint nodded. "Anything else you can tell me about him?"

She thought for a moment. "He was tall and lanky,

but I can't tell you much more than that. It all happened so fast."

Her words came out sounding a little more forlorn than she'd intended. To her surprise, Theo put his big hand on her shoulder and squeezed, offering reassurance. She instinctively leaned into his touch, and when she realized what she'd done, she stiffened and moved away.

Meanwhile, baby Amelia slept on, undisturbed.

"We'll try to find him," Flint said. "Theo, you might look into investing in some sort of home alarm."

"I will," Theo promised.

"Good." Glancing at his watch, Flint put his notepad and pen back in his pocket. "Now I suggest you both get some sleep. We'll talk again after the sun comes up and we're all more rested."

After escorting his brother to the door, Theo returned to Ellie's room to check on her and the baby. Seeing Ellie so terrified and defenseless had awakened every protective instinct he possessed. He'd be lying to himself if he claimed he hadn't noticed how lovely she was, especially since he'd hired her personally. He enjoyed women, especially beautiful ones, and just because that damn rodeo accident had sidelined him didn't mean he had to give up that.

He'd actually figured she'd be a nice diversion while he was stuck here at the ranch. But Ellie Parker surprised him. She'd only been here one week, but when she wasn't working in the kitchen, she might as well be a ghost. Her willowy, athletic good looks had attracted the attention of several of the ranch hands, and Theo had listened to them complain about how she kept to herself. As if she wanted to be invisible.

Which was oddly ironic, because Theo was used to

living life in the spotlight, all the attention on him. One damn crazy-ass bronc and he was off the circuit, his season over for the first time since he'd made it into the Professional Rodeo Cowboy Association and started competing with the big boys. He'd loved the rough competition, the mean, hard-bucking broncs and the hefty payout. For the past three years, he'd ranked in the top twenty of the bareback bronc riders and been steadily climbing. This past year had been his best. This year, the PRCA Bareback Riding World Championship had been within reach.

He wanted that title so bad he could taste it. The pinnacle of his career, the real moneymaker. He'd lusted after that ever since he climbed on his first bronc. And he was damn good at it. He had a knack for knowing beforehand which way the animal was going to buck and spin. He'd figured out how to make his eight seconds count.

The money had been flowing in. After all, it was July, with rodeos with such huge payouts they called it the Cowboy's Christmas. There were plenty to choose from. With an eye on the World, he'd chosen to compete in the ones with the biggest payouts since his placement in the standings depended entirely on total money won.

And he couldn't seem to stop winning. Every day, he called PROCOM, the PRCA's computerized system, and got his numbers. As his standings continued to improve, he supposed in retrospect, he'd gotten cocky. So when he'd drawn the one horse no one had ever been able to beat, a beast known by the cowboys as one of the toughest broncs around, a National Finals horse, it had never occurred to him not to try. After all, he was unstoppable.

The instant they'd exploded from the chute, he realized this bronc wasn't like the others. Something was scrambled in his equine brain. After the first crazy sideways leap, Theo remembered nothing until he'd woken up in a hospital bed.

Even in an occupation where injuries are common, everyone had been concerned. They'd told him he was lucky he wasn't dead. At his lowest moments, he wasn't too sure about that. He'd lived for the circuit, spent his time traveling from region to region, pulling his camper behind his pickup. Now he had nothing to live for, not really. Injured, he couldn't ride, and if he couldn't ride, he couldn't win. Injured, he was nothing, his standings slipping with every rodeo he missed.

He'd retreated to his family's ranch to recuperate and lick his wounds. Luckily, due to Slim George, the ranch foreman who'd been in charge since Theo'd been a small boy, the place ran smoothly.

Which was great, since Theo wouldn't have been much help. After his head injury had left him unconscious—they'd used the word *coma*—for weeks, he'd had a long, slow recuperation. Not just his head, but he'd come within a hair of being paralyzed and the discs in his back were fragile enough that he'd have to be careful the rest of his life.

The doctors had said he'd never ride again, never mind compete. He'd told them all to go to hell and checked himself out of the hospital in Cheyenne as soon as he could, despite his broken ribs and bum knee. Flint had picked him up, sharing some grim news. One of Theo's competitors, a cowboy named Hal Diggins who'd had a cold streak for several months, had injected the bronc with some kind of amphetamine to make it go crazy. Hal had been arrested, and, despite Theo's protests, Flint had moved back to Dead River to help take care of Theo while he recuperated. Later, Theo had learned Flint had wanted to get out of Cheyenne and heal his own wounds.

Despite Theo asking, Flint refused to elaborate on what they might be.

A good and honest cop, Flint had quickly risen through the ranks in the small Dead River Police Department, becoming chief of police and replacing Harry Peters, who'd left to take care of his terminally ill mother in Denver.

It also helped that their sister, Gemma, was a nurse at the clinic. She'd kept Theo on the straight and narrow, made sure he did his physical therapy exercises and took his supplements.

To all outward appearances, Theo had made a full recovery. He could walk and talk, but not ride. No one knew that a huge chunk of him had gone missing, stomped in the sawdust under that last bronc's hooves. His ribs and knee had healed, as had his concussion. But his back would forever be damaged, and he couldn't take a chance hurting it.

Since he had no choice but to try to make the best of it, he threw himself into helping out around the ranch. Only to learn that he sure as hell wasn't needed around here. The place ran like clockwork without him. Any time he tried to get involved in one of the operations, he pretty much just got in the way. Slim George had taken pity on Theo and asked him to take over the hiring, especially since the ranch cook had quit and they needed to find a new one as soon as possible.

Theo had done so gladly, setting up multiple interviews and planning to find a new cook within days. The instant he saw Ellie, with her innocent eyes and her sensual mouth, he'd known he'd like having her around. Hell, maybe in more ways than one.

As long as she understood he couldn't be serious. He enjoyed women's bodies, and dedicated himself to pleasuring them with as much zeal as he applied to the rodeo.

Women he spent time with knew up front what they were getting. A few laughs and a damn good time. They always left satisfied. No one ever got hurt, at least as far as he knew.

The situation with Mimi Rand had come as a complete shock. Theo had known she still shared intimacy with her ex-husband, Dr. Rand. She'd sought Theo out after a particularly spectacular win in Cheyenne. They'd had a couple of drinks and a night of fun.

In the morning when he'd woken, she was already gone.

He had to confess he hadn't paid much attention to what she did after that. Instead he'd done what he always did, focus on the rodeo.

And then he'd been hurt, come home to recuperate, and bam—Mimi showed up at his door with an infant, claiming he was the father. He'd been flabbergasted, asked her point-blank how she knew and instead of answering, she'd gotten a funny look on her face and collapsed.

Leaving him with a newborn and no idea what to do.

Now she was dead. And he figured since her ex had an equal chance of being the baby's father, Dr. Lucas Rand needed an equal opportunity to care for Amelia.

Back in his own room, Theo clicked off the light and tried to sleep. But, just as it once had the night before a big rodeo, his mind kept whirring.

Somehow he must have fallen asleep. He woke to the ringing of his phone. Judging from the wealth of sunlight streaming in from behind his window blinds, it was probably mid to late morning. He squinted, trying to read the caller ID, then gave up and answered.

"Hello," he rasped.

"Theo, you need to call Gemma. She's at work at the

clinic. She's been there all night, ever since Mimi Rand died." The urgency in Flint's low voice had Theo sitting up straight. His brother was normally the most nondramatic person he knew.

"Why? What's going on? Is she all right?"

"Yes." Flint exhaled. "But more people are ill. And it's not the flu. The CDC is involved. It's some kind of virus, a strain no one recognizes." He started to say something more, but someone else spoke to Flint, interrupting him. "I've got to go," he said to Theo. "Call Gemma. She can fill you in."

Immediately after hanging up, Theo dialed his sister's cell. Sounding harried and stressed, she answered, clearly keeping her voice pitched low and speaking quietly so no one else could hear.

"Is this a bad time?" he asked.

"Right now any time is a bad time. We've got old Mr. Thomas here, sick with the same type of thing that Mimi Rand had. His family is freaking out, worried he's going to die. And two children just came in." She took a deep breath. "The waiting room is packed and the phones have been ringing off the hook. People are getting paranoid. It's bad, Theo. Really bad."

"Flint said something about the CDC."

"Yes. Dr. Rand is working with them right now, despite being pretty broken up about losing his ex-wife. I think he still cared for her."

"Yeah." Theo scratched his chin. "I need to talk to him about that. You know she claims this baby is mine."

"So I've heard. Theo, everyone in town was talking about that before people started getting sick. Apparently she told more than one person."

"I barely knew her," he began.

Gemma cut him off. "I don't have time right now," she

said. "You and anyone who came in contact with Mimi Rand need to get checked out. And you especially need to get that baby examined. Something like this would be deadly to an infant."

"I will," he said, but she'd already ended the call.

Pushing himself up out of bed, he felt a flutter of worry in his chest. But he'd never been one to look for problems before they arose. Damned if he'd start now.

Twenty minutes later, having showered and dressed, he made his way down the hall toward Ellie's room. Halfway there, he heard the sound of the baby—Amelia, he reminded himself—wailing.

He increased his speed. Two steps in and the sound stopped. Did babies do that? Frowning, he pushed the bedroom door open, only to see Ellie gently rocking Amelia back and forth.

"Morning." She flashed a tired smile. "She's been kind of restless. She had a bottle an hour ago, but I've used the last can of formula that her mother had in the diaper bag she left, and we're almost out of diapers."

"I'll drive to the store," he promised. With a nod, she turned her attention back to the baby. Even with dark circles under her eyes and her hair a mess, she managed to still look beautiful.

"Have you had breakfast?"

She bit her lip. "No. Neither has anyone else. I overslept and I haven't had time to make it into the kitchen and cook anything, so you probably have a bunch of hungry ranch hands."

He realized he'd need to find either a new cook or a nanny, at least until this thing was resolved. "I'm sure they understand," he lied. "I'll get in there and take care of their morning meal. Heck, I'll tell them it's brunch, since it's nearly lunchtime. They'll survive. And I want you to make sure to get yourself a plate."

A shadow crossed her blue eyes. "I'm sorry. It's just with everything that happened and taking care of the baby—"

"No need to apologize. After I fix breakfast, I'm going into town to talk to Mimi's ex-husband, Dr. Rand. If you'll write down for me what kind I need, I'll be sure to pick up formula and diapers while I'm there."

She nodded, gazing at the tiny infant in her arms. "What do you think is going to happen to her?"

At her question, he dragged his hand across his mouth. "That's what I want to talk to Lucas Rand about."

The rest of the morning flew by swiftly. Still carrying Amelia, Ellie followed him down to the kitchen and directed him in the nuances of preparing the morning meal for six hungry cowboys. She couldn't help but wonder how he managed to look rugged and sexy, even in this setting.

He used two dozen eggs, an entire loaf of bread and two huge slabs of thick-cut bacon. A jug of milk, a huge carafe of fresh, hot coffee and another jug of orange juice completed the setup.

"I usually make them biscuits and gravy too." She sounded apologetic again.

"They'll just have to make do," he said, shaking his head. "Extraordinary circumstances."

Nodding, she crossed to the exterior door and pulled the bell cord, sending the brass bell that hung outside chiming.

Almost immediately after, Theo's hands began filing into the kitchen. A few of them appeared surprised to see their boss there, but once they spotted the food set out on the long wooden table in the adjoining room, they shrugged, grabbed a plate and dug in. If they wondered why the food was so late in coming, no one said anything.

Theo had saved back some of the eggs, bacon and bread and made Ellie and himself a plate. He indicated one of the chairs at the smaller kitchen table and slid her breakfast over to her.

She climbed up, carefully holding Amelia, and once settled, eyed the plate, making no move to pick up a fork.

With a flush of embarrassment, he realized she didn't know how to eat while holding the baby.

"Here. Put her in the bassinette while you eat."

"No." She angled the baby away from him, her chin up, her blue eyes flashing. "You eat first, and when you're finished, you can hold her and I'll have my turn."

For a second, he froze, dumbfounded at the idea of holding such a miniscule little girl in front of everyone. He could do this, he told himself. Surely a man unafraid to climb on the backs of wildest horses wouldn't be undone by an infant. Plus, he'd already held her the night before, though he'd acted solely on instinct.

"Sure," he said, trying for easily.

Ellie rewarded him with a smile that sent his pulse racing. Stunned, he wondered if she knew how adorable she looked. Since she seemed determined, he didn't argue, even though he still felt seriously uncomfortable holding an infant. Instead he started shoveling the food into his mouth, barely pausing for air.

Once he'd cleared his plate, he drained his glass of juice, took a quick gulp of coffee and then held out his arms for the baby, hoping he appeared nonchalant. "Your turn."

One corner of her mouth quirked as she stared at him. "Even they—" indicating the men at the table behind them, who were all intently chowing down "—don't eat that fast."

"I was hungry," he replied, grinning. "Now hand me that baby and eat your food before it gets cold."

Shaking her head, she handed Amelia over, transferring her gently. "Make sure you support her head."

"Yes, ma'am." Once he had her, he gazed down into her tiny sleeping face. She smelled good, like baby powder and milk, and appeared healthy, at least to him. Though fragile. Which made him sort of afraid to move.

"That reminds me," he told Ellie. "There are more people sick with whatever Mimi had. We need to get Amelia checked out."

Fork in midair, Ellie froze. "I didn't think of that." Expression dismayed, she put down her fork. "I don't want her going to the clinic if there are other sick people there. You said Mimi's ex is a doctor. Do you think he'd be willing to check her out here?"

Pleased her concern was for the baby rather than herself, he nodded. "I'll bring that up when I talk to him today. If not, my sister is a nurse and can do it."

He took a deep breath, hating what he had to say next, but knowing it was necessary. "Listen, Ellie, don't go getting too attached. There's a possibility Amelia might not be here too long."

Her eyes widened. Her voice rose. "What do you mean? You can't be considering giving up your own flesh and blood."

The men at the other table stopped talking and turned to stare at them from the other room. Theo grimaced. "There's a very real possibility she's not mine," he said gently. "Mimi was… Well, let's say she wasn't exclusive."

Her downcast look told him she didn't like what she was hearing. "She has your eyes," she said.

"Yes, but green eyes aren't proof of anything."

"I understand," she replied, clearly lying. "Let me have Amelia back, please."

"You haven't eaten yet."

Taking the baby from him, she nodded. "I've lost my appetite."

No one spoke as she marched out of the room.

Once she was gone, Theo's hands all looked at him. Even from the other room, he could feel their disapproval.

He shrugged. "Come on, guys." Giving their empty plates a look, he pointed toward the door. "Time to get back to work."

Though not a single man argued with him, he could tell from a few of their expressions—belligerent, questioning and yes, disappointed—that they wanted to. He hated that they thought he was acting like a jerk—honestly, he wasn't. But this was his life, and it wasn't up for debate.

If baby Amelia belonged to him, Theo would move heaven and earth to ensure that she wanted for nothing. However, if Lucas Rand was actually her father, then Amelia needed to be with her daddy. He didn't need to explain that to anyone.

Chapter 2

The drive into town felt as if it took longer than usual. He figured he'd pick up the diapers and formula after he had a word with Dr. Rand.

Dead River looked like a ghost town. Probably because it was Sunday, and most folks were either at church or home with their families. Main Street, usually pretty busy about this time of day while the stores were open, had tons of empty parking spots and only a few people on the sidewalks. But when he turned the corner onto Third and spotted the clinic's overflowing parking lot, he couldn't believe it. Usually, the clinic was closed on Sundays, except for emergencies.

Gemma hadn't been exaggerating. He ended up parking in the street.

As he approached the glass front door of the one-story, white cinder block building, he nearly stopped short as he saw the mass of people milling around in the waiting area. Surely not all of these people had come down with the virus.

Pushing inside, he stopped, checking everything out. No one looked feverish, or was coughing, sneezing or exhibiting any other flu-like symptoms. As far as he could tell, none of these people actually appeared sick.

His suspicion was confirmed when Cathleen Walker, who worked the intake desk, grabbed his arm. As usual, her clothes looked a bit rumpled, as though she hadn't had time to press them. "Theo, are you okay?"

He nodded. "What's up with them?"

"They want a shot." She grimaced, slipping one foot out of the high heels she continually wore to work and stretching it, before sliding it back into her shoe. "Not a flu shot either—most everybody has already had that. I don't know why, but someone heard we had received an inoculation against whatever killed Mimi Rand and got the others sick."

"And you don't even know what it was, do you?"

"No. But none of these people will leave." She heaved a frustrated sigh. "More and more keep showing up. I've told them, Dr. Moore has told them and even Dr. Granger."

"What about Dr. Rand?"

Her expression changed, softening. "He's in the back, writing up a report on the latest people to fall ill. The poor man is grief-stricken over losing Mimi. He acts like it's his fault he couldn't save her."

"I need to talk to him." Again he glanced at the packed waiting room. "People," he said, raising his voice. "If you're sick, please raise your hand."

Not one hand went up. Exactly as he'd suspected. "Everyone else, go on home. You don't want to risk being exposed to whatever this virus is." He glanced around, picking out individuals among the crowd and meeting their eyes. “Do you understand what I’m saying? If you’re healthy, not only are you using resources that could better be directed toward helping those that are sick, but just being here puts you in very serious danger of becoming infected.”

At his words people began exchanging glances, some chastised, others suspicious, a few even hostile. One or two hurried toward the door, and then a couple more followed. Pretty soon, it became apparent the place was going to rapidly empty out.

“Oh, thank you.” Cathleen sagged against her desk, clearly relieved. “Dr. Granger has been saying if too many more get sick, we’re going to have to set up an isolation area and keep the virus victims separated from everyone else.”

Which made sense, since the clinic was the main place for medical care in Dead River.

“Come on,” Cathleen said, giving him a tired smile and finger-combing her slightly mussed blond hair. “I’ll take you back to see Dr. Rand.”

He followed behind, her high heels clicking on the linoleum. They went past the reception area to where the older patient-records were stored in manila folders. For years, Gemma had claimed Dead River Clinic wanted to go entirely electronic. Apparently they had not yet completed the task of doing so.

“Here we are.” Once again all professional, Cathleen stopped and pointed toward one of the offices. A brown and gold nameplate on the door stated it belonged to Dr. Lucas Rand.

“Thanks.” He lightly squeezed her shoulder, making her blush, which sort of surprised him since they’d known each other from the fifth grade.

Moving forward, he peered into the small office. Dr. Rand spoke into a handheld dictation device. His usually perfect dark hair looked as if he'd been dragging his fingers repeatedly through it.

Theo knocked lightly on the door.

The doctor looked up, his dark eyes full of pain. He clicked off his machine and stood, holding out his hand. "Theo."

Theo shook his hand, trying to figure out the best way to word what he had to say. Finally, he decided the hell with it. He'd talk to Dr. Rand man-to-man.

"About Mimi," he began.

"I can't believe she's dead."

"Me, either." Theo dug his hands down into his pockets and resisted the urge to shift from foot to foot. "I'm guessing you know she had a baby?"

The other man nodded. "Of course. When she first got pregnant, I wrote her script for prenatal vitamins." He choked up, averting his face and swallowing hard as he tried to get himself under control. "I can't believe she's gone."

"I'm sorry."

Dr. Rand sighed. "I tried my best to save her. I couldn't. I let her down. And now her newborn child is motherless."

"About that." Theo tried to figure out the best way to say it, and then decided to just blurt it out. "Is the baby—Amelia—yours?"

Dr. Rand stared at him, his expression a mix of surprise and horror. "Good Lord, no. Mimi and I haven't been together like that in at least a year." He blinked and peered at Theo the same way a scientist might inspect a particularly interesting petri dish full of bacteria. "Um, Theo? I don't know what you're getting at, but it's my understanding that Amelia is your daughter." He flushed and looked away. "At least that's what Mimi told me. And she had no reason to lie."

Mine. For a split second, it seemed to Theo everything tilted sideways. The room suddenly felt too warm. Treading carefully, as it was common knowledge that Dr. Rand had still cared for his ex-wife, Theo cleared his throat.

"Look, Dr. Rand—"

"Call me Lucas."

Theo nodded. "Okay. Lucas. This is awkward, but Mimi never contacted me about being pregnant. I would have helped her."

"I took care of that. I've been paying spousal support anyway, so I just added to it. I don't think she ever intended you to find out, at first. Clearly, she changed her mind."

"That doesn't make sense." Frowning, Theo couldn't make sense of any of this. "Besides, she and I were only together a couple of times. I sincerely doubt that I could be Amelia's father."

Some dark emotion flashed across Lucas's face, before he looked down. When he raised his head to meet Theo's gaze, he expression was calm. "One time is all it takes. You know that."

Theo found himself at a loss for words.

"Look, Theo." Lucas gripped his shoulder. "I've always thought you were a good guy. And little Amelia is a Colton. You should be raising her. Obviously, since Mimi came to you when she realized she was ill, that was her last wish for her baby girl. Amelia needs to be with her family. I work all the time, here at the clinic. I have nothing to offer her, while you…you have a rich heritage, a large family and plenty of support."

Put that way, Theo knew Lucas was right. But how

could Theo be a father? He had no idea how. His own father had been an abusive drunk, who'd only shown up when he needed something and stayed just long enough to break his young children's hearts.

His father's mother—Grandma Dottie—had raised all three of them, and Flint, Theo and Gemma worshipped the ground she walked on. Maybe she could help, Theo thought. Or at the very least, explain to him how a good father should act.

Still rattled, he nodded and turned to go. Lucas tightened his grip on Theo's shoulder, stopping him.

"Theo, I swear I will find the medicine to treat this thing," Lucas vowed. "Or a cure, if it comes to that. In the meantime, have Gemma check you out. I want you to bring Amelia by immediately if she starts showing any flu-like symptoms. Same with you or anyone in your house. We need to treat early, before symptoms become life-threatening."

The other man's choice of words worried Theo. "You talk like this is some new kind of disease."

"It might be." Lucas appeared to be choosing what he said carefully. "I'm doing everything I can to figure it out."

"You're a good man, Dr. Lucas Rand." Theo moved away. "I'll go have a word with Gemma now."

"She's in the back with the sick children." Lucas frowned. "I don't want you going back there. It's not safe."

"Then why is my sister there?" Theo asked sharply.

"She's taking the proper precautions—she has on a mask and gloves. Let me page her and see if she has time to come out."

Theo waited while Lucas did that. After a moment,

Lucas's cell phone rang. He answered, spoke a few words and hung up.

"She said she'll call you later, once her shift is over." A sudden weariness appeared to settle over the doctor. "Thanks for stopping by, Theo. You know the way out, right? I need to get back to work."

Summarily dismissed, Theo took his leave. When he reached the front desk, he saw the waiting room had once again begun to fill up.

This time, he simply made his way to the door. He had a lot to think about, but most important, he needed to pick up formula and diapers.

Once that was done, he headed home.

On the drive there, he called his grandmother Dottie. If he remembered her schedule right, she should be home from church by now. Though she was seventy-five years old, she played canasta with several other widowed women once a week. She'd never remarried, but she kept busy. She ate lunch out with her church friends on Wednesday, and then went to Bible study that night. Church on Sunday, a reading group on another day—he couldn't keep up with her schedule.

The phone rang six times before she picked up. "You're there," he said, relieved. "I thought I missed you and was about to disconnect the call. How are you, Gram?"

"Not too good," she answered, surprising him. "I think I might be coming down with something."

He felt a flash of alarm. "Promise me you'll go to the clinic and get it checked out."

"It'll probably pass." She didn't sound too worried. "If not, I'll have Gemma check me out. If she thinks I need to see a doctor, I will."

Relieved, he asked her if she was sitting down.

She laughed, or attempted to. Instead she made a sound that turned into a hacking cough.

Instantly alarmed, Theo felt his stomach twist as he remembered what Gemma had told him earlier. He told Gram she needed to go to the clinic immediately and get checked out.

"Don't be silly," she replied, after she regained her voice. Even over the phone, Theo could tell she wasn't well. "It's just a cold," she continued. "Nothing to stress about."

"Gram, please. I've got enough on my plate. Don't add having to worry about you to my list." He knew making it be about him was the only way she'd consider doing something for herself. That was his gram Dottie. Always doing for others.

"What do you have on your plate?" she asked, instantly concerned. Of course. He chastised himself. She'd immediately pick up on that.

"A woman named Mimi Rand showed up on my doorstep yesterday morning with an infant. She claimed the baby girl is mine. And then she collapsed." He swallowed hard, almost afraid to tell her the rest. "She was rushed to Dead River Clinic, but she passed away last night. She had a virus. That's why I'm so worried about you. It starts out a lot like the flu. Fever, chills, body aches. A cough, sore throat, maybe even vomiting or diarrhea. Do you have any of those?"

"No."

"I still want you to get checked out. I love you too much to lose you."

"Fine." She sounded grumpy, though touched too. She knew Theo as well as he knew her. "I'll try to go tomorrow. If I start feeling worse, I'll call Gemma and ask her to stop by and check on me."

"Perfect."

"Now, Theo, tell me the truth. I know—knew—Mimi Rand. She was well dressed and well mannered and acted as if she was used to the finer things in life. Probably because she was Dr. Rand's ex-wife. I can't imagine..." She took a deep breath. "Dead?"

"Yes. And Gemma says no one knows what it is exactly that killed her."

Silence while she digested this. Then she cleared her throat and spoke. "Theo, tell me the truth. Is this baby really yours?" She sounded deeply disappointed, which still had the power to crush him.

"I don't know." He told her the truth. "But after talking to Dr. Rand today, it's appearing likely."

"Well, then." Disappointment gave way to her normal, brisk, take-charge attitude. "I'll do whatever I can to help. I wouldn't mind having a young'un to cuddle again. Once I get over this cold, I'll come by and meet... what is her name?"

"Amelia. She's really tiny."

"Amelia. I like it." She coughed again. "I can't wait to meet her."

He hung up, smiling although her cough still worried him. But she was a tough old lady and he figured she knew if she was seriously sick or not.

Ellie had always avoided cocky men who were full of themselves. A lot of cowboys were like that. But from what she'd seen of Theo Colton in the short time she'd been here at the ranch, while he had swagger, and the same rough-and-tumble sex appeal, he wasn't conceited or arrogant. There was a fine line between self-assurance and smug self-importance, and she thought Theo was merely confident and comfortable in his own body. She believed this despite the stories she'd heard the one night she ventured into town to have a drink at the Dead River Bar.

But this morning, hearing how he'd spoken of this precious little innocent baby—*his* baby—at that moment, she'd wondered if she'd been wrong about him after all.

Once he'd left to go to town, she realized he must be terrified. He'd been a big-time rodeo cowboy, a bareback bronc riding champion. She'd spent enough time around horses in her hometown of Boulder to know rodeo cowboys were footloose and fancy-free. They had to be, since they made their living driving from town to town, rodeo to rodeo.

She also knew women of all kinds flocked to them, the way groupies hung on to musicians. All kinds of women. Mimi Rand was proof of that, may she rest in peace.

Now Theo was dealing with the fallout. For him, just knowing that his injuries had cost him all that, everything he'd ever known, must have been bad enough. Now this—finding out he was a father. By a woman who, from what he'd said, he'd barely known.

Gazing at Amelia while she slept in the car seat she'd been brought here in that converted to a portable bassinette, Ellie thought she'd never seen a more darling baby. Wisps of curly dark hair framed her chubby-cheeked face. As she'd done several times over the past hour, Ellie lightly touched the infant's forehead, checking to make sure there were no signs of fever.

So far, so good. No sign of whatever mysterious illness had plagued her mother.

For some reason Ellie thought of her parents. She knew what they'd do in this situation. As lifelong evangelistic missionaries on the African continent, they'd elevated the act of prayer to a fine art. She only wished they'd devoted as much effort to being parents and making them all a family. She hadn't seen them in years, and even in her younger days, she'd stayed with a neighbor while they were off saving the world. They were too busy, too full of what they considered their life's work, to spend time raising a daughter.

Ellie had often wondered why they'd even had her. Most likely, she'd been an accident. Ah well, dwelling on the past never changed anything. And she no longer prayed, because she'd spent her entire childhood praying her parents would want her. When her prayers had gone unanswered through the years, she'd sworn never to pray again.

Even though they'd had a late breakfast, soon it would be lunchtime on the ranch. As the only cook, Ellie knew she had to come up with something to feed the hardworking, hungry ranch hands. Luckily, she'd started on a big pot of chili the day before, and all she had to do was place the large cooking pot on the stove and break out a couple of bags of Fritos and shredded cheddar cheese.

Relieved that she could do this and still take care of Amelia, she knew the evening meal might be more of a challenge. She needed to do prep work now. A couple of days ago, she'd moved four whole chickens to the fridge from the freezer. She could roast those and make a pot of pinto beans and a huge bowl of rice. Simple but efficient.

She gave the chili another stir with the wooden spoon and returned to gaze at the sleeping baby. Footsteps in the hallway made her turn, wondering if the crew had broken for lunch early.

Not the ranch hands. Instead Theo, gazing first at her and then the baby. Ellie's heart did a little stuttering dance as she stared at him. Broad shoulders, narrow waist, muscular arms. And that face, craggy and masculine, with that cute little bump on his nose where it had been broken. He was handsome and sexy, and so far out of her league it wasn't funny. Even knowing this, she couldn't keep from drinking him in with her eyes, even as she tried—and pretty much failed—to appear nonchalant.

"How's she doing?" he asked, his gaze on Amelia.

"Fine." She found a sudden need to turn away and stir the chili. "I've been watching her and there's no sign of a fever. I'm guessing she's not hungry yet since she's been asleep since you left. Did you bring the formula and diapers?"

"I did. They're on the counter." The edge of huskiness in his voice made her look at him. He was still staring at the baby, something very much like tenderness flashing in his amazing green eyes.

Chest tight, she turned back to the simmering pot. "Lunch is almost ready. The ranch hands should be here any moment."

"I told you that you didn't have to cook since you're taking care of the baby."

"Then who would?" Her tone came out sharper than she'd intended. "If I don't, the hands won't have anything to eat."

"Thank you." He came to stand next to her, making every nerve in her body quiver. "I'm sorry. I thought I'd made it back in time to get the noon meal ready."

She didn't comment. It was eleven-thirty and the men ate at straight-up twelve.

When he touched her arm, she gave a little jump. Inhaling sharply, she took a step back from him, hoping if she put a little distance between them, she could regain her equilibrium. When she'd first applied for the job, she was so desperate for work, she'd barely noticed his rugged good looks. After all, she'd been nearly broke with nowhere to live but her car.

Now, almost a full week later, every time Theo came anywhere near her, she went weak in the knees and her entire body tingled.

Cleary, she needed to get over this.

"I've talked to my grandmother." He frowned. "I wanted to ask her to help with the baby, but she sounds like she's coming down with a cold."

"That's not good." Ellie kept her voice steady, a bit startled at the odd rush of possessiveness she felt at the thought of someone else taking care of Amelia. "Maybe it would be better to see if you can find someone else to cook, at least until your grandmother gets better. I don't mind."

He gave her a long look, his green eyes keenly observant. "We'll see. In the meantime, I'll help you with dinner," he said. "How about that?"

"Let's get through lunch first," she said. "If you don't mind, I'll get Amelia changed and fed. There are corn chips on the table, shredded cheese in the fridge and all they need to do is ladle the chili into their bowls."

He nodded. "I can handle that."

"Thank you." Moving briskly, she washed her hands and then grabbed one of the cans of formula and read the instructions, just to make sure.

Once everything was mixed up in one of the bottles, she warmed it slightly in the microwave and shook it to make sure the heat distributed evenly. She squeezed a drop on her wrist, something she thought she'd seen on TV. "Perfect."

More relieved than she'd care to admit, even to herself, she crossed over to where Amelia still slept. One quick glance at Theo, and the knot was back in the pit of her stomach. "I'll just take her upstairs and feed and change her."

"Sounds good." Theo glanced at the clock. "The less exposure she has to others, the better, at least until we get her checked out. I'm going to see if Gemma can come by tonight after work, though I might have her stop by Gram Dottie's first."

The worry and affection in his voice when he spoke of his grandmother warmed her. "Just let me know," she said. "I think I hear the guys."

He gave her a panicked look, nearly making her laugh. Instead she picked up Amelia's carrier, tucking the warm baby bottle on one side. She looped the bag with the diapers over her arm and hurried upstairs just as the back door opened and the hungry ranch hands began filing in.

Amelia woke with a startled little sound when they were halfway up the stairs. After one quick gasp, she scrunched up her little face and let out an ear-piercing wail. By the time Ellie had reached the landing, Amelia had begun to cry in earnest.

Making soothing sounds, Ellie hurried to her room. Once there, she dropped the diapers on the bed and hurried to get Amelia out of the carrier. No amount of rocking or murmuring endearments would soothe her. But the instant Ellie pressed the baby bottle against her lips, Amelia latched on, drinking so fast she hiccupped.

"What a beautiful baby you are," Ellie murmured, her heart full. "I'm so sorry your mama won't get to see you grow up."

Cradling Amelia while she finished her bottle, Ellie wondered at this newfound surge of maternal emotion. She hadn't spent a lot of time around babies, and it amazed her how tiny this one seemed.

Once Amelia finished her bottle, Ellie burped her,

again copying something she'd seen on television. Amelia let out a satisfied belch.

Ellie kicked off her shoes and climbed onto her bed, holding Amelia close. She propped up a pillow and leaned back, resting while she gently rocked her charge.

A few seconds later, Amelia had gone back to sleep. Smiling, Ellie watched her. Once, before her stalker, she'd settled into a sort of Bohemian existence working at a bookstore in Boulder. She'd had friends, she'd been happy, though she'd often felt like she was floating along through life. Her stalker had changed that, and the constant panic had forced her to go on the run. Now she'd landed here. She wasn't sure why, especially since she'd always wanted to travel, but she hadn't felt this content in a long time.

By the time the lunch hour was over, Theo had a newfound respect for the job of ranch cook. Since coming back home, he hadn't had to do much, Mrs. Saul had worked in the kitchen for over twenty years. When the plump white-haired lady had come to him and announced she wanted to retire, the entire ranch was caught off guard. She'd promised to stay until he'd found someone to replace her, and so she had. The transition from Mrs. Saul to Ellie Parker had gone seamlessly.

One tiny baby and everything had been thrown off balance. That was okay, he told himself. Once Gram Dottie took over nanny duty, everything here would be right back on track. He'd just have to pitch in until then. At least he had plans. Big ones, actually. He just had to find the right stock to get his breeding program underway.

Most people didn't realize that the majority of broncos in the rodeos were bred specifically for that role. The best buckers had good confirmation and breeding. Theo figured if he couldn't ride 'em, he'd breed 'em.

Until then, he'd help out in whatever way he could, including cooking. The men had been surprised to see him in the kitchen, but they'd been hungry and dug into the chili. Theo had fixed himself a bowl too, and taken a seat at the table in the other room to eat with them. All the talk was on the upcoming Tulsa State Fair and Rodeo in Oklahoma.

Pretending it didn't bother him talking about something that had been his favorite activity in the world was something he had gotten better at. Theo laughed and joked, argued about who he thought was the best bull rider, hoping and praying they didn't ask him about the bronc riders, whether saddle bronc or bareback. Bareback had been his sport, and even thinking about what he would be missing usually filled him with a brooding kind of anger.

Maybe they had heard this, or perhaps his hired cowboys had a lot of common sense, because bronc riding never came up.

Most of them had seconds, complimenting Theo on the chili. He smiled and told them to thank Ellie. No one asked about the baby, no doubt remembering the way the conversation had gone that morning.

Finally, one by one, they pushed back their chairs and headed out to get back to work. Relieved, Theo gathered up the dirty dishes, rinsed them off and put them in the dishwasher. He made sure the burner was off and left the pot on the stove to cool.

He made a quick call to a local alarm monitoring service and left a message on their answering machine asking for an appointment the next day to have motion detectors and whatever else came with a home alarm installed.

Someone called him back in two minutes, confirming the appointment for Monday afternoon. He imagined they didn't get much business. Here in Dead River, the country folks rarely even bothered to lock their doors.

Theo had been the same. In the past. No longer. He planned to make sure the house was locked up tight each night before he went to bed. An alarm would be additional insurance. Whoever had broken in, whether he'd been after the baby or Ellie, wouldn't be able to get in so easily next time.

As he tried to decide whether or not to take Ellie her lunch upstairs, his cell phone rang. The caller ID showed Gemma.

"Hey," he answered. "I thought you weren't going to call until after you got off work."

"I wasn't," Gemma answered, sounding stressed and more upset than he'd ever heard her. "But Gram Dottie just came in."

"Good. I told her to get her tail in there if she didn't start feeling better."

"Oh, Theo." To his shock, he could tell his sister was on the verge of tears. "She walked in the front door, and then she collapsed. We've moved her back to the isolation area. The doctors think Gram Dottie has the same thing Mimi Rand had."

Chapter 3

Stunned, Theo wasn't sure he'd heard correctly. "What? I just talked to her and she didn't sound that sick. Now you're telling me… How is that even possible?"

"I don't know. No one even knows what this disease is, never mind how it's transmitted. Dr. Rand thinks it's a virus. Either way, it's not good. She's in really bad shape, Theo."

"I'm on my way down there," he said, pacing the length of the kitchen. The rich smell of the chili now made him feel queasy.

"No. You can't. There's a reason we have the victims isolated. You can't risk exposing yourself."

"I don't care about myself." He swore. "You know how much Gram means to me."

"We all feel that way," Gemma said. "And you may not care about yourself, but you have to think of the baby. You can't risk her." She took a deep breath. "Right now you'd be denied entrance anyway. Only essential medical personnel are allowed in, and we have to put on protective-wear as a precaution."

Theo cursed again. "How bad off is Gram?"

"Right now she's stable." Another shaky breath, the sound coming through as more of a warning than any words could be. "The CDC is sending a team. Flint knows this already, but they're talking about a quarantine."

Theo stopped pacing, trying to understand. "A quarantine? Of what, the clinic?"

"No. Dead River. The entire town." And then Gemma, his normally unflappable sister, began to cry.

Theo did his best to console her, well aware she most likely hadn't shared every detail with him. "What about the baby?" he asked, taking a deep breath. "She was with Mimi right before she died. We need to get her checked out."

"You're right," Gemma said. "And you and anyone else who might have come into contact with her. I can't come by tonight, but I work the afternoon shift tomorrow, so I'm off in the morning. How about I swing by the ranch and check her out then?"

"That'd be perfect."

"Then that's what I'll do." With that, Gemma told him she had to go back to work and ended the call.

Stunned, Theo could only stare at his phone. He felt he needed to do something, anything, but he didn't know what. If this virus had been a bronc, he would have climbed on and ridden it into submission. But it wasn't, and in reality, there was nothing he could do but stand by helplessly and watch.

And that summed it up. He was a rodeo cowboy, a bareback bronc riding champion, and not much else. He couldn't even help his own grandmother—the woman who'd raised him—when she needed assistance.

But he could—and would—protect Amelia. His tiny daughter had no one else. He'd somehow figure out a way to be a good father, even though he had no idea how. Again the spicy scent of chili filled his nostrils. This time, the smell filled him with purpose. Ellie had done nothing but work all day. She had to be starving.

He found a cookie sheet that would work as a tray and filled a bowl with corn chips before ladling the chili over that. Topping if off with a generous amount of shredded cheddar cheese, he folded a paper towel to act as a napkin, grabbed a spoon and a can of cola and carried the tray up to Ellie's room.

It was impossible to knock with his hands full, so he didn't bother. The door was cracked. He used his elbow to nudge it the rest of the way open.

Carrying the tray, he paused just inside the room. Both Ellie and the baby were asleep on the bed—Ellie sitting up, her back supported by both pillows, still cradling the infant securely in her arms.

Carefully and quietly, he placed the tray on the dresser and stared at the pair. Bathed in the soft light from the window, Ellie looked almost angelic. Looking at her and the sleeping baby made the back of his throat ache.

Shaking his head, he scoffed at himself. Still, there was a particular glow about her. Maybe it was one of those things females got when they were around babies. Who knew?

He took the opportunity to study her—and his child too. Something about the scene calmed him, the way beauty always did. Ellie's exotic, high cheekbones caught the light, bringing a soft flush to her creamy skin. The delicacy of her face seemed almost at odds with her lean, athletic body. She'd pulled her hair, a soft brown color, back into a ponytail. The soft strands that had escaped framed and highlighted her face.

And the baby… Chest tight, he moved closer to examine her. Perfect little rosebud of a mouth, dusky skin like her mother's. Innocent and perfect, too much so for the likes of someone like him. What did he know about being a father? His dad had become a drunk after their mother was killed in a car accident. His father had been in and out of their lives, showing up just often enough to humiliate his sons. He'd finally abandoned their family, much to everyone's unspoken relief. Gram had taken over, filling the void as best she could. She'd been both mother and father, grandmother and teacher to Flint, Theo and Gemma.

Standing there in the quiet room, midday sunlight warm on his arm, Theo faced the fact that the world he'd taken for granted continued to crumble down around him. Losing the ability to rodeo had seemed like the worst thing that could ever happen, even though everyone had kept telling him he should consider himself lucky that he'd survived.

But now his beloved Gram was seriously ill, and this tiny, helpless human had been entrusted to his care. Him, of all people, who had always taken a certain sort of pride in being the least settled person he knew. Despite his satisfaction with the life he'd chosen, he'd never wanted to fail his grandmother, though deep down inside, he knew he had. Gram had loved him anyway. Now, no matter what, he knew he couldn't let his daughter down.

"Theo? Are you all right?" Ellie's voice, husky with sleep, startled him. Her bright blue eyes were fixed on him, though still groggy with sleep.

"I hope I didn't wake you," he said, feeling surprisingly awkward. "I brought you lunch."

She shifted, sliding back to sit up, careful not to disturb the baby. "Are the hands all fed?"

"Yep. And I cleaned everything up. Later, I'll need you to tell me what I need to do to prepare for the evening meal."

"I will." Her heavy-lidded gaze slid past him to the tray. "But right now I'm famished. Would you mind taking Amelia so I can eat?"

"Sure." This time he didn't hesitate. He figured if he did this often enough, soon he'd be completely comfortable with holding the baby.

The transfer could have been awkward, but Theo just held out his arms and let Ellie take care of it.

"I've got her," he said, half smiling, barely noticing as Ellie moved to take the bowl of chili from the tray and begin eating with a quiet and intent efficiency.

The rumble of his voice caused Amelia's eyes to open. Colton green. Of course. He'd read somewhere that less than five percent of the world's population had green eyes.

"Hi there, little baby," he crooned, trying not to feel foolish.

Looking up from her meal, Ellie made a sound.

"What?" he asked, reluctantly dragging his gaze from the baby.

"She has a name." Ellie's soft voice carried a bit of steel. "Amelia. You don't have to always call her baby or the infant."

"I wasn't aware I did." He shrugged, refusing to let a small detail like that bother him, despite what Ellie thought it revealed. "Sorry."

Too busy finishing her lunch, Ellie didn't respond,

though he could feel her gaze on him as he gently rocked the baby. Gram Dottie would love Amelia, he knew. Now she just had to get well so they could meet.

Something of his worry must have shown in his face.

"Are you all right?" Ellie asked again. "You look... Is something wrong?"

"Yes." He took a deep breath, needing to get it off his chest. "My sister called while you were asleep. Gram Dottie collapsed at the clinic." Despite his best intentions, his voice cracked a little. "The doctors think she has the same thing that killed Mimi Rand. They've got her in isolation."

"Oh, Theo." Ellie's eyes widened. "I'm so sorry."

He nodded, working really hard to keep his expression neutral. "Gemma says they think it's some kind of new virus. The CDC is sending a team and they're even talking about quarantining the entire town."

"What?" Ellie hand moved to her throat. "I've never heard of them doing that, except maybe in movies. It must be really bad."

"Don't panic." His words were for both of them. "We've got some really sharp doctors at the clinic, and Dr. Rand vowed to find a cure. He's working around the clock, despite being really broken up by the death of his ex-wife."

Ellie nodded, her blue eyes huge in her suddenly pale face. Her cheeks flushed, she looked away. "You're right. Of course. There's no need to let my imagination get the best of me. I hope your grandmother gets well quickly."

"She will," he said with a confidence he didn't feel. "Anyway, Gemma is going to come by tomorrow and check us all out. I can't risk the baby's—Amelia's—health by taking her down to the clinic."

"I agree." Her brow creased in a dainty frown. "But it's still safe to go into town, isn't it?"

"Of course."

"Good. I need to pick up a few things." She hesitated, and then continued, sounding a bit sheepish. "Though now that my stalker might have found me, I'm a little bit scared to go."

"Don't be." Here Theo could speak with confidence. "I've called a company to come out and install an alarm. They'll be here tomorrow. And as far as going into town is concerned, I'll go with you, like a sort of bodyguard."

He could tell his words pleased her from the dusky rose that suffused her face. "Thank you," she said. "If you don't mind, I need to make a trip in the morning, as long as it won't interfere with the alarm installation."

"They're supposed to come around two, so if we go early, we should be fine. I'll need to find out what time my sister plans to stop by, but we can work around that. I want to make sure none of us is sick before we leave the ranch and risk infecting others."

She nodded. "Good point. Do you have any idea what the early symptoms are?"

"It's flu-like. From what I remember Gemma telling me, it'd probably be fever and nausea, weakness or tiredness, cough, sore throat, runny or stuffy nose and maybe body aches."

She nodded. "That's kind of what I thought. So far, Amelia hasn't exhibited any of those."

"What about you?"

"Nothing." Tilting her head, she studied him. "And you? Have you been feeling all right?"

He started to answer, then checked himself. "I'm still dealing with fallout from my rodeo accident, but no flu-like symptoms yet."

"I'm sorry." Her soft voice matched the softening in her blue eyes. "What exactly happened to you?" She blushed, then shook her head. "I'm sorry. I don't mean to pry."

Even now, six months later, he could still barely talk about it. To anyone else. But for some reason, he wanted to tell her. "I got thrown by a horse. A crazy, completely out of control bronc. My skull was broken, I had a right clavicle fracture, messed up my hip and my ankle was shattered."

He took a deep breath, forcing himself to continue. "But the worst thing was that my spine got messed up. All the other injuries were fixable. Meaning, I could heal and go back to competing. But that damn spinal cord injury nearly paralyzed me. They told me I can never ride again. I'm lucky I'm even able to walk."

"You don't sound as if you think you're lucky," she commented.

Which meant he hadn't successfully hidden the bitterness. How could he, when it rode so close to the surface?

"Rodeo was my life," he said quietly. "With that gone…"

Her chin came up. He was starting to recognize that habit of hers. Gesturing at Amelia, still cocooned in his arms, she gave him a look that reminded him of Gram Dottie when she was about to make a point.

"With that gone," Ellie threw his words back at him. "You now have time to focus on something else. *Someone* else. Amelia. Your daughter."

Ellie hadn't meant to be so bold. Judging from the total shutdown on Theo's rugged face, she'd gone entirely too far. Still, she didn't regret her words, nor would she call them back.

Amelia had just lost her mother. She deserved a father who'd give her 100 percent.

Theo had given Ellie a hard stare and then turned without a word, placed Amelia in her bassinette and walked away.

Apparently she'd touched a nerve. Well, baby Amelia's situation touched Ellie. She knew better than most how it felt to have parents who treated you as an afterthought. She'd do everything she could to make sure Amelia didn't suffer the same fate.

The rest of the day passed quickly. She bathed and changed Amelia, before taking her down to the kitchen so Ellie could resume the rest of her duties. Despite his offer to help, Theo didn't put in an appearance. Ellie wasn't really surprised, though she was disappointed.

Since Amelia had gone right to sleep, Ellie was able to work unencumbered. Dinner went off without a hitch—she'd placed the chickens in the oven to roast along with some potatoes, carrots and onions, and opened several cans of rolls and baked them just before it was time to eat. For dessert, she'd made a cobbler using baking mix and canned peaches. Not exactly gourmet fare, but it would fill their hungry bellies. She'd fed Amelia while everything cooked.

The meal turned out delicious and the cowboys were loud and appreciative. Theo arrived just after everyone had started to eat. A few of the men paused, but Theo waved them to continue. So they did, still raining compliments down on Ellie.

She smiled, told them thank you, and waved them back toward their meal.

As had been her habit, Ellie stayed slightly apart, near Amelia's portable bassinette. She watched from near the oven, having just made herself a plate and about to sit down at the smaller dinette table. She'd fed and changed Amelia earlier, and despite her earlier nap, exhaustion battled to claim her.

Theo crossed the room to stand near her. Conversation at the long table briefly ceased. But a quick look from Theo and it resumed, though several of them men made no secret of the fact that they were watching.

"I'm sorry," Theo said, pitching his voice low so the others couldn't hear. "I promised to help you with the evening meal and I forgot." He rubbed his leg as he talked to her, making her realize his injuries were no doubt hurting him.

"That's okay." Surprised that he'd even apologized, she slid the plate she'd just filled toward him. "Go ahead and eat. I'll make another plate and join you."

He glanced at Amelia, who, with her tummy full, slept contentedly. "How is she?"

"Still fine." Turning, she busied herself filling a plate with food. Once she was done, she carried it over to the smaller table that sat in the kitchen proper.

After a moment, he followed and took the chair opposite her, his expression shuttered. "I talked to my sister. Gemma's going to be here about eight-thirty tomorrow morning. That'll give her plenty of time to check us all out. The stores in Dead River don't open until ten anyway."

"Sounds great." She glanced at the still-sleeping baby. "What about Amelia? After she's cleared as healthy, can we bring her with us? I can't exactly leave her here alone."

"Of course not. I'll help you with her." Flashing her a preoccupied smile, he dug in. The muscles rippling under his button-down shirt made her mouth go dry. Even here, Theo radiated masculinity and sex appeal. And tension, though he appeared to relax a little as he began eating.

"This is great," he said. "How did you manage to make all this and still look after the baby?"

Secretly pleased, she shrugged. "It's nothing fancy, that's why."

"It's good food. Thank you for managing to act both as cook and nanny. I promise I'll make it up to you as soon as I can."

He sounded earnest and charming, and the sparkle in his emerald eyes was pretty damn close to irresistible. Dangerous thinking, she chided herself. "I may hold you to that," she replied lightly. "Now eat up. There's peach cobbler for dessert."

He made a moan of delight and again she blushed. When she got the warm cobbler out of the oven, the men cheered. She served it herself, wanting to make sure there was enough for everyone.

After the hands had taken themselves off to the bunkhouse, Theo guided her toward the living room couch, handing her the remote before going back to fetch the bassinette, which he placed near Ellie.

"Sit. I'll clean up," he said. "And for breakfast tomorrow morning, Gram Dottie used to make us this baked egg dish that you can refrigerate and just pop in the oven. I helped her once or twice, so I think I remember how to do it."

Surprised and touched, Ellie nodded. "Thank you."

"You're welcome." He flashed a grin so devastating her breath caught in her chest. "Now relax and watch something on TV. I'll join you once I'm finished in the kitchen."

Strange. Too tired to comment, she glanced at Amelia, who still slept. Perfect baby. Leaning back into the overstuffed couch cushions, she pressed the power button on the remote. Since she still didn't know the television channels for this area, she pressed one at random. A legal drama was on, one she thought she might have caught a few episodes of in the past.

The next thing she knew, Theo was shaking her shoulder. "Ellie, wake up. It's late and you need to go on to bed."

Groggy, she blinked up at him, trying to understand. "What…what time is it?"

His lazy smile touched her like a sensual caress. "A little after ten. You fell asleep and looked so peaceful. I didn't want to bother you."

"Amelia." She looked for the baby, not finding her. "Where's Amelia?"

"I carried her upstairs a minute ago. She needed a diaper change and I think I figured out how to do it." He lifted his shoulder in a sheepish shrug. "Though you might want to double-check my handiwork. She's asleep in the crib."

He'd *changed Amelia?* Talk about giant strides, especially from a man who'd barely been able to say his daughter's name. Wisely, she kept her sentiment to herself. She sensed if she made a big deal about it or even commented, Theo would shut down.

"She's going to want her nighttime bottle soon." Pushing herself up off the sofa, she stifled a yawn. "I'll just go ahead and make it, so I'll have it when she wakes."

He eyed her. "How do you know how to do all this, anyway?"

"My parents were very active in the church," she said, shrugging. "When they went off to be missionaries, I stayed with a neighboring family who had triplets. Mrs. Anderson needed all the help she could get. I learned not only how to take care of babies, but I also learned how to cook."

And Ellie had felt glad to be needed. Even if later, as she'd grown older, she'd come to understand she was being used as an unpaid nanny and cook. She hadn't truly minded, as she'd come to love the triplets, but when she'd needed to get a job to earn her own money, she'd asked to be paid. Instead, she'd found herself out on the street. Luckily, one of her high school friends had taken her in until she could find a job and save for a place of her own.

Taking her arm, he guided her into the kitchen and over to a chair. His slow smile made her mouth go dry. "Sit. Tell me what to do and I'll make the bottle."

Wondering if she was still asleep and dreaming, she gave him instructions, unable to resist the tiniest bit of flirting. "It would seem you have a natural talent," she told him, smiling shyly. His answering grin made her feel warm all over.

When the bottle was ready and he'd tested the temperature with a drop on his wrist, the way she'd told him, he handed it over, his fingers brushing against hers and lingering a second too long.

Telling herself it was in her imagination, she took it and pushed to her feet, again swaying slightly. He reached out to steady her, and somehow she ended up pressed against the muscular length of him.

Instantly, her senses leaped to life as she came deliciously awake. Breasts tingling against his rock-hard chest, her entire lower body began to melt as she stared up at him.

Green gaze dark, he lowered his face as if about to kiss her. She caught her breath, her heart lurching crazily, her mouth already throbbing. She wanted him so badly in that moment she shivered, dizzy with longing.

And then he released her, shaking his head, one corner of his sensual mouth curving. "Sorry. Old habits."

Somehow she managed to make it out of that room and into hers without collapsing. Only when she'd closed the door and dropped down onto her bed and covered her face with her hands did she let herself think about what had just almost happened.

The only reason it hadn't was that Theo had enough sense to back away.

Though she had to admit, the casual *old habits* had stung. But then, she chastised herself, what the hell had she expected? Theo Colton wasn't for her. She needed her job and the protection Theo had promised from her crazy stalker. Which meant she needed to get herself under control and forget even thinking about being attracted to him.

Amelia began making snuffling sounds, which meant she was about to cry. Ellie scooped her up, gently pressing the bottle's nipple against her perfect, bow-shaped lips. The baby latched on, suckling like a champion, which made Ellie smile.

Once Amelia had finished, Ellie burped her. One final check of her diaper, which had been put on perfectly, and she put the baby back in her crib, amazed at how quickly Amelia dropped into sleep.

Attending to her evening preparations as quickly as she could, Ellie brushed her teeth, washed up and changed into her pajamas.

She climbed into bed, ready to fall asleep, even though she knew she'd probably dream of Theo. She resolved, if she did, to promptly forget all about them in the morning.

That night and the next morning, Theo refused to even think about what foolish urge had made him almost kiss Ellie Parker. He'd been without a woman too long; that had to be it. After all, Ellie wasn't even his usual type.

He preferred his women curvy and flirty and casual. With her willowy, athletic figure, Ellie not only wasn't his type, but was too serious by far.

And too sweet, he thought. The kind of woman who needed a white picket fence and a husband who was content to work a nine-to-five and come home to her each night.

In other words, everything Theo was not. Little Miss Serious would want it all, including love. He wasn't in the habit of intentionally breaking hearts, and he didn't intend to start now.

Rushing through his shower, he hurried downstairs to get the egg casserole baking in the oven. He also made a pot of coffee, waiting impatiently for it to finish brewing. Outside, the sun hadn't yet risen, and he could tell the outside air would be crisp. His favorite kind of morning, back when he'd wake up and drive out to the rodeo grounds to check out the lay of the land. He'd walk the grounds, a cup of java steaming in his hands, looking for the other cowboys who were out there doing the exact same thing.

Shaking his head, he ruthlessly pushed that thought away the same way he'd quashed his surprising desire for Ellie.

Pretty soon the kitchen smelled like eggs and sausage and coffee. The hired hands begin to drift in, one by one, hanging up their jackets and wiping off their work boots on the mat just inside the back door before heading to their table in the adjoining room.

The casserole seemed to be a big hit, judging from the appreciative comments and requests for seconds. He'd already put the second one in and it had finished cooking just as he scooped the last bit out of the first pan.

The hands finished eating, several of them joking and

laughing and clapping him on the back, calling him a damn good cook. As they filed out, Theo began to wonder why Ellie hadn't yet put in an appearance.

Surely what had almost happened last night hadn't made her skittish?

Fear stabbed him. What if she was sick? Or Amelia? Gemma wouldn't be here for another hour or so. Trying to contain his rising panic, he rushed to Ellie's room, finding the door closed. Taking a deep breath, he tapped lightly. When he received no answer, he went ahead and opened the door.

Inside, he heard water running and realized she was in the shower. Amelia gurgled, awake in her crib. He went closer and swore she smiled at him, flailing her tiny hands. Glancing toward the open bathroom door, Theo leaned over the crib, reaching for the baby. His hands looked huge even to him as he unbuttoned her Onesie so he could check her diaper. It was dry, which meant Ellie had changed her. He noticed two empty baby bottles on the dresser. One had to be from last night. The other meant Ellie had already been downstairs to make her formula and fed her. He had no idea when, but it had to have been before sunrise.

Amelia cooed, and Theo felt his smile widen. He'd never been much for babies—hell, what guy was—but this one seemed cuter than most.

"Well, good morning," he said, in what he thought might be a reasonable facsimile of baby talk. "You look mighty pretty this morning."

And then he'd be damned, but Amelia latched her teeny, tiny, wrinkled pink fist on to his finger and held on as if she knew what she was doing.

Throat tight, he stood still and let her.

A moment later the shower cut off. "I'm in here with

Amelia," he called out, just in case Ellie planned to walk out here naked or something. For his own protection as well, because baby or no baby, he wasn't sure he'd be able to resist a nude Ellie. In fact, even thinking about it...

He forced his thoughts back to the baby, picking her up and holding her close as if she were also a shield.

"Morning." Ellie wandered into the room, wrapped tightly in a towel, wearing another on her head like a turban. She looked pink and young and absolutely delectable.

Glad he was holding the baby, he managed a friendly smile. "I got worried when you didn't come down for breakfast."

"I'm sorry." She sounded anything but. "I got up early to take care of Amelia and then came back up here and feel asleep. You'd promised to take care of feeding the hands, so I decided not to worry about that."

Her gentle dig made him want to laugh. Instead he nodded. "There's still some egg casserole left if you're hungry."

"I'm starving. I'll come down and warm it up after I finish getting ready. Do you want to take Amelia with you or..."

A not so subtle request for him to go. He almost offered to take the baby with him, but then he realized he wouldn't know what to do if she cried or needed something. No, he'd need a bit more practice and experience before he tried handling her alone.

"I'll just put her back in her crib," he said, pretending not to notice her disappointed expression. "Come on downstairs when you're ready. Gemma will be here in a couple of hours."

"Ninety minutes," she corrected automatically. "You said eight-thirty. It's seven now."

"Right." Once he had gently placed Amelia back, he carefully avoided looking at Ellie or going anywhere close to her. His hands were empty now and already he was itching to fill them.

Giving himself a mental shake, he hurried from her room and back down to the kitchen.

Chapter 4

Only when Theo was gone, closing her door behind him, did Ellie release the breath she hadn't even realized she was holding. She didn't know what it was about the man, but he made her want things she had no business wanting.

She'd never met anyone like him. So confident in his masculinity, with sex appeal practically radiating from his skin. She could well imagine how many women he had begging for his touch. The way Amelia's mother apparently had.

No way did Ellie plan to become one of them.

No way.

She hurried through the rest of her preparations, taking a little extra care with her hair, since she'd be meeting Theo's sister as well as going into town.

When she went downstairs, Amelia in her carrier, the empty kitchen had been cleaned and appeared spotless. A plate sat on the stove, covered by a paper towel. She peeked under and saw it was the egg casserole, which looked fantastic.

A quick zap in the microwave, and she sat down to eat, her stomach rumbling.

Her first mouthful had her rolling her eyes in delight. It was good. More than good. Chewing slowly so she could get every ounce of flavor, she finished off her plate in record time and wished there was more.

"Did you like it?" Theo appeared. "It won't hurt my feelings if you didn't."

She had to smile at that. "I need your recipe," she said, paying him the highest compliment anyone could give a cook. "That was absolutely restaurant quality."

He nodded. "Thank you."

"Where is she?" a feminine voice called from the other room. Ellie straightened, turning toward the doorway. A tiny woman with long blond hair breezed into the room.

"Gemma." Theo smiled. "Ellie, this is my sister, Gemma. Gemma, Ellie. She's been taking care of Amelia."

"Pleased to meet you." Green eyes exactly like Theo's flashed as Gemma smiled at Ellie. Spotting the bassinette, she gasped. "Oh, there she is!"

Gemma rushed over, staring down at Amelia while she slept. When she raised her head to look at Theo, her eyes shone. "She's beautiful. I can see Mimi in her some, but mostly she looks like you."

Theo shrugged. "Maybe," he allowed. Ellie considered that great progress, since just yesterday he'd been talking about a DNA test.

Gemma turned to Ellie. "Tell me about her." Quietly intense, she focused on Ellie. "How's she been acting? Any problems taking her bottle? How's her poop? Is she sleeping okay? Or too much?"

"Whoa, take it easy." Theo held up a hand before Ellie could even begin to formulate a response. "Gemma, Ellie's not used to you like we are. Go easy at first."

"It's okay," Ellie spoke up, amused. "Gemma, Amelia seems fine to me. She sleeps a lot, but she's still a newborn. She's eating fine, her poop looks like baby poop and she hasn't been running a fever."

"Thank you." Expression satisfied, Gemma lifted Amelia in her arms. "Is there someplace I can examine her?"

"Sure." Ellie got up. "We can take her to my room. Her crib is set up there."

Leading the way, when she turned to show Gemma into the room, she realized Theo hadn't followed.

Gemma noticed where Ellie was looking. "Don't worry. I'll check him out after this. He knows I've got to examine you, so I'm sure he wanted to give you some privacy."

Feeling herself flush all over for no good reason, Ellie was glad Gemma had begun to undress Amelia.

"Her skin looks normal," Gemma said. "No rashes." She turned the baby over with practiced ease and reached into her satchel for a thermometer. "Let me check her temp."

Ellie waited while Gemma silently counted. She found herself holding her breath as the other women withdrew the thermometer and checked it.

"Normal," Gemma pronounced. "I'd say she's as healthy as could be."

"That's wonderful." Grabbing a clean diaper, Ellie moved forward, only to have Gemma take it from her and change the baby herself. She even buckled Amelia back into her Onesie, crooning nonsense to her the entire time. Amelia loved it, gurgling and cooing back, all smiles.

"You have a way with babies," Ellie said.

"Thanks." Still focused on her niece, Gemma barely looked up. "How often are you feeding her?"

"Every couple of hours," Ellie responded. "I looked it up on the internet and saw she's supposed to eat eight to twelve times a day for the first month."

"Is she eating well every time?"

"Yes." Ellie smiled. "She drains the bottle every single time."

"Definitely healthy." Straightening, Gemma fixed Ellie with a practical eye. "Now it's your turn. How are you feeling?"

"Fine. No fever, I'm eating well. No nausea or sweating. Whatever this virus is, I haven't caught it."

"Do you mind if I take your temperature?"

Smiling, Ellie pointed at the other woman's bag. "As long as you don't use the same thermometer you used on Amelia."

Gemma laughed at that. "No worries. Though that one has been sterilized."

A few minutes later, the examination complete, Gemma also pronounced Ellie healthy. She left Ellie and Amelia and went to check out Theo.

Meanwhile, Ellie took Amelia into the kitchen and fed her another bottle. She had just raised her to her shoulder to burp her when Theo and Gemma returned. Next to his petite sister, Theo appeared even larger and more powerful, the essence of masculinity.

"We have the all-clear," Theo announced. "And now we can go into town and pick up supplies."

"Into town?" Looking from one to the other, Gemma frowned, appearing concerned. "I'm not so sure that's a good idea."

"Why not?"

"The virus," Gemma answered simply. "While it hasn't reached epidemic status yet, it shows signs of heading that way. The CDC is concerned and you should be too."

"We have to get supplies," Theo said. "And unless it turns into some sort of plague, we're not going to stay holed up here like a bunch of paranoid doomsday nuts."

He had a point, Ellie thought. But then again, so did Gemma.

"Stock up on your supplies, then," Gemma told them. "And stay away from the general populace as much as you can."

"You're a fine one to talk." Theo ruffled her hair, earning a sharp look of rebuke. "You're working in the clinic, right there in the middle of all the sick people."

"Fine." Throwing up her hands, Gemma gave in. "But at least keep Amelia away. Can you do that?"

Ellie looked from her to Theo and back again. "We don't have anyone else to watch her."

"Gram was going to help out, but she got sick," Theo added.

"Why can't Ellie go to town alone and you watch Amelia?" Gemma asked.

At a loss for words since she didn't want to go into details about her stalker, Ellie looked helplessly at Theo.

"She can't," Theo said. "And that's that. So we have no choice but to take Amelia with us."

"Then I'll keep the baby," Gemma said brightly, her sharp green gaze going from one to the other. "I'd love to spend some time getting to know my niece, and honestly, I'd feel better if she stayed away from town until we get a handle on this virus."

"Are you sure?" Ellie asked, hesitant to shirk her duty. "I really don't mind."

"Amelia can stay here." Theo took Ellie's arm. "Let's get going so we can get back before Gemma has to go to work."

He hustled her from the room before she could protest. "And make sure you bring your sense of humor."

Dumbfounded, she froze, staring at him. "What do you mean?"

"I know you're worried about the stalker. But for today, I'd like you to try and forget about him. You deserve to have a good time."

"Do I?" She frowned. "If not for me—"

"Shhh." Pressing a finger against her lips, he shook his head. "That's what I'm talking about. I want you to promise."

Staring up at his rugged profile, she felt the weight on her shoulders slide off. "You're right," she said. "At least for today, I'm going to try to enjoy myself."

"Good." The approval in his voice increased her determination to try to pretend her stalker didn't exist. At least for a few hours. She knew she'd have to go back to normal soon enough.

"Do you have everything you need?" he asked.

"Let me grab my jacket." Once she did, she put it on and smiled up at him. "I'm ready."

"Really? What about your purse?"

She shrugged. "I rarely use one. I just stuffed my wallet in my jacket pocket and I'm ready to go."

"What about your lipstick and perfume and all the stuff women always have to carry around with them?"

"I have my ChapStick." She pulled it out to show him. "That's all I need."

The way he looked at her, she wondered if she might have grown two heads.

"Okay," he finally said, grabbing a black cowboy hat from the coatrack and jamming in on his head. "Let's go."

He drove a large black Dually pickup truck, with shiny chrome wheels and an NPRA decal on the back window. When he started it up, the engine rumbled like a hot rod. Inside, there were leather seats, wood-grain trim and every luxury you could get.

She couldn't help laughing.

"What so funny?" he asked, glancing sideways at her.

"I've never seen a vehicle that matched someone's personality as much as yours does."

Putting the shifter in Drive, he shrugged, though he looked pleased. "I spent a lot of time in my truck. I needed to make sure it had everything I liked."

She nodded. "I bet it works great when the snows come."

"It does." He tipped the front of his hat with his index finger. "I know you said you'd just arrived in town when you applied to work at my ranch, but did you get to do any exploring?"

Town. Other people. Maybe even crowds. Just like that, her nervousness slammed back into her, full force. "You know, maybe we should reconsider this."

He glanced at her, and then squeezed her shoulder. "Focus, honey. I asked you if you were able to check out Dead River."

Honey. Even aware the word was a mindless endearment that came naturally to a man like Theo, Ellie felt warm inside.

"Focus," he repeated. "We're talking about town."

After a deep breath, she nodded. "Ok, fine. To answer your question, I was really low on funds. So, no. But I have to say, from what I did see of it, it looks like a nice place."

At that, he laughed. “Nice, huh? That’s what I always thought. One of the reasons I couldn’t wait to get out of here.”

“Nice doesn’t always equal boring,” she felt compelled to point out.

“Maybe not, but Dead River is exactly that. Dead. The lights go out and the sidewalks roll up as soon as the sun sets.”

Surely, Theo exaggerated. “You’re telling me there are no bars?” she asked dryly. “I find that hard to believe.”

One corner of his sensual mouth lifted. “You equate bars with fun?”

Shaking her head, she laughed. “Isn’t that what you meant?”

Shrugging, he looked sheepish. And adorably sexy too. She’d never really had a thing for men in cowboy hats, but Theo looked amazing in his. Ellie hoped that with time, she’d manage to become immune to his over-the-top charm.

As they rumbled from the dirt road to the blacktop, old-school country music wailing away softly on the radio, she couldn’t help marveling at the odd twists and turns her life had taken to get her here.

“I need to ask a favor,” Theo said, sounding oddly hesitant, which was unlike him.

“Okay.” She twisted in her seat as much as the seat belt would allow, and faced him. “What’s up?”

“Would you stay and take care of Amelia on a permanent basis?”

“Permanent?” She swallowed hard, not wanting to tell him as long as there was a stalker out there, she pretty much lived her life day by day.

“Yes. You’re good with her, and Gemma cleared you

as healthy. I know I hired you as cook, but I can easily find someone else to fill that position."

"No." Surprising even herself with her vehemence, Ellie shook her head. "I can do both." She took a deep breath, daring herself to go for the gusto. "But I'll need an increased salary."

A dimple flashed in his cheek. "How much of an increase?"

"How much would you be paying someone else to come in and cook?"

He laughed. "Touché. So you want me to double your salary."

Trying not to wince, she nodded. "Yes."

Flashing her an amused look, he drummed his fingers on the steering wheel as he made a right turn. "Are you up to working two full-time jobs? You know that baby is going to be keeping you up some nights. Getting up before sunrise to make sure breakfast is ready might be a bit of a stretch."

"I need the money." Though her parents had drilled into her the importance of living a Spartan existence, ever since she realized someone was stalking her, Ellie had dreamed of making enough money to fly to another country and disappear. Make that another continent. She wanted to start over, as it were. Maybe doing so would be running away, but she didn't care. She was tired of looking over her shoulder.

She didn't even think she'd let her mother and father know where she was. She wasn't even sure they'd care.

"How about this?" Theo said. "I'm willing to give it a shot, on a trial basis. Provided you promise to tell me if doing two jobs gets to be too much. Taking care of Amelia has to be your number-one priority. Cooking will have to come in second. As long as my hands are fed on time and the food is reasonably tasty, we'll have a deal."

Trying not to be insulted by the reasonably tasty part of his remark, she stuck out her hand. "Deal."

When he slid his big fingers into hers, she felt a jolt. The same kind of shock she'd noticed the few times she brushed up against him, as if his body contained some sort of electromagnetic pull, drawing her to him.

Fanciful and stupid, she chided herself. She needed to focus on reality. This double job, double paycheck would be a good thing. With no living expenses other than clothing and toiletries, making a hefty salary would enable her to sack money away, after she fixed her car. She'd long dreamed of going to Australia. Maybe now she could even start planning.

When they turned the corner onto Main Street, she sat up straighter. Dead River. What a name. Despite that, something about this town called to her, which was the entire reason she'd stopped here in the first place. And then, of course, her car died.

All she'd been thinking of was escaping her life and her stalker, so she'd headed north, planning on traveling through Wyoming on her way to Montana or maybe even Idaho.

But the instant she'd stepped foot in Dead River, she felt as if she was home. Foolish? Maybe. But so far she'd managed to survive by relying on her gut instincts, and they hadn't failed her yet.

She'd seen the help wanted ad clipped on a bulletin board in the coffee shop. She'd called, gotten an interview and here she was. She'd always had an aptitude for cooking. Apparently she also had a knack with babies.

Since she really liked Amelia, and had always loved to cook, it was all good. At least, until her stalker had found her. Now, her very presence here could put them all in danger.

Focus. Theo's admonition had her pushing her worries about what she might have brought to the Coltons' doorstep out of her mind. She'd gotten to go to town with a hunky cowboy. Might as well let herself enjoy it.

Parking in front of a hardware store, Theo grinned at her as he pointed across the street. "See? There's the bar."

Unable to resist the power of that grin, Ellie smiled back as she got out of the truck.

A few people waved at Theo. She noticed most of the men wore either cowboy hats or baseball-type caps. Doug Gasper, one of the guys she'd worked with in the bookstore in Boulder, had called them tractor caps.

She caught a few people eying her with open curiosity, but it felt friendly, in keeping with the overall vibe of the town.

Though the cool air felt crisp, it also felt fresh. She inhaled deeply, a bit of a spring in her step. Pure, like the air near her hometown. But Dead River had a more old-fashioned, close-knit sort of feel.

"I'm going to run in here," Theo said, indicating a barbershop with an old-fashioned barber pole outside the door. "I need to get a trim. You're welcome to come with me, or you can take care of your own shopping. Up to you."

She almost opened her mouth to ask him not to cut his sexy, tousled hair, but she realized she didn't have the right to say she liked his hair the way it was. "I think I'll head over to the drugstore. Meet you back here?"

He grinned. "Either way. If you get done first, that's fine. Otherwise I'll find you up there."

"Sounds good." Before she stepped away, she couldn't resist glancing around. Not that she expected her stalker to show his face in broad daylight, but still. The intruder in her room had made her extremely nervous.

Theo noticed. "Hey, would you rather I go with you? I can always get my hair trimmed another time."

Heaven help her, she actually considered it. But she'd never been timid, and she sure as heck didn't intend to start now. "No," she said, squaring her shoulders. "It's broad daylight. Go ahead and get your haircut. I'll be fine."

A knowing look flashed in his eyes. "Are you sure?"

"Yes." To prove it, she started off in the direction of the Dead River Pharmacy. "See you in a little bit."

Halfway there, she glanced back. Theo still stood outside the barbershop, watching over her like her personal guardian angel.

Inside the drugstore, she turned and looked around. Unlike the huge chains, this small one seemed homey. Clean and well lit, each aisle clearly marked. Relaxing, she grabbed a small basket and headed toward the cosmetics section.

"Can I help you?" An elderly woman in a white coat stepped out from behind the pharmacy counter. "I'm Gloria Hitch."

Ellie shook her hand. "I'm just stocking up. I'm working out at the Colton Ranch."

A smile creased Gloria's lined face. "I thought you were new in town. Welcome to Dead River. Though you picked a mighty bad time to come. I'm sure you've heard about the virus."

"Yes, ma'am." Ellie glanced at a large bottle of Vitamin C tablets. "I'm thinking about taking some preventative measures."

Gloria snorted. "Pills can't help with a virus, honey. Maybe keep a cold away. I'm just hoping one of those doctors at the clinic can figure something out before this thing turns into an epidemic."

The bell over the front door tinkled. Ellie turned, but it wasn't Theo. An older man in a cowboy hat came inside. "Morning, Gloria." He squinted at Ellie. "And who do we have here? Are you one of Brenda Forest's children?"

"She's not," Gloria put in before Ellie could answer. "She working at the Colton Ranch. She hasn't even been in town all that long."

"Where you from, honey?" the old man asked. "My name is Horace, by the way. Horace Gunn."

"I'm Ellie Parker. I'm from Boulder, Colorado," she answered.

"Ellie, you're the second newcomer from that town," he said. "I met a young man at the café yesterday who said he was from there too. Is he here with you?"

A chill snaked down Ellie's spine. "No. Did you happen to catch his name?"

His bushy gray eyebrows drew together in a frown. "I don't think he gave it to me."

Struggling not to show her disappointment, Ellie sighed. "Oh well. I was hoping it was a friend of mine. He was supposed to meet me here," she lied. "But he hasn't made it yet. What did this guy look like?"

"Out of place," Horace answered promptly. "He wasn't a cowboy, that's for sure. Not that everyone around here is, but he looked like one of those dope-smoking, hippy types."

So did half the people in Boulder. "You mean like a college student?"

"Nah, he was older than that." He peered at her, his faded blue eyes sparkling. "Does your friend have long, reggae hair?"

"Reggae hair?" Confused, Ellie tried to understand. "You mean like dreadlocks?"

Horace shrugged. "I guess. I think it was some kind of wig. Is that your friend?"

"No." Ellie tried to sound casual, though she thought she probably failed miserably. "That probably wasn't him."

"Unless he's wearing a disguise," Gloria put in.

"Why would he do that?" Horace's frown deepened.

"So he could surprise her, silly." Gloria turned back toward the pharmacy counter. "Maybe he doesn't want you to know he's in town yet."

Ellie nodded. Gloria was closer to the truth than she realized. Though why anyone would care to wear dreadlocks in a small Wyoming ranching town was beyond her. He'd fit right in if he was in Boulder. Here, he'd stick out like a donkey in a herd of horses.

"Can you describe anything else about him?" she asked, remembering the outline of the intruder who'd been in her room. "Was he tall and lean? Or short and stout?"

"Tall," Horace answered promptly. "And he was a skinny feller. I did notice he had a lot of freckles, if that helps. Does your friend have freckles?'

"No." Pretending disappointment, Ellie shrugged. "That must have been somebody else."

"Horace, your blood pressure pills are ready," Gloria called, winking at Ellie. "Come get them, and let that girl finish her shopping."

Shaking his head, Horace dipped his chin at her and shuffled over to the counter.

Since she had a few more things she needed, Ellie gathered up shampoo and conditioner, a new blow dryer, as hers had given up the ghost right after she'd started working at the ranch and a bottle of generic multivitamins.

She waited behind Horace, who was leaning on the counter telling Gloria all about some dog he'd had back in the 1950s. Clearly having heard this same story numerous times, Gloria rolled her eyes and motioned Ellie up to the register.

Gloria and Horace made a big deal out of Ellie's reusable cloth bag, which Ellie found amusing. In Boulder, people were shocked if you asked for paper or—heaven forbid—plastic.

After she'd paid, she waved goodbye and headed out the door toward the barbershop. On the way there, she stopped to admire the window display in the florist shop. She had just started to turn away when someone came out of nowhere and tackled her, knocking her to the ground.

She hit hard, with a little scream. Panicked, she raised her head, trying to get a good look at her assailant. She saw a black hoody and battered tennis shoes, but since he had the hood up, she couldn't get a good look at his face.

"You belong to me," he snarled, looming over her as if he meant to kick her while she was down. And then, as she opened her mouth to scream for help, someone else came out of nowhere, tackling him.

Theo. He swung at the guy and connected. Wincing with pain, Theo twisted and tried to grab the other man. Instead, Theo crumpled to the pavement.

Taking advantage of this, her attacker ran off.

Shakily, Ellie got to her feet. Her jeans were ripped at the knees, and one knee was scraped and bloody, as were her palms.

The bag she'd been carrying had remained intact, though some of her purchases had been disgorged. Slowly, methodically, she picked them up, tears pricking at her eyes. Broad daylight was all she could think. Her stalker had attacked her in broad daylight.

A lot slower getting up, Theo stood hunched, clearly making an effort to straighten. "Are you all right?" he asked her, limping over to try to help.

"I should be asking you the same question." The instant she spoke, she regretted it.

Though his expression hardened, he exhaled. "It's my damn back. If not for the rodeo injury, I would have had him."

Oddly enough, she felt the urge to comfort him. "It's okay," she began. "He took us both by surprise. Not your fault. I think—"

Hauling her up against him, he kissed her. Hard and punishing, as though he meant to make them both suffer. Stunned at first, she returned his kiss with a recklessness born of adrenaline. When he broke away, leaving her mouth burning as if on fire, they were both breathing faster.

Knees weak, Ellie leaned against the brick wall, trying to regain her bearings.

"We're going to the police station," Theo said to her, as if he hadn't just completely rocked her world. "Come on." Keeping a firm grip on her arm, he steered her back toward his pickup. "Flint should be on duty now. He definitely needs to know about this."

Despite her protests, he loaded her up in his truck and drove her the few blocks to the police station. The one-story, redbrick building looked professional and Spartan, hedges trimmed nicely and the paved lot clean.

After he parked, Theo rushed over to Ellie's side, opened her door and helped her down as if he thought she'd suddenly gotten fragile.

"I'm not badly injured," she said, amused and appreciative all at once. "I can walk."

"Good to know," he said, yet he didn't let go of her arm.

Once inside the glass doors, Ellie looked around with interest. Standard-issue police station chairs, check. There were only six of the plastic and metal monstrosities, separated by a few cheap end tables.

A Formica counter separated the receptionist from the waiting area. The stout, middle-aged woman stood, shaking her curly black ringlets and grinning at Theo. Her name tag said she was Kendra Walker, Dispatcher.

"Theo Colton." She reached across the counter for a hug. "It's been way too long since we've had the pleasure of your company. What are you doing in town?"

"Unfortunately, today I'm here on business, not pleasure," he said, moving enough so she could get a good look at Ellie.

"Oh my." Her heavily made up eyes widened. "What on earth happened to you, honey?"

"We need to talk to Flint," Theo put in before Ellie could speak. "Is he here?"

"Sure." She buzzed them in. "You know the way to his office."

The back area looked like a stereotypical, small-town police station. The same cheap chairs, a couple of metal desks and a few rooms with doors. Theo led Ellie to one of these. A nameplate on the door proclaimed Flint Colton, Chief of Police.

"Theo!" Flint stood when they entered, his face breaking into a welcoming smile. Then he caught sight of Ellie and frowned. "What happened?"

"Someone jumped her. We think it might have been her stalker." Theo swallowed. "I tried to get him, but with this bum back, he got away after knocking her to the ground."

"Are you all right?" Flint asked Ellie. "Do you need medical attention?"

Theo cursed before she could answer. "I should have gotten her checked out at the clinic before I came here."

"Hello?" Ellie waved her hand in front of Theo. "I'm right here. And I haven't lost the ability to speak. Flint, I'm fine. Just a little shaken up, that's all."

Indicating the two chairs in front of his desk, Flint waited until they were seated before taking his own seat. He grabbed a pad of paper and a pen. "Can you give me a description?"

"Not really. He had on a black hoody, and I couldn't get a good look at his face." She took a deep breath. "He's never attacked me before. He just followed me around and left creepy notes and black roses, stuff like that. Until he showed up in my room here, I've never even caught a glimpse of him. And now this."

"Ellie, we're not even sure it's the same guy," Flint cautioned.

She stared at him in disbelief. "Who else could it be?"

"That's what we're trying to find out." His calm and measured voice helped her regain her admittedly shaky self-control. "Granted, Dead River doesn't have a lot of crime, but we have some. The guy today might have been a purse snatcher."

"I don't carry a purse." Ellie remembered the old man in the drugstore and snapped her fingers. She relayed what he'd told her about meeting someone from her hometown.

"Horace met him at the café," she finished. "And he had a pretty good description."

"Horace Gunn?" Theo asked. When she answered

in the affirmative, he smiled. “Figures. He’s a fixture at the pharmacy. He’s sweet on Gloria Hitch. She’s the pharmacist.”

“I met her.” Turning back to Flint, she waited until he’d finished writing.

“A white guy with dreadlocks?” Flint shook his head. “Someone like that would stand out like a sore thumb in Dead River. If he’s your stalker, he’ll be pretty easy to find.”

“Not if he wears that hoody,” she put in. “Whoever broke into my room at the ranch wore a hoody and a ski mask. Plus, today he said I belong to him. So it’s a pretty sure bet it’s the same guy.”

“All right.” Putting down his pen, Flint steepled his fingers on the desk in front of him. “For now, we’ll assume this guy is your stalker. The fact that he attacked you is not a good sign. It could mean that he’s escalating. If so, you will be in danger until he’s apprehended.”

Chapter 5

In danger. Theo tensed at the words, the rush of protectiveness he felt surprising him. "I'll protect you," he declared.

Both Flint and Ellie turned to look at him. Ellie with disbelief, Flint with surprise.

Even as he'd said the words, Theo realized he shouldn't have spoken. Because of his back injury, he hadn't done such a good job protecting her at all. This infuriated him. After all, he'd been told he couldn't even ride a horse—not a bronc, but a regular, tame, saddle horse. Why did he think he could protect Ellie? Most likely, he'd fail.

For a guy who'd never backed down from a fight, this news was sobering.

"I need to go," Ellie said. "As in, leave town. I'm sorry, Theo. But I can't risk putting Amelia or anyone else in danger. If you'll just pay me what you owe me, I'll be moving on."

"You quit?" Theo dragged his fingers through his freshly shorn hair. "We just reached a new agreement. You can't quit without giving me some sort of notice."

Ellie bit her lip. "These are extraordinary circumstances," she began.

"For everyone," Theo put in. "I need your help. I don't have anyone else to take care of Amelia. You can't let her down."

"How can I risk her?" she shot back. "If this guy, whoever he is, is bent on hurting me, he won't let a tiny baby stop him."

"I'm having security installed this afternoon, you know that." Theo heard the edge of desperation in his voice, but it couldn't be helped. With Gram sick, he literally had no one to help him take care of Amelia. He knew absolutely nothing about infants—what little he'd learned had been from watching Ellie. "No one will be able to get into the house undetected."

"That's fine, but what about the rest of the time? I have to come into town occasionally. I can't be a hermit at the ranch."

"When you do, I'll go with you." Theo tried not to let his frustration show. "You'll never be alone. I'll protect you."

Flint cleared his throat, making them both look at him. "Are you two done?"

Looking abashed, Ellie nodded. Crossing his arms, Theo smiled thinly and waited.

"I'll have my men look for either a guy with dreads or a guy in a black hoodie. Meanwhile, why don't you both finish up whatever shopping you have left and head back home? Ellie, are you sure you don't need to go by the clinic and have yourself looked at?"

"I'm sure," she answered. "Just a bunch of scrapes. I can fix them myself at the ranch."

"What about you, Theo? Is your back okay?"

"Fine," Theo growled. "Just fine."

"Okay, then." Flint stood and met Theo's gaze. "I'll call you when I find out anything."

"Sounds good." Again Theo took Ellie's arm. This time, she shrugged him off. He sensed she was furious with him, probably because of the kiss, though it might be because he'd failed her.

He couldn't blame her. He'd not only failed her, but failed himself.

Barely speaking, he drove them to the supermarket and picked up more diapers and another case of formula, just in case. Ellie had wanted to stay in the truck, claiming to be self-conscious about her torn jeans and scrapes. He let her, making sure the doors were locked, glad of the time alone to get his shit back together.

She'd be fine, he told himself, wishing he could believe it. Sunlight, busy parking lot and locked truck would all combine to keep her from harm.

Nevertheless, he rushed through his shopping, and made it back outside in record time. This protective feeling was new and felt…strange. But good. As the older brother, Flint had made sure Gemma and Theo never lacked for anything. Of the three siblings, Flint had been the protector, Gemma the nurturer, and Theo'd been the cool, fun one. He'd never had anyone to look after other than himself. Now he had two people. Amelia and Ellie.

And he'd make damn sure to keep them safe. Back or no back. No matter what it took.

"We need to talk," he said, once they were on the main road heading back to the ranch. "I don't want you to leave. Baby Amelia needs you." Swallowing, he pushed past his fear to say the rest of the words. "Heck, *I* need you. I have no idea how to take care of an infant."

Worrying her bottom lip with her teeth, she wouldn't look at him. "If my being here endangers her, I wouldn't be able to live with myself," she said. "That intruder broke into *your* house, into *my* room. He was standing over Amelia's crib. How is it that you can even think my being here is safe for her?"

"We'll take every precaution to make sure it doesn't happen again. I promise." At least this was one promise he knew he could keep.

When she finally turned to look at him, her expression was troubled. "Why'd you kiss me?"

The simple question took him by surprise. In all his life, he didn't think a woman had ever asked him that question.

He had to think. He knew he could give her the glib answer, say something like *because I wanted to.* Which he had. But he figured he owed it to Ellie to give her the truth.

"When I saw him knock you to the ground, my heart stopped," he answered quietly. "I jumped him. If not for my damn injuries, I would have had him. You would have been safe and that piece of trash wouldn't have bothered you ever again. My blood was pumping, he got away and I let you down. When I saw you watching me, you looked scared and disappointed and…" He dragged his hand through his too-short hair. "I wish I was better with words. I'm not saying it right."

Her soft smile transformed her face. "That's okay. I get it. The adrenaline was flowing. And, Theo, you didn't disappoint me. I barely know you and I just started working here." She cleared her throat. "But I do need you to understand that's not part of the deal."

Realizing she meant sex, he managed to keep his expression neutral. "I never thought it was, Ellie. Look, I'm sorry I kissed you. It won't happen again."

"Thank you," she said. Her obvious relief made him feel even worse.

The security company truck was waiting in the driveway when they pulled up. Theo went to talk with the men while Ellie hurried to her room to check on Amelia and relieve Gemma. Theo told the security crew what he wanted and let them go to work. Headed toward Ellie's room, he was met by Gemma.

"We need to talk," she said, taking his arm and steering him back toward the kitchen. But when she saw the alarm people were installing there, she shook her head. "Where can we speak privately?"

"My office?" he suggested. Years ago, he'd turned a spare bedroom into a sort of trophy room slash office, though he rarely did any work there. Still, when he needed to get on the computer, he had one. As well as a great mahogany-wood desk Gemma had once found him at a flea market.

"Sure." She followed him down the hall.

Once inside, he quietly closed the door and turned to face her. "What's up?"

"We just had a second fatality from the virus," she said, trying to sound matter-of-fact but unable to hide her worry. "Old man Thomas. Remember, I told you he came in yesterday?"

"I remember. You also said you had two children who were sick. How are they?"

She sighed. "One is a six-year-old girl and the other a thirteen-year-old boy. They're still sick. Same symptoms. It doesn't look good. For anyone. Another woman, someone who was passing through and staying at the

Holcombs' Bed-and-Breakfast, walked in saying she had the flu, and died while she was still in triage. More people are dying from this thing. I'm worried about Gram."

Theo swore. "How is she?"

"I checked with Dr. Rand, and he said her condition is stable." Gemma bit her lip. "I'll know more once I get to work and see her for myself."

"What makes it kill some people so fast and others seem to have it longer?"

"We don't know." Frustration plain on her face, she grimaced. "We don't know anything about it. How it spreads, what path it takes. All we know are the early symptoms. Even the people the CDC sent are stumped."

"I'm sorry. We've got our own weirdness going on." He told her what had happened in town and filled her in about Ellie's stalker.

"That's terrible!" Gemma exclaimed. "But if he stands out that much, Flint should have no problem locating him."

"Unless the dreads are a disguise." He shrugged. "He's white, with blue eyes. If they're a wig, once he removes it, he looks like any other rodeo drifter who might blow into town."

"I see your point." Gemma looked away, her expression troubled. "You know, if the CDC really does quarantine Dead River, everyone will be stuck here, including this stalker."

Theo waved off her concern. "Surely it won't come to that. Dr. Rand swore he'd figure it out. Plus, you have all those other doctors there at the clinic. If they put their heads together, they'll come up with something."

"Maybe." But Gemma looked doubtful. She glanced at her watch. "I've got to go to work. Oh, and don't forget. Molly's rehearsal dinner is Friday night."

He nodded. Their young cousin had fallen madly in love with Jimmy Johnson, a newcomer who'd arrived in Dead River a few months ago and taken a job at the auto body shop. After a whirlwind courtship, they'd gotten engaged and the wedding was to be held in two weeks.

"Maybe we should postpone it, because of the virus. That'd be a good excuse to drag things out, give Molly time to think this through. If you're asking me, she's rushing it."

"No one asked you. And I think a family get together is safe. Now, please, just remember, it's Friday."

"Got it. I still don't understand why anyone would want to get married so young."

Gemma laughed. "She's twenty-one. Not that young. And with all this craziness going on, maybe this wedding is just what we need to help distract us."

"Except Gram won't be able to come."

Gemma's smile disappeared, making Theo regret saying anything. "True. And she was so looking forward to it." Again she glanced at her watch. "I've really got to go."

"Thanks for coming and checking us out. Also, I really appreciate you watching Amelia."

"I enjoyed it." Her earnest expression said she meant it. "I might even do it again sometime." Then, with a wave, Gemma left.

Alone again, Theo went into the kitchen and grabbed a diet cola. Suppressing the urge to check on Amelia—since that would entail dealing with Ellie as well—he walked over to the window above the sink and stared out at the rolling hills of his family's land. He'd always wished he could feel some sort of bond with it, the way those ranchers did on TV and in books. But all Theo had ever wanted to do was get away from the place. Flint had been the same way.

He shrugged. He'd long ago come to peace with that part of himself. Now, despite at first feeling as if he had no choice, he realized he wanted to stay. He wanted to build a life here and get his breeding program going.

About time he started moving forward. First he'd need to set up a meeting with Slim George and make sure Theo's plans wouldn't interfere with the successful running of the ranch.

Decision made, he felt better. Like he had a purpose again.

His thoughts turned toward what had happened early today, in town.

When he'd seen the man come out of nowhere and launch himself at Ellie, Theo reacted purely by instinct. He'd managed to get the attacker off her, but he should have had the guy. The man he'd been before the accident wouldn't have had a problem. He'd been fast on his feet. He'd have had Ellie's stalker on the ground, arm twisted behind him, quicker than the kids took down those greased pigs at the county fair.

Now he couldn't move as well, couldn't twist around to save his life and the attacker had gotten away. What Theo would have given to be able to assure Ellie that her stalker wouldn't bother her ever again.

The morning had started out so nice. He'd felt good, taking Ellie into town, giving her a break from caring for the baby who'd been thrust unexpectedly at her.

After his haircut, he'd actually planned to take her to the café for a cup of coffee and a slice of pie. The stalker had ruined that idea.

And then there'd been the kiss. What the hell had he been thinking? Ellie wasn't the type to go for a little recreational sex. Even so, he hadn't been prepared to realize his touch apparently repulsed her.

Though it sounded conceited, even to himself, Theo wasn't used to women turning him down. He didn't want to have sex with Ellie, or so he told himself, but she'd reacted to his kiss as if lips touching were a gateway drug to the rest of their bodies connecting.

Most women actually *wanted* him. The fact that Ellie clearly didn't rankled more than it should. Especially considering that she wasn't his type.

He couldn't help thinking this had something to do with his back injury. Maybe in her mind, he wasn't man enough for her. Normally, he would have found the idea laughable. He wasn't usually so insecure.

But now…he wasn't the man he'd always been. Truth of the matter was, he didn't know who he was anymore. Maybe getting his breeding program off the ground would help with that. Give him a purpose.

Rodeo had been more than his occupation. Riding broncs had been his life. Without that, he was like a foal cut loose from the herd and left to fend for himself in a field full of predators.

The analogy nearly made him smile. He realized he was taking this entire situation—at least the kissing part—way too seriously. Apparently his back injury had made him more sensitive and his feelings more easily wounded too. He grimaced. Time to get over that.

Still, he'd gone way too long without a woman. The injury, his long hospitalization and his return home as a veritable invalid for the first few months had made this virtually impossible. Now he'd suddenly become a father and a virus was threatening the town. Which meant nothing was likely to change.

One thing he knew for sure. Until he could get a handle on this strange attraction to Ellie Parker, he'd need to spend as little time with her as possible. After all, she had enough to worry about—dealing with her stalker and trying to hold down a double job here at the ranch.

Ellie couldn't stop thinking about the kiss. Though it hadn't lasted long—not nearly long enough, as far as she was concerned—the brief contact had melted her to a puddle of quivering desire.

Theo wasn't even her type. At all. She'd grown up around cowboys and had learned to avoid them and their swaggering, blustery self-confidence. But Theo was different. Sure, he practically bristled with masculinity, but he was kind too. She actually really liked him.

But the last thing she needed was a romantic entanglement to complicate things. Especially since she still planned to leave as soon as possible. Despite Theo's assurances and the newly installed alarm system, she simply couldn't take the chance that her stalker might somehow harm this precious infant.

Turning her gaze on baby Amelia, whom Gemma had fed and changed and who now slept, she smiled. No doubt Theo felt as uncomfortable about the entire thing as she did. Maybe it would be best to keep as low a profile as she could, until the incident was forgotten.

Getting back to work preparing food helped Ellie get her composure back. She just didn't have time to worry about it. For lunch, the ranch hands got sandwiches and chips, a lot of them. She used three entire loafs of bread and various containers of cold cuts and sliced cheese.

Once they'd devoured that and trooped back out the door, she sat down and had a quick bite herself, making an extra sandwich for Theo in case he got hungry later. Then she got busy preparing the evening meal. Within an hour, she had a huge pot of chicken stew simmering on the stove for dinner, and buttermilk biscuits ready to be popped into the oven.

A nice dinner for a Monday night.

Amelia woke crying and Ellie took care of getting her fed and changed. Finally, as the infant fell back asleep, Ellie was able to sit down for a moment before popping the biscuits in the oven.

Still no sign of Theo. She supposed that was for the best. At least while she'd been busy, she'd had time to think and to make up her mind.

She wouldn't leave Amelia without someone to care for her. She couldn't do that to the poor baby, or to Theo. She'd stay until everyone got adjusted and then as soon as she could, she'd leave. If she was lucky, she'd slip out of town without her stalker realizing.

Meanwhile, she'd save up every penny she could. And hope and pray no one around her came down with that mysterious virus. Especially this precious baby. Watching Amelia while she slept, she realized she'd need to guard her heart. Not just against Theo, but against Amelia, as well. It would be all too easy to become attached.

The next morning, Theo deactivated the alarm system and wandered into the kitchen for an early morning cup of coffee. As he'd expected, Ellie was already there, making massive stacks of pancakes, which she placed in the oven to keep warm. She didn't look at him when he entered, giving him the opportunity to study her slender, yet shapely form. She'd coiled her long hair in a bun on her head, highlighting her sensual neck. He wondered what she'd do if he went up behind her and slid his arm around her waist and put his mouth to that little bit of exposed skin. Amelia cooed from her little seat, distracting him from his thoughts. Theo swore her eyes latched on to him the moment he entered the room. Ignoring Ellie, he crossed to his daughter, and crouched down in front of her. "Well, good morning, sweetie," he said, doing his best impression of baby talk.

She rewarded him with a bright smile and gurgling sounds. His heart squeezed. He'd never really paid that much attention to babies, but Amelia was exceptionally cute. And bright.

"She only woke up twice last night," Ellie said. "And she fell back asleep as soon as I changed and fed her."

He got to his feet and turned to face her, frowning as he noticed the dark circles under her bright blue eyes. She looked even more delicate than usual, making him want fiercely to protect her.

"Are you feeling okay?" he asked sharply, thinking about the virus and feeling a stab of panic at the thought Ellie might be sick.

"I'm fine." Her dismissive smile didn't fool him. "Just tired. I have trouble falling back to sleep after getting up with Amelia, that's all. I'm sure once I settle into some sort of routine, I'll adjust."

Despite knowing better, he crossed the kitchen to be closer to her. "Ellie, my offer still stands. I don't mind hiring someone else to cook. Just say the word and I'll start looking."

"No." Despite appearing frazzled, she also looked determined. "I can handle this. Plus, like I said, I need the money."

This piqued his interest, but he didn't ask. It was none of his business.

The ranch hands filed in, cutting off any further discussion. Theo pitched in, pouring the hot maple syrup into dispensers and putting them on the table, along with butter. He also dished up the sausage patties that were staying warm in a large electric skillet. Meanwhile, Ellie removed several towering stacks of pancakes from the oven, placing them in the center of the table before turning back to make more.

Apparently ravenous, the men dug in. Theo poured himself a second cup of coffee and watched.

"Aren't you going to eat?" Ellie asked as she flipped the next round to cook the other side.

"I'll wait," he said, smiling easily. "I'll eat when you do."

With a shrug, she returned her attention to feeding his hands. They were a noisy bunch this morning; apparently the cold weather had energized them.

The talk was all about separating the cows. Theo listened, remembering the rare occasions when he'd been home and had gone along for the ride. Now he couldn't even climb up on one of the perfectly trained ranch horses.

Pushing the bitterness away, he took the towering platter from Ellie and carried it to the table.

When he turned around, he caught sight of Ellie, pushing a strand of hair that had escaped from her ponytail away from her eyes. Her shoulders sagged and she appeared exhausted. As she looked up and realized he watched her, she straightened and lifted her chin.

"Your breakfast is ready," she said, flashing a quick smile as she made two plates. "Get it while it's hot."

In the other room, the men were finishing up and making their way outside to get to work.

Theo retrieved one of the syrup containers and butter, carrying it over to the smaller kitchen table. "Here you go," he said, wishing desperately he and Ellie could get back on comfortable ground. He regretted that one impulsive kiss had messed things up. Despite the sharp tug of attraction he felt when around her, he valued the friendship they'd begun.

He waited until they'd both made short work of their pancakes before he leaned forward. "Ellie, maybe we need to talk," he began.

"Good morning!" Gemma's cheerful voice sang out. "Where's my little niece?" Wearing her maroon scrubs, she breezed into the kitchen, smiling. "That smells delicious," she said.

Ellie jumped to her feet. "I'd be happy to make you some," she said."

"Oh, no need." Gemma waved her back to her seat. "I've already eaten. Let me have a look at sweet baby Amelia." Without waiting for a response, she scooped Amelia up and held her close. "Ooh," she said, wrinkling her nose. "Someone has a poopy diaper."

"I'll get that." Ellie took the baby from Gemma and hurried away to get her cleaned and changed.

Gemma watched her go. "She looks tired," she commented. "Is she feeling all right?"

"I just asked her and she said she's fine. No signs of the virus." Theo started gathering up the dirty plates and silverware, carrying them to the sink. "For whatever reason, she doesn't want to give up her cooking job. She insists she can be both—Amelia's nanny and the ranch cook. I think it's too much."

"Maybe so." Gemma cocked her head, her green eyes curious. "I wonder why she's so bent on working herself so hard."

"She says she needs the money."

"Ah. That would explain things."

After squirting in dish soap, Theo began running hot water to fill the sink. "Yeah. So I'm trying to help out as much as I can."

Gemma touched his arm, making him look at her. "Maybe you should help more with the baby instead of the kitchen. Sooner or later, you're going to have to learn how to be a father."

He winced because she was correct, then shrugged. "I'm doing the best I can," he said, meaning it.

Gemma began helping him.

"What brings you out here so early anyway?" he asked.

"Since it's Tuesday, I have to be at the clinic at eight," she said. "Some of the doctors have been working all night, along with the CDC. Everyone is focused on figuring out how to cure this thing."

He nodded, rinsing off dishes and then putting them in the dishwasher. "That's two hours away. And you still didn't answer my question."

"I don't know," she finally admitted. "Little Amelia is like a breath of fresh air in all this sickness. I wanted to see her before I start my day. I also wanted to make sure no one out here is feeling ill."

"We're fine. And I promise to call you immediately if anyone so much as sneezes."

She smiled, though her eyes were still serious. "Flu-like symptoms, Theo. Fever, aches, chills, nausea."

"Got it." He reached around her for the skillets on the stove. "How's everything at the clinic?"

Grimacing, she looked away. "Things are so crazy I don't even want to think about work," Gemma said. "If I do, I might just start crying and never stop."

Awkwardly, he patted her shoulder. "I'm sorry. Hopefully it will get better soon."

Her expression told him she didn't think that was likely.

"At least you have Molly's rehearsal dinner to look

forward to," he pointed out. "It sounds like you need this get together as much as Molly does."

"Maybe." Gemma gave him a sharp look. "What about you? I heard you're pretty much holed up at the ranch."

"I go to town." He tried not to sound too defensive.

"Yeah, now you do. To pick up diapers and formula or take Ellie. I'm talking about even before you found out you were a daddy. People were starting to call you the Colton Hermit. How long are you going to stay holed up here at the ranch?"

Refusing to let her needling bother him, he laughed. "Hey, give me a break. I already agreed to go to Molly's rehearsal dinner."

"And dress appropriately?"

By which she meant no jeans and boots. "You know I don't own a suit," Theo said.

Her skeptical look had him chuckling again. "Surely you at least own a pair of dress slacks."

"Yep." Crossing his arms, he waited, not willing to make it any easier on her.

"Button-down shirt, Western tie, dress slacks and your best pair of boots," she ordered, doing her best Gram Dottie impersonation. Which cracked them both up.

"Fine." He rolled his eyes, exactly the way he'd used to when he was a thirteen-year-old handful. "Whatever."

Which only made them both laugh harder.

"Thank you for that," Gemma finally said, wiping her eyes. "I can't tell you how long it's been since I laughed."

He gave in to impulse and hugged her. "Me too, sis. Me too."

When she looked at him, she was still smiling. "Now, about the rehearsal dinner. We've settled what you're wearing. Do you have a date?"

Recoiling in mock horror, he shook his head. "Oh, hell no."

"Well, then, you might as well bring Ellie and Amelia," Gemma drawled. "God knows we could all use a distraction around here."

"I thought the rehearsal dinner and the wedding would be enough of a distraction," Theo said. "You know how everyone can gossip. Once they get a look at Amelia, the tongues will be wagging."

"Theo, they're already wagging. Everyone knows you have a daughter. If you hide her away, they'll think you're ashamed of her."

He straightened. "I didn't think of it that way. You know I'm not ashamed or anything like that. I'm just trying to adjust to being a father. It's come as a bit of a shock."

She shrugged. "So let the family meet her. Maybe some of them could help you out."

"What about the virus? You said I needed to keep her away from germs."

Gemma's face fell. "You're probably right." The resignation in her posture told him for a brief, glorious moment she'd allowed herself to forget about her job and the growing crisis as the virus spread. Now she'd come back to reality. "I don't want you to do anything that might endanger Amelia. Especially since we still don't know how the virus is spread."

Again, he voiced his doubts. "Is it even a good idea to have a party?"

She grimaced. "Life has to continue to go on. People still shop, go out to eat, to see movies. Our baby cousin is getting married! Molly is so happy and excited we can't deny her this."

"I guess you're right. But we need to tell anyone who's sick—even if it's just with a sniffle—to stay home."

"The CDC has printed up flyers." Her tone had gone back to brisk and efficient, what Theo thought of as her nurse voice. "They'll be distributed all over town on Wednesday. Plus, they're mailing them to every resident in town. Basic, commonsense stuff, like washing your hands often. Hopefully they'll do some good."

"Is the CDC still considering a quarantine?"

For the first time in as long as he could remember, his brave little sister looked scared. "I'm not supposed to tell anyone this, so you can't repeat it. The quarantine will go into effect on Friday. That will be in the flyers. So if you need to go out of town for any reason, do it before then. And make sure you're back by Thursday night."

Chapter 6

The enormity of what Gemma was saying stunned Theo. "Can they really do this? Is it even legal?"

"I don't know," she said simply. "They've been in talks with the mayor and the city council. I'm pretty sure Flint's been involved too, since he's the chief of police."

Theo nodded. "What about people coming from out of town for Molly's wedding?"

"We'll deal with that when we have to." She passed her hand across her eyes. "But I'm guessing they won't be able to come."

"Are you feeling all right?" he asked, suddenly concerned that Gemma herself might be coming down with the virus.

"I'm fine." She met his gaze. "Not sick, I promise you. At the risk of sounding like a broken record, I'm just so tired. And stressed. Everyone at the clinic is. We've been working around the clock. And more and more sick people are coming in. Pretty soon, we're going to have to increase our isolation area or we'll be out of room."

"How many more?" Staring at her in horror, Theo wondered how he'd managed to stay so aloof that he didn't even know what was going on in his own hometown.

Gemma looked as if she was about to cry. "Enough. Look, I don't really want to talk about this anymore. Sometimes I just need to escape, get some time away." She glanced at her watch. "Let me have just this time before I have to head into town to go to work."

"I'm sorry, sis." Placing his hand on her shoulder, he gave a gentle squeeze of reassurance. "One more question, and then I'll drop it. Is Gram improving any?"

A shadow crossed her face. "No. But she's not getting any worse either. That's something."

"I'll take it." Deliberately, he turned the conversation back to the rehearsal dinner. "Too bad. I was going to bring Ellie as my date to Molly's thing. Guess I can't now, since we can't risk exposing Amelia."

As he'd known it would, the prospect of matchmaking provided distraction and brightened his sister's mood. "Sure you can. All we need to do is find a sitter for Amelia."

"A sitter? Why?" Ellie's voice had them both turning. She carried a freshly changed Amelia, though the baby had now fallen asleep.

Theo kept a smile on his face, but inwardly he wished she hadn't walked in on the conversation. Now he had no choice but to brazen it out. "My cousin Molly is getting married. Her rehearsal dinner is Friday night. I was hoping to bring you as my date."

Date might have been the wrong choice of word, Theo thought, as Ellie's face flushed pink.

"I'd rather not," she said, her voice strangled. "Plus, I don't know who else we could trust with an infant as young as Amelia."

"I've got several nurse friends who'd be perfect," Gemma put in promptly. "One or two of them are even pediatric nurses at Dr. Meyer's office downtown. I'll ask them if they can watch her for a few hours."

Theo almost felt sorry for Ellie. She appeared shell-shocked as she looked from him to Gemma. "I really can't," she said. "Sorry."

"Why not?" Gemma sounded perfectly reasonable. And also determined. Theo recognized that tone.

"Well, for starters, I don't have anything to wear."

"You've got time to purchase something. We have a couple of great boutiques in town."

Ellie's horrified expression begged Theo to help her out. He looked away, pretending not to notice. Though in the past, Theo went to parties alone, but rarely left alone, he wanted Ellie to meet people, put down some roots. That way, she might want to stay and he wouldn't lose his nanny. Also, the more people she knew, the more protected she'd be. Until her stalker was caught, he wanted to keep Ellie as safe as possible. He'd point that out to her later, once Gemma was gone.

"Come on, Ellie. It'll be fun." Gemma made it clear she wasn't giving up. "I'll even help you shop if you want."

"I'll think about it, okay?" Placing Amelia back in her bassinette, Ellie turned to face them. Her crossed arms spoke volumes. "That's the best I can do for right now."

Amused, Gemma nodded. "I'll let my brother convince you. I can't speak from experience, but I've heard he can be *very* persuasive when he wants to be."

Theo wouldn't have thought it possible, but Ellie's

creamy complexion turned an even deeper shade of red. He grinned wickedly at her. "Should I test out my powers of persuasion?"

Sounding as if she were choking, Ellie muttered something about needing to freshen up and rushed away.

Theo couldn't help it, he laughed out loud.

"What the heck was that?" Gemma demanded. "Are you tormenting that poor girl?"

He reared back in mock offense. "Just teasing her. Come on, Gemma. You know how I am."

"I do." The way she pursed her lips told him she was debating whatever she might say next. Which meant he probably wasn't going to like it.

"Theo," she began. Yep, she used her scolding voice. He crossed his arms and waited her out.

"Ellie's not at all like the kind of women you normally hang around with. You can't—"

"What?" he interrupted, raising one eyebrow in fake outrage. "What are you implying? That my former lady friends are…what?"

Her gentle smile told him she wasn't buying it. "Come on. You know what I mean. Promise me you won't hurt her."

That was easy. "I promise." He didn't even hesitate. "She and I are getting to be friends, nothing more. I'm not going to sneak into her bedroom at night or whatever you think. She's not even my type."

"Okay, good." Gemma sounded relieved. "I guess I just imagined those sparks flying between you. Just make sure she understands the situation. She seemed awfully flustered a minute ago."

"Yes, ma'am." He gave her a salute. "But I'm pretty sure she gets it already."

* * *

About to walk back into the room after her embarrassingly fast exit, Ellie froze when she heard Theo say she wasn't his type. As her heart squeezed, she wondered what the heck was wrong with her. She already knew she wasn't Theo's type. Really, she did. So she didn't understand why hearing him say it out loud hurt so much.

Pasting a smile on her face, she squared her shoulders and sailed back into the room. "Gets what already?"

This time, it felt gratifying that Theo was the one who appeared ill at ease. "Nothing," he began.

Once again, Gemma cut him off. "Ellie, if Theo's teasing ever makes you uncomfortable, just let him know. Okay?"

Ellie managed a puzzled frown. "Okay, sure. But to be honest, he reminds me a lot of a pesky older brother. Though I never had one, my best friend did."

She looked up in time to see a look of horror on Theo's handsome face.

"Ouch," he said, wincing. "Pesky, huh?"

"Only sometimes," she said back, thinking she might be getting pretty good at this bantering thing. She just didn't know how long she could keep it up.

Baby Amelia let out a wail, saving Ellie from finding out. She hurried over and picked the baby up, making cooing sounds as she checked the diaper. "She's wet, again," she explained. "It's time for her bath anyway. I'll go do that and then feed her. Then I'll get started on the prep work for lunch."

"I've got to run," Gemma said. "Ellie, let me know if you want to go shopping."

"I will," Ellie said, even though was pretty sure she wouldn't. After all, she wouldn't be going; therefore she had no need to buy something to wear.

As Ellie turned to take gather up the supplies to bathe Amelia, Theo's touch on her shoulder stopped her. "Would you mind showing me how?" he asked, his tone and expression serious.

"Show you how?" she repeated, drawing a blank as she tried not to drown in his amazing green gaze.

"To give her a bath." One corner of his sensual mouth lifted. "I'm thinking I need to learn how. You know, just in case."

Somehow she managed not to gape at him. "Sure," she said. "Of course." She swallowed. "I use the sink in the wet bar. It's the perfect size, and much easier to keep clean than the kitchen sink."

He nodded. "How often to you bathe her?"

"Not too often, at least until she's older. Once or twice a week is enough. Too much and her skin might dry out or she could get rashes."

She showed him how to test the water temperature and the correct level to fill the sink. Then, taking a deep breath, she handed him his daughter and the soft baby washcloth and took a step back.

His hands looked impossibly large and tanned as he gently handled his daughter. He washed and rinsed her, making soothing sounds. The melodic tone of his deep voice made Amelia chortle. Seeing this, Ellie knew Amelia would be all right. Little by little, Theo would learn his way. And she could leave with a clear conscience.

Weird how the thought made her chest ache.

After she'd handed him a towel and he'd dried Amelia off, Ellie showed him how to powder her little bottom and then put her in a clean Onesie. Baths always made Amelia drowsy, and her little eyes kept drifting half-closed.

He carried her back to the kitchen and placed her in the bassinette, before getting busy making her bottle.

Ellie supervised, feeling both pleased and oddly bereft as she watched a tough cowboy become putty caring for his daughter. Still, from the frequent looks he gave Ellie, as if to ask if he was doing everything right, it was clear he didn't feel comfortable yet. She knew that would come with time and experience.

The house phone rang, making Ellie jump. Even Theo appeared startled, as he made no move to answer it.

"That's weird," he said. "The only one who still uses that phone is Gram Dottie. Everyone else just calls my cell."

He finally answered, listened for a second and then said, "Sure. Here she is." Turning, he faced Ellie and held out the phone. "It's my cousin Molly. Seems Gemma called her a minute ago and told her you need help shopping for a dress."

Not sure how to react, Ellie accepted the phone. "Hello?"

"Hi. Ellie, I hope you don't mind me calling, but Gemma said we'd like each other and I can use all the friends I can get, you know what I mean?" Molly's cheerful voice brought a smile to Ellie's face.

"Anyway," Molly rushed on. "I need another woman around my age to hang around with." She laughed, sounding slightly breathless. "I'm getting married really soon and it's at the point where I don't trust my own opinion."

Ellie wasn't sure how to respond, so she didn't. Molly didn't appear to notice. She continued talking. "So, what I guess I'm trying to say, is will you be my friend? We can meet for lunch on your day off. What do you say?"

Finally, she paused.

"On my day off?" was all Ellie could think of to say. "Um, I'm not sure I actually get a day off."

"No way," Molly squealed. "Find out."

"Hold on, let me ask." Ellie looked at Theo. "Do I? Get a day off, that is?"

"Sure," he said easily. "Once I know how to take care of Amelia. When do you want one?"

She shrugged, held up a finger and got back on the phone. "Molly, when do you want to meet for lunch?"

"The sooner the better." Molly barely paused for breath before continuing. "How about today? We can shop for a dress after."

Though the idea definitely appealed, Ellie couldn't help worrying about her stalker. "Um, can I call you back and let you know?"

"Sure. My number should be in your caller ID."

Feeling slightly dazed, Ellie pressed the off button and then just stood there staring at the phone. "Wow."

Theo chuckled. "Molly's a force of nature, isn't she?"

"I'll say. And while I'd love to meet her for lunch and then shop, I'm afraid. What if my stalker shows up? I can't put yet another innocent person at risk."

Theo considered her for a moment. "That's easy. Just tell Molly you want to go into Cheyenne. We're about forty minutes away from there. No way will the stalker know where you are."

She felt like jumping up and down with relief. Instead she simply nodded. "As long as I make sure we aren't followed."

"Exactly."

About to hit Redial on the phone, she paused and eyed him. "Are you up to watching Amelia this afternoon? I'll make sure lunch is prepared and dinner. All you'll have to do is heat it up and serve it."

"No problem." He didn't appear the least bit fazed by the prospect. "I can handle it."

Privately, she thought this would be a good thing for

both Theo and Amelia. They could continue to bond, as a father and daughter should. Before he could change his mind, she called Molly back and made arrangements to meet. It turned out Molly had been planning to go into Cheyenne anyway.

"I'll pick you up in a couple of hours," Molly said, sounding as excited as if she'd just won the lottery.

Ellie barely got out an okay before Molly hung up.

When she looked up, she realized Theo was watching her, amusement making his eyes gleam. "Go." He waved her away. "Go and get ready. I've got Amelia."

Grateful, she nodded. "Thank you. I really appreciate this. I've got to get everything ready for the two meals."

"I can do that. You just worry about getting ready."

She stared, stunned. "Are you sure?"

"Of course." His grin contained a hint of wickedness. "But you know this means you have to go to the rehearsal dinner with me, right?"

He had her there. Slowly, she nodded. "I guess so."

The deep richness of his laugh made her grow warm. "You know," Theo said, his tone musing, "I think Molly will be good for you. She might help you loosen up, be less serious."

Serious? Stung, rather than replying, she ignored him and hurried off to her room to get ready.

Ninety minutes later, having done everything she could think of to fix herself up, Ellie returned to the living room. She had on her favorite pair of jeans, the low-heeled boots she'd only worn once and a dangly pair of silver earrings. She'd taken her hair out of it customary ponytail and used her flatiron to straighten it.

She thought she looked pretty good. Young and carefree, at least. Not serious at all.

When she walked into the living room, Theo whistled. "You clean up good," he said.

And of course, she blushed. Something she hated but had no control over. "Thanks," she managed.

A horn honking outside stifled whatever he'd been about to say.

Ellie rushed to the window, staring at the bright red, low-slung sports car idling in the driveway. "A Corvette? Your cousin drives a 'Vette?"

Theo cocked his head. "You don't like Corvettes?"

"I love them," she said. "I always wanted one someday." By which she meant when she was working somewhere where she made a lot more money.

"I bet if you ask Molly, she'll let you drive hers."

The thought made her smile. "I just might have to do that."

Molly looked like her voice. Her trademark Colton green eyes sparkled, and her red wavy hair tried to escape her loose braid.

The instant she caught sight of Ellie, she squealed and hugged her as if Ellie was a long-lost relative. Her infectious joy made Ellie feel as if she'd dropped a boulder that she hadn't even known she carried.

Molly chattered all the way to Cheyenne, which Ellie appreciated since her innate shyness made it difficult for her to find topics of conversation with people she didn't know. Molly clearly had no such problem.

But the time they reached the sign that welcomed them to Cheyenne, Ellie felt as if she'd known Molly all her life.

They visited a few boutiques.

"Surely, here, you'll find something you like." Molly smiled encouragingly.

"I've never really been a dressy person," Ellie confided. "Jeans in the winter, shorts in the summer and that's about it."

"I'll help you." Molly's confident smile reassured Ellie. "I know what kind of dresses will look fabulous on you."

Trailing along behind her new friend, Ellie accepted each dress Molly handed her while trying not to stress with figuring out how she was going to pay, as she hadn't gotten her first paycheck from Theo, yet. She had one credit card that she used only for emergencies, and she rapidly realized she'd have to consider this an emergency or face total and utter humiliation. She could only hope the prices weren't too bad—so far she'd been afraid to look.

"Okay, that should do it." Molly pointed toward the dressing room. "Go try them on. I want to see you in each one."

Resigned, Ellie did as she said.

The first four or five dresses didn't work. Ellie knew the moment she dropped each one over her head. Too tight, too loose, too long, the wrong cut for her long legs and long waist.

Molly giggled, winced, nodded and agreed.

Dress number six looked plain on its hanger compared to the others. Midnight blue, made of some clingy fabric Ellie couldn't identify, the dress didn't look like it'd be the one. Still, she might as well try it on. There were only two more after it, and if she didn't find a dress this go-round, she knew Molly would make her do it all over again.

To her surprise, she realized the instant she looked at herself in the mirror that this was *the* dress. Checking the price tag, she felt relieved to see the dress was under a hundred dollars.

Pushing open the dressing room door, she stepped out to see if Molly concurred.

"Wow." Molly's eyes went wide. "You look absolutely gorgeous. I don't think you should even try any of the others."

"Okay." Ellie looked down at her feet. Throwing caution to the wind, she liked the lighthearted feeling. "I'm going to need shoes to go with this too."

Once they finished their shopping, Molly drove them to a little Mexican restaurant tucked away on a back street near the mall. "I've been here before," she proclaimed. "And I promise it's good."

They talked all through lunch. Ellie learned about the whirlwind courtship Molly had enjoyed with her fiancé, Jimmy Johnson.

"I can't wait until you meet him," Molly gushed. "He's so cute! The first time I met him, the instant he smiled at me, I knew he was The One."

Finishing the last bite of chicken fajitas, Ellie pushed he plate away. "I take it that's the reason you two decided not to have a long engagement. You both knew and decided there was no reason to wait?"

"Yes." Molly's expression grew dreamy. "He proposed two weeks after we met."

Shocked, Ellie looked down to hide it. "How long ago was it that he proposed?"

"A month." Molly's wide smile invited Ellie to partake in her joy. "I know, I know." She fluttered her small hand dismissively when Ellie didn't comment. "It's not long enough. For most people. But for us, we can't wait to live together as husband and wife and get started on a family."

"You're very fortunate," Ellie said, meaning it. "Not everyone finds that kind of love."

"I know." Grinning good-naturedly, Molly grabbed the

check from the waiter. "My treat. And don't you dare try to pay anything, not even the tip. You can treat next time."

More relieved than she cared to admit, Ellie nodded. She had no cash saved up. She hadn't exactly made a lot, working in the bookstore in Boulder. All she earned went for rent and food. Since coming here, she'd opened a bank account and planned to start saving her pay, eventually hoping to have enough to travel far, far away.

With that goal in mind, all she carried was that emergency credit card that now had a hundred and fifty dollars charged to it. She considered herself lucky she'd been able to talk Molly out of making Ellie purchase jewelry and a purse, as well.

Ellie had earrings and a few bracelets she figured would work. And she'd never been one to carry a purse.

After lunch, Molly took them to a nail salon and treated them both to mani-pedis, over Ellie's protests. Though Ellie loved feeling pampered, she knew she'd need to have a frank talk with Molly. If they were going to be friends, she needed to understand Ellie couldn't afford this kind of thing and refused to continually mooch.

Once they were on the road back toward Dead River, Ellie spoke up.

"I'm sorry." Instantly contrite, Molly looked as if she might cry. "I didn't even think. I just wanted to have a girl's day out and…I promise it won't happen again."

Ellie let out a sigh of relief. "I really like you," she said. "And I think we might become good friends while I'm here. But I needed to put that out there, so you knew."

"I can afford it, you know." Molly smiled sadly. "I might work as a waitress, but my sister, Sarah, and I inherited my parents' life insurance when they were killed in a car accident three years ago."

Horrified, Ellie stared. "I'm sorry."

"It's all right." Unbelievably, Molly reached out and patted Ellie's shoulder, as though comforting *her*. "It's been long enough that I can talk about it."

Not sure how to respond, Ellie simply nodded.

"Anyway." Molly lifted her chin, smiling again as she made the turn that would lead them to the ranch. "This has been one of the best Tuesdays I've had in a long time. Tuesdays are my day off. Tuesdays and Fridays."

"I agree," She said, meaning it. Unbuckling her seat belt, Ellie asked, "Would you like to come and meet Amelia?"

"Ooh, Theo's baby?" Molly glanced at her watch and then frowned. "You know, I'd love to, but my sister has scheduled a caterer meeting in half an hour. She's making last-minute tweaks to the menu again. By the time I get home and freshen up…I simply don't have time."

"That's okay." Ellie swallowed her disappointment. She'd have enjoyed showing off Amelia to Molly. "Maybe another time."

"Definitely!" Molly leaned across the seat and hugged her. "See you on Friday!"

After Ellie got out of the car, she stood and watched Molly drive off before going back inside.

Theo was waiting in the living room, holding a sleeping Amelia in his arms. Ellie stopped, taking in the picture, marveling at the warm glow she felt as the sight of the rugged cowboy and the dainty baby.

Not hers, she reminded herself. For one brief moment, she'd had the absurd fantasy that this was her family, her man and child.

"Hey," she said, keeping her dress bag high so it wouldn't drag the floor. "How'd everything go?"

"Fine." He flashed a proud grin, which predictably

turned Ellie's insides to mush. "Amelia and I managed. How about you? Did you have a good time?"

"Yes." Unable to keep from glancing at her watch, she realized it was nearly dinnertime. "Is there something ready for me to serve to the hands for their supper?"

"Yep. I cooked those baby back ribs you had thawing. And baked potatoes and black beans. I've got everything staying warm until it's time."

Exhaling with relief, she nodded. "Thank you."

"Why don't you go and put your dress—and whatever else you bought—up and then meet me in the kitchen?" His wink sent another stab of heat straight to her center. "You'll probably want to check up on my work and made sure I did everything I was supposed to."

Tongue-tied, she turned to do exactly that. Feeling his gaze burn into her back, she struggled not to react. Though she'd count it as a miracle if she made it to her room without stumbling.

Once she'd hung up the dress, she hurried into the kitchen. She saw that Theo had placed Amelia back in her little bassinette to continue to sleep.

"I really like your cousin," she said, opening the massive oven door to check on the ribs and potatoes. "Good. You used tinfoil."

Again he flashed that devastating grin. "This ain't my first rodeo, you know."

Quietly considering him while trying to ignore the way her nerve endings suddenly came awake, she shrugged. "No, I don't know. So you can cook? What's your specialty?"

"T-bones on the grill," he replied promptly. "But I don't cook those on a large-scale basis, for obvious reasons. I also can make a mean chicken enchilada casserole. Gram Dottie taught all three of us to cook."

Another surprise. Turning away to cover her confusion, she stirred the large pot of black beans simmering on the stove. She felt…relieved, actually. She hadn't realized how much her worry about her stalker making an appearance had made her tense. Back at the ranch, with Theo, she could relax. Feel safe. Almost.

"What about bread?" she asked. "We need rolls or corn bread or something."

"I got that covered." He pointed to three unopened loaves of Wonder bread. "Just bread. It goes great with ribs. They'll love it, I promise."

She decided to trust him on that one, mainly because she was too tired to whip something else up.

Everything was ready when the men, tired and hungry, began to file in for the last meal of the day.

The ribs looked perfectly done, restaurant quality. Judging from the comments of the ranch hands, they tasted as good as they looked.

"Aren't you going to eat?" she asked Theo.

"When you do." Pointing to Amelia, who managed to still sleep despite the boisterous group of ranch hands in the next room, he smiled. "Come on. Let's get our plates before they're all gone."

Enjoying the companionable feeling of sitting beside him in the kitchen, with the men chowing down in the other room, Ellie picked up a rib and bit in. Her mouth exploded with flavor. More than just barbecue sauce, she tasted a hint of jalapeño and something else. "What did you mix with the sauce?"

"Dr Pepper," he said.

She laughed. "You'll have to show me how to make it sometime."

After dinner, they worked side by side cleaning up while Amelia worked her pacifier in her bassinette. Ellie loved the feeling of working side by side with Theo, almost as if they were a couple.

Which they weren't, of course. Nor would they ever be. Shaking her head at her own foolishness, she finished stacking the last of the pan in the dishwasher, added soap and turned it on.

"You look happy," Theo observed, making her blush.

"You know, right this moment, I am. It's been a really good day."

He nodded, going to the fridge and grabbing a beer. "There's a John Wayne marathon on tonight. Do you want to watch with me?"

"I love John Wayne," she said, before she thought better of it. Best she remember her place. Spending her leisure time with Theo would only make her want more of what she couldn't have. "But I'm really tired. Amelia still isn't sleeping through the night. I think I'm going to go to my room and read a little."

Was that disappointment she saw in his rugged face? No, most likely a trick of the light. "Sleep well," he said, and left her standing in the kitchen, her foolish heart aching.

Chapter 7

Though he'd been expecting it, Theo still felt stunned the next morning when he found the flyer on his front door bright and early. Wednesday, just as Gemma had said. Everything his sister had warned him about was coming to pass, and it scared the hell out of him.

Carrying it inside, he read in the kitchen as he drank his first cup of coffee. More details were outlined in the flyer. It said the CDC would be announcing the quarantine using multiple media outlets. No doubt they were trying to make sure to reach everyone they could. They had also taken out a front-page ad in the *Dead River News,* put public service announcements to run every hour on the small radio station, mailed out flyers to every single resident and posted the same flyers in the window of every business downtown. They were nothing if not thorough. They'd even listed a toll-free number for people to call if they had questions.

Carefully folding the flyer, he stuck it in his shirt pocket and wondered if he should show it to Ellie or not. Part of him worried she'd leave town, before things got too buttoned down.

But he'd never been much of a liar and he didn't intend to start now. He'd have to take his chances.

Along with freshly brewed coffee, a scent that vaguely reminded him of Thanksgiving tickled his nose. Who knows, maybe Ellie had made pumpkin cinnamon rolls or something.

The kitchen was empty, though the wonderful scent had intensified, which meant Ellie had already gotten a head start on breakfast. Theo poured a second cup of coffee, took a seat at the table and pulled the flyer from his pocket.

He read it again and started over for the third time. His cell phone rang, disrupting his musings. "Did you get your flyer?" Gemma asked.

"I'm looking at it right now." With a sigh, he put the paper down. "You know, once everyone starts reading these, the town will be in an uproar."

"I'm thinking an immediate town hall meeting will be held," Gemma said.

"Probably."

"Are you going to go?" she asked him, her voice worried and weary. With all the craziness at the clinic, she often sounded that way these days.

"No." Sometimes short answers were the best. But of course, being his sister, she had to pry.

"Why not? This is your town too, Theo. I think you need to have an interest in what's going on."

He snorted, unable to help himself. "Thanks, sis. I'll keep that in mind."

Which they both knew meant he had no intention of participating.

"I don't understand." An undercurrent of disappointment had crept into his sister's voice. "You're a Colton. You have a responsibility to this town."

"Do I?" Privately, he doubted that. Anyway, his brother, Flint, carried enough responsibility for all three of them. "Gemma, I already know how the townspeople are going to react to the quarantine. They aren't going to like it. Who would? They'll be angry, the meeting will consist in a lot of shouting and accusations and after a couple of hours of this, absolutely nothing will have changed. Going would be a complete waste of time."

"Fine," Gemma huffed. "I guess Flint will have to represent our part of the family. Like he always does, with no help from you."

Even though he'd just been thinking the exact same thing, Theo let that one pass. "Any other news? How's Gram doing?"

"She's holding steady. No improvement, but she's not worse either. That's what's so crazy about this virus. We don't understand why it takes one path with some people and another with others."

"I'm just glad Gram isn't worse. At her age..." He didn't have to finish. Gemma knew exactly what he meant.

"I've got to go." And she hung up.

Theo knew he was trying, by means of avoidance, to pretend the world around him hadn't gone crazy. In the space of a few short days, he'd gained a baby and turned his new cook into a nanny, and his Gram Dottie was sick with a mysterious virus that had the capability of killing her. Add the quarantine to that, and if he thought about it too long, he might start to wonder if he'd gone downright nuts. If he hadn't had the possibility of his future as a breeder of rodeo broncs to ground him, he didn't know what he'd do. The bad part was that he finally felt ready to get started, and now the town had been shut down.

So he got a third cup of coffee, sat down at the table and read the flyer again. The reading didn't improve with time.

Ellie wandered into the kitchen shortly after Theo ended the call. With a cloth over her shoulder and burping Amelia, Ellie looked adorably disheveled. Just gazing at her made his mood a little better.

Before either could speak, Amelia let out a satisfied belch. "Ah, there we go." Ellie placed the baby in her bassinette, then headed for the coffeepot to pour herself a cup. Once she'd doctored it up the way she liked it and taken a deep sip, she turned to face Theo.

"Breakfast is already made." She did a double take, frowning as she peered at him.

"What's wrong?" she asked. "Why do you look like the world has just ended?"

For a split second, he again considered not telling her. But that wouldn't be fair to her, not after all she'd been through. He had to at least give her a choice.

"You might want to sit down."

Clearly not understanding, she pulled out a chair and sat.

Wordlessly, he handed her the flyer.

Ellie's frown deepened as she read. When she'd finished, and she raised her face to look at him, he recognized the flash of panic in her eyes. "I can't believe this is happening."

"I know." He swallowed. "Not only can no one leave town, but no one can come here either. It's like we're in a bubble."

He saw the moment she realized what this meant.

"My stalker is trapped here with me."

"You don't know that," he hastened to reassure her. "For all you know, the bastard might have gone into Cheyenne to buy more black roses or something. Maybe he's stuck outside Dead River."

Though she nodded, he could tell she didn't really believe him.

"Think positive," he chided. "Gemma said everyone will try to call a town meeting."

"That's a good idea." She sat up straighter. "I think we should go."

He groaned. "You sound like my sister. I don't live in town, so I'm not going. Of course, you can if you want. I'll even watch the baby."

Considering, she finally shook her head. "I'd better not. For all I know, my stalker could be there."

Time to change the subject, before the entire morning was ruined. He eyed her. "What are you making the men for breakfast?"

"Oatmeal," she said promptly. "With pumpkin and brown sugar. It's been cooking in the Crock-Pots all night."

"Now I understand the smell. I thought you'd made pumpkin rolls or something."

"Nope. Oatmeal." She crossed the room and opened two huge Crock-Pots, giving the insides a good stir. "Healthy and perfect on a chilly October morning."

"It smells great." He inhaled appreciatively. "Though to be honest with you, it doesn't sound like something the hands will like."

One corner of her lush mouth tugged up into a smile. "Then maybe it's time they broadened their horizons."

Oddly enough, when the men trooped into the kitchen

and were presented with steaming bowls of oatmeal, every single one of them cleaned his bowl. Theo didn't hear a single word of complaint.

"Here." Ellie slid some in front of Theo. "I added a little bit of milk. Try it. It's good."

She returned to the Crock-Pot and got her own full bowl, taking a seat across from him.

They ate in companionable silence, while baby Amelia cooed in her bassinette. As they finished, the men in the other room filled their own cups with coffee from the large urn and, smiling shyly at Ellie, made their way outside to begin their workday.

"They like you," he said.

She laughed. "You don't have to sound so surprised. They'd like anyone, as long as they were fed well."

While he wasn't so sure about that, he didn't comment.

To his surprise, his bowl was empty before he knew it. "That was really good. Thank you."

Again her laugh rang out, making him smile. "You don't have to thank me for doing my job."

"I know. But I do when you're doing it well. Which you are. You're a damn good cook, Ellie."

Again her porcelain skin turned pink. "Thank you," she said quietly.

Suddenly he wanted to kiss her. So much so that he nearly pushed himself to his feet to go to her. Stunned, he looked down at his coffee, took a deep breath and tried to get himself back under control.

Ellie didn't seem to notice. "I wonder how they're going to enforce it," she said. "Did they call in the National Guard or something? I know Dead River's police force isn't large enough to be up for the task."

The quarantine. He slid the flyer back in front of him

and read it again, feeling as though he was trying to memorize the damn thing.

"Let's take a drive into town," he said. "All three of us—you and me and Amelia. We can check it out ourselves."

Her frown made a tiny line appear between her perfectly shaped eyebrows. "I don't know. Is it safe?"

"We don't have to get out of the truck. I just want to see how people are reacting." And to find out if armed guards were now patrolling the town's perimeter, though he kept that one to himself since he didn't want to frighten her.

After considering for a moment, she agreed. "We might as well pick up more diapers and formula while we're there."

"We just did that."

She laughed again, the sound tickling his nerve endings and making him smile. "Babies go through a lot of diapers and formula. Believe me. We need to stock up. I don't want to ever run out."

Right then and there he resolved to make Ellie laugh as much as possible. She always looked pretty, but when she laughed, she was downright beautiful. Not his type, but gorgeous nonetheless.

"We'll go now," he decided. "Though the other stores don't open until ten, Dead River Pharmacy opens at eight."

Her blue eyes widened. "I need a few minutes to get ready," she said. "If you don't mind keeping any eye on the baby, I'll be back in a few."

"Go ahead." He waved her away. "Amelia and I have some things to discuss anyway."

Once Ellie had gone, he crossed to the bassinette and picked up his smiling daughter. "You're such a happy baby," he said to her. She rewarded him with gurgles and coos.

Lifting her up, he held her suspended, just above his face. She went silent as they studied each other. And then she made a gurgling sound and spit up all over his face and shirt.

At first, Theo stood frozen, afraid to move. He tried to think back, to remember if Ellie had given him instruction on how to deal with baby spit-up. It smelled bad and felt worse.

Finally, he just put Amelia back in the bassinette, grabbed a few paper towels and wiped himself clean. Though he'd have to change his shirt, he felt proud that he'd survived.

Moistening a fresh paper towel, he went back to the baby and gently cleaned up her little face. Because of the way he'd been holding her—note to self, don't do that again—she hadn't gotten any spit-up on her clothes.

Sighing, he continued to drink his coffee, waiting for Ellie to return so he could go and change.

"What happened?" Eyeing his shirt and wrinkling her nose, Ellie glanced from him to the baby and back again. "Let me guess. Spit-up?"

He nodded. "Be right back."

Once he'd cleaned up properly and donned a new shirt, he returned. "I know Mimi brought a car seat when she brought Amelia. Her car is still here. Give me a minute to get it out of there and installed in my truck." He smiled, unable to keep from noticing how lovely she looked.

"Ok." She nodded, looking at him curiously. "Didn't Mimi have any family? I would think someone would have fetched the car by now."

"Good point. I don't know. I'll need to ask her ex, Dr.

Rand. Meanwhile, it'll take me a bit to figure out how to do the car seat. I've never done this before."

She smiled. "I need to pack a diaper bag anyway."

At first glance, the infant car seat seemed a simple thing. After fiddling with it for a few minutes, he decided the infernal contraption had been invented by a sadist. He knew enough to be aware proper installation was of the utmost importance to Amelia's safety.

Finally, he felt satisfied he'd gotten it right.

When he returned to the house, Ellie and Amelia were waiting.

"It's done." He smiled, refusing to hang on to his frustration for any longer than necessary. "So, let's go."

A mile from downtown, he came upon traffic. Red taillights, stopped cars, reminiscent of rush hour in Cheyenne.

Braking, he tried to see what might be ahead. "This is really strange," he said. "Even if there was an accident or something that closed down the road, there's never this many cars heading into town at the same time."

"Maybe it has something to do with the quarantine," she suggested. "It's possible you're not the only one who wanted to go and check things out."

"Or they've already called a town hall meeting, and everyone is rushing to get there." He sighed. "We can turn around and go back home or sit here until things start moving again. Your call."

"We really need diapers."

"Then we'll wait."

Traffic slowly crept forward. It wasn't until they rounded the corner into town that Theo saw the roadblock. "What the..."

State police vehicles were parked on both sides of the road, stopping every car and checking ID.

When Theo finally reached the officer, he handed over his license. “What’s going on?”

“Quarantine,” the man said. “Miss, I’ll need your ID too.”

“Wait a second,” Theo interrupted. “I thought the quarantine was at the city limits. You’re simply blocking access into town proper.”

“Sir.” The trooper looked him directly in the eye. “We have two circles around this town. The National Guard is stationed on every road leading into or out of Dead River, including the rural areas. The state police are manning the roadblocks around the downtown area. Any other questions?”

Theo shook his head. “No, sir.”

“Good.” Turning his gaze on Ellie, the officer held out his hand. “ID please.”

Ellie rooted in the diaper bag, withdrew her driver’s license and passed it over.

“Colorado?” Mouth pursed as if he found the entire state distasteful, he handed it back. “You two are free to go. Please be aware you will have to stop at the checkpoint again should you wish to leave.” He motioned at Theo to pull forward.

Once they’d moved away, Theo let out breath he hadn’t even been aware he’d been holding. “That is just plain weird.” He glanced at Ellie, who appeared a bit shell-shocked herself. “I think I need to stop in and talk to Flint before we go home.”

“I agree.” Looking back over her shoulder, she grimaced. “None of that makes any sense.”

“And it’s not what was outlined in the flyer.”

They pulled up in front of the sheriff’s department and parked. “Do you mind waiting here with Amelia?” Theo asked.

"Not at all."

"I'll be back in a few minutes," he said, unable to keep from noticing how the sunlight turned her reddish-brown hair to molten fire. She really was quite beautiful, though she appeared not to be aware of that fact.

Hurrying into the building, he noted the reception area seemed more crowded than normal. Both of the dispatchers were there, which was odd, as Glenda McDonald usually only worked the night shift.

Waving at Kendra so she could buzz him in, he hurried past the bull pen where the deputies had their desks.

Flint looked up when Theo appeared in his door. "Let me guess," he said, his voice weary. "You want to complain about the quarantine."

"Not really." Hooking his thumbs on his belt, Theo studied his brother, who seemed to have aged years the past few days. "I just wanted to ask about the barricades coming into and going out of town. I knew they'd be patrolling the city limits, but..."

"I don't know." Flint dragged his hand through his closely shorn hair. "I've been informed with no degree of uncertainty that the CDC and the National Guard are in charge of this entire operation. I'm not sure who called in the state police, but it wasn't me."

Theo couldn't believe what he was hearing. "They're keeping you out of the loop?"

Flint shrugged. "Right now, yes. I'm sure once things settle down a bit, they'll do a better job of keeping me informed. I'm actually kind of relieved. I've got enough problems, dealing with a bunch of irate citizens. We're having a town hall meeting later today."

"Gemma said that would happen."

"And I suppose you're not going." There was no censure in his brother's voice, more of a tired resignation.

"I'm not planning on it. I've got enough on my plate as it is. Any word on catching Ellie's stalker?"

"No. I've passed around the description to the National Guard and state police, so if he shows up at one of the checkpoints, they can nab him."

Theo stared at his brother in disbelief. "That's it? You're not actively searching?"

"I'm sorry. Right now, my guys are stretched so thin we haven't been able to do much. You need to keep some of your hands around to guard the house."

Bristling, Theo shook his head. "I can protect Ellie and Amelia just fine, thank you."

Now it was Flint's turn to stare. "Sorry. I didn't mean to imply that you couldn't."

The rush of protective determination he felt floored Theo, though he took care not to show it. "No problem. I guess being a father has made me a bit defensive."

Flint still watched him closely. "Understood. How are they doing?"

"Fine. As a matter of fact, they're both waiting for me outside in the truck if you'd like to come see for yourself."

"Any other time, I'd love to go out and talk to them." Flint sighed. "But as soon as I step out into the waiting area, I'll be mobbed. I know. I went out to get some breakfast at the diner. It wasn't pretty."

"Is there anything I can do to help?"

Flint gave him a considering look. "Not right now, but thanks for offering. Just keep my little niece safe, okay?"

"Will do." Saying his goodbyes, Theo hurried back outside to Ellie and Amelia.

Once they'd pulled back out into the street, Ellie spoke. "People are upset. While I was waiting for you, I couldn't help overhearing a couple of conversations. One group was even talking about organizing a riot."

"A riot?" He shot her a look. "Are you serious? Maybe they meant more like a demonstration?"

"Maybe." But she sounded doubtful and he made a mental note to call Flint later and let him know.

They stopped at the small market to pick up three more boxes of disposable diapers and another case of formula, Ellie apparently being of the belief it was necessary to stock up. Theo couldn't help noticing the way she stuck close to him, or how she constantly looked over her shoulder.

He hated this for her. If he could get his hands on her stalker right now, he'd make sure that idiot would never bother her again. Since he couldn't do that, he did his best to try to make her feel as safe as he could.

After he'd loaded the supplies in the back of his truck, instead of heading straight home, he decided to surprise her. He stopped at a little shop he'd spotted the other day when he got a haircut but forgotten to mention to her in all the excitement.

"What's this?" Ellie asked, peering at the brightly decorated window.

"A children's clothing store. Let's go buy Amelia some new outfits." He waited expectantly. If Ellie was like every other woman he'd known, she'd be delighted and would temporarily forget about her stalker.

"Seriously?" As a slow smile blossomed on her face, he wasn't disappointed.

Smiling back, he nodded. "I'll hang on to her so you can shop."

Amazing, he thought, grinning as he watched her bounce out of the truck, waiting with barely concealed impatience for him to get Amelia out of the car seat. She practically bounded into the store. Once inside, she headed right for the little girls' side.

Luckily, the shop owner had placed a couple of chairs around the room. Theo took a seat in one that gave him a perfect view of the door and sidewalk. Gently rocking a drowsy Amelia, he couldn't stop smiling as he watched Ellie flit from rack to rack, her excitement and joy both palpable and contagious.

After a few minutes, he realized he hadn't seen a single salesperson or cashier. In fact, the store seemed deserted.

Slightly alarmed, he got up and walked toward the back, where the checkout counter was. Beyond that, a door led to the back of the shop.

Unwilling to leave Ellie, he pushed open the door. "Hello?" he called. "Anyone here?"

Ellie hurried over, still flush with excitement. "What's wrong?"

About to tell her, he spun as someone appeared. A short, middle-aged woman came from the back. She wore a white, surgical-type mask.

"I'm sorry," she said, her words muffled by the mask. "With this epidemic, I'm trying to minimize contact with people. When you've made your selections, I'll be happy to ring them up, but I do ask that you keep your distance."

Just like that, Ellie's joy dissipated, reality smacking her in the face. Theo clenched his teeth and managed a terse nod at the woman. In truth, he really would have preferred just leaving without buying anything, but this was the only children's store in town. And since they couldn't drive to Cheyenne, if they wanted to buy Amelia new clothes, they had no choice.

Ellie made her remaining choices with a brusque efficiency. She placed everything on the counter, stepping back so the woman could ring up their purchase.

Once the total had been calculated—nearly three hundred dollars, which sort of shocked Theo, just a little—he fished his money clip out of his pocket, peeled off three bills and tossed them on the counter.

"Keep the change," he said while the clerk shoved the clothes into a bag. When he reached to take it, the woman moved back so fast she nearly stumbled over her own feet.

She didn't say thank you and neither did they. Theo handed the bag to Ellie so he could manage Amelia. Ellie climbed into the cab, her expression pensive. She didn't speak while he buckled Amelia in her car seat.

He didn't either. Backing out of the parking spot, he drove to the barricade, pleased that at least this time, the line was much shorter. A quick glance at Ellie's profile told him she was still internally processing what had just transpired in the store.

Once they'd made it through and were on the road heading back toward the ranch, Ellie finally spoke. "What happened back there really made what's going on with the virus hit home."

"She didn't have to act like that," he said, aching for the way the happiness had been leached out of the day. "She could have handled it differently."

"I don't know. I could understand her fear. She was only protecting herself."

"Then she shouldn't even have opened the store. Staying home would have been better than treating us like lepers."

Ellie's eyes widened. He supposed his vehemence surprised her. He didn't care. He'd enjoyed making her happy, even if only for a little while.

And this realization might have been the most shocking of all. Since when did he try to make a woman happy, other than in the bedroom?

Glancing at her, he saw she'd turned to watch Amelia sleep in her car seat. Well, at least she didn't realize. He took solace in the knowledge that Ellie apparently remained oblivious.

He'd just have to make sure she stayed that way.

Once back at the ranch, Ellie took off with Amelia for her room. Ordinarily she would have spent some time playing with all the new outfits, spreading them out on the bed and looking at them again before hanging them in the closet.

Not now. The stark fear in the store clerk's eyes had made everything feel unclean. Even the pretty, brightly colored baby clothes. Ellie left them in the bag. She'd wash them in the morning before she put them up.

She got the evening meal ready, working on autopilot. Once the men were fed, she ate her own meal, trying to pretend that Theo's conspicuous absence didn't bother her.

After she'd cleaned up the kitchen, fed and changed Amelia and put her down for the night, she was so exhausted she crawled into bed and fell instantly asleep.

The next morning she woke refreshed, her mood once again sunny. Though it was Thursday, it felt like a weekend. After feeding the men—once again Theo was a no-show—and scarfing down her own breakfast, Ellie made a huge pot of spaghetti with meat sauce, which she let simmer all day, filling the house with a delicious aroma that kept her in a constant state of hungry anticipation all day.

By the time the noon meal had been served and there was still no sign of Theo, Ellie began to worry.

Carrying Amelia, since she unashamedly planned to use her as an excuse once she found him, Ellie searched the house. It didn't take long; though the main house seemed pretty large, the open concept design made it easy.

Even Theo's bedroom held no clue as to where he might be. Heart beating fast, Ellie stood in the doorway, wondering if she dared enter.

Finally deciding against it, she turned and went back to her own room.

That night, dishing up the spaghetti with her own mouth watering in anticipation, she gave a little jump when Theo appeared, carrying a notebook. Trying to pretend not to be bothered, she greeted him with what she hoped was a friendly smile and a quick wave.

"Smells like heaven," he said, cocking one eyebrow and leaning his hip against the counter. His windswept hair and outdoorsy appearance made him even more devastatingly handsome.

Her mouth went dry, and she took a sip of water to cover. "Pull up a chair and I'll make you a plate," she offered.

"Don't mind if I do." Again the dazzling smile.

Turning away, she frowned, wondering why he'd gone back to his impersonal, flirtatious attitude. As if they hadn't ever shared a kiss or become friends.

And maybe they hadn't. Become friends, that is. Maybe it was all in her mind.

Either way, she was tired of worrying about it. She was hungry. Damn hungry.

She fixed him a plate and took it to him, then made her own, standing at the kitchen counter to eat her dinner. Hunched over, making notes in his book, he didn't speak and she didn't even try to make him. She hated that somehow she felt guilty. For what, she had no idea.

Which wasn't even logical. And that pissed her off even more.

The hands had finished and were ready for dessert. She'd gone simple with this one—a huge pan of brownies, which she served with vanilla ice cream.

Of course they loved that. Their obvious enjoyment put a smile on her face, the first one of the day.

Only after she'd served them did she turn to see if Theo wanted dessert.

As she did, his cell phone rang. Answering it, he shot Ellie a distracted look and got up, leaving the room. After a momentary flash of disappointment, she made her own dessert and sat down in his spot.

It wasn't really snooping if he'd left the notebook open, right? Spooning ice cream into her mouth, she slid the paper closer and took a look.

He'd made some sort of list. Two words jumped out at her. *Rodeo* and *Bronc.* Her heart sank. Surely Theo wasn't so intent on living in the past that he'd try to resume his former life, despite his previous injuries. If he did, what would happen to Amelia? And to Ellie too, she wondered. Was Theo still the sort of man who'd disappear on his daughter without a second thought?

Chapter 8

Theo didn't know why he felt so angry at Ellie. He'd managed to avoid her the entire day, not liking the unfamiliar feelings she caused. He hated to admit he'd been happy watching her shop, which was weird in itself. Still, he'd felt the happiest he'd been since that damn bronc threw him.

He wasn't sure what to do with this new him. For sure he nearly didn't recognize the person he was on the verge of becoming. Father to the cutest baby girl on the planet. A man who felt protective toward a woman he wasn't even sleeping with, for Pete's sake.

Even worse, every damn time he even looked at Ellie, he got a hard-on so massive he could barely walk.

It wasn't her fault. Objectively, he knew this. She was a sweet, fairly innocent girl with baggage, and she clearly had no idea how she affected him.

When he'd shown up at dinner, tempted by the tantalizing aroma of her spaghetti, he noted her surprise and could tell his behavior had hurt her. While he'd hated that, he couldn't seem to help himself. It was either avoid her as much as possible or talk her into going to bed with him.

Which he did not want. Really. He couldn't afford to run her off. And truth be told, he kind of liked having her around.

His cell phone rang. Gemma. Glad of a distraction, he answered.

"I was beginning to get worried about you," he said.

"Sorry. I've been working pretty much around the clock. No time for a life."

"It's not getting any better?"

"No," Gemma answered. "Not really."

"How's Gram?" Theo asked.

Gemma sighed. "She's hanging in there. No one has died in forty-eight hours. That's something."

"At least it's not getting any worse."

"I wouldn't go so far as to say that," Gemma replied. "We still have new cases coming in."

"What about a cure? Dr. Rand vowed he'd find one."

Her brittle laugh spoke of her exhaustion. "All the doctors are working on that, when they're not treating patients.

"The CDC has people retracing Mimi Rand's steps before she got sick, since everything points to the virus starting with her."

"If it did, I don't understand why Amelia didn't get sick," Theo pointed out. "Illnesses like that seem to be particularly hard on babies and the elderly."

"Believe me when I say they're puzzling over that too. They still haven't figured out a common denominator. If the virus originated with Mimi, how'd she transmit it to the others? And with more and more people becoming infected…"

Theo suddenly realized what she was trying not to say. "We could lose half the town."

"Or more."

"People are going to start panicking."

"I know." Gemma sounded grim. "That's why we're making as little as possible public. We can't afford to have a mass panic. Especially since we're on quarantine."

"People will get hurt." Theo knew what might happen. It would involve beer, and a dare, and a couple of guys in a pickup truck. "I wonder if Flint has enough police officers."

"Since the state police and the National Guard have taken over, I think Flint is out of the equation. You might call him and check."

"Will do. I might be able to make myself useful for once." He didn't mean to let so much bitterness leak out into his voice, especially since he knew his sister would pick up on it.

"Just remember, you're supposed to be recuperating," she gently reminded him. "I know you're still doing physical therapy, but you can't do too much, too soon. Even though I know you want to do more, you've got to take it easy, so you don't risk reinjuring yourself. And you're also a father now. Amelia needs you. Don't do anything to endanger yourself."

"Since we both know Flint wouldn't allow that, I don't think you have to worry."

Gemma laughed with the first real trace of humor in a long while. Flint had actually returned to Dead River to help care for Theo after the accident. And she'd certainly also done her share. Theo's two siblings had been so worried he'd die that they'd dropped everything to make sure he wouldn't.

Theo owed them both a debt he doubted he could ever repay.

Ellie thought she could easily get used to this life. She'd never lived on a ranch before, and she'd always enjoyed taking care of babies, even though she hadn't done so since the triplets. She found herself waking up each morning with a smile on her face, eager to start her day.

Except for one thing. Theo had been avoiding her. If she entered a room, he left it without speaking. Worse, he hadn't been ignoring just her, but baby Amelia. This bothered Ellie enough that she planned to confront him.

If she could find him, that is.

Sighing, she decided to speak to Molly about it. Since their shopping expedition, she and her new friend had spoken on the phone once already.

"Maybe he's scared," Molly suggested, after listening silently to Ellie's complaints.

"Scared? Of what?"

"He's the one who kissed you. Maybe he wants more."

Ellie snorted. "In my experience, that's not how men act when they want more."

"In your experience? How much of that do you have?"

"Probably as much as you," Ellie shot back. "I've had a couple of serious boyfriends and a few not so serious. And the one thing they had in common was they let me know when they wanted more."

Molly conceded the point. "Well, maybe Theo just likes you too much, that's what I'm trying to say."

Ignoring the way her heart skipped at beat at that thought, Ellie took a deep breath and tried not to sound too eager. "What do you mean?"

"Theo's the love-'em-and-leave-'em type. Even before he became a big deal at rodeo, he blazed a scorching path through the girls in this town."

"And once again, you're back to not making sense." Ellie let some of her frustration come through in her voice. "If Theo's truly like that, then he must not find me attractive at all. Otherwise he'd be—"

"Seriously?" Molly cut her off. "You have mirrors there, right? You're gorgeous, girl. Theo's not blind. I think it's just that he's afraid to ruin things."

Though Ellie wasn't buying it, she was intrigued enough to ask, "How so?"

"Think about it. Theo can't commit. He's a good-time guy. Women want more. This is a recipe for disaster. Women tend to get pissed off. Some even have been known to go all-out psycho. He can't lose you. Ergo, he's going to keep his distance."

"I'm going to ask him," Ellie decided, sounding way braver than she felt. "Next time I see him, which should be the evening meal, I'm not going to let him run off without talking to me."

Molly whistled. "You go, you. I'll be silently cheering you on from over here. Call me and let me know how it goes, okay?"

"Okay." After she hung up, Ellie smiled. The conversation had given her a needed boost of confidence. It had been a while since she had a friend. Her stalker had scared away her former best friend, Angela, back in Boulder. Ellie hadn't realized how much she'd missed the camaraderie. Even though she'd only just met Molly, she felt as if they'd known each other forever. Sometimes people just clicked.

She thought of Theo. She'd thought sometimes they

had serious chemistry. Too bad it was apparently completely one-sided.

Ellie began preparing dinner with mixed feelings of anticipation and dread. Good thing the previous cook had stocked up with a major expedition to Sam's Club in Cheyenne before leaving. Ellie had been slow-cooking three huge beef briskets all day, and had a large pot of pinto beans simmering on the stove. She also used five pounds of potatoes to make a potato salad, along with several loaves of sourdough bread.

Instead of homemade barbecue sauce, she had the bottled kind, but she didn't think anyone would mind. And for dessert, she'd made a huge pan of peach cobbler.

The entire meal smelled wonderful. Her stomach growled, reminding her the dinner hour had grown closer.

As the men filed in, she dished up the food at their long table in the dining area. Theo arrived, his expression distant. He filled a plate and sat down to eat at the smaller table in the kitchen. After a moment's hesitation, she did the same.

She ate silently, trying to avoid locking gazes with Theo, but ready in case he tried yet again to slip out of the room without speaking.

The men were loudly appreciative of the meal. Two of them even jokingly proposed marriage, which made her smile. A quick glance at Theo revealed a thunderous frown.

Finally, everyone had eaten until they could hold no more. Amid a chorus of thanks, the ranch hands filed back outside, to head back either to their bunkhouse for the night or to their homes in town.

Theo pushed to his feet and turned to go.

Heart thundering in her chest, Ellie moved to intercept him. "Do you have a minute?" she asked.

He sighed. "Sure. What's going on?"

Now she met his gaze, quelling an immediate stab of longing. "Why are you avoiding me? Is it because of the kiss?"

"Ellie, I—"

"Don't." Suspecting she knew what was coming, she waved away what sounded like the beginning of a feeble attempt at an excuse. "I certainly don't need to be treated as if I have the plague—or the virus."

"You're right." Theo sat down heavily. "I admit, I've been avoiding you for exactly this reason. I didn't want to talk about the kiss. But you're right, we should. So let me begin by promising you it won't happen again."

Stunned, she didn't know how to respond. "Okay," she said, even though it was anything but. "I don't understand why you kissed me to begin with."

Now he flashed a bit of his grin. "Fishing for a compliment?"

"Not at all." Her face flamed at the suggestion. "But clearly you regret it, so I wonder why you even…"

The grin vanished. Expression serious, he leaned across the table. "You might not realize how beautiful you are, but I do. And by now I'm sure you've heard enough about me to realize I'm not the settling-down kind."

Dumbfounded, she could only stare. Right into his sexy-as-hell, bright green eyes. "That's what you think I want?"

"Isn't it?"

Drawing herself up with dignity, she shook her head. "Theo, when all of this is over and I've saved up enough money, I plan to travel. I've always wanted to go to Australia."

Now it was his turn to do a double take. "You want

to do what? Do you realize that's on the other side of the equator and the seasons are opposite of ours?"

"Of course I do." Making a face, she crossed to the sink and began loading dishes into the dishwasher. "Not everyone wants to try to tame the wild stallion."

As jokes went, it came out sounding sort of lame, but she saw the moment Theo got the humor. He shook his head and chuckled. "Point taken. So just to make sure we're clear, we can be friends but no more."

Glad she'd just turned back to the sink, she took a moment to compose her expression. "Sure," she said, sounding both casual and lighthearted, even though she felt the opposite.

"Great." Now the sexy grin came back, turning her insides to mush. "You should know, I've never been friends with an employee before."

And just like that, without even trying, he put her in her place. The truth had the effect of killing her libido. And the talk she'd planned to have with him about spending more time with Amelia? Well, she'd have to try again another time.

Somehow she managed to keep busy cleaning up the kitchen, thanked him politely for his time and gathered up Amelia to get her ready for bed.

She planned to spend the rest of the night in her room, hopefully with a pint of ice cream, trying to cheer herself up.

In truth, she thought she'd have been better off leaving things alone. Now she'd be the one avoiding Theo, at least until she could get over her hurt feelings.

Changing and powdering sweet baby Amelia took her mind off things for a little while. Once she had the baby fed and down for the night, Ellie went in search of that ice cream and a spoon.

As luck would have it, Theo walked into the kitchen just as she was leaving.

"Hey," he said, eyeing her ice cream. "Do you want to share?"

"Nope." She managed a smile to take the sting off her words. "I'm planning on hanging out in my room and eating this while I watch a chick flick." Words guaranteed to send any man running.

"Really? What movie?"

Crap. She hadn't thought that far ahead. She didn't even know what was on. "I'm not sure yet," she said, deciding to go with the truth.

"Do you mind if I watch it with you?"

She froze, not sure how to answer. While it was the last thing she wanted to do at this exact moment in time, if she declined he'd begin to suspect that maybe his words had hurt her. And she had way too much pride to let him figure that out.

"I've already put Amelia in her crib," she said, stalling.

"So? Just bring her bassinette to the living room. She'll be fine."

Before their little talk, she would have jumped at the opportunity to spend alone time with him. But now all she wanted to do was go lick her wounds.

"Okay," she finally agreed. "But I'm not sharing my ice cream with you."

Which made him laugh. Setting her ice cream down, she hurried away to get Amelia with the rich sound of his amusement making her chest hurt.

When she returned a few minutes later, he'd divided the pint into two bowls. "I thought we could share," he told her, sounding completely unrepentant.

"Of course." She glared at him in mock outrage. "I suppose next you're going to want to pick the movie."

Since he'd just shoveled a large spoonful of ice cream into his mouth, he didn't immediately respond. After he'd swallowed, he shrugged. "Nope. I don't care. I just need to relax and escape reality for a little while. You choose."

Relieved, she grabbed her dish of ice cream and plopped onto the couch. "Let's see..." Perusing the on-screen guide, she found one of her favorite movies of all time—*Sleepless in Seattle.* "I haven't watched that one in a while. It starts in five minutes."

Theo sat down next to her. "Sounds good. I've never seen it."

Now it was her turn to be shocked. "You've never watched *Sleepless in Seattle?* It's a classic."

"Maybe for you. My tastes for classics tend to lean toward *Die Hard* or *Fast and Furious*."

"Which are good flicks," she allowed. "But not what I'm in the mood for tonight."

When he didn't reply, she realized her words had unintentionally sounded seductive. Of course her face heated, though she tried to act as if she didn't realize.

The movie came on, to her immense relief. They watched it in silence—awkward at first, but as she began to relax, she thought it became companionable. And nice. With sex off the table, she tried to turn off her über-awareness of him and focus on the movie—and her ice cream. Although she had the strongest compulsion to scoot over next to him and cuddle on the couch. Imagining his reaction to that kept her in place.

When the closing music came on one and a half–plus hours later, she stirred and looked over to see Theo shaking his head in disbelief.

"What?" she asked. "Didn't you like it?"

"That was...ridiculous. People don't really act like that."

Since she liked nothing better than a good movie debate, she grinned, mentally accepting the challenge. "Oh yeah? And do you think people really act like Bruce Willis in *Die Hard?*"

"That's an action adventure flick. It's deliberately over-the-top."

She laughed. "And this is a romance. It too, is deliberately over-the-top."

Arms crossed, he exhaled. "Well, it's stupid. I couldn't buy in to it. Not even for one minute."

"It can happen. You just never know what life has in store for you. That's the whole reason I love this movie. It's optimistic, full of hope."

"Full of nonsense, you mean," he grumbled. "Maybe women think a guy is going to act like that, but I can tell you right now, they don't. That entire ending scenario would never have happened."

"Really?" Animated, loving the exchange and secretly marveling at the way this new "friendship" status made her feel more at ease, she grimaced. "You're telling me you wouldn't have taken a chance to meet the love of your life?"

"Don't you mean my soul mate?" he mocked. "I don't know about you, but I don't know very many men who believe in that crap. It's complete and utter nonsense."

"Wow." Amazed, she gaped at him. "I had no idea you didn't even believe in love."

He stared at her, his green eyes dark and unfathomable. "That's not what I said. At all. I said I don't believe—"

"That every person out there has someone special, waiting for him or her," she interrupted. "I agree, maybe that's a bunch of romantic drivel, but it gives people hope. I don't see anything wrong with that."

Theo groaned. His gaze dropped to her mouth, and then he turned his head and swallowed. "Let's just agree to disagree."

Disappointed, she bravely leaned over and touched his shoulder, making him look at her. "Okay, but I still think—"

She didn't get to finish the sentence. He muttered what sounded like a curse, before his lips captured hers, demanding. After the first initial shock, she returned the kiss with wild recklessness.

His tongue explored her mouth, sending shivers of pure lust exploding in her. For a split second, her emotions whirled, and then she gave in to the pleasure.

Curling her body into his as his hands moved possessively down the length of her back, she dared to caress his muscular shoulders, thrilling at the hard feel of them.

Thoroughly aroused, she squirmed against him, desperately wanting more. Instead he broke off the kiss and pushed himself away, off the couch and to his feet.

"My apologies," he growled, looking an odd combination of furious and aroused.

Confused, she could only stare at him, lips burning and feeling lost, aware her heart shone in her eyes. "What..." Her attempt to speak came out little more than a rasp.

"I promised you that wouldn't happen again." He drew himself up, inhaling sharply. She couldn't help noticing the proof of his arousal, which made her ache.

"Looks like you were wrong." Her weak attempt at humor had no effect on his stony expression. She had the oddest impulse to comfort him. "It's all right, Theo."

"It's not all right," he snarled, turning away from her. "Obviously I need to work on my self-control."

Jumping up, she went to him, touching his shoulder. "What if I don't want you to?" she asked, her heart pounding like a trip-hammer in her chest.

He went absolutely still. "Ellie," he rasped, sounding like a man in torment. "You don't know what you're saying."

And then, before she could respond, he turned away and left the room. A moment later, she heard the sharp sound of his door closing.

Theo tossed and turned all night, furious with himself. He had more self-control than that. He shouldn't have kissed her. Even worse, he shouldn't have enjoyed it so much.

In his life, he'd kissed a lot of women. And each and every one of them had been different. He didn't know why or how, but the instant his lips touched Ellie's, it felt as if electricity had turned his blood to lava.

Thinking that, he shook his head. Listen to him, getting all poetic.

Ellie was a sweet, kindhearted girl. Almost a true innocent. She wasn't used to the kind of erotic playing he used to do. She'd get hurt, he'd feel like an ass and he'd lose the best cook he'd ever had. Not to mention Amelia's nanny, the only one besides Gemma he trusted to watch his daughter.

What a cluster mess his life had become. He wanted to saddle up a horse and just ride aimlessly. Doing that had always helped him think. But he couldn't even ride. With his type of back injury, doctors had specifically cautioned him against getting on a horse again, any horse, ever.

So here he was, a rancher who couldn't ride, a boss who took advantage of his best employee and a really horrible friend besides. Ellie had enough problems with her stalker; she didn't need a sex-starved ex-rodeo cowboy complicating her life.

"But what if I don't want you to stop?" Ellie's words replayed in his mind, over and over, tantalizing him, tormenting him. He closed his eyes and groaned. He had to figure out a way to make it past this craziness and get back on friendly footing.

Watching the movie with her had been a mistake. But after avoiding her for the better part of a day, he'd been missing her company, quite frankly. And when she confronted him, he'd felt comfortable enough to suggest hanging out together.

He hadn't anticipated how every move, every rustle of her clothing, every sigh, would skittle along his nerve endings.

Whatever it was about Ellie that affected him so strongly, he needed to get over it, like yesterday.

But no more avoiding her. That was the coward's way, and Theo had never been a coward.

Ellie had already begun serving breakfast when he walked into the kitchen. The men were dishing their own plates from a huge pan of scrambled eggs and sausage. Another pan contained toast and bagels, and a third bacon.

"Looks good," Theo said, keeping his tone light and cheerful.

Her back to him, Ellie stiffened. Then, turning slowly, she gave him a tentative smile. "Go ahead and fix a plate."

Nodding, he smiled back and did as she'd suggested. Hope flared. Maybe they could regain their casual footing; maybe things could go back to normal after all.

He grabbed a cup of coffee and sat at the smaller table to have his meal. After checking on Amelia, who cooed and squirmed in her bassinette, Ellie made her own plate and sat down across from him.

She avoided making eye contact with him while she ate, which he could understand.

In the other room, the ranch hands ate and talked and laughed. They were a boisterous bunch at meals, but especially in the morning when they hadn't yet expended all their energy at their work.

"I love that sound," Ellie said softly, almost as if she'd read Theo's mind. "It makes me happy."

Again he felt that flush of desire, the tightening of his body. Doing his best to ignore that, he nodded. "When they're happy, the ranch runs better. I've heard nothing but compliments about your cooking."

She blushed prettily and told him thank you. Theo knew he had to get out of there, but he also knew he needed to reassure her that they could interact as friends. Without the crazy passion.

Finishing the food on his plate, he pushed to his feet and carried his plate over to the sink. He refilled his mug with coffee and then gave Ellie a friendly wink and a wave before leaving the kitchen.

Once out of there, he took a deep breath, relieved to see his hands weren't shaking. Around her, he felt like an addict in need of a fix. Good thing he had something to occupy his mind this morning.

The ranch hands were sorting calves today, and while Theo couldn't actually participate, he planned to watch. They were his cattle, after all. Even though the mama cows didn't take kindly to the brief separation from their babies, branding and castrating had to be done. It was a well-organized event, and everyone had their roles to play.

Ellie had been told to make sandwiches for lunch and

one of his men would pick them up and bring them out to the corrals.

The day passed quickly. By the time the calves had been reunited with their anxious mamas, Theo was covered with grit and sweat. Still, he felt happy and alive.

Back at the house, he showered for a second time and put on clean clothes.

His cell phone rang. Flint. Maybe his brother could provide a welcome distraction.

"Can you meet me in town?" Flint sounded exhausted. And pissed. Theo knew his brother well enough to recognize that tone.

"Is there a problem?" he asked, wary despite feeling secure that he personally wasn't responsible for Flint's foul mood.

"Yes, there is, but I'd rather not discuss this over the phone. I'm off duty at three, and I'd love a beer. Or two."

"Okay." Theo checked his watch. A little after two, which meant he had plenty of time to get cleaned up and make his way to town. "Um, you do remember that tonight is Molly's rehearsal dinner, right?"

"That's why I'm leaving work early. It's also part of what I want to talk to you about." Now Flint sounded even more furious. Which meant things had gone from bad to awful. Theo figured it probably had something to do with the virus.

"I'll meet you there at three," Theo said. The Dead River Bar was a couple of blocks from the police station. It wouldn't take Flint long to get there.

"Sounds good," Flint replied, and ended the call.

Theo supposed he ought to tell Ellie he was going out. After all, she'd agreed to accompany him to the rehearsal dinner.

Halfway toward her room, he stopped. Since when did

he need to start checking in with a woman who worked for him? Shaking his head, wondering what had just almost happened, he turned on his heel and went the other way.

Theo hadn't visited the Dead River Bar since before he left town to live out on the road, chasing the rodeo circuit. Unlike other sports, rodeo season was year-round, now that there were so many indoor arenas. He hadn't been home much, before his accident. If he remembered right, the place packed them in on Friday and Saturday nights, when there was a live band, drink specials and appetizers for half off until nine.

Lucky for him, not many people stopped in for a drink so early in the day. All the stools at the bar were empty.

Sally Jean Mabry, part owner and sometime bartender, hurried over. "Long time, no see," she drawled. "Heard you were beat up pretty bad." She raked her gaze up and down him, then gave him a slow smile. "You look pretty good to me."

He laughed. Easily old enough to be his mother, Sally Jean had always been a flirt. Some people even called her a cougar, but Theo had never been one to judge. After all, it took two to tango.

"Flint's meeting me in a few minutes," he said. "While I'm waiting, how about a nice, cold beer." He didn't have to specify what kind. Everyone in his family drank Coors.

Flint arrived a few minutes later. Sally Jean took one look at his face and poured him a tall one, sliding it over to him. She hurried away without an effusive greeting.

Theo sipped his beer and waited, giving Flint a chance to decompress. Gripping his glass with both hands, Flint took a long drink, before wiping his mouth with the back of his hand. "I needed that," he said. "Christ, this has been a day."

Theo nodded, aware that if he waited it out, Flint would eventually unload. Plus, he knew from experience that it could be dangerous to speak when his brother was like this.

The two men sat side by side, not talking at first. Theo took the opportunity to check out the rest of the bar, to see if it had changed any since he'd been there last.

He was pleased to note it had not. Red pleather booths, the wooden tables scarred and worn. Of course the old Western bar, which had supposedly been brought in from a saloon up in Deadwood, South Dakota, was still in place, the dark wood polished and solemn looking.

Only one other patron was inside the place, and he sat in a booth by himself, back where the lighting created pockets of shadows. Narrowing his eyes, Theo checked him out. He didn't recognize the guy, but there were no dreadlocks at least.

Still, he considered going over and trying to make small talk with the stranger. If Flint hadn't been in such a black mood, Theo would ask him to do it. Even though Flint no longer wore a uniform, he no doubt still had his badge somewhere on him.

"Molly's wedding is off," Theo finally said, his voice little more than a growl. "She's really upset."

Chapter 9

"Off?" Privately, Theo thought his cousin must have finally come to her senses. She was too young to be getting married. "What happened?"

"Her piece-of-crap fiancé cleaned out her bank account." Flint shot Theo a dark look. "For whatever reason, she put his name on it. Now her money is all gone. I'd like to find the son of a bitch and punch him in the face. She's brokenhearted."

"Jimmy Johnson?" Despite having the same name as a famous football coach, Jimmy had seemed a nice enough guy. Theo had met him a few times. What he lacked in height, he made up for in personality. Outgoing and talkative, he'd seemed better suited to have been a salesman than a guy doing auto work in a body shop.

"Are you sure?" Theo asked when Flint didn't respond. "He doesn't seem the type. Plus, he really appeared to love Molly."

"The first thing I learned when I became a cop is nine times out of ten, appearances are deceiving." As he stared morosely into his beer, a muscle worked in Flint's jaw. "I've got men looking for him now."

"Well, he can't have gone far," Theo pointed out. "With the quarantine and all."

"True." Flint took another long drink, before turning to face his brother. "Who runs off with a quarantine in place? He never was the sharpest tool in the toolbox."

"Maybe he thinks he can figure a way to sneak out."

"Maybe." Flint sighed. "There are others who apparently think the same way. But those CDC people aren't messing around. I know you saw the National Guard the other day. They've set up even more roadblocks and barricades. They're determined no one is leaving this town."

Theo winced. "Which means Ellie's stalker is also stuck here." He couldn't help glancing back toward the guy in the booth. The booth was empty. The stranger had gone. Only thing, to get out he would have had to walk past the bar. Theo would have noticed him.

"Hey, Sally Jean," Theo called, making Flint wince.

"Ready for another?" she asked, gliding around behind the bar.

"Not yet," Theo said. "Hey, did you happen to see where that guy went? The one who was in the last booth?"

Sally cursed. "No. That turd better not have left without paying his tab." She practically flew toward the empty booth. "Ah, good. He left enough to cover his beer and a generous tip. That's what I get for thinking the worst."

Theo waited until she'd returned and put the cash in the till. "Sally, I didn't see him leave. Did you guys put in another door that I don't know about?"

She frowned. "No. The only other exit is if you go

through the kitchen, and there's a sign on the door that plainly states Employees Only."

"And we know how everyone pays attention to signs, don't we?" Theo didn't bother to hide his sarcasm. "Obviously the guy didn't want to be seen. It wasn't Jimmy Johnson, was it?"

"No, of course not. That boy doesn't drink."

"Really? How sure of that are you? He's twenty-two years old and every time I've been around him, he acted like the life of the party."

Her mouth twisted in an admiring smile. "You got me there. I should have said he didn't drink in here." She shrugged. "For all I know, he could've been pounding down a twelve-pack every day."

"Okay, thanks." Flint turned his attention on the rest of his beer, which was dwindling fast.

"Anyway," Sally continued, as if she didn't notice his still-black mood. "Won't you be seeing him tonight at the rehearsal dinner?"

Theo watched his brother carefully, curious to see what he'd do. He knew, like everyone else in Dead River, if Flint told anything to Sally Jean, everyone in town would know about it within hours.

Instead of answering, Flint drained his beer. "Speaking of that, I think we'd better go." He slapped a five and two ones on the counter. "This is on me," he said to Theo. "Thanks, Sally Jean. We'll see you around."

"No problem." Scooping up the money, Sally Jean nodded at him coolly, though her intent gaze followed Flint as he moved toward the door.

"You coming, Hot Shot?" Without waiting for an answer, Flint crammed his battered cowboy hat on his head.

Grimacing, Theo gulped down the rest of his beer and followed.

Once outside, where Flint waited for him, Theo motioned toward his truck. “Do you want to ride out to the ranch with me?”

“Let’s walk first. I need to think.” Flint had always gone for a walk when he was trying to puzzle something out.

Theo glanced at his watch. “You also need to start making some calls. Everyone’s going to be arriving at the Blue Bear Restaurant in a couple of hours.”

“I know.” Flint grimaced again. “Gemma already knows. She can’t leave work, but someone needs to be with Molly, helping to calm her down.”

“Let me check with Ellie when I get home.”

“Ellie?”

“Yes. She and Molly hung out the other day. Went shopping, had lunch, got their nails done—all that kind of stuff women do.”

“That would be awesome.” For the first time, Flint sounded relieved. “Head on home and see if Ellie minds going over there. From what I hear, Molly’s locked herself in her house and refused to talk to anyone, even her sister.”

Especially her sister. Both brothers knew how Sarah could get. The woman always had to be right. No doubt one of the first things she’d said when hearing the news was “I told you so.”

Flint and Theo parted ways and Theo drove home. Though he usually took his time, barely driving the speed limit, this time he broke every speed limit.

When he walked in the front door, Ellie greeted him, clearly agitated. “Molly called,” she began. “And my car still isn’t running right. I haven’t had the time—or the money—to take it in and get it fixed yet. And Molly really needs me.”

"I know." He squeezed her shoulder, fighting the urge to let his hand linger. "I'll take you over there. The car seat is still in the backseat of my truck."

Ellie nodded. "I don't mind taking her with me. It might distract Molly to have a baby to fuss over."

Though he'd actually planned on watching Amelia while Ellie and Molly visited, Ellie's idea had merit. "That's a really good idea."

"Unless you think it'd be better for her to stay home."

They both spoke at the same time. Ellie smiled self-consciously, wearing her sadness for Molly like a scarf. Theo smiled. "Your choice. You decide what you think would be best." He liked that she could care so much for his cousin, a woman she'd only just met.

Though she'd only known Molly a day, hearing the anguish in her new friend's voice had Ellie holding back tears. She'd promised to be there as soon as she could. Molly had even offered to pick her up, but Ellie didn't want her driving in her condition. Poor thing couldn't even speak a complete sentence without breaking down and sobbing.

When Theo had arrived back home, Ellie was prepared to plead her case. She'd missed both the lunch and dinner for the hands once already, when she'd gone shopping with Molly, and now she would be leaving the cooking to Theo once again. On the bonus side, after hearing him talk about his chicken enchiladas, she'd cooked several chickens that morning and put them aside. She'd planned to ask Theo to show her how to make the dish.

Once she had the diaper bag packed, she hurried to the kitchen, where she'd made up several bottles. Putting those in a small, soft-sided ice chest, she double-checked to make sure she had everything before picking up Amelia and wrapping her securely in a warm blanket.

"We need to pick her up some more clothes next time we go to town," she told Theo when he returned. "She'll need a coat, and some little shoes."

"I'll give you my credit card and you and Molly can do that, if that's okay with you," he replied as they walked outside. "Go today. That might help Molly cheer up."

"Not today." She sighed. "Molly is really broken up. I'll see if she wants to make plans to do that on my next day off."

"It won't be a day off if you're taking Amelia shopping." He took the baby from her and buckled her securely into the infant car seat. "Consider it part of your job."

Once again, if she did that, she wouldn't be cooking. She pondered this as she climbed up into the cab and buckled herself in. Maybe Theo was right and she did need to rethink her plan of holding on to both jobs.

Except she really needed the money. Not only to fix her car, but to save for her grand escape.

"I'll do it on my day off," she said firmly. "That way, it won't make me miss cooking any meals."

He sighed but didn't respond.

At first, the bouncing of the big pickup had Amelia squealing. But once they left the dirt road and hit pavement, the motion lulled her to sleep. Ellie couldn't keep from smiling as she turned to check on her small charge.

"She's beautiful, isn't she?" Theo said, pride and something that sounded an awful lot like affection coloring his deep voice.

"She certainly is. And a really easy baby too, I think.

At least, she seems that way, compared to caring for the triplets."

"You're way ahead of me." He gave her a rueful smile. "There are no babies at all on the rodeo circuit."

"What was that like?" she asked, hoping the question didn't make him shut down. "I know there's a lot of driving involved."

"I never minded that. I got to see a lot of new towns, though I never stayed in one very long. But there's an adrenaline rush I can't really describe." His pensive expression seemed wistful. "I had my routine and I really enjoyed it. It really bothers me to think it's all still going on and I'm not a part of it."

Though Ellie nodded as if she understood, she didn't really. She'd never felt that passionate about anything. She'd taken a few classes at CU after high school, but since she didn't know where to focus, she soon lost interest and stopped going. She'd worked at a bookstore on Pearl Street, and part-time as a waitress in an Irish pub in the same area. But to find a job that meant everything... that was something she'd figured was for other people.

The idea of traveling to a place with sandy beaches, a turquoise ocean and year-round warm temperatures was about the only thing that even came close.

They pulled up to a neighborhood flanked by adobe walls. Inside, the houses seemed larger and more ornate, though the yards were incredibly small.

"Once of the first things Molly did once she got over the shock of losing her parents was pay cash to build a new home," Theo said. "Security has always been important to her. Though now that Jimmy cleaned out her bank account, I don't know how she'll pay the insurance and taxes. She doesn't make that much as a waitress."

"Cleaned her out?" Aware her mouth was open, Ellie closed it. "Are you saying her fiancé stole from her?"

"His name was on the bank account, so not technically. But yes. What he did was wrong. And when we catch up with him, we're going to make him pay back whatever he hasn't spent."

Molly hadn't mentioned this. All she'd said was the wedding was off, that Jimmy had broken up with her.

"That's terrible," Ellie mused. "What kind of man does this?"

"Not a good one, that's for sure."

They parked in front of a beige adobe house, with a red tile roof and matching front door. "Wow," she said, impressed. "What a great house."

"Yeah. I heard she fixed it up real nice too." Theo jumped out, went around to Ellie's side and opened the door, just as he had when they went shopping. Again unable to hide her surprise, she thanked him, which earned her a startled look. Just because most of the men she knew didn't know how to be a gentleman, didn't mean it was unusual to someone like Theo.

"You know what?" he said when she went to get Amelia out of the car seat. "I'll keep her. You comfort Molly."

Ellie froze. "But you still have to get supper on the table for the men. I can't ask you to watch the baby too."

"You didn't ask. I insist. I need to spend more time with my daughter."

Put like that, how could Ellie refuse?

"Thank you," she said. "You're a good man, Theo Colton."

He flushed, whether from pleasure or embarrassment, she couldn't tell.

"I'll call you when I'm ready to come home," she said,

resisting the urge to kiss him on the cheek. Then she blushed too, realizing she'd used the word *home.*

"See you," she said, turning away to cover her discomfort. As she walked the last few feet up to the front door, she heard the truck drive away.

Molly flung the door open just as Ellie was reaching for the doorbell. Her puffy face was streaked with tears.

"Thank goodness you're here," she exclaimed, pulling Ellie inside. "I was just about to do a shot of tequila. You can join me."

Ellie considered telling her she didn't do shots, but seeing the pile of used tissue on the coffee table, she decided maybe she'd do just one. Later.

"Before you do that," Ellie said, dropping onto the sofa and patting the spot next to her. "I want you to tell me everything that's happened."

Swallowing hard, Molly promptly burst into tears.

It took the better part of an hour to get the entire story. Molly hadn't known Jimmy long, true. But she'd believed him when he'd claimed to recognize her instantly as The One.

"It was so romantic, you know," Molly said, then blew her nose and added another tissue to the pile. "He wanted to save for a ring, but I'd always wanted to wear my great-great-grandmother's ring. It's a family heirloom. And it's gone," she wailed. "I haven't told anyone in the family yet."

"Gone?" Ellie glanced at Molly's ringless hands. "Wouldn't you be wearing it?"

This question brought on another bout of weeping. Once Molly got herself back under control, she grabbed the bottle of tequila, poured a shot and downed it. Wiping her mouth on the back of her hand, she exhaled. "It needed to be sized. We were going to go this morning and have that done. The rehearsal dinner was supposed to be tonight, for pity's sake." And then she began weeping again.

Ellie patted her back, her heart aching for her friend. "I wish there was something I could do to help you."

"Yeah." Molly raised her red, puffy eyes. "The only good thing is he's got to be around here somewhere. With the quarantine, he can't leave town. Flint will find him. And then I want him to look me in the eye and tell me why he did this."

Privately, Ellie thought the reason was clear—greed. This Jimmy Johnson had seen a golden opportunity and had taken advantage of a trusting young woman.

"True," Ellie said. "I hope he hasn't sold your ring or spent all your money."

"That too." Molly poured another shot and held it out to Ellie. "Here."

"I don't think—" Ellie began, then caught sight of Molly's pleading expression. Sighing, she accepted the glass and took a deep breath before downing it. Immediately she shuddered, scrunching up her face at the taste. "There." She placed the glass back on the table. "I did it."

"Good." Molly took one more. "I want to drink enough to forget. Or get angry. Angry's good. Better than pain."

"Yes, it is. But…" Ellie took a deep breath. "I'm not sure getting drunk is the answer."

"Seriously?" Molly shot her a look of disbelief. "This is killing me. I've got to do something."

Ellie nodded, conceding the point. "Whatever you want. I'm here for you."

"Good. Then drink up." Molly poured and handed Ellie another shot.

"I don't think I want this," Ellie began.

"Drink with me," Molly said, her large green eyes filling with tears, which she defiantly wiped away. "Distract me. Tell me stories. What's life like, living out at the ranch?"

"Normal. I'm taking care of the baby and trying to keep my first job as ranch cook. So far, it's not going well." She studied the shot glass, narrow-eyed, before downing it. The alcohol seared a path down her throat.

"At least living out there, you're not dealing with the constant fear of everyone who lives in town." Molly grimaced. "A lot of people are scared to leave their houses."

"Oh, I'm afraid too," Ellie said, after setting down her shot glass. She held up her hand when Molly went to pour her another. What was this, three? Or four? Ellie couldn't remember. "No more. I don't want to get sick."

Molly nodded, wincing. "The room's spinning. Maybe we should take a break." She sighed. "What are you afraid of? Your stalker?"

"So many things. Including him." Ellie tried not to sound maudlin, but on the rare occasions she drank, her emotions and innermost feelings always seemed to bubble to the surface. She sighed, then managed a wobbly smile. "This virus has me pretty terrified too."

"Yeah." Molly picked up the tequila bottle, examined it and put it back down. "So many people are sick and dying. Poor Gemma is working herself to the bone."

"I pray every day that Amelia won't catch it," Ellie confessed. "And I'm worried about Theo's grandmother. He clearly loves her."

"She's a strong woman. She's hanging in there. What about you?" Molly regarded her curiously. "For a day or two, I was paranoid that every little ache or pain might be a symptom. Mimi Rand was young and healthy, and she died. I'm not ready to die."

Ellie stared at her new friend. "Me either." She considered the tequila bottle, then decided what the hell? "Pour me one more shot."

After she'd downed it, she sat back and shook her head. "That would suck, to die this young."

"I'd want some warning myself." Following suit, Molly took another shot, as well. "Because at least if I knew, I could try to do some of the stuff I needed to do before I died."

"Me too," Ellie said, a bit too enthusiastically. "And there's one thing I definitely would want to do before I left this earth." Then, realizing who she was speaking to, she clapped her hand over her mouth. "Never mind."

"Oh, no. You're not getting off that easily." Like a bloodhound on the scent, Molly leaned in. "What is it? What's the one thing you'd do that you don't want me to know about?"

"I can only tell you if you swear to me you won't tell another soul."

"Tell anyone?" Molly waved her arms dramatically. "Who am I gonna tell? You're my best friend. If anyone's going to get dished the latest dirt, it'd be you."

Ellie giggled, which surprised her. She never giggled. Well, hardly ever. But she had just drunk four—or more, she'd lost track—shots of tequila. "Okay," she said, vaguely wondering if this was a good idea. "If I found out I was going to die, I wouldn't want to go until I'd made love with Theo."

"Theo?" Molly gasped. "Seriously?"

Ellie nodded, feeling her face heat. "I know he's your

cousin and everything, but he's…" She closed her eyes, wishing she'd kept her mouth shut. "Never mind."

"Oh, no, you don't." Molly touched her arm. "I can see the appeal. Heck, Theo's had every female in town fawning over him."

This caught Ellie's interest. "Really? I hadn't noticed."

"Well, not so much these days." Molly shrugged. "But before, when he was a big rodeo star. He always had a bunch of women throwing themselves at him. Like Mimi Rand."

Amelia's mother. Ellie wished the thought would magically sober her up. "I didn't intend on getting drunk," she sighed.

Molly shrugged. "You're not driving, so why not? Theo will understand."

"Maybe." The thought of facing Theo while tipsy made Ellie wince. "He keeps kissing me, then getting mad about it. I just hope I don't do something stupid, like jump his bones."

As soon as she spoke, she knew she'd had way too much to drink. "I won't, of course."

"I know you won't." Molly wagged her finger. "That's your problem. You're too afraid."

"Maybe. But I think I know Theo well enough now to know he won't take advantage of an inebriated woman."

For some reason Molly seemed to find this hilarious. "Fine, then," she said when she finally stopped laughing. "You can seduce him another time, when you're sober."

"Seduce him?" Horrified, Ellie started to shake her head, stopping when the room began to spin. "Oh no. I don't plan on doing that."

"Why not?"

Ellie shrugged. "For one thing, I don't know how. I've never seduced anyone in my life."

Molly stared at her, her eyes going wide. "You're not a…"

"A what?"

"A virgin." Molly whispered the words.

That cracked Ellie up. She laughed and laughed until tears ran down her face. "Oh, heck, no. I've had a boyfriend or two. But I never had to seduce anyone. I wouldn't even know how."

"I can teach you," Molly said solemnly, though her eyes twinkled. "As a matter of fact, you can be my pet project."

"No, no, no." Feeling dizzy, Ellie waved her away. "No, we're not going to do that."

"You have to." Batting her eyelashes, Molly pouted. "How can you take away the one thing that can distract me after my fiancé dumped me right before the wedding?"

Put like that, Ellie knew she had no choice. Molly gave her a wobbly grin. "Then you're in?"

Reluctantly, Ellie nodded. "I'm in." And wondered what she'd just gotten herself into.

"Yay!" Molly clapped and jumped to her feet. Or tried to. But her feet tangled and she fell back onto the sofa. "Maybe I'd better make us some coffee and try to sober up."

"Food would be better." Suddenly ravenous, Ellie attempted to stand. "Do you have anything to eat?"

"Sure." Molly waved her question away. "First, I want to try to figure out a plan for your seduction of Theo."

This time, Ellie knew better than to argue. She figured

she'd let Molly talk, agree with everything and Molly would have totally forgotten about it by morning.

"We're going to buy you some sexy lingerie," Molly declared, her smile not quite banishing the shadows behind her bright green eyes.

"No. We're not." Ellie shook her head for added emphasis. "If I go into one of the shops in Dead River, everyone will not only know, but rumors will start flying around town. It'd be different if we could leave and go to Cheyenne."

"Fine." Molly thought for a moment, then snapped her fingers. "I know. We'll buy it on the internet."

Ellie thought of her one credit card and grimaced. "Not too expensive, okay?"

"Sure." Molly grabbed her laptop. With a few expert clicks, she navigated to a website. "Here you go. Take a look."

Ellie studied the page of negligees and shook her head. "Not these."

"Really?" Molly's perfectly shaped eyebrows rose. "What exactly did you have in mind?"

"Well, if I'm really going to do this, I need something that's the opposite of my personality. Something daring." She thought for a moment. "None of these pastel colors. I want red or black."

Molly laughed. "Wow. You surprise me." She jumped to her feet. "Just a second. Wait right here."

A moment later she returned, carrying a box from a popular store. "I had a bridal shower a couple of weeks ago," she said, her voice wavering before she cleared her throat and bravely lifted her chin. "I got this as one of my gifts. Clearly, I'm not going to be using it. I think it might be exactly what you're looking for."

"Oh no. I couldn't do that."

"Why not?" Molly squinted at her. "What am I going to do with it? Might as well put it to good use."

Ellie used the only excuse she could think of. "We're not the same size. I'm taller than you."

Hearing that, Molly laughed. "Open the box. It's sort of one size fits all."

With trepidation, Ellie did. After she parted the pink-striped tissue paper, she lifted the two scraps of red cloth and stared in disbelief. "Um." Not sure what to say, she could feel her face heating with embarrassment.

Which only made Molly laugh harder. Doubled over, she laughed until tears streamed down her cheeks and she couldn't catch her breath. Finally, she wiped her eyes and tried to rearrange her features into a pseudo solemn expression.

"Ellie, just take it home with you. Try it on. If you don't like it, throw it away. But I can guarantee you if you're serious about making Theo lose his mind, then this outfit will do it."

Ellie finally nodded. Wrapping the wisps of sheer material in the tissue paper, she returned it to the box and put it in her purse.

"Now about that food," she said.

They feasted on frozen pizza and carrots and hummus. And odd combination, but satisfying anyway. With this, they drank ginger ale, as the fizzy drink sounded better than coffee or water.

After she got some food in her, Ellie felt much better. Still a bit dizzy, but no longer on the verge of getting sick.

"Want to do more shots?" Molly asked, grinning. "Just kidding," she said, laughing in reaction to the shocked look Ellie gave her. A moment later, she weaved across the room and enveloped Ellie in a hug. "Thank you."

"For what?" Ellie asked, stunned.

"Cheering me up. You really helped."

"I aim to please."

Ellie glanced at her watched, stunned to see it was nearly midnight. "I'd better call Theo to come pick me up. I didn't realize it was so late."

"Just spend the night," Molly suggested. "He can pick you up in the morning. I have a lovely guest room."

Shaking her head, Ellie gave her new friend a rueful smile. "As great as that sounds, I'd better not. Theo's already had to step in and make a couple of the meals for the ranch hands."

"So? He needs to do something. Better than sitting around feeling sorry for himself." As soon as she spoke, Molly clapped her hand over her mouth, eyes wide. "Oh, jeez. Don't tell him I said that. It's the tequila talking."

"I won't." Regarding Molly with open curiosity, Ellie knew she had to ask. "Is that what people think?"

Molly sighed. "I wish I'd kept my big mouth shut."

"I told you, I'm not going to repeat anything. I just wonder. It seems like Theo went through a lot."

"He did, he did," Molly hastened to reassure her. "I was being snarky. Mainly because he gave me a hard time for continuing to work as a waitress even though I had the trust fund. But I knew that money wouldn't last forever. So I paid cash for my house and my car and banked the rest. I don't make a lot waiting tables, but I enjoy my job."

"I've worked as a waitress." Ellie grimaced. "And a barista in a coffee shop, a salesclerk in a bookstore and now a ranch cook and nanny. Experience makes life richer."

"Exactly!" Beaming approval, Molly sighed. "I knew there was a reason we hit it off so well. We think alike." And then she sat down, leaned against the back of the couch and fell asleep.

Ellie could do nothing but envy her. More than anything, she wished she could claim the overstuffed armchair and do the same. Instead she got out her cell phone and punched in Theo's number.

Chapter 10

Ellie and Molly must have had a good time, despite Molly's crisis. When Ellie called him a little past midnight, she'd spoken with a slight slur to her words. He'd told her he was on his way. Carrying a sleeping Amelia out to his truck, he buckled her in her car seat, careful not to wake her.

When he pulled up in front of the house, Ellie hurried outside, a little unsteady on her feet. She opened the passenger-side door and jumped up into the cab.

"Hey," she said, a bit too brightly. "Thanks for picking me up."

He smiled and nodded, able to smell the liquor. "Did you manage to help make Molly feel better?"

"I think so. Between me and the shots of tequila, she wasn't feeling any pain."

He laughed with genuine enjoyment. As he watched her blink, apparently struggling to stay awake, he realized he hadn't laughed much at all until she'd come to work for him. Since then, even with all the craziness going on around them, he'd found himself smiling or amused at least once a day.

"Shots, huh?" he asked as they pulled away from the house. "I wouldn't have pegged you for a shot-drinking kind of girl."

"I'm not. At all. But Molly insisted, and she was so miserable..." Her words trailed off and she yawned. "But in the end, we had a good time. Luckily, she had some munchies, so I could lessen the effect of all the alcohol."

"Was she still crying over that low-life fiancé of hers?"

"Not by the end of the night. She barely even talked about him."

"What did you talk about?" he asked, more to make conversation than anything else.

Ellie didn't respond. When he glanced over at her to see why, he realized she'd fallen asleep with her head pillowed against the doorjamb. Just like Amelia, who hadn't woken up once in her car seat.

Chuckling, he turned the radio up and hummed along to the music all the way home.

Once they'd left the pavement for the rutted dirt road leading to his ranch, the bouncing and swaying of the truck shook Ellie awake.

"Theo?" Voice husky, she sounded confused. And sexy as hell. Lust stabbed him instantly. He decided to try to ignore that.

"Um-hmm?"

"Are we almost home?"

"In a minute or two, darlin'." Slipping into the easy endearment he used with most women—at least those who weren't his employees—he turned to look at her. She looked befuddled, as if everything was slightly out of focus. "I bet you're dying to get in your own bed and sleep it off."

"Well, actually no. I don't feel good. I think I'm going to get sick." And then she leaned forward and violently vomited all over the floorboard of his truck.

Hangovers were a fate worse than death, Ellie learned. The next morning when Amelia's hungry cries woke her, Ellie felt as if her skull might crack open. Her headache pulsed with every angry beat of her heart. She pushed herself out of bed, rushing to brush her teeth immediately, hoping to banish that awful taste in her mouth.

That done, she changed Amelia and staggered to the kitchen to make her a bottle. Luckily, the baby girl stopped crying the instant Ellie lifted her. Ellie didn't know how she would have survived if she hadn't.

Finally, with Amelia sucking eagerly on her bottle, Ellie sat down. What on earth had happened last night? She remembered leaving Molly's house with Theo, and then…

Oh no. Her stomach rolled as she realized she'd gotten sick inside Theo's truck.

When the coffee finished, she poured herself a cup and contemplated the stove. She had to make something for the men to eat for breakfast. Not an easy task when even the thought of food made her feel queasy.

That said, she made an executive decision that today would be a cold cereal and fruit day. They might complain, but they'd have to make do. That was the best she could manage.

Once everything had been set out, she took Amelia and headed back to her room. She needed to lie down for a little while. Hopefully when she next woke, she'd feel better.

One thing for sure—she was never going to drink that much again. Ever.

Somehow she made it through the day. Napping for a few hours helped settle her stomach and restore her appetite, and when she got up again and changed Amelia, she headed to the kitchen to make herself a sandwich.

She'd just sat down and taken a bite when Theo sauntered in, grinning, and looking sexy as sin. "How are you feeling today?" he asked. "I'm going to guess not great, since I saw you put out cornflakes for the guys this morning."

Swallowing, she took a sip of her ginger ale and managed a weak smile back. "Did they complain much?"

"Not after I told them what you did yesterday. Then they understood."

"You didn't," she protested, even though she knew he had.

He crossed to the bassinette and picked up a happy, gurgling Amelia. "Gemma said to tell you to make sure and drink lots of water today."

Gemma. Ellie closed her eyes. "You told her?"

"She called." He didn't sound worried. "She's glad you spent time with Molly."

"About last night," Ellie began.

"How much of it do you remember?" he teased, a devilish sparkle in his green eyes.

"Enough." With a groan, she took another sip of her ginger ale. "I'm sorry about your truck."

"Yeah, I am too. I left it for you to clean up today."

At the thought, her stomach rebelled. She swallowed, eyeing her barely eaten sandwich, and then pushed away the plate.

Unable to tell if he was serious, or still teasing, she sighed. "Really?"

"No." Rocking Amelia gently, he looked a study in contrast. Rugged, devil-may-care cowboy combined with tender, loving father. Ellie found the combination darn near irresistible. Which made it even harder to understand if he really wanted to leave and go back to the rodeo.

"Eat your sandwich," he urged. "And I'll help with the preparations for lunch."

Grateful, she nodded, then winced at the stab of pain. "I need some ibuprofen," she said. Theo crossed the room without a word, opened a cabinet and brought her a bottle. After she'd swallowed a couple of pills, she got busy finishing her lunch.

Theo watched her silently while she ate, which made her want to squirm. Luckily, he alternated his attention between his baby girl and Ellie, so she was able to manage to choke down the rest of her food.

"So, how is Molly taking this?"

She sighed. "She seems more mad than brokenhearted, though she's hurt. She's more worried about the ring than the missing money."

He went still. "What ring?"

Cursing her slip of the tongue, she knew there was no help for it but to go on. "She hasn't told anyone in the family yet. It's her great-grandmother's ring or something."

"More like great-great-grandmother's." Theo sounded grim. "That thing's been in the family for generations."

"Is it valuable?"

"Very." He shook his head. "But there's no way he can even attempt to pawn it here in Dead River. Everyone in town knows who it belongs to. No doubt he intended to skip town and take it with him. I guess he thought he could somehow leave despite the quarantine."

Ellie got up and carried her plate to the sink. She felt a little bit better having eaten. "Well, Molly is broken up about him taking it."

"I imagine she is. How did he get a hold of it?"

"They were taking it to get resized. I'm guessing she left it lying around and he took it." Ellie sighed. "What kind of person does something like that? It's bad enough that he's dumping her practically at the altar, but to *steal* from his own fiancée?"

"He's a piece of work, that's for sure," Theo agreed, keeping his tone mild for Amelia's sake. "I knew she was rushing into things, but everyone else insisted she was in love."

Not sure how to respond, Ellie simply nodded.

"We need to let Flint know about the ring," Theo said. "I'm sure he's already looking for the SOB, since him jilting our cousin is a slap in the face to our family. Stealing the ring is him giving us the finger. Colton pride and all that."

Though his tone sounded a bit mocking, Ellie judged from his expression he meant what he said. "About Flint," she began. "I think I need to call Molly and tell her what I've done. She should be the one to tell Flint, don't you agree?"

He shrugged. "Either way, Flint needs to know." Glancing at his watch, he stood, still expertly holding Amelia. "I'll put her down and then let's figure out what you want to serve for lunch. Flint's supposed to stop by around noon."

In the end, Ellie ended up directing Theo in the browning of a large quantity of hamburger meat. They were making sloppy joes and would be serving them on hamburger buns, along with potato chips and pickles, for lunch. She took care to stand a fair distance from the stove, as even the smell of the frying meat made her feel nauseated again.

After the meat had browned and the grease drained off, she supervised Theo mixing up the tomato paste and seasonings. Even watching the fine hairs on his muscular arms as he cooked made her feel dizzy with longing.

Once he'd stirred that in and everything was simmering, she slipped away to phone Molly and let her know what she'd done.

"How are you feeling today?" Molly asked, sounding none the worse for wear. "You were pretty far gone when you left."

"I know." Ellie grimaced. "I'm not used to drinking. I got sick in Theo's truck."

"You did what?" Molly squealed, making Ellie wince in pain. "Oh no, I bet he was livid."

"I don't remember," Ellie admitted. "And I've felt horrible all day. Theo's even cooking the ranch hands' lunch for me."

"Is he? Now, that's true love."

Despite knowing Molly was teasing, Ellie felt her face heating. "Anyway, I messed up. In talking to Theo a little while ago, I slipped and told him about the missing ring."

"Crap." Molly went silent. When she spoke again, she sounded a bit stressed. "That means I need to call Flint. I've been dreading doing that. He's sure to lecture me." She grimaced. "Even though he's my cousin, he likes to act like a big brother. Maybe because I don't have any brothers. Who knows."

Seeing a chance to make amends, Ellie smiled. "Actually, Flint is supposed to be here for lunch. I can tell him for you, if you'd like."

"Really?" The infectious energy was back, just like that. "You'd do that for me?"

"Of course."

"Doesn't he scare you?"

"Flint?" Puzzled, Ellie glanced at Theo, still stirring the meat and not making any effort to hide his eavesdropping. "No, Flint doesn't frighten me. He seems like a nice guy."

"Ha." Molly snorted. "Sure, if you don't mind telling him, have at it. And when he calls me to gripe, I just won't answer the phone."

"Whatever makes you happy," Ellie said, smiling. "I'll take care of it."

"That was a weird conversation," Theo said.

Ellie shrugged. "Flint intimidates her."

"Seriously? That's weird. He's her cousin."

"Who apparently is fond of delivering lectures on how she should live her life."

Theo laughed, the rich masculine sound caressing her insides and turning her knees to water. "He's good at that. He only does it because he cares."

"Only does what because he cares?" Flint strode into the kitchen. "Damn, that smells good."

"Theo made it," Ellie said. "It's a big pot of sloppy joes."

Removing his cowboy hat, Flint looked from Ellie to Theo and whistled. "About time somebody taught this boy how to cook."

Theo laughed again. "It's not exactly French cuisine."

The men arrived then, interrupting whatever response Flint had been about to make. Ellie got busy serving them, amazed at the way Theo stood right by her side and helped. Flint stayed out of everyone's way and watched them, his face expressionless. "If anyone has questions about the quarantine," he announced, "I'll try to answer them as best I can after you eat."

Once all the ranch hands had their plates, Ellie gestured to Flint. "Come on, and I'll make you a plate."

The three of them ate at the small kitchen table. The easy camaraderie of the men in the other room buoyed Ellie's mood. "They sure are a happy bunch," she mused, pitching her voice low enough so that only Flint and Theo could hear.

The two brothers exchanged a glance. "They should be," Theo said. "I take care of my guys."

Ellie figured now would be as good a time as any to tell Flint about the ring. "Um, I talked to Molly," she began.

Theo looked down. From the way his shoulders were shaking, she figured he was trying to hide laughter. Ignoring him, she went on. "Anyway, she's pretty broken up about her fiancé running off right before the wedding."

"And cleaning out her bank account," Flint put in, exactly as she'd guessed he might.

"About that…"

Theo guffawed, trying to cover it with a cough. She gave Flint a nervous smile, wondering what Theo found so funny. "Anyway," she continued, bracing herself just in case. "Molly's more worried about the ring."

Flint froze, exactly the way Theo had done when she'd told him. "That jerk stole Molly's ring?" His voice had gone deadly calm.

Ellie nodded. "She wants it back."

"You're damn right she does." Judging from his clenched jaw, Flint was as angry as Molly had predicted. "We all do. I wish I'd known it was missing. I've got men watching for him, but I'm about to get into my car and go try to spot him myself. That ring has been in the family for generations."

Before Ellie could reply, he turned to eye Theo. "Mind telling me what you find so funny about this?"

Theo shook his head, not the least bit intimidated. "Sorry. It's just that Molly told Ellie you frighten her. Because of that, Ellie got a bit nervous to tell you. I think she thought you were going to start yelling or maybe throwing things."

Flint frowned, clearly puzzled. "I scare Molly? Why?"

Ellie looked down, wishing Theo hadn't started this line of conversation. Taking a deep breath, she raised her gaze, looking from one brother to the other. "You don't scare her, really. She even said you act more like a big brother than a cousin."

Ignoring Flint's grin, she continued, "Look, it's already bad enough that I slipped up and told you about the ring. She told me that in confidence. I had to call her and tell her what I'd done. Then Theo here listened in, and that's why he's saying she's afraid of you."

"Oh, really?" Crossing his arms, Flint looked from her to Theo and back again. "So there might be the possibility he made this up."

"Definitely." She glared at Theo, daring him to contradict her. Grinning back, he kept his mouth shut.

In the other room, the ranch hands had finished eating and were making their way out. Several of them stopped to exchange a few words with Flint, asking questions about when he thought the quarantine would be lifted. As the sheriff, Flint did a good job reassuring everyone, while not giving any concrete answers.

When they'd finished with Flint, they exchanged a few words with Theo, and waved at Ellie on their way out, thanking her for the grub.

Once they were all gone, Ellie hurried in to gather up the dishes. To her surprise, Theo came and helped. They worked side by side in companionable silence while Flint sat sipping his cola and watched.

"Thank you for the meal," Flint said, once they'd finished. "I actually came by to discuss the progress—or lack thereof—the doctors are making on determining how and where Mimi contracted the virus. So far they seem to be in agreement that she was ground zero—where it all started."

"Nothing, huh?" Disappointment colored Theo's tone. "The CDC came by and took her car yesterday. I guess I was hoping they'd have some answers by now."

"If they do, they haven't passed them on."

"What about her family?" Ellie asked. "Surely they need to know what's going on."

Theo and Flint exchanged a glance. "Mimi was an only child, according to Lucas Rand. Her parents divorced when she was a teenager. Her mom married some wealthy guy from England and moved to London. And her father has been living on the beach in Mexico for years. As far as I can tell, Mimi rarely spoke to them."

Theo shrugged. "That's what I figured. If they cared, I would have had them calling to ask about Amelia by now." He looked at his brother. "Speaking of the CDC, have they been successful in determining what it is and how it's spread?"

A muscle worked in Flint's jaw as he eyed them.

Ellie waited with bated breath to see if he would answer.

"No. As unsatisfactory as this might be. They aren't any further along, except for one thing. They think it might be man-made. A human-engineered virus."

Stunned, Ellie didn't know what to say. She looked at Theo, who appeared equally shocked.

"Like a terrorist?" he asked. "But why would someone like that pick Dead River to start a biological attack? We're just a small town in Wyoming."

"Whoa." Flint held up his hand in warning. "You're getting way ahead of yourself. No one said anything about terrorists or biological warfare. Just that this virus might have been created in a lab. If so, in all likelihood, it probably escaped by accident."

"If someone created it, then there must be an antidote," Ellie put in. "Though I'm sure all those medical types already realize this."

"I'm sure they do. Anyway, the quarantine still stands. There have been no reports of the virus anywhere else in Wyoming or any other state, for that matter."

Ellie's heart sank. "That's good, but not for us."

"Yes." Flint's expression briefly looked bleak, before he schooled it back. He met Ellie's gaze. "I take it you and Molly have become friends?"

Slowly she nodded, not sure where he was heading with this line of conversation. "I think so, yes."

"Good." He smiled and then winked, reminding her of Theo. "She needs a good friend. Someone she can trust."

Blushing, Ellie nodded. She looked up to find Theo watching her, his extraordinary eyes blazing. They locked gazes, and she shivered with a hunger so visceral it felt physical.

Flint cleared his throat. "I'll be going now," he said. "I'll keep you posted if we make any progress on finding Jimmy Johnson."

Theo looked away, breaking their locked gaze. "Theo, if you need any help, I'll be glad to assist. Just give me a holler."

"Will do." Flint grabbed his hat and let himself out.

Theo crossed the room and began going through the mail, which had been left on the counter.

Alone with him, Ellie found herself inexplicably tongue-tied. His broad shoulders and narrow waist made her ache to touch him. Not to mention his sexy, jean-clad behind. She wondered what he'd do if she went behind him and slipped her arms around him. Just the thought heated her blood.

Turning, he eyed her, making her wonder what was going on inside his mind. "You've got mail," he said, holding up a letter.

Puzzled, she moved closer. "From who?"

"It doesn't say. It's got a Dead River postmark."

Just like that, she knew. "Let me see it."

Silently, he handed her the envelope and a letter opener.

Willing her hands not to shake, she slit an opening. Inside, a single sheet of lined notebook paper had been folded three times, perfectly even.

"I'm almost afraid to look," she confided.

"Do you want me to do it?"

"No." She shook her head. "But thanks for asking."

Heart pounding, she unfolded the paper. For all its outwardly neat appearance, the writing inside was the antithesis. A single sentence, scrawled in what appeared to be black crayon, slanted across the lines.

"'You're mine—until death do us part.'" She read it out loud, fear stabbing her heart. And anger too. "This needs to stop," she said.

"I agree. I think it's time we figure out who your stalker actually is," Theo announced, sounding a hell of a lot more confident than she felt at the prospect.

Still, the idea of doing something, no matter how fruitless, sounded better than nothing.

Getting up to feed Amelia her midday bottle, Ellie looked at him, both intrigued and doubtful. "Oh yeah?

How are we going to do that, exactly? The police in Boulder have already tried."

"Then they didn't try hard enough."

"They did, though at first they didn't take me seriously. I've been over this with them and on my own, as well. A hundred times."

He pulled out a chair and straddled it. "Hear me out. We need to go through people you've known in the past. He might be a bad blind date, or maybe someone who asked you out and who you turned down."

Ellie shook her head. "I don't know about that."

He eyed her, head tilted, looking so cocky and sexy it took every ounce of willpower she possessed to keep from crossing the room and planting a kiss on his sensual mouth. Ever since the night they'd kissed, she'd been battling the urge to see if he wanted to do it again, to do more. Only knowing Theo as she did, she knew if he really did, he'd have been in her room long before now. While this hurt, she'd decided he would have to be the one to make the next move.

Assuming there was one.

"Please," he said, the deep rasp of his sexy voice turning her insides to mush. "Let me at least try."

"Fine." Amelia had finished her bottle, so Ellie lifted the baby to her shoulder and began burping her. "Let me finish with her. Once I put her down, we can discuss this."

He nodded, continuing to watch her. Her heart skipped a beat as she tried to pretend not to be bothered by the intent way he stared.

Once Amelia was settled, Ellie returned to the table. Theo had a pad of paper and a pen.

He'd returned the letter to the envelope. "I want to show it to Flint," Theo said.

"Ok."

"Are you ready?"

She shrugged. "I guess. But I promise you, it will be a really short list."

"We'll see. Where did you go to high school?"

"Boulder High. And most of my classmates went on to college."

"At CU?"

"Yes. Since they were still there in town, a few of us continued to hang out together."

"But you didn't go to college."

Another one of her regrets. Keeping it light, she nodded. "I couldn't. After I turned eighteen, the family I'd been living with asked me to leave. I was too busy trying to support myself to go to school. The only kinds of jobs for people like me are working in the food industry, or retail. I did both."

"Can you think of any coworkers, bosses even, who might have been fixated on you?"

Ellie laughed. "No."

Despite her response, Theo pressed her. "Come on, Ellie. Think. Surely someone asked you out, even if it was in a kidding sort of way."

"I once had a manager who I had to report for sexual harassment," she admitted, feeling reluctant. "But he quit and moved away. I'm pretty sure he's not my stalker."

Pen poised, Theo nodded. "Still, let's write him down. What's his name?"

"I can't remember. And I'm telling you the truth. Tom or Tim, maybe?"

"Fine. Let's move on. Ellie?"

She blinked, focusing her attention back on the task at hand. She'd die before she'd admit that she'd been eyeing the way the muscles on his arm flexed when he wrote.

Cleary, she didn't affect him the same way he affected her.

"I'm thinking," she said. "High school, there might have been a couple of people I turned down for a date. But very few. And the only job I had where I had to constantly fight off inebriated men was when I worked as a waitress on the graveyard shift. All the drunks came in to eat after the bars closed."

"There you go." Pen poised, Theo waited, clearly expecting her to name names.

"I didn't know them," she pointed out. "And while there were a few regulars for sure, I never got more than a first name."

"Can you list them?"

"Theo." She rolled her eyes. "No, I can't. Believe me, I've tried. I have no idea who my stalker might be."

"Have you given up?"

Stunned, she froze. Had she? "No," she answered. "At least I don't think so. I loved living in Boulder. I loved my life. But I was at my wits' end, so I fled, aware that I might not ever be able to return. I felt hopeless, and desperate. I can't tell you how many times I've gone over this in my mind, trying to figure out who might be stalking me, and why."

"Bear with me, okay?" He dragged his hand through his hair, giving him a rakish look. Just sitting across from him made her insides tingle. "Give me the names of anyone who might have made you feel uncomfortable."

Without even thinking, she rattled off a list of names. "The Boulder police have already checked them out." She watched as he wrote them down anyway.

"Do you know where any of them are now?" he asked.

"No. But I'm guessing you could look on Facebook."

He nodded and made another notation. "And the guy in

the hoodie who jumped you, did his body size and shape match up with any of these men you listed?"

"Not that I could tell. But to be honest, that was the first time I've even seen him. Normally, he just leaves weird, depressing poetry and those damn black roses."

"He broke in here," Theo pointed out. "And next he tried to jump you in town."

"He seems to be getting more aggressive since I came here. I don't know why."

Theo gave her a long look. "My guess would be he feels threatened. You almost got away from him, and now you're starting a completely new life."

"Maybe so."

He folded the paper and got up. "At least we've made a start. I'll pass this list along to Flint and have him check them out. At the very least, we should be able to tell if any of them have left Boulder."

"Thank you." She smiled, even though she didn't have much hope her stalker would be on that list. And with everything going on in Dead River with the quarantine and Molly's ex-fiancé, she figured Flint and his men had too much on their plate already.

Right now she'd settle for protection. If Theo could just keep her stalker away from her and baby Amelia until the quarantine was lifted, she'd leave town.

Though the possibility of spending the rest of her life looking over her shoulder seemed a bleaker one than it had when she'd left Boulder. She didn't want to think why.

Chapter 11

The rest of the week passed calmly. Ellie cooked, Amelia continued to thrive and Theo continued to charm Ellie. Several times she felt so content she caught herself dreaming of what it would be like to have this life forever.

Dangerous thinking, that.

Still, alone in her room at night, her body throbbed and ached for Theo. The kiss they'd shared had only ignited a desire for more.

Friday afternoon, Molly called. Ellie answered eagerly, glad to hear from her new friend.

"Meet me in town," Molly said, sounding excited. "We'll stop at the diner for dinner and then head to the bar for drinks and dancing."

"Oh, that sounds lovely." Glancing at Amelia still sleeping soundly in her crib, Ellie knew she'd have to decline. "But I can't. I don't have anyone to watch the baby."

"Get Theo to do it. She's his daughter."

Ellie snorted. "He's not here. I haven't seen him all afternoon."

"Being a nanny isn't 24/7."

"I know." Glancing around to make sure she wasn't overheard, Ellie confided in her friend. "I think Theo is afraid he can't take care of her. Plus, I'm not sure he wants to. I found a notebook he was writing in. I believe he intends to go back to the rodeo."

Molly gasped. "He can't. The doctors told him if he jostles his spine, he could be paralyzed permanently."

"Maybe he just doesn't want to believe it."

"No." Molly sounded thoughtful. "Theo's an intelligent man. You must have misunderstood."

"Maybe."

"Then ask him to watch her."

Ellie sighed. "I'll think about it. He really does need to spend more time with her. He actually is pretty good at it."

"There you go. You know, maybe he is trying to make you think he's incapable, so you'll stay."

For an instant, hope slammed into her, making it difficult to breathe. But reality reared its head. "No. Theo's not like that. The one thing he's always been is honest. If he really wanted to make sure I'd stay, he'd just ask."

"Okay. But still, you can't be on call every second of your day. You're allowed time off."

"True." Ellie smiled at the belligerence in her friend's voice.

"Good. Then you're coming with me. How about a sitter? Gemma was just saying the other day she wanted to spend more time with her niece."

"I'm tempted, but..."

"But what?"

"I have a stalker, remember? What if I run into him?"

"You won't." Molly sounded determined. "I promise to make sure you're never alone. Nothing's going to happen. I'll get a hold of Gemma. Let me call you back." And she ended the call before Ellie could protest.

Ellie's first thought was to worry about what Theo would think. Her second was to remember his promise about her having time off. If she waited to go until the evening meal had been served and all the hands were taken care of, then he wouldn't have room to complain.

Two minutes later, her phone rang again.

"Guess what?" Molly said. "Gemma would adore watching over little Amelia. She said she really needs a break from bad stuff, and a baby would be just the ticket."

"I can't go until seven or eight," Ellie said, beginning to get excited herself. "I've got to feed the hands and then change and put on makeup."

"Perfect! Do you want me to pick you up or would you rather meet me there?"

Ellie winced. "I still haven't gotten my car fixed. And I haven't seen Theo at all today, so I can't ask to borrow his truck." As if she would.

"I'll pick you up," Molly chirped. "That way I can pop in and say hello to the baby while I'm there."

"Sounds great. See you later."

Humming happily, Ellie hurried over to her closet to decide what to wear. Thanks to Molly, she suddenly felt happy and young again. Even better, she paid off her credit card bills from before and could afford to spend a little on a girls' night out. She made a mental note to use her next paycheck and see about getting her car repaired.

Theo or no Theo, Ellie decided she'd have a darn good time. As long as she didn't run into her stalker. No. She was done letting him ruin her life. She'd take precautions to stay safe, but she refused to let him destroy her night.

Gemma arrived just as Ellie had finished cleaning up the kitchen. The dark circles under Gemma's eyes attested to the amount of time she'd spent working at the clinic.

For the first time since Molly had come up with the plan, Ellie felt a twinge of guilt. "Maybe this isn't a good idea," she said.

"No worries." Gemma waved her off. "What I need more than anything is to breathe the sweet scent of baby and let Amelia's pure innocence remind me of better times."

"Are you sure?" Ellie shifted her weight from foot to foot.

Fixing Ellie with her Colton green eyes, Gemma smiled. "Positive. Now go get ready."

Still, Ellie didn't move. "She's already been changed and she's due another feeding around nine o'clock. We've got plenty of diapers, and she's had a bit of diaper rash, so I've been putting ointment on."

"Got it." Gemma waved her hand, shooing her from the room. "She'll be fine. Don't worry."

Worry? The word galvanized Ellie into action. Turning on her heel, she hurried off to her room. What was wrong with her? Amelia wasn't her baby, just her charge. Yet here she was, feeling like an overprotective mother, afraid to leave her baby and go out for an evening.

Shaking off her misgivings, she jumped into the shower to begin the preparations for her night out.

An hour later, she stood in front of her dresser mirror. Skintight jeans, cowboy boots and a Western shirt tucked in. She almost didn't recognize herself. Not only did she have on makeup, but she'd straightened her long hair and wore it down, something she rarely did since accepting the job here. A pair of dangly silver earrings and five or six bracelets completed her outfit.

Squinting, she finally decided she looked okay. Turning, the heels of her boots clunking on the wooden floor, she grabbed her purse, and headed out to wait for Molly.

For some reason she'd thought Theo would make an appearance while she waited. Oh, who was she kidding? She'd hoped to run into him, just so he could see what she looked like when she was all fixed up.

Of course he didn't show. Mildly angry at herself for feeling so disappointed, she went back into the den, where Gemma sat on the couch playing with Amelia.

"Wow," Gemma said, clearly impressed. "You look nice."

"Thank you." Trying not to sound too glum, Ellie sat in the chair. "Have you talked to Theo lately?"

Could she have been any more obvious? Blushing, Ellie tried to act as if her question had no hidden meaning.

Unfortunately, Gemma apparently could see right through her. "Are you two fighting?"

"Fighting?" Ellie shook her head. "That would imply a relationship. He's my employer."

Gemma studied her for a moment. "Then why'd you ask?"

Feeling her face heat an even deeper shade of red, Ellie looked away. "I just haven't seen him at all today. Usually he at least comes to see his daughter, but his truck's been gone since early this morning."

And there, she put it right back where it belonged. The father-daughter relationship.

"He's probably helping Flint with something," Gemma said. "I'm sure he'll pop in and see this precious girl tonight."

Which would be fine with Ellie.

The doorbell chimed.

"That will be Molly," Ellie said, hurrying to answer.

"Hey! Don't you look fabulous!" Molly hugged her, hard and fast, before breezing inside. The instant she caught sight of Amelia, Molly squealed. Simultaneously, Gemma winced and Amelia jumped, letting out a wail and starting to cry.

Ellie rushed over, barely stopping herself from snatching Amelia out of Gemma's arms to comfort her.

"Shhh, it's all right," Gemma soothed, rocking Amelia expertly. Almost immediately, the baby's sobs became hiccups, then quieted.

"You're really good with her," Ellie said, trying not to sound jealous.

"Thanks." Gemma smiled. "I work with a lot of infants at the clinic."

"She's adorable," Molly chimed in, appearing not the least abashed at all the ruckus she'd caused. Spinning, she grabbed Ellie's arm. "Are you ready?"

Glancing one final time at Gemma and Amelia, Ellie nodded. "Sure. Let's go."

Molly chattered nonstop all the way to town. Ellie didn't see any sign of the brokenhearted, jilted bride, and she was glad. Apparently Molly was resilient. Either that or she'd mastered the art of hiding her emotions.

They pulled up in front of a brick building with a neon sign proclaiming it as the Dead River Bar.

"What about the diner?" Ellie asked.

"It's just a block away. I'd rather park here and walk there and back. Neither of us has on heels. Is that okay with you?"

Glancing down the street, Ellie shrugged. "It seems

well lit and there are enough people out and about, it should be safe."

"Of course it's safe." Molly stared at her a moment, before comprehension dawned. "You're worried about your stalker, aren't you?"

"Yes. If he was here when the quarantine came down, he's trapped here with us."

"It'll be okay." Molly squeezed her shoulder. "I've got your back."

Getting out of the car, Ellie tried to shake off her apprehension.

"Hey." Molly took her arm as they walked side by side. "Don't let him ruin your night. No one should have that much power over someone else."

Easier said than done. Ellie smiled and tried to act nonchalant, but she couldn't help checking behind them and keeping a constant eye on their surroundings.

They made it to the diner without incident. "See?" Molly said, letting go of her arm and grinning. "No problem."

Inside, the place smelled like bacon and burgers. There were red booths circling the place, with tables in the center. At one side was an old-fashioned counter with stools.

"Where do you want to sit?" Molly said. "I like the booths myself."

"Sounds good." Ellie pointed to one that was not in full view of the outside window. "How about there? And I'm sorry, but I've got to sit where I can see the door."

Though Molly sighed, she didn't comment.

Once they were seated and the waitress had brought menus, Molly put hers down and touched the back of Ellie's hand. "I hope for your sake, he's caught soon."

"Me too." Molly sighed. "Now, let's not talk about him again. I'm here to have a good time."

After their meal, they walked back to the bar. The sidewalks had gotten even more crowded, which seemed unusual in such a small town at night, and Ellie said so.

"Oh, that's because one of our local bands is playing tonight," Molly said, grinning with excitement. "The Dead River Diamonds."

"Makes sense, I guess." Ellie had never heard of them, but that didn't matter. The townspeople were showing their support. Pretty nice, as far as she was concerned.

The bar charged a five-dollar cover, something Molly told her was unusual. "But this is a special night."

Inside, the place had begun to fill up. Molly made a beeline to a bar table on the edge of the dance floor. "Killer seats!" she crowed. "I can't believe we lucked out and got these."

Glancing over her shoulder, Ellie made a point of checking out all the exits, a habit she'd gotten into after her stalker had shown up one too many times. They were on a direct path from the front door, but once the bar got crowded, she wouldn't have a great view of anyone entering.

They'd barely gotten seated when a tall, angular waiter with multiple piercings stopped to take their orders.

"Hey, Chad!" Molly greeted him happily. "I didn't know you still worked here."

"Just on special occasions," he replied, smiling back. "What can I get you ladies to drink?"

"This seems like a beer night," she said, winking at Ellie. "What do you think, Ellie?"

"Sure." Ellie didn't care what she drank. She wasn't planning on having a lot of it, whatever it was. Out in public like this, she couldn't afford to let her guard down.

They sat and sipped their beers as the bar filled up. Men began carrying in instruments and getting them set up on a raised wooden stage. According to Molly, the band would start at nine. Which wasn't too far away now.

Molly's excitement must have been contagious, as Ellie began to get antsy. Why not? She loved music, enjoyed dancing and the place had not gotten so crowded that her stalker could try anything here. And it wasn't as if anyone had known she'd be here either. She might as well relax and have a good time.

Promptly at nine, five guys with shaggy hair and beards strolled out. The crowd greeted them with thunderous applause and whistles, which they acknowledged with waves and grins.

The first chords filled the room. Expression rapt, Molly leaned forward. Stunned, Ellie began tapping her foot along to the beat. No wonder half the town had come to hear this band play. They were really good.

A few seconds into the first song, and people began appearing on the dance floor. Ellie watched with enjoyment, sipping her beer and rocking along on her bar stool. The sound was a catchy combination of country and rock, entirely danceable and the kind of music she would sing along with in the car if she knew the words.

A tall man with a bushy mustache and a brown cowboy hat touched her arm and asked her to dance. She glanced at Molly, who was chatting away with Chad, and then agreed.

Out on the dance floor, she let her body sway to the music, smiling up at her partner. As he spun her, she got a good view of the crowd through the smoky haze. Her heart skipped a beat as a familiar face caught her eye.

Theo. Her heart sank—for no good reason—as she realized he was with a woman. Mortified, she turned her back to him, praying he didn't recognize her.

The song ended. The man—she thought he said his

name was Sam—wanted to dance again to the next one, but she declined. Hurrying back to her seat, she took a long drink of her beer, startled to realize she'd nearly finished it. Weird, as she wasn't overly fond of beer.

Still talking to Molly, Chad noticed and hurried off to bring them another round.

Molly caught sight of her face. "What's wrong?"

"Theo's here." Ellie swallowed, aware her friend wouldn't get her distress. "With a date."

"So?" Raising an eyebrow, Molly drained her own mug. "What's the big deal? It's not like you're dating, are you?" Then, before Ellie could answer, Molly's mouth formed a shocked, round O. "Oh. Em. Gee. Did you use that negligee?" she asked, looking stunned. "Have you two done the nasty?"

"No. Absolutely not." Ellie shook her head. "And the only reason I'm sort of unhappy to see him is that he doesn't know I took the night off." Okay, this was a bald-faced lie, but this wasn't the time or place to tell Molly how distant Theo had been.

"Pshaw." Waving her hand, Molly glanced toward the crowd, apparently trying to spot him. "He won't care. Especially since Gemma is taking care of Amelia."

"He's on a date." Ellie tried not to sound miserable, and she prayed the music drowned out her feeble attempt to act as if she didn't care.

"Really?" Now Molly stood on the bottom rung of her chair, scanning the hazy room. "Who with?"

"Some redhead."

The band announced they'd be taking a short break. Canned music began to play over the speaker system, the volume much lower.

"I see them. Hey, I know her." Molly waved. "Theo! Over here."

Great. Ellie wanted to crawl under the table. She considered excusing herself and rushing away to the ladies room, but Theo had already spotted them.

Frowning, he made his way through the crowd toward their table, his date tagging along behind him.

"Hey, you two." He smiled, but his green eyes were cold as he looked at Ellie. "I'm surprised to see you here. Where's Amelia?"

"Gemma's babysitting her," Ellie said, resisting the urge to apologize or explain.

"Lucy!" Jumping up, Molly hugged the redheaded woman. "I didn't know you and Theo were seeing each other."

"We're not," Theo said. "I came to hear the band and Lucy here decided to befriend me." The layered sarcasm in his tone left no doubt how he felt about that. Ellie squirmed for the other woman.

"Now, Theo, you know we have some catching up to do," Lucy drawled, apparently oblivious. "We might as well have some fun while we're at it. Buy me a drink, and I'll find us a table."

"I think that's going to have to happen another time," Molly put in smoothly, clearly deciding to be Theo's wingman. "My cousin, Theo, was supposed to be meeting us here tonight. Sorry. I guess you can catch up with him later."

Pouting, Lucy gave Theo one last lingering look of longing. When he didn't respond, she sighed and sashayed away. Ellie silently watched her go, wondering why she didn't feel sorry for her.

"Thanks," Theo said, grabbing a chair from another table and pulling it up between Molly and Ellie. His black cowboy hat shadowed his face, and he wore a fashionable button-down white shirt with a gray-and-black swirling design around his broad shoulders. He looked dangerous and sexy as hell. "I'll buy the next round," he said.

As far as Ellie was concerned, there'd be no next round. She tried to figure out a way to talk Molly into leaving. But when Chad showed up and plunked her mug of beer in front of her, she took a sip just to have something to do.

"Having fun?" Theo asked. His aloof expression had vanished, replaced by the friendly, flirty Theo she'd come to know.

Still uncertain, she nodded. "The band is really great."

"I saw you dancing," he said, the teasing sparkle in his eyes inviting her to smile along with him. Instead she looked down, her insides churning with a confusing mix of emotions.

He leaned closer, speaking in a voice pitched low enough that only she could hear. "You look beautiful," he told her, his husky tone making a mess of her insides.

How should she respond to that? "So do you," she blurted, mortified when he laughed. She decided she'd go hide in the ladies' room. But before she could jump up, Molly announced she was going to the restroom. "You wait here with Theo and hold the table," she told Ellie, grinning mischievously to let Ellie know she was disappearing on purpose. With a quick wave, Molly disappeared into the crowd.

"You could have held the table," Ellie muttered at Theo.

He shrugged. "I can, if you want to go with her."

Sorely tempted, instead she found herself unable to move, as if her legs had grown roots. "I can wait."

"So, how have you been?" he asked kindly, his expression full of polite interest. As if they didn't live in the same house.

"Fine." Her impersonal response told him what she thought of that. "Thank you for asking."

Some of her frustration must have come through in her voice. "What's wrong?" he asked, sounding concerned.

Taking a deep breath, she decided to tell him. "Well, for starters, where have you been? You just kind of vanished."

"Missing me, were you?" Again the flash and teasing grin, which made her stomach lurch in instant response.

"Amelia has," she countered, proud of herself for the quick comeback. "She needs her daddy."

Just like that, his smile vanished. The sharp pang of guilt she felt nearly made her apologize, but for once she managed to hold her tongue.

"I'll always be there for her," he said, his expression serious, his green gaze intent. "You know that. It's just been crazy around town and I had to help out with a few things."

His ruggedness and masculinity made him the most attractive man in a sea of cowboy hats. Damn, he looked good. Mouth suddenly dry, she nodded and took a gulp of her beer.

"The band's coming back," Molly pointed out as she slid into her seat. Seeing her opportunity, Ellie excused herself and pushed through the crowd toward the ladies' room.

Once there, she eyed herself in the mirror. With her heightened color, she thought she looked like a woman in heat. Trying to shake it off, she headed into a stall.

When she emerged and washed her hands, she appeared a bit calmer. Taking a deep breath, she sucked it up and headed back toward the table.

Halfway there, a man stepped in front of her, blocking her way. "Hey, darlin'," he slurred.

"Excuse me," she said firmly, stepping around him.

"Wait a second." His hand shot out, grabbing her arms so hard she stumbled backward, into him. "Now, that's much better."

His hands were everywhere while he turned her to face him. Acting purely on instinct, she brought her knee up, slamming it into his groin.

Immediately he let go and doubled over, his face contorted as he flung a stream of curses at her. Heart pounding, she tripped over her own two feet, trying to move away.

When she looked up, Theo was there. He hauled her up against him and then stepped in between her and the other man. "You got a problem, buddy?"

Still gasping for air and trying to recover, her assailant took a look at all six foot two of Theo and began backing away while shaking his head.

Relieved, Ellie sagged against Theo.

"Are you all right?" he asked, holding her close enough for her to feel every muscle in his body.

"Yes." Her answer was more to keep him from going after the other man. If Theo got in a bar fight, she figured there'd be all kinds of trouble. "No harm, no foul."

Though he appeared unconvinced, he finally nodded and, keeping his hand in the small of her back—possessively, she thought—followed her back to the table.

Molly and Chad were deep in conversation and Ellie figured her friend had missed the entire thing. Which was good, as all Ellie wanted to do was forget about it.

The band started playing a slow song just as Theo began to pull out Ellie's chair.

"Let's dance," he said, pushing her chair back under the table.

Though Ellie wasn't 100 percent sure her legs would

hold up, she wanted nothing more than to dance with Theo, so she nodded.

He pulled her into his arms and she thought she'd died and gone to heaven. They began to move around the dance floor, gliding really, as she followed his lead.

She'd never been with a man like him. Never. Muscular and tall, a man who made his Wranglers look like designer jeans. He moved with a sexy, masculine confidence that was addictive. She fought the urge to dance closer, rubbing herself all up on him like one of his groupies, or a cat in heat.

Despite reminding herself that he was her boss, aware he was something she could never have, she felt dizzy with craving him.

Finally, the song—and the slow torture—ended. Breathless, she hurried back to the table. The instant she took her seat, Molly jumped up and dragged Chad out onto the dance floor.

"She doesn't seem to be hurting too badly," Theo observed.

"I think she's keeping busy so she doesn't have to think about it," she said, suddenly thirsty. She took a couple of gulps of her beer, wishing for water.

"Just a second." Theo got up, went to the bar and returned with a tall glass of ice water, which he slid over to her.

"How'd you know?" she asked, amazed.

"Because I can tell by your face that you're not a beer drinker." He smiled, watching as she gulped down the water.

"Thank you," she said when she'd nearly drained the glass.

"You're welcome." Arm over the back of Molly's

empty chair, he surveyed the room. "Are you ready to go home?"

Longing swept her, but she shook her head. "I can't. I came with Molly."

He glanced at Molly, dancing up a storm on the dance floor. "I don't think she'd mind."

Ellie blushed as she realized what he meant. "Do you really think Molly and Chad…?"

Though he gave a mild shrug, his eyes sparkled. "We all do what we have to in order to distract ourselves."

Feeling hot all over for no good reason, Ellie resisted the urge to fan herself.

"I'll have to check with her." She already knew if Molly thought there was even the most remote chance Theo and Ellie would get together, she'd merrily send them on their way with a wink and a shove. Not to mention two wispy scraps of cloth.

Ellie tried to calm her racing heartbeat and focus on something else. Like finishing her water and then taking teeny-tiny sips of what remained of her beer.

When Molly finally returned, out of breath from dancing and sans Chad, who apparently had to go back to waiting tables, she eyed the two of them. "What's up?"

"Nothing," Ellie said, aware she was blushing again.

Luckily, Theo didn't appear to notice. "I asked Ellie if she wanted to catch a ride home with me," he said.

Molly grinned. "Rrrreally?" she purred.

"But not just yet. I'm not ready to leave right now," Ellie put in, sounding more breathless than she'd intended.

Both Molly and Theo laughed.

"Fine," Theo said. "I'll stay until you're ready to leave, and then I'll take you home. There's no reason Molly should have to drive all the way out to the ranch when I'm right here."

Looking from one to the other, Molly continued grinning like a madwoman. "True. He has a point."

"Whatever." Pretending to be supremely disinterested, Ellie kept her gaze firmly fixed on the band.

"Actually, Ellie..." Molly leaned over, appearing sheepish. "Chad gets off work at midnight. He and I were thinking about going to a private party at his brother's house. Of course you're welcome to come, but you won't know anybody. It's your call."

What Molly had just described might have been fun, on any other night, for any other person. But Ellie wanted to go home—or back to the ranch. She seriously missed Amelia, which confounded her. And she'd never been a big partier.

"I'll just ride home with Theo," she said. "But I want you to promise me you won't drive drunk."

"I won't." Molly held out her hand. "Pinky-swear." They locked pinkies, which felt both childish and fun. "Worse comes to worst, I'll just stay over there and go home in the morning."

"Then it's settled?" Theo touched Ellie's shoulder, making her jump. "Ellie's coming with me?"

"Yep." Molly still sounded way too cheerful, making Ellie eye her. Was she matchmaking again?

Her next statement confirmed it. "Hey, Ellie, don't forget that little present I gave you, okay?"

By which she meant the sexy negligee.

If possible, Ellie's face turned even redder.

"What present?" Theo asked, which made Molly dissolve in a fit of giggles. Theo looked from one to the other, his eyebrows raised.

"Never mind." Ellie's voice came out sharper than she'd intended. "It's a private joke."

"Whatever." He cocked his head. "Just let me know when you're ready to leave."

Suddenly, Ellie wanted to leave right now. Ignoring the knowing way Molly eyed her, she stood. "Let's go."

Hand on the small of her back, Theo urged her toward the door. Just then, the band began to play a slow, romantic ballad that had been popular a few years ago.

Theo stopped. "Do you want to dance one last time before we head out?"

Did she? She made the mistake of glancing at him. He exuded masculinity. Sexuality and self-confidence. No wonder women threw themselves at him everywhere he went.

Her heart skipped a beat. Sweet torture. She wasn't sure she could endure going body to body with him again, without doing something she definitely would regret.

"No, thanks," she managed. "I'm pretty tired." Her words sounded like a lie, even to herself.

His gaze searching her face, he finally nodded. "All right."

This time, when he settled his hand in the small of her back to guide her toward the door, she felt the heat of his touch burning through her shirt.

Outside, the night air contained a chill, helping cool her overheated body. She breathed in, glad Theo had found her. Being with him made her feel protected and safe.

She felt almost giddy as she climbed into his truck. For just one instant, she let herself pretend they were escaping the bar for a romantic rendezvous. Even imagining the things they might do if that were the case made her mouth go dry and her body wet.

She didn't think she'd ever wanted a man as much as she wanted him.

And that alone was reason enough to try to have him.

Again, Molly's words came back to tease her.

It might have been the alcohol giving her false bravery, but she thought she just might give that little negligee a try.

Chapter 12

As they approached the barricade, Ellie sat up straight. She didn't want whatever officer was manning the checkpoint to think she was intoxicated, though she imagined that might be the least of their worries right now. No one had been informed what purpose exactly the barricades served. It was one thing to keep people from leaving Dead River. But entering too? She didn't understand what they were trying to keep out.

Since there were few vehicles out this late, they pulled up, spoke, and after a quick glance inside the truck, they were waved through. Ellie relaxed, feeling sleepy.

A few seconds later, Theo glanced at his rearview mirror. "That's weird," he said, almost to himself. "A minute ago, we were the only ones out. Now another car just went through the checkpoint and is behind us."

Mildly concerned, she turned to see. Two headlights,

about three car lengths behind them. "Hopefully it's just someone else going home for the night."

"Yeah, maybe." Theo gave her a reassuring smile. But she couldn't help noticing his white-knuckled grip on the steering wheel.

Praying it wasn't her stalker, she tried not to overreact. Still, she had to force herself to take deep, calming breaths.

Theo smiled reassuringly. "I'm sure it's nothing."

She nodded.

They continued to drive a steady speed. Theo made the turn from the highway onto the two-lane paved road. They were in familiar territory. The gravel road that led to the ranch was about two miles away.

"Damn it." The curse exploded from Theo. "They're gaining on us. I'd think they were just wanting to pass, but I've been doing close to eighty miles an hour."

"What is it?" she asked, twisting to try and see. "A car or truck?"

"It's another truck, about the same size as ours."

Heart pounding, she gasped as she saw the headlights growing closer until they were right on their rear bumper. "Oh, I hope he just wants to pass."

Jaw grim, Theo accelerated. "If so, there's certainly been plenty of opportunity to do so. They've been hanging back until now."

Panic clawing at her, Ellie couldn't look anymore. Turning to face front, she checked her seat belt and watched the speedometer inch past eighty-five, ninety, before she looked away. Awfully fast. She found herself clutching the door handle, her teeth clenched, praying it would turn out to be nothing.

"He's keeping up with us." Theo had barely gotten

the words out when *bam!* The truck slammed into their rear bumper.

Ellie gasped. Her seat belt held, cutting into her chest and making her cry out.

"What the hell..." Theo stomped on the accelerator. "This is crazy."

And then she knew. "It's my stalker, isn't it?" she rasped. "He followed us."

"Could be." Theo's grim expression confirmed her fears. "I think the sick son of a bitch is trying to run us off the road."

Though she knew she shouldn't, she peered at the accelerator. They were pushing ninety-five.

"If we wreck at this speed..." She didn't have to finish the sentence. They both knew what would happen.

"Hang on," Theo said. "I'm going past our road and taking the turn that leads back to the main highway. I'm going to have to slow down. There's no way we can make a turn at this speed."

She nodded, bracing her hands against the dash. "I'm ready."

"Here we go." Gradually easing off the accelerator, he slowed them down, also using the brake. "The turn is coming up."

He cursed. "That son of a bitch is going to ram us again."

The words had barely left his mouth when the other truck slammed into them. This time, it hit them hard, sending them spinning out of control.

"Hang on," Theo shouted. "And pray."

Ellie closed her eyes, terror threatening to strangle her. They were going to wreck. Wreck badly.

Everything seemed to slow down, time suspended in measured motion. Theo. Oddly enough, Ellie's first concern was for him. He still hadn't fully healed from his rodeo accident. She didn't know what kind of damage a crash like this might do.

"Damn him."

Spinning, spinning. Cursing, Theo fought to keep them on the road. The other truck hit them again, this time on the right front wheel well, just before the passenger door. That impact was just enough to send them tumbling into a roll.

Ellie screamed. She closed her eyes as Theo's truck turned over with a sickening crunch of metal. The windows shattered, shards of glass raining on them. She shrieked again and again, an endless voicing of her terror and pain.

"Ellie!" Theo shouted, his voice harsh and raw.

The sickening crunch of metal and shattered glass seemed deafening. Miraculously, they rolled all the way over and came back up, wheels on the ground, roof crumpled, windows broken, the engine quiet. Stopped.

Shards of glass covered her, along with a lot of cuts. Stunned, she tried to process what had just happened. One, she didn't hurt at all. Yet. Dimly, she realized she was most likely in shock.

"Are you all right?" Theo asked. Dazed, she could only nod. Something wet obscured her vision, and when she used her hand to wipe it off her eyes, her hand came away red with blood.

She screamed again, then choked it off midstream, hyperventilating as she clutched at Theo's arm.

"You're fine," Theo soothed, his deep voice unbelievable steady. "Ellie, please try not to panic."

Exhaling sharply, he took a deep, shaky breath. "As far as I can tell, neither one of us is seriously hurt." He reached out and turned the key, even though the engine was already dead. "Just in case," he said. "Ellie, honey. Please. Look at me."

Blinking, she managed to close her mouth, though involuntary whimpers escaped her in a continual stream. Struggling to focus she locked gazes with him.

"Now breathe," he told her. "Just breathe."

In. Out. As she did, everything came back into focus.

"Now," Theo continued. "We need to get out of here. Just in case. Can you do that?"

"I think so. But the guy who hit us," she managed, her numb fingers fumbling to unhook her seat belt. "Where is he?"

"I don't know." Theo struggled to open his door. He cursed when he couldn't. "It's too damaged," he said. Instead he used his elbow to push out the rest of the glass in his window.

Theo had cuts too, she belatedly realized. A lot of them. In addition, one of his eyes was black and blue and beginning to swell.

But they were alive. That's what mattered.

"See if you can open your door," he said. "If not, once I'm out, I'll come around to your side and try to free you."

"Or else I can crawl after you," she said, feeling more like herself. "I don't think anything is broken." Of course, for all she knew she could have bones poking out of her skin. She'd read when people went into shock, they didn't feel pain.

She guessed she'd now learn if that was actually true.

"Let's give it a try." Twisting in his seat, Theo grimaced. He opened his mouth to speak, but before he could, a face appeared at Ellie's window.

Jumping, she squawked a strangled scream, recoiling back against Theo.

"You belong to me," the apparition snarled. Ellie

squinted, and then realized he was wearing a mask, the kind of thing someone would don on Halloween. Deliberately trying to frighten them.

"Remember that. No one else can have you." Then, just as she was starting to wonder if she'd begun hallucinating or something, he tossed a single black rose on her lap. Her stalker.

"Next time, he dies. Maybe you too."

"What do you want?" Ellie cried. But he turned away and didn't answer. And then he was gone.

Theo cursed, trying again to push his door open. Once more, he failed. A moment later, they heard the sound of a truck taking off and roaring away into the distance.

Shaken, Ellie stared down at the black rose amid the glass shards. "He nearly killed us," she said, her voice sounding weak and trembling. "What he's doing makes no sense."

Theo reached out and plucked the rose from her lap and tossed it out his window. "He's here in town. With the quarantine, he won't be able to leave. And now his truck is damaged too. It shouldn't be too hard to find him."

Still feeling kind of numb, she didn't immediately respond. When she moved again, it was to wipe more blood from her eyes. "Where is this coming from?" she asked, frustrated and scared.

"You have a head wound." He opened the glove box and rummaged around, emerging with some fast food napkins. "Here. Use these." He pressed one to her face, right above her temple. "Press and hold. Head wounds bleed a lot, but you need to stop the bleeding."

Glad to have someone telling her what to do, Ellie did as he said. "Thank you," she murmured. "What now?"

"Well, since he's gone, let's see if this truck will start. If it does, I want to try and drive it back to the ranch."

She nodded, sending shooting pain through her head, and winced.

The engine caught on the first turn of the key.

"Starts just like nothing happened," Theo said, sounding amazed. Ellie tried to focus on that, but her vision blurred.

"Ellie? Are you all right?"

Feeling as if she'd separated from her body, Ellie tried to smile, but her lips felt cracked and she couldn't. "Maybe. Maybe not. Right now I can't tell. I think so. But just in case, maybe we should see if Gemma can check us out before she goes home. You know, just to make sure nothing is broken."

"We will." He reached out to squeeze her shoulder, then stopped himself. "I don't want to hurt you."

Though she nodded, Ellie could think of one thing. "What if Amelia had been with us? She could have been killed."

"She wasn't," he said firmly. "And until that bastard is caught, she won't be going anywhere with either of us. Right now try not to worry about what might have happened, okay? Focus on what did. We're safe, we're okay. Can you do that for me?"

About to nod again, Ellie thought better of it and settled for a sigh. "I'll try."

Theo kept his fury hidden—Ellie had already been through enough because of her psycho stalker. Now not only had she nearly been killed, but he knew she'd spend a lot of time worrying about what had happened to him and his truck, blaming herself. When none of this was her fault, at all. So help him, if he could get his hands on that guy…

What kind of crazy fool did stuff like that? He'd

known the guy wasn't right in the head; he was a stalker after all. But to profess undying love and then nearly kill the object of his affections? The guy was a psychopath, and his behavior had escalated. Now he was much more dangerous than Theo had originally believed.

Theo knew one thing. He had to protect Ellie. He'd enlist Flint's help, but with or without his assistance, Theo planned to hunt the creep down.

Ellie drifted in and out of consciousness as they limped home. He worried she had a concussion or some other, more serious injury, but he couldn't do anything about that. They'd never make it back to town, and the clinic was closed anyway. No, Gemma was their best option.

As for himself, Theo felt reasonably sure he had a few cuts and bruises, nothing serious. Maybe a bruised rib or two. He'd had worse. Of course, he hadn't actually tried walking yet.

When they finally pulled into the ranch drive, he parked in front of the house and cut the engine. Breathing a sigh of relief, he tried one more time to open his door. It still wouldn't open, apparently too badly damaged.

Glancing at Ellie, he knew she'd need his help getting out. He'd have to go out his window and risk getting cut on any remaining pieces of glass. Just as he'd started hefting himself up and out, Ellie opened her eyes and looked blearily at him. "Are we home?"

Home. Hearing her say the word like that brought a tightness to his chest. "Yes, honey. We're home."

If she caught the use of the endearment, she didn't react. Instead she tried her own door handle, exclaiming when she was able to wedge it open, not fully, but enough.

"Can you get out on your own?" he asked. "If so, hold on to the truck until I can help you. I'll be right over there." And he pushed himself the rest of the way out his window, dropping to the ground and stifling a grunt of pain.

Testing his legs, he held on to the door. He needed to see if his legs would support his weight. Once he knew they would, he kept one hand on the truck for support and hurried over to her side. Her door still sat partly open.

"Take my hand and let me help you," he said. "Do you think you can do it?"

"I think so." Taking his hand, she managed to slide into the open space and out.

"Can you walk?"

"I don't know." Taking his arm, she took a tentative step forward. "It appears that I can."

She held on to him all the way into the house. Once inside, he sat her down at the kitchen table. "Let me call Flint. Then I'll go wake up Gemma and we'll see about getting you cleaned up."

"What about you?" she asked. "You're all cut up too."

Not as badly as her, though he kept that information to himself. "I'll clean up after you."

He dialed Flint, not liking the way his hands shook. Delayed reaction, he guessed. His brother picked up on the second ring.

"What's up?"

Speaking tersely, Theo relayed what had just happened.

"Thank God Amelia wasn't with you. He's escalating," Flint said. "And if he wasn't dangerous enough before, I now consider him extremely so now. We'll charge him with vehicular assault."

"Good," Theo said. He suddenly realized he ached in places he hadn't even realized he'd hurt.

"Are you and Ellie all right?"

"I think so. We're home now, but we're both pretty banged up. I need you to have your guys look for a white pickup, a Dodge Ram, I think. It'll have some front end damage."

"Do you want me to come over and take a statement?"

"Not tonight," Theo said, trying his damnedest to sound calm and composed. "She's pretty shook up. You can come talk to both of us tomorrow, okay?"

"Fine. What about medical treatment?"

"Gemma's here. She babysat Amelia for Ellie, though she's most likely asleep. I'll wake her up and have her check us out." Despite his best efforts, Theo knew he sounded shaky—hell, he *was* shaky.

"I just can't believe the SOB tried to kill you." Even Flint, seasoned lawman as he was, sounded traumatized.

"Well." Theo took a deep breath. "If you want the honest truth, I think he just wanted to scare the crap out of us. He could have kept ramming us, and done even more damage. He could have shot us, assuming he had a gun."

Flint swore. "What he did was bad enough. We need to find him and get him locked up. Until then, I want you and Ellie both to take extra precautions."

"We will." Theo hung up. A moment later, Ellie emerged from the bathroom, swaying slightly. Theo hurried over and helped her to the couch. "Wait here. I'm going to wake Gemma and have her check you out."

"You too." Ellie stared up at him. The dark hollows under her eyes made him ache to comfort her.

Instead he did the wise thing and hurried to fetch his sister.

The next morning, Ellie came awake with a gasp. Bad dream. She stretched and winced, hurting all over. And then she realized it hadn't been a nightmare after all.

Her stalker now wanted to kill her. For what reason, she had no idea, but then she'd never understood what motivated him to follow her around and leave black roses and weird messages.

Clearly, he thought he owned her. The thought made her shudder, as she could see how he'd think if he couldn't have her, no one could.

He planned to kill her. Never more had she felt the panicked urge to flee, to take everything she had and sneak out in the middle of the night. If not for the quarantine, she might. Not only had she become far too attached to sweet Amelia, but she couldn't risk endangering the precious newborn.

And Theo. He'd almost been killed, merely because he'd given her a ride home.

She shuddered, fighting back waves of panic. She'd die before she let anything happen to him or his perfect daughter. Since she knew she couldn't leave, at least not while the National Guard patrolled the town's borders, she'd have to figure out a way to fight back.

Though she'd wanted only to flee, that was no longer an option. Plus, her stalker had now tried to hurt someone she cared about. She had no choice now. No matter what, she wasn't going to let her stalker win.

The next morning, Flint came out to take both Ellie's and Theo's statements. For whatever reason, Ellie started shaking as she recounted the events of the night before.

To her surprise and relief, Theo came and put his arm around her shoulders, offering his strength and comfort.

Flint narrowed his eyes as he looked from one to the other, but he didn't comment. He'd just about finished writing everything up when his cell phone rang.

"Excuse me a moment," he said. "I need to take this." Answering the call, he left the room.

Glad of the respite, Ellie turned to Theo. "Thank you," she said quietly. "I'm still pretty raw."

"I know and that's understandable." He winked, grinning at her instant blush. "You're going to be fine. Flint will catch that guy. He's really good at what he does."

She nodded, so distracted by the warmth in his green eyes that she couldn't speak.

"Damn it." Flint returned, his eyebrows drawn together in an agonized expression. "I've got to go. There's been an emergency."

"What happened?" Theo asked.

"I left my rookie deputy, Mike Barnes, alone in the station, guarding Hank Bittard."

"That guy you arrested for murder?" Theo asked.

Grim-faced, Flint nodded. "Yes. I had him there awaiting transfer to the county jail. I'm not sure how, but Hank attacked Mike and escaped. He left Mike for dead. One of my other deputies found him and called the paramedics. They took Mike in to the clinic, so that's where I'm headed."

Ellie gasped. "Oh no. How badly is he hurt?"

Jamming his cowboy hat on his head, Flint met her gaze and then shook his head. "It's going to be touch-and-go. I've got to go check on him before I can round up men to search for Bittard."

"Do you need any help?" Theo asked, clearly wanting to go with his brother. Ellie wondered why he didn't.

"Not right now. I will need you to help me organize some search parties later, okay?"

"No problem."

Halfway to the door, Flint stopped and turned. "Listen, you need to be extra vigilant. This property is on the outskirts of town and near the woods. Bittard will probably keep a low profile. He'll want to slip out of town quietly the instant the quarantine is lifted."

Ellie glanced at Theo, who nodded. "I understand," he said. "We'll watch for any signs of him."

"Just be careful." Flint left.

"Thank goodness you installed that alarm," Ellie said. "I'm not sure which scares me more—an escaped murderer or my stalker."

"I think they're both about equal," he replied. "I want you to try to rest up, and try not to think about any of this."

She grimaced. "Easier said than done."

"You'll have ample opportunity to heal," he said. "I've asked one of the ranch hands' wives to fill in as cook for a couple of days."

About to protest, Ellie decided not to. Even though nothing had been broken when the truck rolled over, she had several nasty cuts and bruises. Plus, her entire body felt as if she'd served as a punching bag for a particularly angry boxer.

She did prefer staying busy, though, so that she didn't have time to dwell on things. Like her growing attachment to both Amelia and Theo. She really would have preferred not to think about that, or the fact that her stalker presented a danger to both of them.

So she took care of the baby, acted polite to Theo and anyone else she came in contact with and mostly kept to herself to lick her wounds. She took her meals in her room, noting with a bit of perverse satisfaction that her temporary replacement wasn't nearly as good a cook as she was.

Theo checked on her, but his visits were brief and perfunctory, letting her know he battled his own demons.

Finally, after three days of self-imposed isolation, she

felt good enough to resume her life. She gathered up a happy, gurgling Amelia and went in search of Theo. She found him in his office, intent on something he was reading on his computer screen.

"Absolutely not," he said, when she told him she wanted to resume her cooking duties.

Pride warred with common sense, but she finally gave him the truth. "I really need the money."

"Fine, I'll double your nanny salary. But until you're all healed, I don't want you cooking."

Shaking her head, secretly pleased at his coddling, she smiled. "Have you tasted the meals lately?"

One corner of his mouth quirked in response. "Of course I have. But you'll be cooking soon enough. I just want you at 100 percent."

"Fine," she huffed. "But what am I supposed to do with myself?"

His smile widened and for a second she thought he might actually flirt with her. Instead he held out his arms for Amelia. Once she'd transferred the baby, she watched with her heart in her throat as this beautiful, rugged cowboy cooed and spoke baby talk tenderly to his daughter.

In a flash it hit her. She loved him.

Stunned, Ellie took a step back. How had this happened? What on earth was wrong with her?

Somehow she found her voice. "Do you mind watching her for a few minutes? I've got something I need to do."

He barely looked up as he agreed.

And she fled.

Instead of going back to her room, she stepped outside, breathing in great gulps of fresh air. Had she completely lost her mind? All her life, she'd pictured the type of man she'd eventually love, and Theo was about as far from her imaginary lover as a man could be.

Worse, he'd told her up front, he wasn't the settling-down kind.

Still, she loved him. And she needed to wrap her mind around that.

Absorbed in the beauty of his little girl's tiny hands and perfect button nose, Theo remained conscious of Ellie watching him interact with the infant. He often wondered if she thought he was doing it right.

And when she'd gotten that strange expression on her face and rushed off, he was pretty damn sure he wasn't.

A good thirty minutes passed before she returned. Amelia had dozed off to sleep in his arms.

"Do you want me to take her?" Ellie asked softly.

He searched her face. She seemed normal now, back to her usual competent and beautiful self. "Sure."

Once he'd transferred the baby, he decided to voice his doubts. "Sometimes I wonder if I'm any good at this. I have no idea what I'm doing."

"You're going to be fine," Ellie said, her smile patient and so lovely it tugged at his insides. "Just give it time."

Something about the softness of that smile made him want to tell her the truth.

"I have no idea how to be a father," he told Ellie, his voice cracking. "After my mom died, my dad picked up the bottle and never looked back. Some parents are strong and know they have to take over raising the family with the other one gone. Not my father. He dumped us off on Gram Dottie and took off. He only showed up often enough to make an ass of himself and embarrass us. Like the time he came to my senior prom stone-cold drunk. He stormed out on the dance floor and humiliated my date."

"And you," she said softly, wincing. "I can't even imagine."

"Yeah." He knew his expression was bleak, but he didn't see any need in pretending his life had been something it wasn't. "He's the reason both Flint and I got out of town as soon as we could."

"And now you're both back."

He shrugged. "That's life. Sometimes it just does a one eighty from what you had planned."

"Did Gram used to live here on the ranch?"

"Yes. But she moved to town a few years ago. Slim George has kept the place running ever since I can remember."

The tenderness in her gaze had him wanting to kiss her. To distract himself, he forced a half smile. "What about you? What are your parents like? I imagine they've been beside themselves trying to help you deal with that crazy stalker."

She made a sound low in her throat that sounded like harrumph, but he couldn't be sure. For a brief second, he thought she was going to stonewall him and retreat into her own private world.

Finally, she made a face and answered, "My parents are the opposite of what your father is like, at least to all outward appearances. They're missionaries, devoted to spreading their religion to all parts of the world. When I was really small, they made an effort to try to be parents, and took me with them. But after I contracted malaria in Africa, they dumped me off in Boulder with friends from their church."

The raw pain in her voice had him clenching his hands into fists to keep from touching her.

Unaware, she continued. "They didn't even bother to come back for holidays, like Christmas, or for my birthday. The family that I stayed with said I needed to understand the gospel came first."

He winced. "I take it you had no desire to follow in their footsteps?"

"Oh, hell no." Her eyes widened. She seemed shocked that he'd even suggested such a thing. "I understand having convictions, but if they didn't want to be parents, why'd they even bother having a child. Even if I was an accident, which I'm pretty sure I was, being a parent is a responsibility and a privilege. I spent my entire childhood wondering what I'd done to make my parents not love me anymore."

Her words both moved him and stunned him. "That's terrible," he said. "I'd never do anything like that to my child."

"Which proves you're going to be fine."

"I don't know. Since I can't rodeo anymore—"

"Hush." Ellie stomped her foot. "No matter how badly you might want to, you can't go back to rodeo. For a man who has so much, you act like you have nothing. You're alive, you have family who loves you, a productive and profitable ranch and a beautiful baby girl. What more do you want?"

He started to respond, then thought better of it.

"You don't know, do you?"

Slowly, he shook his head. "No. I don't."

"Look at you," she continued, her expression fierce. "You say you don't know how to be a father, but you've already owned up to the responsibility and are doing your best. You understand Amelia has no one else."

Her praise made him feel worse. "I'm worried I won't do right by her. I'm bound to make mistakes."

She gripped his hand, sending a shock wave through him. "You're human, Theo. We all make mistakes. As long as you love her and are there for her, everything will be fine."

He curled his fingers around hers, holding on as though for dear life. "You don't know how badly I hope you're right."

Chapter 13

Ellie didn't know what to think about the tender moment she and Theo had just shared. Even later, after she'd headed to her room for the night, she knew the image of his tanned fingers wrapped around hers would be burned in her mind.

He would make a fine father. *And a wonderful husband,* part of her mind whispered.

The thought surprised her. She'd never even considered marriage. To anyone, not just Theo. The fact that she even was thinking about it now scared her, so she tried to push it from her mind.

Despite everything, or maybe because of it, she fell asleep almost as soon as her head hit the pillow.

With only Amelia to take care of, Ellie's body healed. She slept well, and even if she preferred to eat food she'd cooked herself, she had to admit it was nice not to have to head down to the kitchen at the crack of dawn to cook for the ranch hands.

She completely forgot about the negligee until she spied the fancy box poking out from under her bed a few days later. She pulled it out slowly, glancing at the open door to make sure no one was there. Opening the box, she lifted the tiny scraps of material and tried to figure out where they went. Even the thought of appearing like this in front of Theo made her entire body heat.

Not going to happen. This so wasn't her. She started to put the negligee back into the tissue paper, intending to slide the box back under her bed. Then, taking a deep breath, she changed her mind.

She wanted to try it on. She'd never in her life purchased or even tried on anything like this. Never even imagined how she'd look in one.

Might as well see.

A quick glance assured her Amelia still slept soundly in her crib.

Before she lost her nerve, she closed the door and kicked off her shoes and unzipped her jeans, stepping out of them as well as her panties. She pulled her shirt over her head and discarded her bra.

Then she picked up the little wispy creation and tried to arrange it on her body.

To her surprise, it settled over her and clung to her shape as if it had been made just for her.

Ellie almost didn't recognize the woman she saw in the mirror. Just for fun, she struck a pose. Hip cocked, breasts out and up.

Fun.

A sharp tap sounded on her closed bedroom door.

"Ellie?"

Theo. Just like that, her heart began beating a rapid

tattoo in her chest. She eyed herself in the mirror, an almost unrecognizable version of the Ellie she faced every day.

Could she do it? Did she dare?

"Ellie? Are you in there?"

"Just a moment," she called. She could open the door, and finally see his reaction to the negligee. Or…she could ask him to wait while she got dressed. Her choice.

Quivering, she pressed her hands to her stomach. It would be so worth it if she risked it all, and won. And so humiliating if he didn't react at all.

She needed to know. If he truly didn't want her, the time had come to find out and stop mooning over a man she couldn't have. For once in her life, she wanted to go for the gusto. Take a chance. Be brave.

As soon as she realized she'd made her choice, she began trembling. No matter. Crossing the room to the door, she cracked it a little and peered out, hoping she could do this.

Theo stood in the hall, his expression a combination of impatient and concerned. "Are you all right?"

Oh, wow. Ellie thought her heart might just pound right out of her chest. She inhaled, swallowed and then opened the door wide, revealing her entire body. "Come in."

Instead he froze. He locked gazes with her, his pupils dilated, before his gaze slowly slid downward.

"What?" He sounded weak. "Are you doing?"

"Oh, this?" She made herself spin, fighting the urge to cover herself with her hands. Her nipples were so achingly hard even the tiny scraps of cloth rubbing against them felt supercharged. "Molly gave it to me, so I thought I'd try it on. What do you think?"

Still he didn't move. Had she gone too far? If he resisted even this, her blatant, albeit inexperienced, attempt to seduce him, then she might as well give up. Forever.

He took a step toward her, reaching out to touch her, his expression almost reverent. "You look," he rasped, sounding like a man in torment, "amazing."

Hope warring with desire, she smiled. At the smoldering fire in his gaze, a tingle of excitement gave her the courage to pull him into the room.

"No fair," he protested, though it sounded like a token attempt at best, especially since he reached for her at the same time.

He slid his hand across the exposed skin on her belly, making her shudder with delighted need. Caressing her breasts, he lingered over the sensitive nipples. When he bent his head to take one in his mouth, she gasped.

Her body throbbed as she arched her back. Theo used his lips and tongue to sear a path up her throat, until he claimed her mouth and kissed her.

And then she was lost.

He shed his clothes and gently lowered her to the bed while she struggled not to claw at him, to urge him to just take her, for heaven's sake.

Instead, he touched her lightly, teasingly, which felt almost painful, making her whimper as she curled herself into his body, pulling him over her. Needing more. So much more.

Slowly, maddeningly, he explored her thighs, with a feather-light touch. She groaned as she felt the swollen hardness of his arousal pressing against her stomach. Reaching blindly, she cupped her hand around the length of him, thrilling to the touch.

Theo groaned as she began to move her hand up and down. "Don't," he said. "Not yet."

But she was done with slow and steady. Her insides

were melting. "I want you inside me," she said, arcing against the magic touch of his fingers as he explored.

"All in good time," he gritted, his arousal jerking against her touch. She shifted, moving her body so the tip of him pressed against her, and undulating so the engorged tip of him rubbed against her slick woman parts.

Theo groaned again and then, with a muttered curse, gave in and pushed into her.

Pleasure—pure, explosive and powerful—ripped through her as he began to move.

Mindless with need, she wouldn't let him go slow, though he tried. She moved and rode him from underneath, her body trembling just on the edge of ecstasy.

With a cry, she came apart, shattering in a wave of soul-drenching, perfect and sweet agony.

Her spasms of joy brought Theo to his own release shortly after, his body throbbing as he emptied himself into her.

Nestling against him while he held her, their slick bodies cooling, Ellie realized she could stay there forever.

And for that reason alone, she knew she had to get away as soon as she could.

Furious with himself, Theo had to notice the irony of the emotion. The man he'd once been, the popular rodeo star and ladies' man, would have celebrated his victory and mentally carved another notch in his bedpost.

For whatever reason, he was no longer that man. In fact, despite the way he missed bronc riding, he never wanted to be that way again.

The bad thing about all of this was he knew Ellie would end up hurt. And he cared about her, maybe too damn much.

He managed to avoid her at breakfast, sneaking down

into the kitchen for a bagel and coffee half an hour before the new cook would be there to start making breakfast for the ranch hands.

Bad thing was, he knew he couldn't dodge her for too long. Actually, he didn't want to. He just needed to come up with a way to explain that what had happened between them was an aberration and wouldn't happen again. It couldn't happen again. The more and more she gave of herself to him, the deeper their connection, their attachment.

And despite the growing realization that he wished he could be the kind of man she needed, he wasn't. He doubted he could ever, no matter how hard he tried, change enough to be that man.

Poor Ellie had run to Dead River to escape danger, but it had followed her. And now things had gone from bad to worse, with the virus essentially shutting down the town.

In addition to that, now they not only needed to worry about a stalker, but about an escaped murderer. Hank Bittard had nearly killed the rookie deputy, and Theo had no doubts the man wouldn't hesitate to kill again.

Sometimes he felt as if his life had become a soap opera. Once everyone was occupied with breakfast, he figured he'd slip out of the house and head to town.

A sharp tapping on his bedroom door jolted Theo out of his thoughts. He turned, about to ask who was there, when he heard Amelia begin crying right outside the door. This cry sounded different. More of a shriek, as though she was in pain.

Heart pounding, he barreled to the door and threw it open. A disheveled and worried-looking Ellie stood in the hall, rocking a wailing baby.

"She's sick," Ellie said, sounding on the verge of tears. "Burning up. I took her temperature rectally, and it's a little over 101. I looked online and read that I shouldn't give her baby Tylenol without talking to a doctor. Can you call Gemma or one of the doctors at the clinic?"

He spun and grabbed his phone. Since he had Gemma's cell phone number stored, he punched it. A second later, she answered, sounding groggy.

"Amelia's got a fever. Ellie needs to know if we can give her infant Tylenol."

"A fever? What temperature?" Just like that, Gemma came instantly awake.

"One hundred and one. Ellie took it rectally."

Gemma swore. "A fever that high in such a young infant would warrant a sepsis work up in an E.R. One hundred and one is extremely worrisome in a newborn because her immune system is immature. What else is wrong? Any vomiting or diarrhea?"

He asked Ellie, who told him no, fear making her voice quiver. He knew the feeling.

"Right now we need to get her temperature down. Go ahead and give her infant Tylenol, along with a lukewarm bath."

Gemma waited while he relayed the information to Ellie. Meanwhile, the unspoken word hovered between them.

Virus.

All three of them knew how deadly a virus like the one that'd killed Mimi Rand could be to a tiny infant.

"It's not the virus," Theo said finally, determined not to give that particular terror power over him. "It's not."

"It can't be," Ellie agreed with him. "It's been too long since she was exposed."

Only Gemma was silent. Theo hadn't realized how desperately he needed her to agree until she spoke.

"Let's hope not. But since Amelia's mother died from it, we've got to go with the assumption that it is."

Theo glanced at Ellie and realized she was silently crying, tears streamed a silver path down her cheeks.

His throat closed up. "I can't lose her, Gemma," he said, his voice rough. "We can't lose her."

"And we won't." Gemma had gone back to her brisk, efficient nurse voice. "Get started on the bath and the infant Tylenol immediately. Take her temperature again in thirty minutes and call me back. Understand?"

Murmuring his assent, Theo ended the call and hurried after Ellie, who was already on her way to the bathroom.

Her hands shook as she handed him the Tylenol to open. Once he'd filled the dropper, he gave it back to her, watching as Ellie squeezed the recommended amount in Amelia's open mouth. This infuriated her, and she scrunched up her tiny red face, gearing up to let out a good screech. Ellie tried to soothe her, managing to get her quieted down somewhat, though it was clear Amelia didn't feel well.

Ellie sighed, still rocking the snuffling baby. She met his gaze, her own steady. "Will you hold her while I run her bath?"

For an answer, he held out his arms. The instant she placed the restless infant in them, he could feel the heat radiating from Amelia's tiny body. "She's really warm," he commented, his chest tight.

"She is." Ellie raised her head to look at him. "I really hope the medicine and this bath help."

"We have to believe it will." He let his determination fill his voice, aware that he had to be strong for all their sakes. "I don't want to have to take her in to the clinic. Right now, that's no place for a baby."

Ellie turned back to the bathwater, checking and double-checking the temperature. “I have to make it the perfect temperature,” she said. “Definitely not too warm or too cold. Just lukewarm, enough to get her body temperature down.”

Once she was satisfied she had it right, she took Amelia from him and divested her of her clothes. Briefly hesitating, she inhaled. “Get ready. I suspect she’s not going to like this.”

And Ellie lowered Amelia into the water.

After the first initial shock, Amelia began squirming and wailing in protest. “Shhh, baby girl,” Ellie soothed, continually pouring water over her. “We’re only trying to help you.”

After a few minutes of this, Ellie gently lifted Amelia out of the water and toweled her off. “In a few minutes, we’ll take her temperature again.”

Watching Ellie taking such tender care of his daughter, he thought his heart would explode. Amelia had to be all right. She couldn’t have caught the virus. In that instant, he realized he’d gladly trade places with his baby. He’d lay down his life if it meant saving her.

For the first time since he’d been a young boy and Gram Dottie had dragged him to church on a regular basis, Theo lowered his head and began to pray.

“All right,” Ellie said briskly, startling him. “I think it’s been long enough. Let’s see if we were successful in getting her fever down.”

She moved with cool efficiency, as though already certain of their success. He recognized this as a way to keep terror at bay.

Watching as she inserted the rectal thermometer, managing to keep a squirming Amelia in place, she watched the clock. The second hand seemed to creep around as she counted off one minute, then two and finally three.

"Here we go." She held up the thermometer and squinted at it in the light. "Oh, Theo." And her eyes filled with tears.

"What? Is it bad?" he asked, reaching for it to see for himself.

"No. It's normal again." She gave him a watery smile. "We just need to keep an eye on her and make sure it doesn't climb back up again. As long as she has no other symptoms, I think we can safely say it's not the virus."

Theo's knees felt weak. He leaned over and gave his still-fussy daughter a kiss on the forehead. "Thank God," he said and rose and kissed Ellie for good measure.

She blushed but barely paused a beat as she diapered and redressed Amelia. "I'm going to go rock her in the rocking chair for a while," she said, ducking her head shyly. "If you don't mind, will you call Gemma back and let her know?"

He thought she'd never looked so beautiful and nearly said so but managed to keep quiet. "Sure. I'll call her in a minute."

Watching as she carried Amelia out of the room, he wondered what the hell he was going to do. He'd gone from having nothing to having an almost family. And all of a sudden, he realized he might be able to have it all, if he was willing to take a chance and try.

After making a quick phone call to Gemma, he went out to the barn to brush a few horses, maybe even take one or two out and lunge them for exercise in the round pen. Anything to make him feel like himself again. He couldn't even look at breeding stock until the quarantine was lifted.

Theo needed to find his equilibrium and needed to do

so soon. Only then could he think clearly, and figure out what he truly wanted.

That night, after dinner had been eaten and the dishes put away, Ellie brought Amelia into the den to watch television. Though Theo knew such a simple act would feel far too intimate, he'd also been compulsively checking on his daughter throughout the afternoon, fearful her fever would return. Ellie seemed to understand this, no doubt because she had similar fears of her own.

They settled on the couch, Amelia on a blanket between them, and watched a singing talent competition. Theo couldn't have cared less about the show, but he needed somewhere to park his gaze so he wouldn't feel compelled to study every nuance of Ellie's expression.

Amelia seemed normal, wide awake and happy with her pacifier. As she grew, she became more and more beautiful, and even without the DNA test, Theo believed with all his heart she was his. Not only did she have the Colton green eyes, but she had his chin.

When he finally allowed himself to relax, contentment stole over him. He could get used to this, quiet evenings with the family.

The instant the thought occurred to him, he wondered why he didn't feel the familiar urge to bolt. Then, not wanting to ruin a perfectly good evening by overanalyzing things, he pretended to watch the show.

Ellie took Amelia's temperature again before putting her to bed. Theo watched, willing it to be normal. And it was.

"I think we're over the hump," Ellie said, beaming. "But I'll keep watch on her tonight."

He wanted to tell her to try to get some sleep, but since he knew she wouldn't, he settled for asking her to promise to wake him if anything was wrong.

"I will," she said softly. Then she leaned over and kissed him on the cheek. "Good night, Theo."

Stunned, he murmured the same in response and left her room. Only when he'd closed the door to his own room did he allow his hand to touch his cheek.

He went to sleep smiling.

And when he woke in the morning, his mood annoyingly cheerful, he realized he was in deep trouble.

After grabbing breakfast and checking on Amelia, who Ellie informed him was completely back to normal, he headed outside to check on his hands. They were bringing cattle down from the summer pastures, a task that had always been one of Theo's favorites when he was growing up. He longed to go, despite knowing it was not possible.

Most of the hands had already ridden out, and the few that remained were about to go. After being assured that everything was under control, Theo returned to the house.

At loose ends, he decided to go into town, even though he realized it was another way of avoiding his growing feelings for Ellie. Just as he couldn't yet consider he'd eventually have to deal with them, or he'd lose her.

He just had to figure out what he wanted. While his ranch continued to be prosperous, he wasn't sure Ellie would want a broken rodeo cowboy like him. Even if he did eventually have a successful breeding program.

Just as he picked up his keys off the dresser, Flint called. Seeing his brother's name on the caller ID, Theo figured it was time to talk about organizing a search party.

"What's up?" Theo asked.

"Gemma called me. How's Amelia?"

"She slept through the night." He sighed. "Ellie's

watching her like a hawk. I'm about to head into town myself. I want to make sure we have plenty of infant first aid supplies."

"Can't you have one of your guys do that? I really need to meet up with you."

Instantly alert, Theo froze. "Sure. What's going on?"

"The whole town's gone freaking crazy." Hoarse, Flint didn't sound like himself.

Theo felt a stab of fear, wondering if his brother had taken sick.

"Are you okay, man?" Theo asked. "Any fever, body aches?"

"Of course not." Flint sounded offended that he'd even asked. "More than anyone, I'm aware of the need to check in at the clinic at the first sign of the virus."

Relieved, Theo exhaled. "Then what's happening?"

"You mean beyond the fact that the National Guard has become power-hungry, the state police are right there with them and the townspeople are going stir-crazy? Oh, and not to mention one of my deputies is critically injured and there's an escaped killer on the loose?"

Theo winced. "Sorry. Is there anything I can do to help?"

"Not with that. Unless you can wave a magic wand and make this damn virus disappear. It seems to be multiplying rapidly."

Theo's heart stopped. When he'd talked to Gemma the day before, he was so worried about Amelia that he hadn't asked her anything about the virus. "How bad is it? Is it getting worse?"

"Yeah." His brother sounded grim. "More and more people are getting sick. Everyone else—those who don't have the virus—are being asked to stay home and wait out their symptoms." He took a deep breath. "Even so, the clinic's isolation area is bursting at the seams. The CDC has brought in temporary trailers to house more patients. They've also got some for the doctors and nurses to use, as many are working twelve-or-more-hour shifts all week trying to care for all the sick people."

"What about deaths? How many more people have died?"

"Last I heard it was close to a dozen."

Stunned, Theo wasn't sure how to respond.

"And then there's those idiots who decided the quarantine doesn't apply to them." The frustration and anger in Flint's voice came loud and clear over the phone. "Some of them are even our relatives. Couple of them got liquored up and decided to try to run the barricade. Damn fools almost got shot."

Theo cursed. "As if you don't have enough to worry about."

"Right." Flint went quiet. When he spoke again, he sounded worried. "It's going to happen again. Sooner or later someone's going to get hurt. Or killed."

"You really think they'll try again?"

"Maybe not them, but someone. You know how we Wyomingites are. They were even shouting the state motto, Equal Rights. Never mind that symbolizes the political status women have always enjoyed in our state."

"Was beer involved?" Theo asked, already knowing the answer.

"Isn't it always?"

"How's Mike? Is he still at the clinic?"

"Yeah. The good news is, they upgraded his status from serious to stable. Bittard stabbed him quite a few times."

"Any sign of him?" Theo asked.

"Not yet. I've been too busy to get together a search party. That's partly why I called you."

"Just say the word and I'll get it put together." Theo didn't tell his brother how badly he needed a distraction.

"Okay. Can you come by my office this afternoon?"

"Definitely," Theo agreed. "I was just about to leave."

"I can't meet for about an hour."

"No problem." Theo figured he'd stop by the café for lunch to kill time. "I've got a few other things to take care of."

After a pause, Flint asked how Theo was doing. "You sound a little weird."

Theo shrugged, then realized his brother couldn't see him over the phone. "Not bad. Considering. It was pretty damn scary when Amelia got sick."

"Are you getting used to being a daddy?"

If anyone else had asked that question, Theo might have come back with a flippant remark. But Flint shared the same past. More than anyone else, he knew Theo had no fatherly example to emulate.

"Little by little. Ellie's helping me learn," he allowed.

"Ah, Ellie." Something in Flint's tone…

Theo frowned. "What do you mean by that?"

"Just that you and she seem…close."

Familiar with his brother's teasing, Theo laughed, though he felt himself grow a little hot under the collar.

"She's really pretty," Flint continued. "Not your usual type, but I'd say an improvement."

"She's sweet, kind and a hard worker," Theo allowed. "But you know I don't mix business with pleasure." He winced, aware of the blatant lie. "She's my nanny and until the accident, she worked as the ranch cook, not my girlfriend."

Flint snorted. "Since when have details like that ever stopped you?"

"I don't know what you mean," Theo lied again. "But seriously, I can't afford to mess this up. If I didn't have her to take care of Amelia..." He shuddered. "I wouldn't survive."

Flint laughed. "Yeah, smart move, Hot Shot. Keeping your pants on. I have to say, I'm proud of you."

"Don't be." Unable to keep the glum note out of his voice, Theo continued, "Because I didn't."

"You slept with her?" Flint sounded shocked.

"We didn't do much sleeping." Though that was Theo's standard reply, this time it came out sounding flat.

"You don't sound overjoyed."

Theo sighed. "I have a feeling, no matter what I do from this point, she's going to get hurt. You know how women have a way of getting upset when you don't give them everything they want. I'm a one-night kind of guy. And she's—"

"White picket fence and minivan," Flint finished, making Theo laugh.

"Not really, though I bet she might want that someday. She talks a lot about traveling." Deciding it was time to change the subject, Theo asked about Molly's ex-fiancé. "Any luck locating him?"

"Nope. My only consolation is I know he hasn't left town. He stopped by the body shop to pick up his last paycheck on Friday afternoon. After the quarantine went into effect."

"He still picked up his paycheck after cleaning Molly out?"

"Yep." Flint's tone told what he thought about that. "I can't wait to get my hands on him."

Someone spoke in the background.

"I've got to go," Flint said. "See you in about an hour, give or take."

Theo agreed and ended the call. He grabbed his Stetson and put it on. Jingling his keys, he headed out.

He nearly made it to the front door, but Ellie's voice stopped him. "Are you going into town?"

Slowly, he turned. Despite steeling himself, his heart skipped a beat at her blue-eyed prettiness. "Yep. Why? Do you need more formula and diapers?"

Her slow smile didn't entirely hide the hurt in her expression. "Amelia really runs through them. I'm afraid I'm going to have to ask you to pick up a double batch."

"What about more infant Tylenol?" He flashed an impersonal smile when what he really wanted to do was kiss her goodbye.

"Oh, good idea. And I need one more thing, if you don't mind."

The slightest hesitation in her voice made him tense. He waited, wondering if she meant to ask to go with him.

"Would you mind picking up a few Halloween decorations?"

This stunned him. "What for?"

"It's my favorite holiday. I usually decorate. As a matter of fact, I have a list of supplies and I can get them, if you want to watch Ellie. Either way, we're running low on a few things."

He actually wished she could come with him. Of course, there was no way he wanted Amelia anywhere near town. Plus, he had the meeting with Flint, and a search to organize.

"I'll have one of my hands do the shopping for you, okay? I've got to meet up with Flint and won't have time."

Face expressionless, she nodded. Amelia fussed, and

she turned her attention to the baby. "So far, she seems okay. No sign of fever or anything else."

"That's a relief," he said, and meant it. "Gemma said she'd try to come by and check her out, but she sounded so exhausted, I told her not to. I promised we'd call her if anything changed."

She nodded and turned away. But not before he caught himself longing to kiss the hurt from her bright blue eyes.

Theo took the opportunity to escape, feeling gutless, which unsettled him. He was many things, but a coward wasn't one of them. He stopped back by the barn, tagging one of the younger hands who'd just finished sweeping out the tack room and asking him to head up to the house, get the list and handle the shopping. Already disappointed at not being able to help round up cattle, the boy brightened at having an actual task.

Once that was handled, Theo got in his pickup and headed to town.

Chapter 14

The young ranch hand who showed up a few minutes later seemed nervous. Ellie smiled to put him at ease and handed him her list. She'd crossed off the Halloween decorations, as she didn't want to make anyone else try to decide what to buy. That was half the fun, after all.

She had a feeling this year Halloween wouldn't be the same.

Molly called, full of the news that her ex-fiancé had been spotted in town. Flint had two men searching for him right at this moment. "I might just maybe get my heirloom ring back," she said. "Plus, I really want to make him face me and explain why he did what he did."

"That might be interesting." Ellie could imagine what a fireball Molly would be, demanding to know why Jimmy had broken her heart.

"What about you and Theo?"

Ellie swallowed. "What about us?"

"Ellie! Did you try the negligee?"

Closing her eyes for a moment, Ellie debated whether or not to lie. What she and Theo had shared was private, but on the other hand, he'd been acting so strange since then, she'd like a second opinion.

"Yes," she finally allowed, wincing as Molly squealed.

"Then I can assume it accomplished the intended purpose?"

"It did."

Silence. Then Molly ventured, "You don't seem too happy about it. What's wrong?"

"We made love and it was…wonderful. I really think we had a connection." Ellie sighed. "But since then, Theo's been even more remote. It's like it never happened."

"You need to talk to him."

"I will," Ellie promised. "I don't know, maybe I'm afraid he'll think I'm making a mountain out of a molehill. I mean, isn't Theo the love-'em-and-leave-'em type?"

"Oh, Ellie." Molly sighed. "You knew that going in. I thought you just wanted to have a little fun."

"I was, I am…" Miserable with the lie, Ellie sighed. "I don't know. I'm a little confused right now. Anyway, enough about me. What's new with you?"

"Well, Flint has people looking for Jimmy and the pawnshop has been put on notice in case my ring shows up."

"That's good." Relieved, Ellie sighed. "Flint's not so bad, actually."

"No. I guess I was being silly. But I confess, I wanted to hug him when he told me what he wanted to do to Jimmy once he catches him. Of course, since Flint's the sheriff, he can't. But still."

"I hope he finds him soon."

"Me too. But since everyone in town is on the lookout for him, he can't spend much of my money. So there's that." Molly sounded upbeat. "And he must still have the ring. No doubt he's hanging on to it until he can get out of town and pawn it in Cheyenne or somewhere."

"I wonder if he'll try to sneak out of town."

"I wish he would. The way they're patrolling the borders would mean he'd get caught much more quickly. So far, every single person who's tried to leave has been caught."

"Seriously?" Impressed and appalled, both at the same time, Ellie shuddered. "I don't hear any of that stuff since we're so isolated out here at the ranch. What else is going on in town?"

Molly told her the townspeople had decided to cancel Halloween, because of the virus, which made Ellie wince.

"That makes me sad. It's my favorite holiday."

"Really?" Molly sounded surprised. "Even more than Christmas or Thanksgiving?"

"Yep. I've always loved Halloween. When I was younger, it had started as rebellion, since my parents disallowed Halloween, claiming it was a holiday for devil worshippers."

Molly gasped. "That's intense."

Used to this reaction, Ellie shrugged, even though Molly couldn't see her. "They're super religious. Right now they're missionaries in Africa."

"Oh. That makes more sense." Again Molly gave a light trill of laughter. "So that's why you love it so much? Rebellion?"

Ellie laughed. "Not anymore. As I grew older, I came to honestly love the decorations and the costumes, and the mystical aspects of All Hallows' Eve. I really like the artwork from Dia de Muertos, the Mexican Day of the Dead."

"Wow," Molly said. "I just like giving out candy."

"Oh, me too. Or at least, I used to."

"What about costumes?" Molly asked. "Since you love Halloween so much, I bet you have some amazing ones."

"Not really." Ellie had only dressed up once herself. As a bride. She smiled at the thought, remembering how excited she'd been when the family she was staying with had taken her trick-or-treating.

And how furious her parents had been when they learned of the event later. She'd been told she was never to wear a Halloween costume again. And she hadn't.

She told none of this to Molly. It was old news, history, and she refused to let it be part of her new life.

"Even though I don't dress up," Ellie said, "I still enjoy the holiday. Not that I think we'd get many trick-or-treaters out here at the ranch—we're a bit too isolated for that."

"You should try wearing a costume. I mean, another time when Halloween isn't canceled. The bar normally has a great costume party, and it's a lot of fun. They aren't having it this year."

"I'd like that," Ellie said softly. "Though I'd have to buy something to wear. Maybe another time."

"You could borrow one of mine." Enthusiasm made Molly pitch her voice higher. "I have a ton. Heck, I'm pretty sure even Theo has dressed up once or twice."

"What, as a cowboy?" Ellie couldn't resist, laughing along with Molly.

"No," Molly squealed. "Something else. But I can't remember what."

"I'm so glad you called," Ellie said, once they'd finished laughing. "I needed a bit of a distraction, even if you did give me bad news. I was really looking forward to Halloween."

"You can come to my place," Molly offered. "If they hadn't canceled everything, I'd normally get tons of little rug rats here. Even without it, you and I can celebrate. It'd do you good to get off the ranch."

"I might take you up on that." The idea brought Ellie's excitement back. "I'll have to check with Theo, since I'd want to bring Amelia."

"Did you get her a costume?"

Ellie grinned. "Yes. I ordered her an adorable infant princess outfit. Originally, I planned to let her wear it on an excursion into town for the big night. Which now, since they've canceled it, won't happen."

"Well, just let me know," Molly said. "And I'll keep you informed if Flint's men have any luck finding Jimmy and my ring."

Ellie noticed she made no mention of her missing inheritance. "I will," she said, hanging up.

The rest of the afternoon, without food prep and cooking to keep her busy, moved slowly. Thoughts of Theo filled her mind constantly. They seemed to have reached a new point in their relationship—she thought. Though from the way he acted, in his thoughts nothing had changed.

In fact, she'd had enough of this evasive stuff. When he got home, she planned to confront him. Even though she knew he probably had a lot on his mind with all the goings-on in Dead River, it appeared they were going to be together awhile longer, and she had a right to know where they stood. Actually, she needed to know.

Molly's news about Halloween had felt like the last straw. While she could understand the reasons for canceling the holiday, she'd been looking forward to it for months.

Trick-or-treating might be gone, but nevertheless she felt determined to celebrate one of her favorite holidays, no matter what. Even if she had to go buy her own bag of candy and eat it all herself.

After he passed through the barricade on the way into town, Theo couldn't believe his eyes. Dead River looked deserted, like a ghost town. Occasionally, as he drove slowly down Main Street, he'd see someone leaving a store and hustling to their car, but by and large the sidewalks were empty.

Even the few people he saw looked different. They were alone, for starters. Single individuals only, not even a few couples or groups of three. And their movements appeared afraid, almost furtive. They moved about quickly, hunched into themselves, clearly in town only out of necessity.

This was such a stark contrast to the other evening, he couldn't help wondering what new calamity had befallen the town.

He pulled into the diner parking lot, relieved to see quite a few cars. People had to eat, at least. Once he stepped inside it was like changing the channel on the television—leaving the surreal gray-scape of an old *Twilight Zone* episode for a modern, color show.

The diner appeared at least two-thirds full, not bad for a weekday afternoon, even under normal circumstances. He sat in his regular spot, a small booth by the kitchen door, which was empty as usual. Others might avoid sitting here, but Theo loved having a view of the hustle and bustle of the kitchen.

Wilma hurried over. As one of the long-term employees, she got to choose her section, and she always worked this area. Theo liked her too, as she was briskly efficient and friendly, without overdoing it.

"Hey, Hot Shot," she greeted him, having long ago picked up on his childhood nickname. "Are you having the usual?"

Theo cocked his head, pretending to have to consider. "Sure," he finally said, grinning. "Why would I mess with a good thing?"

She grinned back and set down his iced tea. "I already put the order in the minute I saw you walk through the door."

Another reason why he loved her. She knew him so well he imagined she might faint if he ever ordered something beside his bacon burger and fries. Of course, why would he?

"How's business?" he asked.

"Better than it is at a lot of other places." She gestured around the room. "The past couple of days, people have been acting like the virus is floating everywhere, waiting to grab them if they left their house." She sighed. "I imagine they must be getting tired of that. It's been slow. Today's the first day we had a decent-sized lunch crowd. I guess it'll be back to normal tomorrow."

He nodded and took a drink of his tea. "So, what's new? I mean we've been under the quarantine and dealt with the virus for a while now. Why is everyone acting so weird?"

Wilma leaned in closer. "Between that and Hank Bittard having escaped, plus Jimmy Johnson robbing sweet Molly blind, I think people are on edge. More than once, I've heard someone comment that if the virus doesn't get them, Hank will."

Theo found himself feeling sorry for his brother. He

could only imagine what kind of hell Flint's life must be, with the citizens of Dead River on the edge of panic.

Wilma headed off with a wink to help another table. While Theo waited, he took the opportunity to observe the other customers. As far as he could tell, everyone seemed relatively normal. A bit subdued, maybe. And perhaps there were more diners eating alone instead of with friends or family.

A few minutes later Wilma returned with Theo's burger, setting it in front of him with an admonishment to eat up. Since he was hungry, he gladly complied.

After lunch, Theo drove to the sheriff's department. The parking lot there also seemed unusually empty. He guessed people were taking their concerns to the state police or the National Guard. As he parked, he couldn't help wondering if Flint felt relief or frustration about that.

After Kendra buzzed him back, Theo crossed the nearly deserted squad room to Flint's office. Talking on the phone, Flint gestured toward a chair. A few second later, he finished his call.

"Thanks for coming in," he said, exhaustion plain in his face. "I've just about had it up to here with the military. They keep using the phrase *martial law.*"

Shocked, Theo stared. "Did I miss someone declaring a state of emergency?"

"No. You didn't. And they won't. At least not out loud, in public. Not with our citizens verging on panic. But with the National Guard shooting people when they try to escape, and their continued refusal to listen to reason, I think maybe someone somewhere has done so internally."

"What are you going to do?"

Flint spread his hands. "There's nothing we can do. They've got us under a rock and a barrel, to say the least. So I'm just trying to focus on the things I *can* control.

Like recapturing Hank Bittard. And locating Jimmy Johnson, and Ellie's stalker."

"I understand." Though Theo really didn't. But that was another reason he was glad he wasn't sheriff. If he couldn't be a rodeo star, he guessed a cattle rancher or a horse breeder wasn't such a bad thing to be.

The revelation stunned him. All along he'd considered his breeding program a second choice. Now, it sounded pretty damn appealing, actually.

"Theo, are you listening to me?" Flint demanded.

Blinking, Theo gave his brother a sheepish grin. "Sorry. What were you saying?"

"I was asking you if you'd mind lending me a few of your ranch hands—plus yourself—to head up a search for Bittard."

"I'd rather look for Jimmy," Theo said grimly. "But since a killer is more dangerous than a thief, I don't mind at all. When do you have in mind?"

Flint shrugged. "As soon as possible. I know your guys are bringing the cattle down from the higher pastures and I don't want to mess with that."

"I'll check with Slim George about the schedule and let you know."

"Thanks."

"I drove downtown," Theo began, not at all sure he should mention anything. "The place seemed pretty deserted."

"I know. With all the declarations and bulletins, the CDC has everyone pretty scared." Dragging a hand through his close-cropped hair, Flint shrugged. "I can't say I blame them. They've even canceled Halloween, for Pete's sake, including the annual Dead River Bar party. They're believing all the B.S. the CDC is putting out."

"How do you know it's not true?"

Flint's mouth twisted in a mocking smile. "That's the thing. I don't. But the way they're acting, they apparently believe everyone in Dead River is pretty much doomed."

"I refuse to believe that," Theo said. "We're not. Especially if Dr. Rand or one of the others can find a cure."

"True."

Since there wasn't much else to say, Theo got to his feet. "Is Gemma all right?" he asked.

"I suppose so. I'm sure we would have heard from her if she wasn't. All I know is every time I talk to her, she sounds dog-tired. I know they've brought in RVs for the clinic staff to sleep in. They've got people working around the clock there. Not just ours, but the CDC people too."

On the drive home, Theo reflected how life could turn on a dime. When he'd gotten hurt trying to ride that crazy bronco, he had no idea in the instant before he hit the sawdust that his life as he knew it was over.

Nor had he realized when Mimi Rand showed up on his doorstep with a baby how his world would spin another 360.

And then Ellie. He'd felt that tug of attraction the day he hired her, but he hadn't known how much she would impact his life.

All this time, he should have been counting his blessings. Now he just needed to figure out where he wanted to go from here.

The quarantine could be lifted any day now. With Ellie's stalker still at large, he knew she'd leave town first chance she got if she thought she was protecting Amelia.

He didn't want her to go. Not just because he needed a nanny and a cook, but because he needed her. The time they'd spent side-by-side in the kitchen and caring for

Amelia had made him realize what a relationship could be like. What building a life together could look like.

Though he needed to find out if Ellie felt the same.

And neither the damned stalker nor the virus had better not rob him of that chance.

Ellie heard Theo's truck returning. When the house was quiet, the sound of tires on gravel was unmistakable.

She brought Amelia into the den and perched on the sofa. Theo's hand had brought her the necessary supplies over an hour ago.

"Did you get everything you needed?" Theo asked as he strode into the room.

Ellie took in his cowboy hat and boots, unable to keep from admiring the way his Wranglers fit his tight butt. For a second, she lost track of what he'd asked her.

"Oh yes. The diapers and formula and other stuff."

"Right. And the Halloween decorations."

She smiled to hide her disappointment. "No decorations. I crossed them off the list. I didn't want to put that poor kid through the chore of trying to choose."

Regarding her with a quizzical look, he finally nodded. "So now you're not going to decorate at all?"

"No. I talked to Molly about Halloween," she said, keeping her voice bright. "Like I said, it's one of my favorite holidays."

After a moment, he nodded. "I guess you heard they've canceled it in town."

"Yes. I'm still going to dress Amelia up."

"You are?" At her nod, he cocked his head. "Let me guess. You've got your own costume planned. Something elaborate and showy."

"No." She frowned. "I never dress up."

"Never?" His narrow-eyed gaze told her he wasn't

sure she meant it. "Molly always does. There's usually a big party at the bar, and from what I hear, Molly has had a fancier costume each year."

This made her smile. "I can imagine," she said.

"Then why don't you? I think you'd actually enjoy it."

Why didn't she? So she'd had one bad experience as a kid. Maybe it was time to let go of the past and make one more change. "You know, I believe you're right. I would." She shrugged. "But since Halloween is canceled, it's a moot point now."

"I guess you're right." Oddly enough, she could have sworn he looked disappointed. "But you should still dress Amelia up. I don't think we should let that stupid virus ruin her very first Halloween."

"I agree. I'm going to let her wear her costume. Molly invited me over to her house, so I thought I'd bring Amelia with me, if it's okay with you. Even though there won't be any trick-or-treaters, I think it'd still be fun."

He gave her an odd look. "But this is Amelia's first Halloween. I'd kind of like to spend it with her. And you know—" he gave her a sheepish sort of smile "—take pictures, all that."

Stunned, she simply stared at him, her chest tight.

"You can go to Molly's if you want," he continued. "But leave Amelia here with me." He flashed a crooked smile. "You can even dress her up in her costume before you go."

Suddenly, the thought of going to Molly's held zero appeal. Not only was Theo learning to be a daddy, but he'd come to love his infant daughter. They'd make Halloween a family event, the one aspect of the holiday she'd never been able to recreate.

Longing stabbed her. Once again, she was on the outside looking in. Theo and Amelia were a family of two.

Ellie was merely the nanny. And no amount of wishing or wanting would change that.

Still, she wanted to experience this, even if it was mostly pretense on her part. No matter how great the potential for hurt.

"Would it be all right if I stayed with you two?" she asked, her voice tentative. "I'd really like to be a part of Amelia's first Halloween, also."

Just as Theo was about to reply, a sharp knock sounded on the back door.

Before either of them could react, the door flew open. One of the ranch hands rushed in, clearly agitated.

"Theo, you need to get out here," he said. "We spotted a stranger over on the west pasture near the woods. The guys think he might be that escaped killer, Hank Bittard."

Instantly alert, Theo nodded. "Let me get my gun. Are any of them men armed?"

The other man nodded.

"Good. Give me a second. I've got to unlock my gun safe."

Ellie watched wide-eyed as Theo disappeared. A moment later, he returned, carrying a deadly-looking rifle.

As he headed for the door, Theo glanced at Ellie. "You stay here with Amelia. Set the alarm after I leave."

Ellie nodded, her heartbeat ragged. The intruder might very well be this Hank Bittard person, who from all accounts was armed and dangerous.

But he could also be her stalker. She wasn't sure which one would be worse.

Following his man down the ravine where the stranger had been spotted, Theo held his rifle ready. He hoped he wouldn't have to use it, but better safe than sorry.

In the meantime, he called Flint's cell. As soon as his brother answered, Theo relayed the info.

"I'll be right there," Flint said. "Don't do anything foolish. This guy's a killer and has nothing to lose."

Theo agreed and ended the call, cursing the ache in his still-healing bones that made it difficult to keep up with his ranch hand. He took consolation in the knowledge that at least, if needed, he was a crack shot with a rifle.

Once they reached the edge of the woods, they met up with three of Theo's other men, all armed.

"He went in there," one said, pointing toward the old hiking trail that led to one of Theo's summer pastures.

"Good. We'll split up," Theo decided. "Two of you go that way, and we'll go the other."

As they murmured their assent and started moving away, he called after them, "Be careful. And don't get too trigger-happy, understand?"

Carefully and quietly, Theo and his guy searched. After thirty minutes or so, they met up with the other two.

"Nothing."

While they debated whether to search some more, Flint pulled up on the road beside the pasture. He had his lights flashing and left them on as he got out of the car. Climbing the fence, he strode over to them.

"Any luck?"

"Nope." Theo pointed toward the area they'd searched. "We split up and came up with nothing. I think if it's Bittard, he's probably trying to make a run for it through the trees. Eventually, he'd come out on one of the forestry roads. I'm guessing there's no way the National Guard can police every single mile."

"No, they can't." Flint looked grim. "But you've heard the helicopters and low-flying planes. They're doing regular flyovers using heat-seeking eyewear. If anyone tried to get out, it's likely they'll be caught. Just this week alone, they've stopped two groups—one of four teenagers and the other three hunting buddies."

Stunned, Theo exchanged glances with his men. "Why didn't we hear about any of this?"

Flint shrugged. "What's the point? The last thing I need to do is incite more panic. I think we should—" His belt radio crackled. Someone spoke, but the speaker kept cutting in and out and the rest of the words were so full of static they were unintelligible.

Cursing, Flint used his cell phone to call in. As he listened, his normally tanned skin turned ashen.

Ending the call, he turned to Theo. For the first time Theo could remember, he saw panic in his brother's eyes. "Theo, get in my truck. It'll be faster. We gotta go. Now."

Without hesitation, Theo headed for the truck, Flint right beside him. Once they both were inside, Flint started the engine and hit the gas. The truck fishtailed on the gravel road. Flint straightened it out, his expression grim.

"What's going on?" Theo asked.

Flint swallowed. "A 911 call came in from your house. It was Ellie. She didn't manage to talk, but she left her phone on speaker. It sounds like an intruder broke in and is holding her hostage."

Ellie had just finished changing Amelia when a peculiar shadow on the wall had her straightening. She turned to see the man in the hoodie standing in the doorway between her room and the hallway.

She froze, her heartbeat hammering in her throat.

"Afternoon, Ellie," he drawled, pulling down his hood so she could get a good look at his face. High balding forehead, narrow nose and thin lips. Doug Gasper.

"You," she gasped, moving to stand protectively between him and Amelia's crib. She'd left her phone on the changing table, and she pressed the call screen, hitting 911 and speaker quickly before turning back around.

Doug had worked with her at the bookstore. "You're my stalker? I don't understand. We were friends."

"Were we?" he asked, his tone mild as he peered down his nose at her. "Maybe that was the problem, right there, in a nutshell."

Bewildered, she eyed him. She had trouble believing he was dangerous. "Us being friends was a problem?" She crossed her arms. "Doug, we had dinner together at least once a week. I thought you were one of my best friends. You even comforted me when my stalker left roses or one of those poems."

He didn't reply, just continued to stare at her.

The implications of this struck her. She and Doug had talked for hours at each dinner. She'd denigrated her stalker with his creepy black roses and frightening and awful poetry. Doug had pretended sympathy, when in reality he must have been furious that she didn't appreciate his efforts.

A chill snaked up her spine. Clearly, she'd severely misjudged him.

"I still don't understand why," she finally said. "I thought you liked me. Why would you do all that stuff to me?"

"Liked you?" He moved closer. She realized to her shock that he had a gun in his hand. "You never did get it, did you, Ellie? *Like* never factored into it."

Swallowing, she was afraid to ask what he meant.

A tic moved in his cheek as he sidled around to stand beside her, his back against the changing table. "Ellie, you were mine from the first moment I saw you, but you didn't realize it. Or care."

"I always cared," she protested, praying he wouldn't notice her cell phone. "We were friends, Doug."

"I thought I could win you," he snarled. "But the first time I left you a poem, instead of appreciating it or wondering who your secret admirer might be, you said horrible things about it. About *me*."

Ellie inhaled sharply, struggling not to recoil. She sensed that the slightest wrong move would set him off. Whatever happened, she knew she must keep him away from the crib. And oddly enough, now that she had Amelia to protect, she was no longer worried about what he might do to her.

The baby, however, was another story.

"You're wrong," she said. "I remember that first poem. I can recite it from memory." She ought to. After all, she must have studied the damn thing hundreds of times trying to decipher its meaning.

He narrowed his brown eyes. "I don't believe you."

Keeping her tone measured and level, she began. "The darkness comes when I look in your eyes. No longer blue, but the inky color of the deepest corner of hell. You are mine and I find myself longing to bathe in your eternal fire, damned forever." She swallowed. "Come on, Doug. I don't think you can honestly tell me that anyone wouldn't find that terrifying."

His frown made a deep line appear between his bushy eyebrows. "It's romantic," he declared. "I can't help it if you don't appreciate a good literary work."

Wisely, she refrained from commenting.

"You never appreciated any of my efforts," he continued, his gaze burning. "The black roses were an ironic portrayal of the commercialization of red roses to symbolize love. I thought you'd get that, but instead you acted as if you found them creepy."

Trying to formulate a reply, Ellie jumped as the back door flew open and footsteps pounded down the hall toward them.

Moving swiftly, Doug grabbed her, holding her around the neck in front of him, his pistol pressed against her temple. She began to perspire, praying he didn't have an itchy trigger finger.

Chapter 15

Theo and Flint rushed into the room, stopping short as they took in the scene. Shocked, Ellie noted that both men had weapons drawn.

"Get Amelia out of here," Theo ordered. Flint glanced at him, and then hurried to do exactly that.

"No," Doug said, the single word stopping Flint in his tracks. "The baby stays."

"Why?" Ellie pleaded. "She's not mine. She has nothing to do with you and me. Let her go."

He pressed the muzzle harder into her temple, making her gasp with pain. "I might need her for a bargaining tool."

"Bargaining for what?" Flint asked, his voice deceptively calm. "What do you want?"

"My woman, for starters." He squeezed the arm he had around Ellie's neck, choking her. She began to struggle as her air supply was cut off, seeing stars.

"Let her breathe," Theo shouted. Though at first glance he appeared composed, Ellie could see the desperate fury in his eyes.

For some reason this reassured her. Doug wasn't going to get away with this. Theo wouldn't let him.

"Doug?" she rasped, her throat slightly raw. "If you really want my undying love, you've got to be more romantic than this. What kind of story would this be to tell our children?"

Doug froze. She prayed he'd buy the complete and utter nonsense she'd just sprouted. It depended on how deep his delusions were.

"You're wrong," he finally said, sounding furious. "I might just kill you, and your baby, before I shoot myself. That way we'll be together forever."

A chill spread through her, turning her blood to ice. Doug sounded crazy enough to do exactly what he said.

"Now, hold on," Flint said, his tone reasonable and reassuring. "None of us want it to come to that. What would be the point?"

"You know nothing," Doug argued. Facing Flint, he slightly loosened his grip on her neck. Heart pounding, Ellie figured it'd be now or never.

She twisted her head back into his face, ducking and ramming her elbow up at the same time, knocking his pistol arm away from her head and using that momentum to jab again, this time her elbow into his stomach. Out of reflex, he fired. The shot went wild.

Theo jumped him, wrestling him to the floor, holding him down while Flint cuffed him. Doug continued to spew curses and nonsense about destiny and true love. Shaking his head, Flint led him out of the room.

Ellie's legs gave out and she crumpled, suddenly unable to stop shaking. Crouching beside her, Theo scooped her up, holding her close and murmuring soothing words.

"Amelia?" she managed to ask. "Is Amelia okay?"

"She slept through it all." His husky voice reverberated against her ear. "And believe it or not, she's still asleep."

Ellie nodded, shaking violently. She closed her eyes and let herself sag against him as she pushed back panic. She couldn't allow herself to think of how close she'd come to dying. Worse, how close Amelia had come to being hurt. She knew that would come later, no doubt tonight when she was alone in her bed trying to sleep.

At least Amelia and Theo were safe. That was the most important thing. And then it hit her. She couldn't imagine a life without the two of them, her makeshift family. Somehow she'd allowed a tiny baby and her cowboy father to worm their way into her heart. Which meant she had set herself up for a world of hurt.

To her consternation, her eyes filled with tears, which overflowed and began running down her cheeks. She turned her face into Theo, crying in earnest, her entire body shaking with the force of her sobs.

"It's over now," he said, smoothing his hand down her hair and massaging her shoulder. "Flint's taking him to the station and booking him. That crackpot won't bother you again."

And then she realized she no longer had a stalker.

"It's finally over," she managed, hardly able to believe it all, still floored with the realization of how much Theo and Amelia meant to her. Even though she was now free, she knew she wasn't. "He almost killed me."

"I wouldn't have let him," Theo said, his voice fierce. She remembered the feel of the cold metal against her temple and knew he wouldn't have been able to do anything.

No doubt he knew this too, which was why he continued to hold her.

She wiped her eyes, sniffling and wishing she had a box of tissue. Pushing against Theo, she struggled to stand, unable to keep from checking on Amelia once more.

The baby still slept peacefully, oblivious of the craziness that had just occurred around her. Thankful, she clutched the edge of the crib, wondering why her legs felt hollow.

Theo came up behind her, his hand gentle on her shoulder. "Are you all right?"

Refusing to look at him since she knew if she did, she'd start crying again, she shrugged. "I don't know," she answered honestly, hating the quaver in her voice.

"Come in the kitchen and let me get you a glass of wine."

"As tempting as that sounds, I don't want to leave Amelia." Glancing at her hands, she realized she clutched the edge of the crib so hard her knuckles were white.

When he didn't reply, she raised her head to see him gazing down at his daughter, naked tenderness softening his rugged features.

Longing stabbed her, mixed all up with joy and relief and an odd sense of finality. "I'd like to rest," she said, again avoiding meeting his eyes. "Sometimes I nap when she does. I really need to lie down."

"Okay." Was that regret coloring his voice? "I'll be around if you need to talk, all right?"

Answering with a quick nod, she turned away and crossed to her bed, where she methodically began folding down the blanket, and then the sheet, using the busywork to keep her occupied until she heard the sound of the door closing behind him.

Then she crawled into her bed, buried her face in her pillow and allowed herself to weep.

"Ellie." As if he knew, somehow Theo was beside her, gathering her close, kissing the tears from her cheeks. Holding her tight, as if he never meant to let her go.

She kissed him back, mindless in her desperation, needing to feel alive. To feel real, to let her body speak for her heart. She clawed at his shirt, wanting nothing but skin between them.

Somehow they divested themselves of their clothing. Theo seemed to share her need, instinctively understanding that this was not a time to go slowly.

They met halfway, body to body. Not sure how, she ended up on top, mindless with desire. She rode him hard, letting herself go wild with her head back, a primal sound of need and wanting escaping her throat. She gave herself over to him, to his body and to his life.

When she reached the peak, she let herself go, hurtling toward fulfillment with a cry and a shudder. Theo wasn't far behind.

Holding each other close, they fell asleep in each other's arms.

Amelia's hungry cry woke Ellie a few hours later. She sat up and blinked for a moment at Theo, sound asleep in her bed. She slid from under his muscular arm and hurried to get to the baby before her crying escalated.

Feeling pleasantly sore, Ellie carried Amelia into the kitchen and began to prepare her formula. Outside, she saw dusk had fallen. Which meant she and Theo had missed the evening meal.

But inside the refrigerator, Mrs. Jay had made two plates, covered in cellophane. Ellie smiled, silently thanking her.

After Amelia had finished her bottle, Ellie burped her. Then she went to wake Theo so they could eat. Grinning wickedly, Theo trailed his gaze over her, as hot as any caress. Wearing only his boxers, he followed her into the kitchen. He ate fast, though Ellie picked at her food. She couldn't concentrate, not with him sitting across from her practically naked.

The instant they'd finished, Theo stood and came over and kissed her. "I'll be waiting in your bed," he murmured, his voice husky with desire. "For you."

Her entire body blushing, Ellie nodded. She carried Amelia back to her room and changed her, feeling incredibly self-conscious with Theo's half-lidded gaze on her. She put the already sleepy baby in her crib, then turned to face him, already unbelievably aroused, dizzy with need.

"Come here, you," he said, holding out his arms.

So she did.

Wonder of wonders, Amelia slept through the night for the first time that evening. Sunlight had already begun to stream through the window when she made her first, gurgling baby sounds.

Ellie glanced at Theo, who still slept with one arm holding her close to him. Again she managed to wiggle out from under him without waking him, and changed Amelia before carrying her into the kitchen for her morning bottle.

A quick glance at the calendar, and she smiled. Halloween. Even though Dead River had canceled the holiday, she still got that expectant feeling she always had on holidays or her birthday. As if something wonderful would happen that day. Even though Dead River would not be celebrating, Ellie and Amelia and Theo would.

She thought it might be the best Halloween ever.

Theo kept his eyes closed when Ellie got up to tend to Amelia. This, he realized. This was how he wanted to start every morning from now on. With his arms around Ellie.

He'd spent way too much time bemoaning everything he had lost. The rodeo was out, his career, his life, vanished in the buck of a crazy bronco. Suddenly, he realized he could have a new life.

Ellie's words came back to him. *"For a man who has so much, you act like you have nothing. You're alive, you have family who loves you, a productive and profitable ranch and a beautiful baby girl. What more do you want?"*

Her, he realized. He wanted her. Ellie, to promise to stay with him and love him for the rest of her life.

She had no idea how he felt. He certainly had never told her, and he couldn't help but wonder how she'd react once he did. He knew she wanted to travel. What he didn't know was if she'd consider traveling with him rather than alone, at least once the quarantine was lifted.

No risk, no gain. That had always been his motto, part of what had made him so successful in pro rodeo.

Humming, he got up and headed for the shower. After he emerged, energized and clean, his cell phone rang.

Flint. "I need to officially take your and Ellie's statements. Can you come down and give them? You can even wear a costume if you want. Hell, it might brighten things up. It's Halloween, even if all festivities have been canceled."

"Halloween?" Ellie's favorite holiday. And just like that, he knew what he had to do.

He thought for a moment. "What's all this about a costume? You know I don't have any. I never dress up."

"I know. But I have, once or twice in the past. If I wasn't sheriff, I'd damn sure be wearing one of them."

Theo hesitated, and then decided what the hell? "I might want to borrow one. Would that be okay?"

"Sure." Flint sounded a bit mystified, but he didn't press for specifics. "So you'll pick it up when you bring Ellie in to give me your statements?"

"About that…I probably could come in, but I don't think we both can. I don't want to risk Amelia getting sick, especially after last time. And Ellie's too fragile right now to leave alone."

"Can't say I blame you." Flint sighed. "But what about the costume?"

"I'll send one of the hands over to get it." He decided not to mention to his brother that he had a bit of special shopping of his own to do. He knew Flint would tease him mercilessly if he did.

"Fine," Flint said. "I guess I can just take your statement over the phone. And when Ellie feels up to it, just have her call me. How about that?"

"Works for me," Theo replied. "But you were here. You know everything that happened."

"I do. But I still need you to go over the event in your own words."

Barely resisting the urge to roll his eyes, Theo did. After he'd finished, he headed into the kitchen to find Ellie. He planned to watch Amelia so Ellie could shower. Then once she'd done that, he'd have her call Flint. He figured he'd wait until dinner to tell her he was planning something special for their first Halloween together.

In between, he needed to call Molly and send the same hand he'd be sending to Flint's to run by her house.

Ellie's cheeks reddened as he walked into the kitchen. "Good morning," she said, sounding shy.

He grinned, unable to keep himself from planting a kiss right on her still-swollen-from-last-night lips.

"Mornin' darlin'," he drawled. "How about I keep an eye on Amelia, so you can have a shower?"

Swallowing, she nodded. "That would be nice."

He thought she'd bolt or rush out of the room, but instead she reached up and cupped his face with her hands. "Thank you," she whispered, brushing her mouth over his, sending a jolt of desire straight to his groin. Then, looking pretty darn pleased with herself, she strolled away, hips swaying.

Theo grinned, watching her go. He waited until he heard the sound of the shower before he picked up the phone.

Molly sounded surprised and pleased when he heard his request. "I don't know if she'll go for it," she said. "But I really do think it would be great if she did. I'll help you in any way I can."

When he told her what costume he wanted for Ellie, she laughed. "That's perfect. I'll have it ready for you. When are you going to get it?"

"I'm going to send someone now," he said. "Since tonight is the night, I want to surprise her."

"Sounds good," she said. Relieved that she didn't ask any more questions, he headed out to the barn to get all of the details taken care of. After that, Theo went down to the kitchen to see what kind of meal Mrs. Jay, his temporary cook who might be about to become permanent, planned to make for the evening meal.

"A nice pot roast," she said, smiling. "With new potatoes and carrots. Will that be all right with you?"

He nodded. "And biscuits?"

"Of course."

"What about dessert? Since it's Halloween, would you mind making some sort of special, themed dessert?"

Her smile widened. "Of course not. I know just the

thing. My boys used to love Halloween when they were younger."

"Thank you," he said, turning to go. "Then I'll leave you to it."

"We're having chicken sandwiches for lunch," she called after him.

With a wave as his answer he left, his mood buoyant. If everything worked out as planned, Mrs. Jay would be offered a permanent job before she left for the day.

Theo skipped lunch, afraid he'd slip up and do something to make Ellie wonder what he had planned. More than anything, he wanted to surprise her so he could witness her joy firsthand.

If things went the way he hoped, Amelia's first Halloween would be the first of many holidays he and Ellie shared.

Claiming he needed to stop by the feed store, he drove to town and stopped at the lone jewelry store, Dead River Diamonds. The proprietor, Mr. Mauricio, squinted in surprise when Theo walked in.

"I've already told your brother I'd let him know if anyone tried to sell me your family heirloom ring," he said.

"That's not why I'm here," Theo said, walking to a case and peering down. Suddenly intimidated by all the dazzling choices, he looked at Mr. Mauricio for help. "I need to buy an engagement ring of my own," he said, glad the store was empty. "For a very special lady."

The older man's face lit up. "Why didn't you say so? What cut in the diamond?"

"Bear with me, I've never done this before." He watched while the jeweler brought out a tray of sparking rings and pointed to a square-cut diamond, surrounded by a complete circle of smaller diamonds. "I like that one."

"Good choice." Mr. Mauricio named a price and then

followed up by stating he could offer an installment plan if Theo liked.

Smiling, Theo declined and wrote the man a check for the full amount.

"You can bring it back to be sized, at no charge." He handed Theo the ring in a black velvet box. "I sure hope your lady likes it."

Thanking him, Theo tucked the box in his jeans pocket and left. After he left the jewelry store, he stopped by the drugstore and bought decorations. Not scary spiders and skeletons, but streamers and lights and everything he could think of to make the living room magical.

Back home, he felt like a kid on Christmas morning as he tried to keep busy while unobtrusively watching the clock. He took the decorations to Mrs. Jay and asked her if she'd put them up when Ellie was out of the room. Giving him the smile of a conspirator, she agreed.

The ranch hand he'd sent to pick up the costumes arrived and handed them over, both in plastic dry cleaning bags. Theo hurried to get them to his room before Ellie saw.

Finally, it was time for the evening meal. Since they always ate pretty early, he knew the hands would be gone before dark.

"This is delicious, Mrs. Jay," Ellie said, smiling. She practically glowed with happiness tonight, despite the town's cancelation of Halloween and despite nixing her plans with Molly to stay home with Theo and Ellie.

Watching her while trying not to stare, he also thought she looked radiantly beautiful. Her pretty blue eyes shined with excitement.

Theo barely tasted his meal, though he was hungry since he'd skipped lunch. He managed to clean his plate, aware that tonight just might be the biggest night of his life.

"I can't wait to see Amelia in her costume," Ellie said, glancing over at the bassinette where the baby dozed. "I'm planning on taking some pictures and posting them on Facebook."

"I didn't know you were on there," he said, surprised.

"I wasn't." Her smile dazzled him. "But now that I no longer have to worry about a stalker, I've reactivated my account."

"I'll have to send you a friend request."

She stared, clearly astonished herself. "You have a Facebook account?"

He laughed. "Yes. It used to be for promoting my rodeo career. I used to have a virtual assistant to handle all my online activities. Of course, once I had the accident and lost my career, I had to let her go."

She nodded, watching him closely. "I'm sorry."

"Don't be." And he meant it. For the first time, he felt no despair when talking about his former rodeo days or his accident. "That's all in the past," he said. "I'm concentrating on looking forward, to the future."

"Me too." She lifted her chin. "Of course, that won't even be possible until they lift the quarantine."

Just like that, his confidence deflated. He knew he didn't know what she wanted out of life, other than she'd said she'd always wanted to travel to Australia. Would he be wasting his time asking her to spend the rest of her life with him?

No matter. He had to know. Theo had learned early on that the bigger the risk, the better the reward. Ellie had become his everything, and no way in hell was he going to let a bit of uncharacteristic self-doubt prevent him from going after what he wanted.

Mrs. Jay announced the time had come for their special dessert. As was customary, she served the ranch hands first. Guffaws and hoots greeted whatever she gave them. Amid teasing and laughter, the men got busy eating.

A moment later, Theo saw what all the commotion had been about. Mrs. Jay had made cupcakes, decorated to look like spiders.

When Ellie saw this, she clapped her hands with happiness. "Perfect," she said, jumping up and planting a quick kiss on the older woman's cheek. "Thank you so much. I love Halloween, and you've just helped make it even more special."

Theo watched in amazement as the normally confident cook blushed. "You're welcome, dear."

He choked down his cupcake, making the appropriate complimentary comments.

The men got up to leave, grumbling about how the annual Halloween party at the bar had been canceled. They were planning to have a poker game instead.

"You in, boss?" one of them asked Theo.

"Not this time," he answered. "It's my baby girl's first Halloween and I want to spend it with her."

The man smiled his approval, put his hat back on his head and left.

Ellie offered to help Mrs. Jay with the dishes. The older woman declined, shooing Ellie along. "You go celebrate with Amelia and Theo," she said. "Once I finish cleaning up, I'm taking myself home. I'm sure going to miss all the kids coming around for candy."

"Maybe they'll let them do it another day," Ellie said. "Once they find a cure for the virus."

"Maybe so." Mrs. Jay turned back to the dishes.

Ellie crossed to the bassinette and picked up Amelia. "I'm going to go get her cleaned up and changed and then put her in her costume." Her excited smile told him how much this meant to her.

He followed her down the hallway, stopping her with a touch on her arm when she got to her room. "Just a minute," he said. "I've got something I want you to put on once you're finished."

Though she gave him a quizzical look, she nodded.

Hurrying into his room, he opened his closet door and removed the elaborate and gaudy princess costume Molly had provided. It came complete with a sparkling crown and jewelry. Since Ellie and Molly were about the same size, he felt confident it would fit.

"Here you go." He handed her the plastic-wrapped gown. "Courtesy of Molly."

"A costume?" Her eyes sparkled with delight, though she appeared confused. "What for?"

"I thought we'd all three dress up tonight," he said, his heart thumping loud in his chest. "I really want this to be special for Amelia—and you."

Though she nodded and ducked her head, he could tell she was pleased. What woman—especially one who loved Halloween—wouldn't want to wear such a beautiful dress? Even if they weren't going to a party, she could pretend for a few hours.

Once she'd closed her door, he hurried to his room to don his own costume. He was going to be prince to her princess, and when he got down on one knee to offer her the ring, he wanted it to be the most magical moment of her life.

And hopefully of his.

Dressed, he checked himself out in the mirror. Surprised that he didn't feel even the slightest bit foolish, he didn't think he looked half-bad.

Satisfied, he turned to go check out the living room and see if Mrs. Jay needed any help.

"I'm nearly finished," she chirped when she saw him, and then her eyes went round. "You look stunning."

He grinned and thanked her, looking at the streamers and balloons and tiny orange lights. "This is perfect. You did a great job."

"That's good." She ducked her head, clearly pleased. "Especially, since I've never decorated inside for Halloween before."

She finished up and took herself off for home, still smiling, almost as if she knew what he intended.

A few minutes later, Ellie emerged. Theo heard the sound of her door opening and tensed. Telling himself to relax, he faced the hallway, eager to see her reaction when she saw what he had done.

But when she turned the corner, he found himself transfixed instead.

"Wow!" Ellie as a princess gliding into the room, transfixing him with her beauty. "This place looks amazing."

Speechless, he nodded, though he only could look at her. The deep purple velvet of the dress highlighted the perfection of her porcelain skin, which glowed with heightened color. Her soft brown hair hung in long, seductive swirls over her shoulders.

He lowered his gaze to her creamy throat begging for kisses above the low-cut bodice of the gown. She was exquisitely feminine. Slender, willowy, yet somehow dainty.

His.

Finding himself at a loss for words, he struggled to figure out the right thing to say.

At his silence, her lashes swept down over her cheeks. "What do you think?" she asked shyly.

Then, as he opened his mouth to respond, she held up Amelia, wearing an infant version of the princess gown, only in a cheerful, bright pink.

"Isn't she lovely?" Ellie said, smiling with joy. "I even bought this little flower headband to go on her sweet, bald head."

Enchanted, he crossed the room and took little Amelia from her. "She's beautiful," he said. "Just like you."

Though she blushed at his words, she didn't look away. "You're a prince," she said, her blue eyes sparkling.

"I am."

"I would have thought you'd go as a cowboy," she said. "But then I guess it wouldn't really be a costume, since you're a cowboy every day."

Normally, he would tease her. But the black velvet box inside his pocket made him tongue-tied. Panicking slightly, he realized he should have rehearsed this, maybe even practiced. A man only got one chance to propose, and he damn sure had better get it right.

Not yet, though. He planned to wait until the moment was right. First, he wanted to give her the special Halloween night she'd wanted.

"We never have trick-or-treaters out here at the ranch," he said. "And since Dead River canceled their festivities, including the annual party at the bar, I thought maybe you and I could have our own Halloween party."

She gave him a tentative smile. "Okay."

"You know, I have to tell you again how gorgeous you look. If the costume party at the bar hadn't been canceled and we'd gone, you would have had men fighting to dance with you."

Her delighted laugh lightened some of the tightness in his chest. "What about you?" she asked, her smile turning teasing. "You make a mighty handsome prince yourself."

Unable to resist, he placed Amelia in her bassinette and gave her the pacifier. Then he held out his hand. "May I have this dance?"

Her eyes widened. "But there's no music."

He lowered his voice. "We can make our own."

Shaking her head, nevertheless she slipped her fingers into his. He pulled her close, one hand on her waist, and twirled her around the floor.

Laughter floated up from her throat as she spun, her skirt flaring out. He caught her and brought her back, realizing the moment could never be more perfect than it was at this very instant.

"I need to ask you something," he asked, his voice thick and unsteady.

Smiling up at him, she tilted her head. "If it's about my dancing, then no. I never did learn how to slow-dance properly."

Enchanted again, he nearly staggered at the intense flare of his emotions. "Not about your dancing," he managed. Letting go of her hand, he dropped to one knee.

Ellie stared at him, her hand creeping up to her throat, her lovely eyes huge in her pale face. "Theo…"

If he'd thought about it too much, he knew in this moment he might fumble taking the ring box from his pocket. But as certainty filled him, his hands were steady and sure.

He opened the black velvet box, letting her see the ring he'd chosen. "You've made me realize what kind of future I can have with you by my side. I'm tired of living in the past, especially since everything I want and need is right here, with you and Amelia. I'd be honored, Ellie Parker, if you'd agree to become this rancher's wife."

When she didn't immediately respond, he knew something had to be bothering her. Because deep in his heart he had to believe that Ellie loved him almost as much as he loved her.

"What is it?" he asked. "Is it because you wanted to go to Australia? We can do that for our honeymoon. I still have lots of money socked away from my prize-winning rodeo days. So if you're still wanting to travel Down Under—or anyplace else—we can take vacations there together."

"You know, I think I'd like that." Her sweet smile appeared a bit mischievous, though her eyes had grown wet with unshed tears. "Though I mainly wanted to get away because of my stalker. Now that he's out of the picture, I'm pretty darn happy right where I am."

Despite her words, she still looked troubled. "But Theo, I have to ask you something. I saw a notebook you had, and it looked like you were planning on trying to go back to the rodeo. Is that the case?"

Puzzled, he shook his head. "I can't go back, even if I wanted to. I'm not sure what you saw..." And then he realized what it had to have been. "I plan to start a breeding program to supply rodeo broncos. With my knowledge of rodeo and of ranching, I'm pretty confident I'll be a success. At least, once this quarantine is lifted, that is."

Her dazzling smile made him catch his breath. "That's absolutely wonderful," she said. "And you're completely right—I believe you will be very successful."

"Thanks." Eyeing her, he cleared his throat. "About my proposal?"

"Ah yes." Her smile broke into a watery grin. "About that. I'm thinking there's something you haven't yet said. I don't know if you're wanting to marry me just because of Amelia, or if you really want me for yourself."

She was right. Amused and chastened, he nodded. "You're correct. So here's the truth. I love you more than words can say, Ellie. I love you more than you could ever love a broken-down cowboy like me."

"Don't say that!" She dropped down beside him, cupping his face gently with her hands and caressing his mouth with hers. "I adore everything about you, Theo Colton. And yes, I'd love to be your wife."

Elation sang through his veins and he kissed her back. Then he broke away, slipping the ring on her finger. They both admired it for a moment and then, arms wrapped around each other, he reclaimed her lips.

The doctors might not have figured out the cure to the virus, and the future of Dead River might be uncertain. But this, his love for her would always be steady and sure.

"We're a family now, Ellie," he promised her, against her lips. "Together, we'll make it through all this craziness. You, me and our daughter."

She gave him a watery smile. "I believe we will." And then her expression turned mischievous. "You know what? Theo, what do you say we get married wearing these costumes?"

He gazed back, his heart full of amused wonder. "You know, I think that might be perfect. Once this virus gets cured, we'll have a costumed wedding, in honor of your favorite holiday."

Half laughing, half crying, she wrapped her arms around him again and buried her face against his throat.

"I want to spend the rest of my life showing you how much I love you."

Ducking her head, the rosy color in her cheeks told him his words had pleased her. "Me too," she replied. "That is, I want to do the same with you."

He couldn't help it, he laughed and pulled her close. "You're something else, Ellie."

"So are you, Theo Colton." She kissed him again, without hesitation, and full of love. "So are you."

Smoothing his hand down the silky length of her hair, he marveled at how quickly his life had changed for the better. "One year ago, I thought I'd lost everything. And now I've been given a second chance. My life is richer than I ever could have imagined."

"Mine too." She raised her head, a seductive softness in her baby blue eyes. "And I can think of a great way to celebrate."

Before he could ask, she kissed him once more and proceeded to show him exactly what she meant.

* * * * *

Award-winning author **Amelia Autin** is an inveterate reader who can't bear to put a good book down... or part with it. She's a longtime member of Romance Writers of America, and served three years as its treasurer. Amelia resides with her PhD engineer husband in quiet Vail, Arizona, where they can see the stars at night and have a "million-dollar view" of the Rincon Mountains from their backyard.

Books by Amelia Autin

Harlequin Romantic Suspense

Man on a Mission

Cody Walker's Woman
McKinnon's Royal Mission
King's Ransom
Alec's Royal Assignment
Liam's Witness Protection
A Father's Desperate Rescue
Killer Countdown
The Bodyguard's Bride-to-Be
Rescued by the Billionaire CEO
Black Ops Warrior

The Coltons of Texas

Her Colton P.I.

Silhouette Intimate Moments

Gideon's Bride
Reilly's Return

Visit the Author Profile page at Harlequin.com.

HER COLTON P.I.

Amelia Autin

For my stepmother, Mary Dorothy Callen Autin,
who makes the world a special place
for everyone who knows her. For my stepsister,
Patti Padgett Mouton Fagan, who made my father
immensely proud of the woman she became.
And for Vincent...always.

Chapter 1

She's not going to get away with it. That was all Chris Colton could think as he listened to the tearful story Angus and Evalinda McCay unfolded before him. Holly McCay wasn't going to get away with keeping her in-laws from their beloved twin grandsons, all they had left of their son after he died.

Chris leaned back in his chair in his northwest Fort Worth, Texas, office and glanced at the pictures the McCays had handed him. One was of blond-haired, brown-eyed Holly McCay and her now-deceased husband, Grant. The other was of the McCay twins, Ian and Jamie.

"But they don't look like that anymore," Evalinda McCay said sadly. "Our grandsons weren't even a year old when that picture was taken, and that was more than six months ago. Holly won't even let us see them. She's been like that ever since Grant..." She dabbed a tissue at her eyes.

"Don't worry, Mrs. McCay," Chris said, steel in his voice. "I'll take this job myself—I won't hand it off to an associate. I'll find your grandsons for you. And your daughter-in-law, too."

Angus McCay cleared his throat. "I don't like to speak ill of my son, Mr. Colton, because he's gone and can't defend himself. But he was blind to what his wife was really like. She trapped him into marriage—"

"They hadn't even been married seven months when Ian and Jamie were born," Evalinda McCay clarified in a shocked tone.

"Grant's will made her the trustee for their boys," Angus McCay continued, as if he hadn't been interrupted. "And…well…"

"The money is all she cares about," his wife threw in. She put her hand on her husband's arm. "I know you don't like to put it so bluntly, Angus, but you know it's true." Her gaze moved to Chris. "Holly took the boys and left town three weeks before Christmas. Right before *Christmas*…" She choked up for a moment before continuing. "Grant's fortune is tied up in a trust for Ian and Jamie, but Holly is the sole trustee. Which means she can spend the money any way she sees fit, without any real oversight."

Angus McCay added, "And since she won't tell us where she is…won't even let us *see* them…" He sighed heavily. "We don't even know if they're alive, much less healthy and happy."

"We tried to get custody of the boys through the courts right after Grant died," Evalinda McCay said, her wrinkled face lined with worry. "But grandparents don't seem to have any legal rights these days. Our lawyer said he's not optimistic—not even to force Holly to let us have some kind of visitation with Ian and Jamie."

"The police won't help us, because Holly hasn't done anything wrong," Angus McCay said gruffly.

"Except break our hearts, and Ian's and Jamie's, too, for that matter—but there's no law against that," Evalinda McCay put in.

"You don't have to say any more." Determination grew in Chris. If it was the last thing he did, he'd find Holly McCay and her eighteen-month-old sons for Mr. and Mrs. McCay. Not just because no one had the right to deprive good and decent grandparents like the McCays access to their grandchildren. But because the children deserved to know their grandparents. That was the real bottom line.

Not to mention it made him sick to think of Holly McCay isolating her children from their relatives for money. His foster parents hadn't abused him, but he'd known ever since he was placed with them when he was eleven that they were in it only for the money the state gave them.

"We tracked Holly here to Fort Worth, but then the trail went cold. That's why we decided to hire you, Mr. Colton," Angus McCay said now. "You know this part of the state—we don't." He glanced at his wife, who cleared her throat as if to remind him of something. "And there's another thing. It's all over the news here in Fort Worth about the Alphabet Killer in Granite Gulch."

Chris stiffened, wondering if the McCays knew about his family's connection to the serial killer. But Angus McCay continued without a pause and Chris relaxed. "We know Granite Gulch is forty miles away, and we know all the targets so far are women with long dark hair. But who knows? That could change at any time. And Holly... well...despite everything, she *is* our daughter-in-law. If anything happened to her..."

He trailed off and his wife picked up the thread of the

story. "We heard on the news the last victim was Gwendolyn Johnson, which means the killer is up to the *H*s now. And Holly's name begins with *H*. No matter what she's done to *us*, Mr. Colton, she's Ian and Jamie's mother. They've already lost their father before they ever had a chance to know him. I shudder to think of those two innocent babies orphaned at such a young age." She turned to her husband and nodded for him to continue.

"We don't know what it will cost," Angus McCay said, "but we have some money saved. Whatever your fees are, we'll double them if you make this job your top priority. And we'll give you a bonus if you find Holly within a month. We *have* to find her, Mr. Colton. And the boys," he added hastily.

"That won't be necessary," Chris said, thinking to himself that Holly McCay didn't deserve in-laws as caring as the McCays obviously were. "I won't even take a fee for this one—just cover the expenses and we'll be square. But I'll find your daughter-in-law and your grandsons for you, Mr. and Mrs. McCay. You can take that to the bank."

Evalinda McCay unbent enough to smile at Chris with approval. "You're a good man, Mr. Colton. I knew we were doing the right thing contacting you." Her smile faded. "When you find Holly, please don't tell her anything. She might take the boys and disappear. Again. No, I think it's better if you just let us know where she is and we'll take it from there. If we can just see her…talk to her…if she can see us with our grandsons…she can't be that hard-hearted to keep us away when she knows how much Grant's boys mean to us."

Chris nodded. "Yes, ma'am." He wasn't convinced Mrs. McCay was right, but he wasn't going to say so. If Holly McCay had fled right before Christmas, taking her twins—and their money—with her, she definitely *could* be hard-hearted enough to prevent the McCays from being a part of her sons' lives. *It's all about the money for her*, he thought cynically. *Just like my foster parents. It's all about the money.*

Holly McCay pulled up in front of her friend Peg Merrill's house, parked and turned off the engine. But she didn't get out right away. She adjusted the rearview mirror of her small Ford SUV with one hand and tugged her dark-haired pixie-cut wig more securely into place with the other. She hated the wig, even though she'd repeatedly told herself it was a necessity. It was already too warm for comfort, and it was only the first day of May. What would she do when the north Texas heat and humidity blasted her in July?

Ian and Jamie hated the wig, too, because it confused them. Just like the other disguises she'd donned had confused them before they came to Rosewood. Her eighteen-month-old twin toddlers were too young to put their emotions into words, but Ian had started acting out recently, refusing to put away his toys or eat the food on his plate without coaxing. Even his favorite mashed potatoes—which he called "smashed 'tatoes"—didn't seem to tempt him.

And Jamie had begun clinging in a way he never had before. Almost as if he was afraid his mother would disappear from his life. He didn't even want her to leave him with Ian to play with Peg Merrill's kids while she went grocery shopping in nearby Granite Gulch—and Jamie loved playing with Peg's children. Until a month ago he'd never been the clinging type.

Holly sighed softly. *If only*, she told herself for the umpteenth time. If only Grant hadn't died. If only he hadn't left *all* his money to their twin boys in an unbreakable trust, but instead had made provision for his parents. If only Grant's parents weren't so…so mercenary.

Not just mercenary, Holly reminded herself, shivering a little even though it was a warm spring day. *Deadly.*

She gave herself a little shake. "Don't think about that now," she muttered under her breath, doing her best Scarlett O'Hara imitation. She pasted a smile on her face and glanced at the mirror again to reassure herself she presented a normal appearance. Ian and Jamie didn't need a mother who was always looking over one shoulder. Who was paranoid that somehow the McCays had tracked her down to— *Stop that!* she insisted. *You're not going to worry about that itch between your shoulder blades… Not today.*

She was going to have to worry about it soon, though. And make some hard choices. If she packed up Ian and Jamie and everything they owned—which wasn't all that much, just what would fit into her small SUV—and moved away from their temporary home in Rosewood, she'd be on her own again. No Peg to help her by watching the twins while she ran errands, like grocery shopping or driving the forty miles into Fort Worth—or the seventy-plus miles into Dallas—to withdraw cash from one of the branch banks there.

But it wasn't just Peg's help with Ian and Jamie she'd miss. Peg was like the older sister Holly had always dreamed of, and she would miss that…a lot. Besides, what would she tell Peg? She couldn't just disappear without a word, could she? Peg would worry, and it wouldn't be right to do that to her friend. Especially since the Alphabet Killer had everyone in Granite Gulch and the surrounding towns terrified.

Holly sighed deeply, gave one last tug to her wig, then scooped up her purse and headed for Peg's house.

Down the street, Chris sat slumped in the seat of his white Ford F-150 pickup truck, parked two houses away beneath the shade of a flowering catalpa tree. He watched Holly McCay walk up the driveway, skirt Peg's SUV parked there and make for the front door. The male in him noted her slender but shapely figure in jeans that lovingly hugged her curves, and her graceful, swaying walk. The PI in him ignored both—or tried to.

He shook his head softly, forcing himself to think of something other than the way Holly McCay looked. *It's a good thing she isn't a professional criminal*, he thought instead, *because she's lousy at it.*

Oh, she'd done her best to avoid detection, he'd give her that. The short dark-haired wig she was wearing was an effective disguise of sorts. And she'd paid cash for everything—there'd been no paper trail of credit or debit purchases to follow. No checks written, either. But she'd transferred a large sum of money from her bank in Clear Lake City south of Houston to the Cattleman's Bank of Fort Worth, where she'd opened a new account when she moved to the Dallas–Fort Worth area. *That* had left a paper trail she hadn't been able to avoid, since she'd used her own driver's license and social security number. That was how the McCays had tracked her this far.

True, she'd varied the bank branches she'd used to withdraw funds, so no one could stake out one branch and wait for her to show up. That showed she was smart. But she'd slipped up by withdrawing cash from the Granite Gulch branch. Yeah, she'd done it only once, but it stood out in neon letters, since it was out of the pattern—all the other branches had been in Fort Worth or Dallas. And once Chris had known that, he'd searched Granite Gulch and the surrounding area for a woman with twin toddlers who'd recently moved in. No matter what color her hair was, no matter how much she tried to fade into obscurity, everyone remembered the twins. Especially eighteen-month-old identical twin boys as cute as buttons.

And Holly McCay was still driving her Ford Escape with its original Texas license plate tags registered in her name. *Duh!* Once he'd located a woman with twins in Rosewood, the next town over from Granite Gulch, he'd staked out the Rosewood Rooming House, where by all accounts she lived, and bingo! There was her Ford SUV with those incriminating tags.

She was registered at the rooming house using her real name, too, which had made confirmation a piece of cake. He'd almost picked up the phone to call the McCays and tell them he'd located their daughter-in-law…but he hadn't. He wasn't sure why. Was it because a warning light had started blinking that very first day when they turned over everything they knew about Holly's banking transactions? Information they shouldn't have had access to…but somehow had?

Or maybe it was the self-satisfied expression on Evalinda McCay's face when she thought Chris wouldn't see it, when he'd been perusing the financial reports they'd handed him and he'd glanced up unexpectedly. The expression had been wiped away almost instantly, replaced with the look of worried concern she'd worn earlier. But Chris's instincts—which he trusted—had gone on the alert.

He'd been a private investigator for nine years, ever since he'd received his bachelor of arts degree in criminology and criminal justice from the University of Texas at Arlington. From day one he'd trusted his instincts, and they'd never steered him wrong. Only an idiot would go against his instincts in his line of work, and for all his laid-back, seemingly good-old-Texas-boy persona, Chris wasn't an idiot.

He'd also run a credit check on the McCays the same day they'd come to see him—standard procedure for all his clients these days. He never took anyone's word they had the wherewithal to pay him—he'd been burned once early in his career and had learned a hard lesson. The credit report on the McCays had come back with some troubling red flags. They were living beyond their means. Way beyond their means, and had done so for years, despite Angus McCay's well-paying job as a bank president down in Houston. Even though Chris was taking this case pro bono and wouldn't be paid except for expenses, that credit report had given him pause.

Now he was glad he hadn't called the McCays for several reasons, not the least of which was that he knew Peg Merrill, had known her all his life. If she and Holly were friends, then Holly *couldn't* be the woman the McCays had made her out to be. Peg had an unerring BS meter—she'd nailed Chris on a few things over the years—which meant Holly couldn't have fooled Peg about the kind of woman she was. To top it off, Peg reigned supreme in one area in particular—motherhood. The worst insult in her book was to call someone a bad mother. No way would she be friends with a woman who was a bad mother.

Besides, Peg was his sister-in-law. Former sister-in-law, really, since Laura was dead. But he wasn't going there. Not now. Sister-in-law or not, Chris didn't want to be on Peg's bad side. Especially not on a pro bono case he'd already been having second thoughts about.

Chris waited until Holly McCay strapped her twins into their car seats and drove away before he got out of his truck. He shrugged on his blazer to hide his shoulder holster, then settled his black Stetson on his head and ambled toward Peg's house, determined to find out whatever he could about Holly McCay from Peg.

"Chris!" Peg exclaimed when she opened the door. "This is a surprise. Come on in."

"Unca Chris!" Peg's two-year-old daughter, Susan, made a beeline for Chris when he stepped inside, and he bent over to swing her up into his arms. A cacophony of barking from three dogs—one of which had been Chris's gift to Laura not long before she died—prevented anyone from being heard for a couple of minutes, but eventually Peg's two dogs subsided back to their rug in front of the fireplace in the family room.

Chris settled into one of the oversize recliners, still cuddling Susan against his shoulder while his other hand ruffled Wally's fur. "Hey, boy," he murmured, gazing down at the golden retriever Laura had adored. If his heart hadn't already been broken when Laura died, it would have broken at losing Wally, too. Chris had given Laura the puppy thinking they'd soon be moving from their apartment into a house with a large fenced yard. But that dream house sat vacant now—Chris couldn't bear to live there without Laura. And an apartment was no place for a growing dog, especially since Chris was rarely home. So when Peg and her husband, Joe, volunteered to adopt Wally, Chris had reluctantly accepted their offer. At least he'd still get to see Wally, he'd reasoned at the time—he was always welcome at the Merrill house.

Chris and Peg chatted about nothing much for a few minutes. About Bobby, Peg's napping one-year-old son, who was already starting to walk. About Joe's thriving gardening center in Granite Gulch, the Green and Grow. About Chris's highly successful private investigation business—which he'd thrown himself into even more thoroughly after Laura's death—and the fourth office he'd nearly decided to add in Arlington.

When Susan's eyelids began fluttering, Peg reached to take her daughter from Chris, but he forestalled her. "I'll put her down for her nap," he told Peg, doing just that. When he came back, Peg handed him a frosty glass of iced tea prepared the way he preferred it, with two lemon wedges, not just one.

They'd just settled back into their spots in the family room, Wally at Chris's feet, when Peg put her own glass of iced tea down on a coaster on the end table and said, "So what's wrong?" She didn't give Chris a chance to answer before she continued, "I didn't want to say anything in front of Susan—you would *not* believe how much she understands already. I told Joe he needed to watch his language now that Susan is so aware—and she mimics everything he says…*especially* the bad words." Chris laughed, and Peg said, "But something's up. You wouldn't be here in the middle of the week, in the middle of the afternoon, if something wasn't wrong."

Chris shook his head and smiled wryly. "You must have second sight or something." He hesitated, considering and then discarding his original idea of pumping Peg for info about Holly McCay on the sly. "The woman who was here a little while ago—"

"Holly?" Peg's surprise was obvious.

"Yeah. Holly McCay. I've been hired by her in-laws to find her."

Chapter 2

Two days later Holly drove away from Peg's house with her vision blurred from unshed tears. She'd left the twins in her friend's care one last time, but that wasn't why she was practically crying. She hadn't told Peg—she'd chickened out at the last minute—but she wasn't going to do errands. She'd wanted Ian and Jamie to have one last opportunity to play with Susan and Bobby…while she packed up the contents of their room in the Rosewood Rooming House and loaded everything into her SUV. Then she would pick up her boys, hand Peg the note she was trying to compose in her mind so Peg wouldn't worry about them…and they'd be gone.

Chris followed Holly away from Peg's house, keeping enough distance between his truck and her little SUV so she wouldn't spot the tail. He was surprised when she didn't stop at any of the stores in Granite Gulch but kept driving. She kept driving even after she reached the state highway that was the boundary between Granite Gulch and Rosewood. Puzzled but not really worried, Chris let the distance between their two vehicles increase, because there weren't any cars out this way to hide the fact that he was following her.

When Holly pulled into the Rosewood Rooming House parking lot, Chris was faced with a dilemma. He drove past, then doubled back as soon as he could, just in time to see Holly entering the rooming house's front door.

"What the hell is she doing?" he muttered to himself, wondering if she'd forgotten something and would be back outside soon. He made a U-turn a hundred yards down, parked close enough so he could watch the front door and Holly's SUV, but far enough away from the rooming house so he wouldn't be spotted, and waited. And waited.

A fleeting thought crossed his mind that the Rosewood Rooming House wasn't really the safest place for a woman on her own with two young children. Not only was the rooming house full of transients, but Regina Willard—whom law enforcement had pretty much identified as the Alphabet Killer—was known to have roomed here not that long ago. *Not* his baby sister, Josie, thank God. The Alphabet Killer hadn't been caught yet, but at least now everyone in town knew it wasn't Josie.

Thoughts of Josie reminded Chris that she was still missing, even after all these years he'd been searching for her. His two most spectacular failures as a PI both had their roots in his family history—Josie...and his mother's burial place. He touched his heart in an automatic gesture. The pain he felt over those failures ranked right up there with Laura's death and his guilt over that.

If his serial-killer father could be believed, however,

his mother's burial place might at last be discovered, something all the Colton children devoutly wished for. When their father had killed their mother, he'd hidden her body. She'd never been found, not in twenty years. But Matthew Colton had provided four clues to where Saralee Colton's body was buried. Not that the clues made any real sense…so far. But they were clues. He'd promised one clue for every child who visited him in prison. Annabel had been the last to visit their father, and her clue—Peaches—had been just as enigmatic as the first three: Texas, Hill and *B*. The siblings had theorized that maybe—*maybe*—the clues were pointing to their maternal grandparents' home in Bearson, Texas. But that house sat on acres of land. Even if their mother was buried somewhere on her parents' property, they weren't really much better off than they'd been when they started this sorry mess.

Chris sighed. This month was his turn to visit their father in prison. He didn't know why Matthew was putting his children through this torture—other than the fact that he could because they were all desperate to locate their mother's body and give her a decent burial—but it almost seemed as if their father was getting a perverse pleasure out of it. "The serial killer's last revenge," he murmured. Matthew Colton was dying. Everyone knew it, especially Matthew himself. "It would be just like that bastard to torture us with these disparate clues…then die. Taking his secret to the grave." He relieved his anger and frustration with a few choice curse words…until he remembered he was supposed to be giving them up. He'd resolved two days earlier that he was going to clean up his language for Susan Merrill's sake, and Bobby's, just as Joe Merrill was supposed to do.

"Heck and damnation," Chris said now. It didn't have the same impact.

* * *

Regina Willard groaned as she rolled out of her uncomfortable sleeping bag and staggered outside to relieve herself. She hated this hideout, hated being forced by the Granite Gulch Police Department and the FBI to hurriedly leave the Rosewood Rooming House. Her place there hadn't been luxurious by any means, but at least she'd had a comfortable bed and civilized facilities at her disposal. Not this hole-in-the-ground living quarters without any running water.

She thought fleetingly of her half brother, Jesse Willard, and his thriving farm. The last time she'd talked to him, years ago, he'd tried to encourage her to move on. To stop grieving for her lost fiancé. Jesse didn't understand. That bitch had stolen the only man Regina could ever love, and she'd had to pay. No matter how the woman disguised herself, no matter how many times she changed her name, Regina recognized her…and made her pay.

Regina shook her head. She kept killing that woman, but the bitch refused to stay dead. So Regina had to keep killing her again and again. If she killed her enough times, eventually she would *stay* dead. Then she could relax, move away from this area and try to forget.

She blinked, then rubbed her eyes, trying to focus. How many times had it been altogether? She ticked them off on her fingers. "Seven," she said at last. She chuckled to herself. Yes, she'd been forced into hiding out in this shelter in the middle of nowhere, but not even the vaunted FBI had been able to stop her. She was on a mission, and no one would stop her until the bitch was dead. Permanently.

Holly packed swiftly. While her hands were performing that mindless task, she tried to make plans. *Where to go?* she thought. *New Mexico? Arizona?* Or should she just keep driving until she'd put thousands of miles between herself and the McCays? She'd never lived in the United States outside Texas, and a little niggling fear of the unknown made her heart skip a beat as she envisioned going to a completely strange place. Not just the difference between Houston and Fort Worth, but *completely* different. Yes, she'd visited South America as a young child with her missionary parents, but that was a long time ago—Texas had been her home ever since she'd started school.

Leaving again hadn't been an easy decision for Holly to make—she didn't want to leave. Not just for her own sake but for her boys, too, who had reached the age where they noticed changes in their lives. But the time had come to move on.

She wasn't really concerned about the Alphabet Killer, despite the fact that the killer was up to the *H*s now. All seven of the killer's victims had long dark hair, and while Holly's wig was dark, it was very short. Not that she was careless of her safety—she wasn't going to risk being the exception to the killer's rule.

But she wasn't running from the Alphabet Killer. She was running from the McCays. The McCays…and their attempts on her life.

She hadn't wanted to admit it at first. But when one near miss had led to a second, then a third, she'd been forced to look at the McCays with suspicious eyes. *Someone* wanted her dead. Who else could it be? She didn't have an enemy in the world. But she *was* the trustee for the twins' inheritance from Grant. Which meant she controlled the income earned on nearly twenty million dollars. Over and above the cash invested conservatively, the trust also owned stock in Grant's software company—

now being run by others, but still doing well. So the trust had unlimited growth potential.

She'd always known Grant's parents—especially his mother—were cold and calculating. Grant had known it, too, although they'd never really discussed it—not when they were kids, and not after they were married. It was one of those things they'd just taken for granted. Was that why he hadn't left them anything in his will? Because he knew they were more interested in the fortune he'd earned from his breakthrough software design than they were in him or their grandsons?

She had no proof the McCays were trying to kill her, though. Nothing to take to the police except a growing certainty it couldn't be anyone else. Especially after the McCays tried to gain custody of the twins through the courts and had lied about Holly in their depositions—warning bells had gone off loud and clear. But even if she'd gone to the police, what would they have said? Those near misses could have been a coincidence. Accidents. The McCays were solid, middle-class, upstanding, churchgoing citizens. The salt of the earth. Or at least that was the image they projected. How could she even think of making a slanderous accusation against them… especially for such a heinous crime as attempted murder?

Which was why she'd packed up the bare necessities three weeks before Christmas, buckled her sons into their baby car seats and headed north toward the Dallas–Fort Worth metroplex with fierce determination. She hadn't really had a plan—plans could wait, she'd told herself—but she knew she had to put herself out of reach of her in-laws until she had time to think things through. She'd thought she could lose herself in Texas's second-largest metropolitan area.

But she wasn't a criminal on the lam, and she had no

idea how to go about getting a fake ID. Not to mention she couldn't carry huge wads of cash with her in lieu of using her credit and debit cards. She had to withdraw money from the bank periodically—a bank account she'd opened with her real social security number and driver's license.

She'd moved a week after she'd opened the new bank account—as she'd moved every time she got the feeling the McCays were getting close. But she hadn't switched banks. She'd picked the Cattleman's Bank of Fort Worth precisely because it had hundreds of branches throughout the DFW area, including small branches in grocery stores. And Holly had used many of them to throw the McCays off the scent…assuming they were still trying to track her down. But she had to assume that. She didn't dare assume otherwise.

Which meant her time in tiny Rosewood, right next door to Granite Gulch, where Peg lived, had finally come to an end. Rosewood was so small she'd thought the McCays would never find her in this out-of-the-way place, since she was still paying cash for everything and varying which bank branches she was using to withdraw that cash.

She loved the small-town atmosphere here, and after she'd made friends with Peg at the Laundromat—*thank God Peg's washing machine broke down that day!*—she'd started to feel at home. So she'd convinced herself she was safe. But for the past three days she'd had…well… *the willies*, she told herself, for lack of a better term. A feeling she was being watched. Followed.

It *could* be the Alphabet Killer, she supposed. But she didn't think so. Either way was a disaster in the making, and she wasn't going to stick around to find out for sure one way or the other.

Holly stashed two suitcases into the rear of her SUV, then headed back to the rooming house for another load.

She held the door to her room open with one foot as she picked up a box of toys and books, then tried to scream and dropped the box when a tall blond man in a black Stetson loomed in the doorway.

A large hand covered her mouth, stifling her voice, and all Holly could think of in that instant was *No!* No, she wasn't going to be a victim. She wasn't going to let herself be raped or murdered or—

She tore at the hand covering her mouth, but the man plastered her against the wall inside her room and kicked the door shut behind him. Then just held her prisoner with his body as she desperately tried to free herself. She gave up trying to fight the hand that muzzled her and went for his eyes instead. But he ducked his head, placing his mouth against her ear as he said in a deep undertone, "Stop it, Holly! I'm not going to hurt you—I'm trying to save your life. Peg Merrill's my sister-in-law."

She froze. Her heart was still beating like a snare drum, but she stopped fighting at Peg's name. And when she did that, she realized the stranger wasn't using her immobility to his advantage. She tried to ask a question, but the hand over her mouth prevented her.

"If I take my hand away, are you going to scream?" he asked, still in that same deep undertone. Holly shook her head slightly and was surprised, yet not surprised, when he did just that—he removed his hand. But it hovered near her face, as if he'd clamp it back in place if she screamed.

She swallowed against the dry throat, which terror had induced, then whispered, "Who are you?"

"Chris Colton. And yes," he answered before she could ask, "Peg's really my sister-in-law."

"I don't understand. Why are you here? Why did you force your way into my room?"

An enigmatic expression crossed his face, and he looked as if he was of two minds about answering those questions. "If I let you go, are you going to run for it? Or are you going to give me a chance to explain?"

A tiny dart of humor speared through her, despite the dregs of terror that still clung to her body. "You'd catch me before I ran three steps," she said drily. "So I guess I have no choice but to listen to what you have to say."

He surprised her again by laughing softly, but "Smart woman" was all he said. He took a step backward, then another and another, slowly. As if he was expecting her to make a break for it. But Holly wasn't stupid. If he was there to kill her, she'd be dead already—her strength was no match for his. And if he was there to rape her, he'd never have let her go.

Besides, she'd felt the bulge of his gun in its shoulder holster when he held her pinioned against the wall, but he hadn't drawn his weapon and used it against her. This meant he was probably telling the truth. Probably.

"I don't understand," she said again. "If Peg sent you, why didn't she tell me she was going to? I was just there, and she didn't say a wor—"

"She didn't send me. Not exactly. And I know you were just at her house. I followed you there…and back. I've been following you for days."

"Why?" She managed to tamp down the sudden fear his revelation triggered. So she *wasn't* crazy. She *had* been followed.

He removed his Stetson as if he'd just realized he was still wearing it. Then ran his fingers through the hair the hat had flattened. "Because the McCays hired me to find you."

“What?” She barely breathed the word.

His face took on a grim cast. “I’m a private investigator, Holly. The McCays came to my office a week ago. They spun me a cock-and-bull story about you, which I almost swallowed hook, line and sinker. Almost.” He looked as if he were going to add something to that statement, but didn’t.

“Let me guess. I’m an abusive mother, and they want to rescue Ian and Jamie from my clutches.”

“No.”

A wry chuckle was forced out of her. “Well, that’s a change. That’s the story they told the court when they tried to wrest custody of my boys from me after Grant died.” Curious, she asked, “So what was their story this time?”

Chris glanced down at the Stetson in his hand and ran his fingers along the brim. “You’re the trustee for the boys’ inheritance from their dad,” he said when he raised his eyes to meet hers again. “You wanted to use the money on yourself instead of for the boys’ benefit, and you took Ian and Jamie away from their loving grandparents so no one could call you to account. And you won’t let the McCays even know where you are… where the boys are. Won’t let them be a part of your children’s lives.”

Holly closed her eyes for a second, laughed again without humor and shook her head. “All of that is true, except for one thing,” she admitted. “I *am* the sole trustee. And I *did* run with Ian and Jamie—three weeks before Christmas, did they mention that?” Chris nodded. “And I *haven’t* told the McCays where we are…for a perfectly good reason. Because—”

“Because they’re trying to kill you.”

Stunned, Holly asked in a breathless whisper, "How did you know that?"

One corner of Chris's mouth twitched up into a half smile. "Because I'm damned good at what I do, Holly. Because the minute I found out you were friends with Peg, I knew the McCays were lying through their teeth, and I wanted to know why. I hate lies and I hate liars. But even more than that, I hate being taken for a sucker. So I did a little more digging…on them. And found out a hell of a lot more than they want the world to know."

"I can't believe you believe me."

"It's not so much a matter of believing *you*, it's putting the facts together and believing the story they tell—no matter what that story is. No matter if the story seems incredible on the face of it."

Holly buried her face in her hands as emotion welled up in her. For months she'd had no one she could confide in about her suspicions. No one she could share her worry with. She hadn't even told Peg. And this man, this *stranger*, was telling her she'd been right all along.

When she finally raised her face to his, her eyes were dry. She wasn't going to cry about this, not now. She'd cried enough tears over the McCays, almost as many tears as she'd cried over Grant's death. Her lips tightened. "That means I'm doing the right thing taking the boys and leaving town."

Chris shook his head. "I didn't tell them I located you. And I won't."

"But don't you see? Even if you don't tell them where I am, if they hired you they know I'm in this area. And the next PI they hire might not… What I mean is, not everyone will suspect their motives. Not everyone will believe the truth."

Chris stared thoughtfully, then nodded. "You're right.

But I can't let you run away again. Not knowing what I know. I'd never be able to forgive myself if…" He seemed to reach a decision. "I think the best thing would be for you and your boys to check out of this rooming house… but stay where I can keep an eye on you until we can set a trap for the McCays."

Holly shook her head vehemently. "I can't do that to you and your wife—put you in danger that way."

All expression was wiped from Chris's face in a heartbeat. "My wife is dead."

She gasped and covered her mouth with her hand. "I'm so sorry," she whispered eventually. "I didn't know. You said Peg's your sister-in-law, and since you and she don't have the same name, I assumed…" Her words trailed off miserably.

"Peg never mentioned her younger sister, Laura?" Holly shook her head again. "I guess I shouldn't be surprised," Chris said. "Peg and Laura were particularly close. She took Laura's death hard." He didn't say it, but Holly could see Peg wasn't the only one who'd taken Laura's death hard. But that closed-off expression also told her this wasn't a topic of conversation Chris wanted to pursue.

Is that why Peg bonded with me so quickly? Holly wondered abstractedly. *Because she saw in me the little sister she'd lost?*

"So you're not putting my wife in danger," Chris said, drawing her attention back to the here and now. "Most of my family is in some kind of law enforcement, too, and I can recruit them to help me set a trap for the McCays. Of course, everyone's focused on capturing the Alphabet Killer right now, so the McCays aren't going to be a top priority. Especially since there's no concrete evidence against them. In the meantime, though, I want you and your boys in safekeeping."

"Ian and Jamie aren't in danger," she was quick to point out. "Just me."

"Are you so sure?" Chris's eyes in that moment were the hardest, coldest blue eyes she'd ever seen. "If the McCays are willing to kill you to gain custody, who's to say they wouldn't eventually arrange 'accidents' for the boys, too, once they had them in their control?"

"Their own grandchildren? I can't believe—"

Chris cut her off. "Believe it. Once you've taken the first life, the next one is easier to justify in your mind. And the next." A bark of humorless laughter escaped him. "I should know. My father is Matthew Colton."

Holly's brows drew together in a frown. "I don't think I—"

"Matthew Colton, the original bull's-eye serial killer. He was infamous in his day. The Alphabet Killer is a copycat of sorts, marking her victims the way he did." His face hardened into a grim mask. "My father killed ten people twenty years ago. Including his last victim—my mother."

Chapter 3

"Oh, my God!"

Shock was obvious on Holly's face, followed quickly by the emotion Chris hated the most—pity. He'd had a bellyful of pity in his life—from the time he was eleven and became a quasi-orphan, right up through Laura's death almost two years ago. He didn't want pity and he didn't need it.

"My father killed nine men who reminded him of his hated brother, Big J Colton," he said brusquely, "before he killed my mother...whose only crime was that she loved him. So don't tell me the McCays couldn't possibly kill their innocent grandchildren."

"I...won't." The fear in Holly's eyes surprised Chris, because it wasn't fear of him. It wasn't even fear for herself as a target of the McCays. No, the fear was for her children. Then her face changed, and the fear morphed into fierce determination to protect her children at all costs, no matter what. If Chris had needed one more bit of proof Holly McCay was a good mother, he'd just received it.

"They're not getting anywhere near Ian and Jamie," Holly stated unequivocally. "What do you want me to do?"

He glanced away and thought for a moment, then nodded to himself. His eyes met Holly's. "I've got a house on the outskirts of Granite Gulch. No one lives there, but Peg looks after it for me, so it's not…abandoned." A wave of pain went through him and his right eye twitched as he remembered this was Laura's dream house, the one he'd built for her right before she died. The house she'd never had a chance to live in. The house he couldn't bear to occupy after her death. "It stands all by itself on several acres, and it's up on a ridge—you can easily spot someone coming almost a mile away. I can't think of a safer place for you and the boys to hide out."

"Just us?"

"And me. Until we can set a trap for the McCays, I don't want you out of my sight if I can help it."

"What about your job? You can't just—"

Chris's jaw set tightly. "I run my own business. I haven't taken a day off since Laura's funeral, so I think I can manage this. Besides, I do a lot of my work over the phone or on the computer. I can work from the office in the house. We designed the house—" *...with that in mind*, he started to say, but his throat closed before he could get the words out.

Holly didn't respond at first, just assessed him with an enigmatic expression on her face. The silence stretched from ten seconds to twenty, to thirty. Nearly a minute had passed before she said, "Okay. I appreciate the offer.

And I'll accept it on my children's behalf. If it was just me…that would be a different story, but it's not."

A half hour later everything Holly and the twins had with them was loaded into her SUV, with the exception of the two fold-a-cribs she'd bought when she moved to Rosewood. Chris stashed those in the back of his truck, and Holly realized if she'd taken Ian and Jamie and run, she would have had to leave the twins' cribs behind—they just wouldn't fit.

"I'll follow you to Peg's," Chris said as he raised the hatch and clicked it firmly closed. "But first, we'd better stop in town and get some groceries. The utilities at the house are on—so we'll have water and electricity—but there's no food."

Holly nodded. "Sounds good."

"And while I'm at it, I'd better stop off and pack a suitcase, and pick up my laptop from my apartment. I live above the Double G Cakes and Pies."

"Oh, I love that place!" she exclaimed. "Mia—the woman who runs it—she always gives Ian and Jamie special cookies she makes just for them."

Chris smiled. "Sounds like Mia. She and my sister Annabel are best friends—they were foster sisters together." His smile faded, replaced by the closed expression that was becoming familiar to Holly, and she knew instinctively this was another topic of conversation he'd never intended to bring up. Foster care joined the growing list of subjects to avoid…unless Chris brought it up himself.

As they drove the short distance to Granite Gulch, Holly wondered about Chris. About his motives for doing this—protecting her boys and her. She also couldn't help wondering about his wife, Laura, and what had happened to her. Car accident? Some kind of illness, like cancer?

Peg had never mentioned Laura that she could recall. But it wasn't just idle curiosity. She really wanted to know, because it was obvious Chris had been in love with his wife.

Holly glanced in the rearview mirror at the man in the truck behind her and sighed. If only Grant had loved her the way Chris had loved his wife. If only…

She couldn't help feeling a dart of envy comparing Chris to Grant. Not that Grant hadn't been a good man—he had been. So very different from his parents. No, the problem was that Grant had been her best friend growing up, and while he'd loved her, he hadn't been *in love* with her. Not the way she'd been in love with him.

She'd grieved for Grant. Those first few months after his death she'd been devastated…but she hadn't been able to grieve for long. The McCays had seen to that.

Was that why I recovered from Grant's death so quickly? she asked herself now. *Because Grant's parents tried to gain custody of Ian and Jamie and that took all my energy and concentration? Because when that didn't work they tried to have me killed, forcing me to take my babies and flee?*

The first time a car unexpectedly swerved into her lane on the expressway just as she was approaching an overpass, Holly had dismissed it as merely poor driving on someone's part. The second similar attempt only two weeks later had raised her suspicions, especially since she thought she recognized the car. But the third try on her life had been the clincher—someone had deliberately attempted to run her down in the grocery store parking lot, and she'd escaped with her life only by diving between two parked cars as the vehicle in question sped away without stopping.

Holly glanced in the rearview mirror again. *Or is the*

reason I'm not still grieving because Grant never loved me the way I wanted him to love me? The way I loved him.

She would never know. All she knew was that not quite a year after Grant's death she was ready to move on with her life…if the McCays would let her.

Holly buckled Ian into one car seat while Chris buckled Jamie into the other. She'd been surprised at first at how baby-knowledgeable Chris was, but she quickly realized she shouldn't be—Peg's kids adored their "Unca Chris," as Susan called him. Which meant even though she'd never met Chris at Peg's house in the three months the two women had been friends, he had to be a fairly frequent visitor.

Holly turned back to thank Peg just as the other woman came out of the house with a bag of dog food balanced on one hip, a bag of doggy treats perched precariously on top and a leashed Wally dancing joyously beside her.

"What the—" Chris began, but Peg cut him off.

"Holly's kids adore Wally, and he's attached to them, so that will help the kids acclimate faster. Besides, it won't hurt to have a guard dog out there, Chris. You know that. It's why you got Wally for Laura in the first place."

Chris's slow smile did something to Holly's heart. She wasn't sure what it meant, but she wouldn't have minded having that smile aimed at her.

"Thanks," Chris said, relieving Peg of the dog, the dog food and the doggy treats before planting a kiss on her cheek. "Come on, boy," he said, opening the door of his F-150 and letting Wally scramble up onto the front seat as Chris plopped the dog food on the floor.

Holly turned to Peg. "Thanks for watching the boys

for me," she said softly. "I wasn't going to leave without telling you—please believe that."

Peg smiled and hugged her. "I do." She stepped back and her smile faded. "But you can't run forever, Holly. I know it's not easy, but sometimes you just have to face up to the truth and take a stand. Chris's idea is better any way you look at it. You owe it to your boys to have the McCays put away so y'all can stop running."

"I know."

The two women embraced once more, and Peg whispered in her ear, "Chris needs to do this, Holly. I can't explain, but he needs to do this. So just let him take care of you and your boys."

Chris drove at a sedate pace—unlike his usual hell-bent-for-leather style—watching Holly's SUV in his rear-view mirror, making sure he didn't lose her. And as he drove he wondered about her. Not the facts and figures he'd uncovered in his investigation—he already knew far too much about her past, much more than most people would find out in a year of knowing her.

He knew where she'd grown up, what had happened to her parents, where she'd gone to college and where she'd worked after graduation. He knew she'd been a stay-at-home mom when her husband had been sideswiped on the I-45 in Houston, triggering a massive pileup that had killed three people…but not the drunk who'd instigated the accident—a driver who'd been using a revoked license, and who now resided in the state prison. He knew how much Holly had received from her husband's insurance, and he knew how much her twins had inherited from their father in the trust the McCays had told him about—just about the only truth in their pack of lies.

But he didn't care about all that. What he wanted to

know was what made her tick. She obviously loved her sons. Had she loved their father? His investigation hadn't uncovered any men in her life other than her now-deceased husband, which put her head and shoulders above most of the women he'd been hired to investigate. While the bulk of his work was doing background checks for a couple of major defense contractors in the Dallas–Fort Worth area, as well as extensive white-collar-crime investigation, no PI could completely avoid divorce work. Infidelities were profitable.

But the cases that eviscerated him were the noncustodial kidnappings. He'd had half a dozen of those cases in his career, three of which he'd taken pro bono, the same way he'd taken the McCays' case. What he wouldn't accept—could *never* accept—were people who deliberately separated children from the rest of their family for no real reason except selfishness. Not just parent and child, but also brothers and sisters.

His foster parents had done that. They'd deliberately isolated him from most of his siblings growing up. They hadn't been able to keep Chris away from his twin sister, Annabel—Granite Gulch had only one high school, and they'd had classes together from day one.

But his foster parents had done their best to keep them apart anyway—even grounding him on the slightest of pretexts and piling him with a heap of after-school chores in addition to his homework—but Annabel had needed him. And beneath his laid-back exterior, Chris had always been something of a white knight. His twin had come first…even if it meant being perpetually grounded.

Chris had managed to reconnect with the rest of his siblings once he was an adult—all except his baby sister, Josie—but he could never get back those growing-up years he'd spent without his four brothers. Without those close familial bonds brothers often formed. That could have made a difference in all their lives, especially given their tragic family history.

That was why he'd taken those pro bono cases in the first place, one of which had come early in his career, when he'd been struggling to make ends meet. But he couldn't turn down a case involving children. Which was why he'd almost fallen for the McCays' sob story. Which was also why he was taking on the toughest case of his career to date—protecting Holly, Ian and Jamie McCay.

"Four bedrooms, Holly," Chris said as he shifted Ian into his left arm and unlocked the front door, then keyed in the code to disengage the alarm system. "Take your pick. Let me know which one you want for the twins, and I'll set up their fold-a-cribs. One of the bedrooms is—"

He broke off for a heartbeat, then attempted to finish his sentence, but Holly said quickly, "I want them with me." She cuddled Jamie, who was starting to fret. "I know all the baby books say it's a bad idea, but ever since…well, ever since we left Clear Lake City, Ian and Jamie have stayed in the same room with me. First in the motels and then in the Rosewood Rooming House. I'm afraid they'll be scared if I try to change that tonight, especially since this is a new place to them and all." She smiled down at the toddler in her arms. "Yes, Jamie, I know you're hungry. Give Mommy a few minutes, please. Okay, sweetie?"

"If that's what works," Chris said, "then it'd probably be best if you took the master bedroom. It's a lot bigger than the others, more room for both cribs."

"But that's *your* bedroom," she protested. "I don't want to put you out of—"

Chris shook his head. "I've never lived here. Never

slept a night in that room. So you wouldn't be putting me out."

I did it again, Holly thought as that closed expression replaced Chris's smiling demeanor. She put Jamie down, and he clung to her leg. "I'm sorry." Her voice was quiet. "You're going out of your way to help us, and I…I keep saying the wrong thing."

Chris lowered Ian to the floor but kept a wary eye on him so the toddler didn't wander off. "Not your fault," he said gruffly. He herded Ian toward Holly with a gentle foot. "Why don't you give these two some lunch while I get everything unloaded? I'll bring in the groceries and the high chairs first."

Chris set up the fold-a-cribs in the master bedroom while Holly fed the twins. As he'd told Holly, the master bedroom held no memories for him, except…Laura had picked out the furniture. She'd picked out everything in the house…without him. Her dream house, she'd laughingly called it. But he'd been too busy to go with her, so she'd gone without him. She'd driven into Fort Worth with her sister, armed with the platinum credit card Chris had given her, and she'd furnished the house, room by room.

That was where she'd been exposed to viral meningitis. Somewhere in Fort Worth she'd come into contact with a carrier of the disease. Much later the Center for Disease Control had reported a mini outbreak of viral meningitis in Fort Worth—too late. Laura had never mentioned the subsequent symptoms she'd experienced to Chris—the severe headache, fever and neck stiffness—and he hadn't noticed. He'd been too busy to—

His cell phone rang abruptly, startling him out of his

sad reverie. "Chris Colton," he answered, recognizing the phone number.

The voice of one of the administrative assistants in his Fort Worth office sounded in his ear. "Chris? It's Teri. Angus McCay just called. He wants to know the status on his case. I told him you'd call him. Do you need the number?"

"No, I've got it, thanks. Oh, and, Teri, I'll send an email, but can you let everyone in all three offices know I won't be in for the next few days? Something personal has come up I need to take care of. They can reach me by phone or email if it's urgent. And if any other client calls come in, have Zach or Jimmy deal with them."

"Sure thing, Chris."

He sensed the question Teri wanted to ask but wouldn't. His staff knew not to ask because that's the kind of manager he was—he kept his personal life and his business life completely separate. Chris disconnected, then thumbed through his phone book until he found the listing for Angus McCay and picked the office number. The phone rang only twice before it was answered.

"Angus McCay."

"Chris Colton here. You called me?"

Angus McCay cleared his throat. "I know you told us you'd let us know if you found Holly, Mr. Colton, but… it's been a week and we haven't heard from you. My wife…well, she wanted me to call you and see if you've made any progress."

"Not to worry, Mr. McCay," Chris assured him, his mind working swiftly. "I tracked Holly to Grand Prairie, but she gave me the slip." He deliberately named Grand Prairie because Holly *had* stayed there…just not recently. And Grand Prairie was southeast of Fort Worth, nowhere near Granite Gulch. "I'm hot on her trail, though. I think she might have moved northeast to Irving." Another place Holly really had stayed…briefly. "Just sit tight, and I'll let you know as soon as I have something concrete."

"It's not just our grandchildren at stake, you know. They still haven't caught the Alphabet Killer and…well… you see how it is. Holly's name begins with *H*."

Yeah, Chris thought. *Keep beating that drum. How stupid do you take me for?* "I don't think you have to worry about that, Mr. McCay. Both Grand Prairie and Irving are closer to Dallas than to Fort Worth, and the Alphabet Killer isn't striking anywhere near there."

"Okay, well…just remember, if you find Holly, we don't want you to do anything to scare her off. Just let us know and we'll fly up from Houston immediately. If we can just see that the boys are okay…if we can just talk to Holly…"

"You bet," Chris told him. "I'll keep you posted. And don't worry, Mr. McCay. Holly won't slip through my fingers next time." He disconnected just as a sound from the doorway made him swing around. Holly stood there, white as a ghost, a twin balanced on each hip.

Chapter 4

"You…you said you believed me about the McCays," Holly managed, despite the way her heart was pounding so hard she could barely breathe.

Chris tucked his phone back in his pocket. "I do."

"Then why… What were you telling my father-in-law? It sounded like you—"

He cut her off. "Just throwing him off the scent, Holly. I had to tell him something, and part of the truth is better than an outright lie—I *did* track you to Grand Prairie… after I'd already located you in Rosewood. And I wasn't lying…you *did* move on to Irving after you left Grand Prairie. But you only stayed there two weeks, too."

"How do know that?" Her voice was barely above a whisper.

One corner of his mouth curved upward in a half smile. "I told you, I'm damned good at what I do. After Irving you moved to Mansfield, then Arlington. After

Arlington you stayed almost a month in Lake Worth before you moved here."

He walked toward her as he said this, and she backed away on trembling legs, clutching Ian and Jamie as if they were talismans. *I was so careful*, she thought feverishly. *How could he know all that?*

She hadn't realized she'd spoken aloud until Chris gave her an "are you kidding me?" look and said, "You make a lousy criminal, Holly. But that's a compliment, not an insult."

When Holly bumped into the hallway wall outside the bedroom doorway, she realized she was trapped. But all Chris did was take Ian from her, hefting him under one arm like a football and gently swinging him until Ian laughed at the game. "Time for your nap, bud," Chris told him. "You and your brother." His blue eyes met Holly's brown ones, and there was a gentleness in his face. An honesty she couldn't help but believe. "I'm not going to hurt you, Holly. Ever. And I'd never do anything to hurt your sons."

Holly was so mentally exhausted and emotionally drained that after she read the twins a story, sang them two songs and tucked them up in their cribs, she lay down on the bed, telling herself she'd rest for just a moment. Then she'd unpack their suitcases, wash the lunch dishes, put away the dry-goods groceries she and Chris had bought and decide what to make for dinner. But before she realized it, she was out like a light.

At first her dreams were of happier times, when the twins were newborns and Grant was there. He'd been so proud and nervous at the same time, like most new fathers. Then her dreams segued into nightmares, starting with the devastating news of Grant's death…the lawyers trying to probate Grant's will and the McCays attempting to contest it…followed swiftly by the McCays trying to seize custody of the twins, along with control of the trust Grant had set up for his sons. A dazed and bereft Holly had been forced to fight, not only for custody and to carry out Grant's last wishes but for her good name, too.

That time in her life had been a waking nightmare. She'd won the preliminary battles in the courts and thought she was finally on firm ground…until those three close calls. Any one of them could have been an accident, but three? After the last one, when she'd shown up at the McCays' house shaken and trembling to pick up the twins, she'd sensed the McCays' surprise…that she was still alive. And she'd known in that instant they were trying to kill her.

In the way of dreams, Holly suddenly found herself at the Rosewood Rooming House with Chris. He was holding her, but not the way he had in real life. This time his strong arms were surrounding her in comforting fashion as he pressed her head against the solid wall of his oh-so-warm chest and promised her she was safe. "I won't let them hurt you," he said, referring to her in-laws. "And I won't let them get custody of Ian and Jamie."

The sense of relief she felt was incredible, and all out of proportion to her real life. Holly didn't subscribe to the theory that a woman couldn't take care of herself, that she needed a man to look after her. She was a software engineer, for goodness' sake! She'd supported herself after her missionary parents had been killed in one of their trips to South America—leaving very little in the way of life insurance—and had put herself through college. After graduation she'd held down a challenging job for NASA at the Johnson Space Center in Clear Lake City, Texas, before she'd taken maternity leave when the twins were born. She didn't need "rescuing" from her life...as a general rule.

But that was before the McCays had tried to kill her. The situation she found herself in now was so totally outside her experience, so much like one of the thrillers Grant had loved to read but that Holly had always avoided, that she recognized she couldn't do it all on her own. Single mother? Check. Guardian of her children's financial future? Check. Putting attempted murderers behind bars? Not so much.

Maybe that was why when Chris had held Holly in the shelter of his arms in her dream and promised she and the boys were safe, she'd believed him...because she *wanted* to believe him. Because she *needed* to believe him.

Then he'd kissed her.

No one had ever kissed her that way, with an intensity that shattered everything she'd thought she knew about men and women. Chris's kiss exploded through her body, as if she were gunpowder and he were a lighted match. He was hard everywhere she was soft, and it made her want to get closer...impossibly closer. Her nipples tightened and her insides melted as Chris tilted her head back and his lips trailed down, down, to brush against the incredibly sensitive hollow of her throat. Then lower.

Holly moaned in her sleep and curled onto her side, pressing her legs together against the throbbing she felt there. And the dream suddenly vanished.

She woke to the mouthwatering aroma of baked chicken, Ian and Jamie's chorus of "Ma-ma-ma-ma-ma" as they stood and banged on the sides of their cribs to get her attention and the guilty memory of Chris's dream kiss. Not the kiss so much as her reaction to it, she acknowledged as a flush of warmth swept through her body. As if…

A tap on the door frame drew her attention, and there stood Chris in the doorway, almost as if she'd dreamed him into existence. Holly quickly hid her face with her hands and rubbed at her eyes, pretending she needed to wake up that way. She didn't—she just didn't want Chris to see her flaming cheeks.

"Dinner's ready" was all Chris said, and as he walked farther into the room, Holly scrambled off the bed. "I'll take Ian for you," he said, lifting the older of the twins—older by three minutes—out of his crib.

"How do you know that's Ian?" she asked, moving to grab Jamie. "They're identical. Most people can't tell the difference. Peg can, but it took her a week."

The intimate smile Chris gave her curled her toes. "Ian looks up when he sees me. Jamie looks away."

"That's it? That's how you can tell them apart?"

"Well…that and the fact that Ian's ears stick out just a little more than Jamie's, and Jamie's hair is just a shade lighter than Ian's."

Holly stopped short, glancing from the toddler in Chris's arms to the one in her own arms. "You're right," she said after a minute. "I never realized about the ears… but you're right."

"So how do you tell them apart? Motherly instinct?"

She adjusted Jamie to balance him against her hip and popped a kiss on his rosebud mouth. "I can't really tell you," she confessed. "I just know."

Chris nodded as if she'd given him the answer he expected. "Motherly instinct," he repeated, but this time it wasn't a question. He turned toward the doorway. "Come on, dinner will be getting cold."

"I was going to make dinner," she protested as she followed Chris into the kitchen, feeling guilty.

"You were fast asleep every time I came to check on you, and I didn't have the heart to wake you." Chris settled Ian in one of the two high chairs he'd pulled up beside the kitchen table and strapped him in. "Hang tight, buddy," he told the boy as Ian began banging on the tray and shouting, "Din-din-din-din-din!"

Jamie took up the chant as Holly got him settled. "Sorry," she told Chris over the boys' urgent demands. "I usually feed them a little earlier. I must have been more exhausted than I thought."

"Adrenaline will do that to you," Chris said as he grabbed two child-sized plates that were sitting in the microwave, added the baby cutlery she'd used at lunch from the rack on the drain board—*he must have washed the lunch dishes*, Holly realized with another little dart of guilt—and whisked the plates in front of Ian and Jamie. Baked chicken, cut into baby-sized bites, sat next to miniature mounds of mashed potatoes. Peas with a tiny dollop of melted butter rounded out the servings.

"Are you sure you're not a nanny in disguise?" Holly joked as the twins' eyes lit up and they dug in, soon making a mess out of feeding themselves. "How do you know—"

"Don't even *think* about finishing that sentence," Chris told her in a stern voice, but the twinkle in his eyes gave the lie to his tone. "I'm the second oldest of seven. That many kids in a family—you need a lot of hands to get all the work done. My twin sister, Annabel, and I used to help Mama with the younger kids, especially my baby sister, Josie."

He turned away to take the rest of the chicken out of the oven, but not before Holly saw a troubled expression slide over his face. *More land mines*, she warned herself. *He doesn't want to talk about his childhood.* That made sense given what he'd told her this morning—that his father was a notorious serial killer who'd killed Chris's mother, too.

She cast about in her mind for a safe topic of conversation as she filled a plate for herself from the chicken pan and the pots on the stove, and Chris filled Wally's bowl with fresh water. "I didn't realize you're a twin," she said as she seated herself at the table.

Chris started to respond, but Holly leaned over to Jamie, who was rolling his peas across his high-chair tray and then smashing them flat with the tip of one chubby pointer finger. "You're going to eat those, mister," she told him in a no-nonsense voice. "So you just peel them up and pop them into your mouth." She waited until Jamie obediently scooped up two peas and ate them before she glanced up at Chris. "Sorry. It's a constant battle with boys this young. They want to feed themselves, but… What were you going to say?"

"I was just about to say that yeah, I'm a twin myself. Not identical, of course, but there *is* an unbreakable bond."

"I've seen that with Ian and Jamie already."

"Not surprised. It starts early."

"What does your sister do? Is she a PI like you?"

Chris shook his head. "She's a cop." He hesitated. "My brothers and I—we didn't want that for her. I know it's chauvinistic in this day and age, but this is Texas. We wanted her to be safe, you know? I had a big argument about it with her. And—" he had the grace to look ashamed "—none of us except Sam attended her graduation from the police academy. She graduated top of her class, too." He took his plate and settled in a chair at the other end of the table.

They ate in silence for a minute, then Chris said roughly, "I know how it sounds, but we've already lost one sister. Josie. We don't want to lose the only one we have left."

Treading cautiously, Holly asked, "What happened to Josie?"

"No one knows. We haven't heard from her in six years." His brows drew together in a troubled frown. "And even before that she practically refused to have anything to do with us for years." He thought for a moment. "I guess she was about twelve when she told the social worker she didn't want us visiting her anymore."

"How old were you?"

"Twenty. The summer before my junior year in college." He sighed. "But even before that she… When Trevor turned eighteen—Trevor's the oldest, three years older than me—when he turned eighteen, he tried to get custody of Josie, take her out of foster care. But she refused. We figured it had something to do with her foster sister, Lizzie. They were particularly close. And Lizzie says they were both attached to their foster parents."

He sighed again. "I also tried to get custody when I turned eighteen and graduated from high school. I'd have passed on college if that's what it took—scholarship be damned. But I didn't have any more luck than Trevor." He looked down at his plate, forked a bite of chicken and swirled it in the mashed potatoes, then ate it.

Holly pried peas off Jamie's tray, piled them on his plate and tapped an imperious finger. "Eat those, mister." She glanced over at Ian to make sure he was eating what was set before him without difficulty, then looked up at Chris. "What happened then?"

"Even with the scholarship it wasn't easy, but I managed. I worked to put myself through school, and when I graduated, I came back here to Granite Gulch. Laura was waiting for me—we'd been engaged since my junior year in college—but I told her I needed to try one more time with Josie…who turned me down flat."

That hurt him. Chris didn't have to say it; Holly just knew. "Josie didn't say why?"

"Nope. Basically her message was 'Leave me alone.'" He paused. "I don't blame her in one way. She was only three when our father murdered our mother—I doubt she even remembers her or us as a family."

But you do, Holly thought. *You remember...and it hurts you to remember.*

"So it only makes sense she didn't want to have anything to do with her brothers and sisters—we're not her family anymore. Then six years ago…" Chris began, but when he stopped, Holly raised her eyebrows in a question, so he continued. "Josie ran away six years ago. At least that's the best we can figure. I've been searching for her off and on ever since."

Now Holly thought she understood what Peg had meant when she said Chris needed to do this, needed to shelter Holly and her boys from the McCays. Chris carried a load of guilt over his missing sister. *Probably some guilt over his mother, too.*

"You said there were seven of you, and that Trevor's the oldest. What does he do?"

"FBI profiler."

"Wow. Impressive."

Chris nodded, but Holly got the impression there were some unresolved issues between Chris and his older brother. *I wonder what that's about.* She wasn't going to ask, of course. But maybe he would volunteer something later on. "After Trevor it's you and Annabel, right? And Josie's the baby. Who else?"

"Ridge. He's two years younger than me."

"Unusual name."

Chris laughed. "It suits him. He's in search and rescue. He's big and bad and nobody messes with Ridge."

Kind of like you, Holly thought, but she kept it to herself. "And after Ridge?"

"Ethan. He's twenty-seven, and he is *intense*. He kind of keeps himself to himself, if you know what I mean." Holly nodded. "He's a rancher. His ranch is…oh, about ten miles from here. The isolation suits him, but he's going to have to get accustomed to having more people around—his wife, Lizzie, is expecting a baby any day now."

"Oh, that's nice. You'll be an uncle again." She counted up in her mind, then said, "One more. Another brother, right?"

"Yeah. Sam. He's a police detective, right here on the Granite Gulch police force, just like Annabel. He's twenty-five, and he just got engaged in January to the sweetest woman, Zoe. You'd like her."

"Wait. Zoe Robison? The librarian?"

Ian piped up, "Zo-ee, Zo-ee!" and Jamie copied him. Holly quickly looked over at her boys and realized they were pretty much done. They'd left a disaster that would need hosing down to clean up, but at least they'd managed to eat most of what was on their plates. What hadn't been eaten was now adorning them. She shuddered at the mashed potatoes Ian had massaged into his eyebrows.

"You know Zoe?" Chris asked.

Holly jumped up and grabbed the washcloth from the sink. "She runs the Mommy and Me reading program at the library," she explained as she wiped Jamie's hands and face, then did the same for Ian. "Ian and Jamie adore her, and yes, she's really sweet."

Chris waited until Jamie was clean, then he unstrapped the boy and lifted him out of the high chair, setting him on his feet. When Ian was ready, he got the same treatment.

"Leave this," Chris told Holly. "I'll clean up and put the dishes in the dishwasher."

"I should do it," she protested. "Ian and Jamie are the ones who made such a mess." She grimaced as she took in the condition of the floor, which had a few peas scattered beneath the high chairs—the ones Wally hadn't gobbled up—not to mention a couple of gooey globs that looked like mashed potatoes.

"You probably want to give the boys a bath before too long."

"You mean before they track the mess into the rest of the house?"

Chris grinned. "Yeah, that's exactly what I mean."

"You really don't mind cleaning up in here? I feel awful leaving this for you."

"Don't sweat it." He was already swiping a damp paper towel over the mashed potatoes and picking the remaining peas up off the floor as she spoke. Chris's cell phone rang at that moment, and he threw the peas into the garbage disposal before he checked the caller ID. "Annabel," he told Holly. "I should take this. Excuse me." He pressed a button. "Hey, Bella, what's up?"

He stiffened almost immediately, and Holly watched his lighthearted expression fade away as he listened to his sister on the other end. Two minutes passed, then three, before Chris said, "I'm sorry to hear it. What does Trevor say?" He made a sound of impatience, then nodded as if Annabel could see him. "Okay. I understand.

Besides Trevor and Sam, who else knows?" He listened for a minute, then said, "Nothing I can do, but thanks for letting me know. Watch yourself, okay?"

He disconnected but didn't put the phone away. He hit speed dial, waited a few seconds, then said, "Peg? It's Chris. Have you been watching the local news?" Apparently the answer was no, because he added, "Turn it on. Now. Annabel just called me. They found another body with the bull's-eye marking. Yeah, number eight—Helena Tucker."

Chapter 5

Chris hung up with Peg, then glanced at Holly. She was kneeling on the floor, an arm around each twin, clutching them tightly. "Sorry," Chris said, thinking she was trying to keep the boys from hearing his side of the conversation. "I forgot there were little ears around." The face Holly raised to his was ashen, and guilty. "What?" he asked.

"It's terrible," she whispered. "I should be praying for that poor woman. But all I could think about when I heard her name was that I could stop worrying."

Chris shook his head. "You didn't really think you were in danger, did you? Yeah, your name begins with *H*, but hell—" He caught himself up short, remembering too late his vow to watch his language. "Heck," he amended, "you don't have long dark hair. Your hair isn't even really dark—I have the pictures to prove it."

"I know. I wasn't *really* worried, but…fear isn't always logical. It was just there in the back of my mind, you know? And the newspaper reported that the woman who's suspected of being the Alphabet Killer—I forget her name—"

"Regina Willard."

"Right. She once stayed at the Rosewood Rooming House, same as me."

"I know." Chris suddenly thought of something. "Before I forget, I wanted to tell you there's no internet service here at the house yet. And no cable. Water, gas, electricity and phone—yeah. I couldn't turn the water off—unless I wanted to let the landscaping shrivel up and die. Not to mention Peg needs water when she comes out here to take care of the place. And electricity and phone service are necessary for the alarm system. But no cable or internet landline. I called to get them turned on when we were at Peg's, but it'll be a few days."

"That's okay," Holly informed him. "I haven't watched TV since I left Clear Lake City. And I only browse the internet at the library anyway, so it's not a hardship to do without. But what about you?"

"I can survive without cable for a few days. And I've got mobile internet access for my laptop and smartphone—I need it for my PI business. So, I'm good."

Ian and Jamie both squirmed to get free at that moment, and Chris said, "Better get them their baths. Go on," he insisted. "It won't take me more than a few minutes to clean up in here. Then I have some work to catch up on. I'll be in the office."

A half hour later Holly ruefully fished her dark pixie-cut wig out of the tub in the master bathroom, where Ian had dunked it after he tugged it off her head. She rolled the wig in a towel to dry it as much as she could, then hung it on a hook over the shower. "Laugh," she told Ian in a mock-threatening tone as she lifted him out of the tub and wrapped his wriggling body in a towel. "You just wait until you grow up. I'm going to take delight in embarrassing you by telling your friends all the things you did to me.

"No, Jamie, we don't eat soap," she said, changing subjects, quickly removing the bar of soap from his vicinity. She scooped him out of the tub and wrapped him in a towel, too. She played peekaboo with both boys and their towels for a couple of minutes, then gathered them close as intense motherly love for her babies washed through her. "You're little monsters—you know that—but I love you madly," she told them. "And I wouldn't trade you for anything in the world."

Clean, Ian and Jamie looked like little angels, their golden curls fluffed into tiny halos. Holly brushed their barely damp hair, ruthlessly suppressing the curls, before using the brush on her own head when she caught sight of herself in the mirror. She wasn't vain about her appearance—well, not much—but she didn't want anyone seeing her with her hair a flattened mess. She refused to acknowledge who she meant by "anyone," but in the back of her mind lurked the memory of her dream that afternoon. The dream, and the kiss. Not to mention her erotic reaction to it.

Holly let the twins run naked into the bedroom, dabbing futilely at the large, damp patch on her pale blue T-shirt where Jamie had—deliberately, she was sure—splashed her with soapy bathwater. Then she followed her sons into the other room.

She dressed them in the pull-ups they still wore at night because they weren't *quite* potty trained yet, then in their nightclothes. "Come on," she told them, taking their hands in hers. "Let's go say good-night to Mr. Colton. Pretend you're really as angelic as you look so he won't mind sharing a house with us."

Chris leaned back in his leather desk chair and absently fondled Wally's head as the dog lay quietly beside him. "Look at this, boy," he murmured. "You think...?" *This* was a news article on his laptop's computer screen—a story about the daring capture of a fugitive on the FBI's Ten Most Wanted list. A dangerous man who was an alleged associate of a drug lord who'd been dead for six years—Desmond Carlton. The name Carlton was enough like Colton for the story to have caught Chris's eye, and he shook his head at a vague memory. Then he picked up his smartphone and hit speed dial.

"Hi, Chris," Annabel said when she answered. "What's up?"

"Carlton," he said abruptly. "Wasn't that the last name of Josie's foster parents?"

"Um...I think so. Yes, it was. Why?"

"I was just reading something on *Yahoo News* about a man who ran with Desmond Carlton six years ago."

"The guy who was on the Ten Most Wanted list? The one the FBI just captured?"

"Yeah, him."

"Why is that important? Other than someone else will be promoted to the list tomorrow, now that he's in prison where he belongs, the creep."

"I don't know," Chris said slowly. "But as I was reading the story the name Carlton rang a bell. That, and the fact that Desmond Carlton has been dead for six years. Six years, Bella. Think about it."

"You don't mean... Josie? It's got to be a coincidence."

"I don't like coincidences. And I don't trust them. Especially two coincidences together." He thought a minute. "Do me a favor, will you? Find out what prison this guy is in. I might want to have a little chat with him."

Annabel's soft drawl took on a hard edge. "You don't want to ask Trevor? He's FBI. He could probably get in to see this perp whether or not he wants visitors." When Chris didn't respond, his sister said, "Are you still holding a grudge against Trevor? I thought you agreed it wasn't fair to him."

"Trevor's got enough on his plate right now," he pointed out, "what with trying to find Regina Willard. Especially now that she just added number eight to her victim list—the pressure to catch her has got to be intense."

"It's not just the FBI, you know," Annabel said drily. "The Granite Gulch Police Department is involved in this case, too."

Chris winced. His sister didn't say it, but it had been Annabel's solid police work that had identified Regina Willard as the Alphabet Killer. The woman hadn't been caught yet, though not for lack of trying on Annabel's part.

But the real reason Chris didn't want to ask for Trevor's help wasn't that his older brother was too busy—that had just been an excuse. Chris *was* still holding a grudge... but he wasn't going to admit it to Annabel. Okay, it was an old wound from his childhood that he should have gotten over long since—he knew that. The adult in him knew that. And yeah, it wasn't fair to Trevor—Annabel was right about that. And true, he and Trevor had finally reconnected years back...mostly.

But deep inside him resided that eleven-year-old boy who'd idolized his older brother, who'd felt betrayed when the family was split up and Trevor made no attempt to maintain the connection with him when they all went into foster care. Yeah, they'd seen each other a few times a year at the home of Josie's foster parents—court-mandated visits—but that wasn't the same thing at all. Chris had pretended it hadn't hurt…but it had. Badly. He was still trying to excise the scar tissue that had left on his psyche, but he wasn't there yet.

Then there was the whole Josie thing. When Trevor turned eighteen, he'd tried to get custody of Josie…or at least that was the story. But how hard had he tried, really? Chris didn't know, and the uncertainty of that ate at him. Josie would have been only seven back then. She'd turned Chris's offer down when *he* turned eighteen, but by that time it was already too late—she'd been ten, and had spent seven years with the Carltons. Maybe it was unreasonable, but Chris laid the blame for losing Josie squarely on Trevor's shoulders.

"But you're right," Annabel said, breaking into his thoughts. "Trevor's got enough to worry about. I'll see what I can find out."

"Thanks, Bella."

"No problem." Silence hummed between them, until Annabel said out of the blue, "I can't stop thinking about the day I saw her."

"Josie?"

"Mmm-hmm. I can't *swear* it was her, but—"

"But that gold charm you found clinches it," he finished for her.

"Yeah." She sighed. "Ridge and Lizzie believed it was her when they had their own Josie sightings."

"I know. At least she's alive. For the longest time I…" Chris's throat closed as he thought of how he'd imagined the worst. Young women disappeared all the time.

Murdered. Their bodies disposed of in the most callous ways. It had killed him to imagine that was Josie's fate.

Annabel seemed to understand Chris couldn't talk about it, and she changed the subject. "Speaking of sightings, Mia told me she spotted you coming out of your apartment this morning carrying a suitcase and your laptop bag. You taking a trip? Something to do with your work?"

Chris hesitated, then remembered his heart-to-heart conversation with Annabel last month and his promise that he would take her seriously as a police officer going forward. She'd earned that right and then some. "No," he told her. "Remember that missing-person case I mentioned the other day? The one I was taking pro bono?"

"The widow who ran off with her twin sons? The one the in-laws are trying to track down?"

"Yeah, her. Turns out I was way off base."

His sister snorted. "Told you there was more to the story."

"Don't rub it in." Chris massaged the furrow he could feel forming between his eyebrows. "Anyway, long story short, I found her. But she had a damned good reason for running—her in-laws tried to kill her."

Annabel gasped. "Are you kidding me?"

"Nope. She's been living in the Rosewood Rooming House with her boys for the past three months, but she was just about to run again." He took a deep breath. "So I convinced her it would be safer for the three of them to live in my house for the time being…with me."

"Your house? You mean the one you built for Laura?"

"Yeah. I couldn't let her run, Bella. I wasn't going to tell the in-laws I found her, but I couldn't let her run. If she did and the in-laws hired someone else…" He knew he didn't have to draw his twin a picture.

"So you're living there with her?"

"And her sons," he was quick to point out. "Just until we can set a trap for her in-laws."

"We?"

"I was thinking Sam, you and me. Unless you don't want to." He knew when he said it what Annabel's answer would be. Set a trap for would-be murderers? If they pulled it off, it would be another professional coup for his sister.

"Count me in."

Annabel's enthusiastic response made Chris smile to himself. "I haven't asked Sam," he told her, "so don't say anything to him yet, okay? This all just happened this morning."

"No problem. Just let me know when and where. So, what's her name?"

"Holly. Holly McCay. And her boys are Ian and Jamie."

"Cute names. What's she like?"

Chris smiled again. Knowing his sister, he'd known the question—or one very similar—was coming. "You'd like her. She's very down-to-earth. Very unassuming. And a good mother. You're not going to believe this, but Holly and Peg are friends," he said, knowing the message that would convey. "Other than Peg and me, you're the only one who knows where Holly is right now, and until we can prove anything against her in-laws, that's the way I want to keep it."

"Works for me. When do I get to meet her?"

Children's voices from the hallway outside his office alerted Chris that Holly and her boys were approaching, so he cut off his conversation with Annabel. "I'll let you know," he told her quickly and disconnected. He swung his chair around and stood up, but Wally was faster. The dog bounded across the room toward the hallway, tongue lolling out, tail wagging.

"Holly, I—" Chris began but stopped as if he'd been poleaxed when a blonde woman appeared in the doorway with Ian and Jamie. Long blond hair that owed nothing to artifice. Long blond hair that shimmered under the lights with a hundred different layered shades of gold. Long blond hair parted slightly off center, paired—unusually—with pale brown eyes. The eyes he'd seen before, but not with the blond hair. *Holy crap*, he thought as desire unexpectedly slashed through him, but all he said was, "What happened to the dark-haired wig?"

Holly laughed ruefully. "Ian thought it was funny to pull it off and dunk it in the tub."

He didn't mean to say it, but the words just popped out. "Your pictures don't do you justice."

She laughed again, but this time a slight tinge of color stained her cheeks. "Thank you… I think." She stood there for a minute staring at Chris as if caught in the same trance as he was, and her not-quite-steady breathing drew attention to her breasts rising and falling beneath her damp T-shirt. But when the twins tugged free of her hold to play with Wally, the spell—or whatever it was—was broken. "We came to tell you good-night," she explained, the color in her cheeks deepening.

"Oh. Right," Chris said, forcing his eyes away from Holly and down to the toddlers and the dog. Their well-scrubbed cherubic faces were misleading, he knew—if they were like most boys, Holly's twins were no angels. But they were all boy, just as Wally was all dog. Boys and dogs went together like…well…like boys and dogs. And Chris had a sudden memory of his younger brothers Ridge and Ethan—four and two to Chris's six—and his dog back then, Bouncer, a golden retriever, just like

Wally. It was a memory from his early years that didn't stab at his heart for once, a memory that made him smile for a change. He glanced at the clock on the wall and said, "Kind of early for bedtime, isn't it?"

"I start early," Holly explained. "I read them stories, then they get lullabies, and…" She smiled. "All of that can take an hour or more before they finally settle down and go to sleep."

He didn't know what made him make the offer, but he said, "How about I read them their bedtime stories?" When Holly looked doubtful, he added, "I'm a pretty good bedtime-story reader. Peg's daughter, Susan, would vouch for me if she was here."

Holly chuckled. "Okay," she agreed. "I wouldn't mind a few minutes to myself for a change. Let me get the books. We have a ton of library books—I was going to return them on my way out of town today," she rushed to explain, as if she didn't want him to think of her as a library thief. "And we have some books I bought for the boys. I let them pick the books they want me to read."

She was back in no time, carrying a stack of books that Chris quickly relieved her of. "Their favorites are on top," Holly told him. "But I usually just spread the books out and they choose based on the cover."

"Fly," Jamie said. "Want fly."

"A Fly Went By?" Chris asked him, juggling the stack until he found the Mike McClintock title three books down from the top. He handed it to Jamie, who hugged it.

"You remember that book?" Holly asked, surprised.

"Hell—heck, yeah," he amended. "That was one of Josie's favorites. I read it to her so many times I think I have it memorized."

"Me, too." Holly smiled at Chris, a somehow intimate smile, and something he hadn't felt in forever tugged at his heart. Holly's smile made him realize there was more to life than merely putting one foot in front of the other. More to life than the work he'd thrown himself into with even more dedication after Laura's death. Except for his relationship with Peg, Joe and their kids, except for his relationship with his sister and brothers, his life revolved around his work. Work that gave meaning to a life that held little else.

But Holly's smile reminded him he was a man, first and foremost. A man who hadn't made love to a woman in close to two years, who hadn't even given it serious thought in all that time.

He was thinking of it now, though. He was definitely thinking of it now. In spades.

Chapter 6

Holly escaped to her bedroom, her cheeks burning. The intently male look Chris had given her the moment before was branded into her memory. *He wants you*, she told herself as she quickly stripped and stepped into the shower. *Just as you want him.*

The hot water pummeled her body, which had become hypersensitized merely from that one look from Chris, and felt like a man's caress. Which was *crazy*! She didn't react to a sexy man that way. Yes, she'd been physically attracted to Grant—far more than he'd been physically attracted to her, since Grant had looked on Holly more as a sister than anything else—but she'd been in love with Grant. She couldn't have carnal urges like this for a man she'd just met that morning… Only, she did. *Don't lie to yourself, Holly*, she warned. *You want him. Admit it.*

"Okay," she muttered, soaping her body and rinsing

off quickly. "Okay, so I'm a normal woman with normal needs and it's been more than a year since I…"

Not just a year since she'd made love. It had been a lot longer than a year since a man had looked at her with that burning intensity in his eyes, his face. An expression that conveyed how unutterably desirable she was to him, and at the same time triggered those same needs in her.

Holly washed her hair just as quickly as she'd washed her body. *No one's* ever *looked at you like that*, she admitted to herself as she rinsed, and the memory made her nipples tighten into tiny buds that ached beneath the warm spray.

She wasn't afraid Chris would do anything she didn't want him to do…but that was the problem. She wanted him to do things to her she'd never imagined having a man do to her. And she wanted to do things to him she'd never believed in her heart women really wanted to do for men. And that was a *huge* problem.

She'd been nothing but Mommy for so long she'd thought she was immune to men. She'd thought wrong.

Chris knew Peg didn't allow her dogs on the furniture—not a dictum he would have made, but Wally wasn't really his dog, so he enforced the rule anyway. Since the twins wanted Wally close enough to pet while Chris read to them, he solved the dilemma by plopping down on the floor in his office with his back to the sofa. Wally lay across his legs and a boy sat on either side of him as he read. He'd finished *A Fly Went By* and had nearly reached the end of Dr. Seuss's *Green Eggs and Ham* when Holly returned.

Her long blond hair was damp and had been sleeked back away from a face that held not a vestige of makeup that he could see, not even lip gloss. But the minute she walked into the room the temperature rose to an uncomfortable level.

Holy crap, he thought as he read aloud the last two sentences, then closed the book and said, "The end."

He'd thought his sudden attraction to Holly had been nothing more than an aberration, the normal reaction of a man who'd gone too long without receiving an attractive woman's smile. He'd been way off base.

But there was something inherently…unsavory…about lusting after a woman when her eighteen-month-old sons were cuddled on either side of him, enthralled by his renditions of children's stories. So Chris tamped down his desire and smiled up at Holly without letting her see how much she affected him. "You're just in time," he told her. "We're done here."

Jamie scrambled to his feet, tripped over Wally's thumping tail and picked himself up again, patting Wally's backside as apology. "Sor-ry, Wally, sor-ry." Then he turned to his mother and demanded, "Ma-ma sing now."

"Later," she replied, bending over and picking him up, settling him against her hip. "Did you thank Mr. Colton for reading to you?"

Ian piped up, "Unca Cwis." He patted Chris's arm, and repeated, "Unca Cwis."

"Sorry," Chris said swiftly. "I told them to call me that. That's what Susan calls me, and I figured it was easier than saying 'Mr. Colton.'"

"Not a problem," Holly replied, then asked her boys, "Did you thank Uncle Chris?" A chorus of childish thank-yous followed her pointed question before she explained to Chris, "They don't have any real uncles. No aunts, either. Grant was an only child, and so was I." She sighed and added wistfully, "I always wanted a brother or a sister. So did Grant. I think that's one of the reasons we were such good friends growing up."

"You can have one of mine," Chris joked. "I've got plenty." He paused for a second. "Not Annabel. Not my twin. But you can have one of my brothers." He tilted his head to one side and thought about it for a moment, as if seriously considering his offer. "Not Sam, either. Or Ethan. They're too young—you don't want a younger brother. How about Ridge? He's twenty-nine, same age as you."

"Ridge, as in 'big and bad and nobody messes with Ridge'? That brother?"

"Yeah, him."

Holly shifted Jamie to her other hip. "I'm not sure I want a brother who will scare away all my dates," she teased, getting into the game. "I'll bet you heard that same line from Annabel. Am I right?"

Chris winced and held up both hands in mock surrender. "Guilty as charged," he admitted. "But it was for her own good. Honest. And I didn't scare away *all* her dates, just the ones who had something nefarious in mind."

"Mmm-hmm." She nodded. "I'll bet. What would Annabel say, though, if I asked her?"

He chuckled softly. "Funny you should ask me that. My sister just got engaged last month, so I guess I didn't scare them all away. Her engagement was kind of late in the game, though, especially since that's all my brothers and I wanted for her—that she find Mr. Right and settle down."

"Finding Mr. Right doesn't happen for all women." The suddenly serious way she said this made Chris wonder. "I should get these two down for the night. Come on, Ian. Say good-night to Mr.—to Uncle Chris, and let's go."

Ian patted Chris's arm to get his attention and in a plaintive tone asked, "Cawwy me?"

"Carry," Holly corrected automatically. "And you don't need to be carried, Ian. You're a big boy."

Before she could put Jamie down and make him walk, too, the same as Ian, Chris stood and swept Ian into his arms. Then he effortlessly lifted the toddler up onto his shoulder. "Hang on, buddy," he told Ian as the boy chortled with glee at being so high up.

"Me too, me too!" Jamie pleaded, holding his arms out to Chris, and Holly was so startled she almost dropped him. Jamie never voluntarily went to *anyone* other than her, so for him to want Chris to carry him was a shock.

"You don't have to," she protested in an undertone as Chris took Jamie from her arms.

"Fair's fair," Chris retorted, hefting Jamie onto his other shoulder. "Nobody wiggle," he told both boys. "And watch your heads as we go through the doorway."

Holly followed Chris through the hallway to the master bedroom, sighing a little at how easily he carried the twins. Ian and Jamie were off the charts for eighteen months, and it was getting harder and harder for her to carry one boy, much less two. But it wasn't just that. She also ruthlessly suppressed the little pang of motherly jealousy that her twins preferred Chris over her, even in something as simple as this. *If Chris was their father it would be different*, she reasoned. *I wouldn't be jealous. Would I?*

She wasn't quite sure, and that bothered her. She wanted so badly to be a good mother, wanted to raise strong, independent boys who would become strong, independent men. She didn't want to be one of those mothers who spoiled her children but kept them emotionally dependent on her, tied to her apron strings. *Not that you wear an apron*, she thought with a flash of humor. But that phrase perfectly described what she *didn't* want for her boys.

So this is a good thing for Ian and Jamie, she reasoned. A little masculine attention from a man she already knew would be a good role model…after knowing him for only a day. She stopped short at the realization that, yes, she'd known Chris for only a day. Not even an entire day at that.

Chris and the twins disappeared into the master bedroom, and she hurried after them. She was just in time to see Chris swing each boy down from his shoulders into his crib and was surprised he got them right. Jamie was in his crib, the one with baby pandas adorning the sheets, and Ian was in the crib with dolphins on the sheets. *He doesn't miss a thing*, she realized. *He notices...and he remembers.*

There was something very appealing in that revelation.

Chris had started down the hallway back to his office when he heard a warm, sweet contralto voice coming from the master bedroom, singing a lullaby he recognized with a sense of shock. And though he told himself not to, that he had no business intruding on Holly's private time with her children, he was drawn back to the doorway.

The room was dark, but the light was on in the master bathroom and the door was cracked open—a makeshift night-light for the twins. Chris could make out Wally's shape on the floor—the twins had begged to be allowed to have Wally sleep with them, and Chris hadn't been able to refuse. Neither had Holly. So Chris had used a folded-up blanket as a dog bed for Wally and had placed it meticulously equidistant between the two cribs.

But he wasn't really looking at the dog. And he wasn't really looking at the twins. All he really had eyes for was Holly, her back to him as she sang the haunting cowboy ballad he knew as "Utah Carl."

Chris closed his eyes, and in his mind he was four years old, listening to his mother, Saralee, singing that very same song to a two-year-old Ridge as she rocked him to sleep. She'd been almost nine months pregnant at the time—*that would have been Ethan*, he realized now—but despite her financial worries and her constant pregnancies, his mother had never let her children know her life was hard. The love she'd felt for each and all of them had shielded them from the knowledge of the trials she faced on a daily basis, not the least of which was loving Matthew Colton and standing by him through thick and thin.

There hadn't been a lot of money in the Colton household, but none of the children had known it at the time. There had always been enough money for the important things—school clothes, books, birthdays and Christmases. And Saralee had made sure all her children knew they were loved, from Trevor right down to baby Josie.

The ballad came to an end, but Holly barely skipped a beat, moving right into another song Chris also remembered from his childhood. A desolate ache for that long-ago time and for the mother he still mourned ripped through him, and his face contracted in pain. His eyes were damp when the song ended, and he quickly rubbed his fingers over his eyelids to remove that betraying moisture.

Then, before Holly could start another song, he slipped noiselessly away from the doorway. He went into his office and shut the door behind him. Firmly. As if he could shut the door on his memories the same way.

* * *

It was almost midnight and the house was shrouded in darkness when Holly turned over restlessly in bed. Ian and Jamie were fast asleep—she could hear their rhythmic breathing—and she envied them. If only she could sleep with that same innocent abandon. If only she could sleep believing all was right with the world.

"Shouldn't have had that nap this afternoon," she whispered to herself, although she knew it was a lie. It wasn't the nap preventing her from sleeping, it was her conscience.

Holly's missionary parents had raised her to know right from wrong. And to believe that actions have consequences. Which meant that sometimes—like now—her conscience uncomfortably reminded her that if she hadn't done what she'd done…maybe things would have been different. Maybe she wouldn't be running for her life.

Grant's death wasn't her fault. No way was she responsible for that. But the McCays? If she'd never gotten pregnant, if she'd never married Grant, then the McCays would have inherited Grant's wealth when he died, and they would have no reason to want her out of the picture.

"That's stupid," she told herself sternly. "You're not responsible because they're so mercenary they're willing to kill to get you out of the way."

But…

Friends to lovers was a popular theme in romance novels, but it didn't always work out that way in real life. Best friends Holly and Grant had attended the University of Texas at Austin together and had both earned software engineering degrees. Then Holly had landed that plum job at NASA, while Grant—always more adventuresome than she—went out on his own, starting his own software company.

They'd seen each other often, at least once a week. Holly had known about the women Grant was dating but had consoled herself that as long as he was playing the field she didn't really have to worry he was getting serious about any one woman, the same way he'd been in high school and college. And she'd done everything she could to remain a key part of his life.

One mistake on Grant's part on a night when he'd had too much to drink, and Holly had soon discovered to her secret joy she was pregnant. Grant had done the honorable thing and proposed when she'd told him. After all, he'd reasoned, they'd been best friends forever, so what better basis for a strong marriage? Especially since they'd eventually learned Holly was expecting not one but two babies.

I should have known better, Holly told herself now. Loving Grant secretly the way she had, she'd agreed to his proposal, hoping their babies would bring them together. Hoping that someday he'd realize he loved her, too, the way she loved him.

It hadn't happened. And while they'd both loved Ian and Jamie, their marriage had been…shaky…threatening to destroy their lifelong friendship. *My fault*, she acknowledged now. *I thought I could make Grant love me. But you can't* make *someone love you. Either they do, or they don't.*

Grant's breakthrough software design had hit the market at just the right time, and suddenly his company was raking in millions when Holly took a maternity leave of absence from her job. Holly had intended to return to work when the twins were three months old, but found she just couldn't leave them when the time came. And since Grant had certainly been able to afford it, Grant and Holly had decided she would be a stay-at-home mom until the boys were older.

Then Grant was killed in a car crash when the twins were six months old, leaving Holly mourning what had never come to be, and now never would.

Grant had left Holly comfortably well-off but had left the bulk of his estate in a trust for his sons—something Holly had known about and approved of when they'd both made their wills a month after the babies were born. No provision had been made for Grant's parents, who had first fought the will, then fought to gain custody of the twins from Holly so they could get their hands on the income from the trust. But Holly's in-laws hadn't been willing to wait for the court's final ruling…

Holly sighed and turned over again. Rehashing old history in her mind was no way to fall asleep. She could never resolve the past. Couldn't change it, either. She just had to live with it, accept that she'd made mistakes and move on.

But thinking about moving on was dangerous, too, especially when the man she was interested in moving on with was Chris Colton. *So much emotional baggage*, Holly thought. *Holy cow, I thought* my *past was troubled.*

She started listing all the reasons getting involved with Chris was a bad, bad idea, but soon gave up…because she didn't care. Because the reasons *for* getting involved with him far outweighed the reasons not to, starting with the way he was with her boys. Not to mention the way he'd looked at her when he'd seen her without the wig for the first time…and her reaction.

Holly sighed again as she saw him in her mind's eye—so tall and impressively male, with muscles that rippled beneath the black T-shirt that fit him like a glove, the same way his jeans did. "Not helping," she muttered.

After ten more sleepless minutes she gave up. She tossed off the covers and rose from the bed, wrapped her robe around her and belted it tightly, then crept barefoot out of the bedroom and headed quietly for the kitchen. She'd tossed a box of her favorite herbal tea with oranges and lemons in their shopping cart this morning, and if that didn't help her sleep nothing would.

The tea bags and a mug were easy to find. Holly thought she might have to boil water in a pot—she didn't care for microwaved tea—but when she looked for a pot in the cabinet beside the stove, there was a brand-new teakettle. As she filled it with water and put it on the stove to boil, she couldn't help wondering about this house furnished with everything anyone could reasonably want… standing vacant. Uninhabited. Chris had told her Peg looked after it for him, so she wasn't surprised everything was spotless—as if the house's loving owners had merely stepped out and would return momentarily.

But it wasn't just that the house was well tended. Someone *had* loved this house once, even if Chris had never lived here. And it didn't take a genius to figure out that someone had to be Chris's deceased wife, Laura. But if Chris had never lived here, that meant Laura probably hadn't, either. And Holly's heart ached for the woman she never knew, the woman who had put so much time and effort into creating a home for the man she loved… and then died. A home her husband couldn't bear to live in without her…but couldn't bear to get rid of, either, because it had been *hers*.

Tears sprang to Holly's eyes as empathy and a kind of envy converged in her heart. *What would it be like to be loved that much?* she wondered with bittersweet intensity. And she knew in that instant she would sacrifice anything except Ian and Jamie to be loved like that.

The teakettle chose that moment to start whistling, and Holly dashed the tears from her eyes. Then she turned the flame off, grabbed a pot holder and poured hot water over the tea bag in her mug.

A deep voice from the doorway said, “Holly?” and she whirled around, almost dropping the teakettle in startled panic.

Chapter 7

Chris hadn't been to bed yet. After he'd left Holly singing her sons to sleep, he'd tried to do some work, but the memories evoked by Holly's lullabies were too sharp, too poignant. Though he tried to focus, his mind kept sliding back to his childhood. To his mother, of course. But also to his father.

Saralee had been a near-perfect mother, but Matthew hadn't been a bad father. Stern. Harsh on occasion. Busy, as a man would be trying to support such a large family on what a handyman could earn, and trying to keep the ramshackle Colton farmhouse from falling to pieces around them. But…he'd taken Chris fishing sometimes, had taught him how to ride a bike. Had even taught him how to handle a rifle and a shotgun and not blow his own damn fool head off.

Chris would also never forget the day he'd turned six and Matthew had given him the best birthday present a boy could ever have—his golden retriever, Bouncer. Chris hadn't known then that Bouncer was the partial payoff Matthew had received for a job he'd done for a rancher who couldn't pay him in cash. Chris also hadn't known money was so tight for the Coltons that year that Saralee had despaired of where the money would come from for birthday presents for Chris and Annabel. All Chris knew back then was that Bouncer was *his*, and he'd loved that dog almost as much as he'd loved Saralee and Annabel. Almost as much as he'd loved Trevor.

Bouncer had been his constant companion for more than five years. Losing his dog had cut a gaping hole in Chris's heart. If he'd had Bouncer, the other losses—his mother, his father, his brothers and sisters—wouldn't have hit him so hard. But the foster parents who'd taken Chris into their home for the money the state paid them weren't willing to take on a dog as well—not without compensation. Bouncer had been sent to an animal shelter…and euthanized.

The boy he'd been had never recovered.

Now Chris stood in the kitchen, staring at the woman who'd opened the door to so many painful memories from his past he almost resented her for it. But then he realized she wasn't to blame—it wasn't her fault his father was a serial killer, had made Chris's mother his last victim and set in motion a chain of events no one could have predicted. And he couldn't blame Holly for being a good mother to her sons, either, for singing the bedtime songs Saralee had sung to her own children more than twenty years ago.

No, the only one to blame in all of this was Matthew Colton…whose murderous blood ran in Chris's veins.

"Sorry," he told Holly. "I didn't mean to startle you."

She shook her head. "You don't have to apologize. It's

my own fault—I shouldn't be so jumpy. It's just that I wasn't paying attention, because I was thinking about—" She stopped abruptly.

"Thinking about the McCays?"

She shook her head again, then turned and put the teakettle down. "No. I was thinking about this house. About..." She hesitated. "About Laura. About how much you must have loved her. And I was thinking I would give anything to be loved that much."

Chris moved into the room until he stood right in front of Holly, staring down at her. So clean and wholesome. So sweet and desirable. "Yes, I loved Laura... but not enough," he said roughly. Holly's face took on a questioning mien, but all he said was "You don't want to know, Holly. But don't have any illusions about me. Laura wasn't a saint, but she was far and away too good for the likes of me."

The ache in Chris's heart grew until it threatened to overwhelm him. The urge to touch Holly, to kiss her, to lose himself in her arms was so great he almost did just that. And something in her soft brown eyes—a yearning empathy—told him she wouldn't stop him if he *did* try to kiss her. But if he touched her, it wouldn't end with kisses. It wouldn't end until he'd disillusioned her, until he'd proved to her she'd been wrong to trust him. Because he *would* hurt her...just as he'd hurt Laura. Not physically—he would never do that—but emotionally. And hurting Holly...hurting *any* woman ever again... would destroy him.

He took a step backward, putting distance between himself and temptation. "Don't look at me like that. And for God's sake, don't pity me." It hadn't been pity he'd seen in her eyes, but...

"Not pity," she told him quietly. "You're wrong if you

think that. And you're wrong if you think anything your father did is a reflection on you, or that you could turn out like him," she added, unerringly going right to the heart of Chris's deepest fear. "Grant was a wonderful man—*nothing* like his parents. Should I not have loved Grant because his parents are the way they are?" Her voice dropped a notch. "Ian and Jamie are McCays, too. Should I blame them because their grandparents tried to kill me?"

Holly turned around and picked up her mug. She fished the tea bag out of it with a spoon, threw the tea bag in the trash, then turned back to Chris. "Think about it," she said. "Good night, Chris."

Chris stared at the doorway through which Holly had disappeared as he acknowledged she was right—his father's sins were his alone. Chris didn't need to atone for them. Just because a killer's blood ran through his veins didn't mean he was a killer. Chris had always known that deep down, but…but what? He'd let society's scorn for a serial killer's son color his perception of himself? He'd let the people of his hometown judge him for actions not his own?

Saralee's blood also ran through his veins, and she'd never hurt anyone. The people of Granite Gulch hadn't focused on that, though, just on what Matthew had done, and all the Colton children had paid the price to a greater or lesser extent. But Chris wasn't Saralee any more than he was Matthew. He was his own person. His character had been forged by the life he'd lived, and the sense of right and wrong his mother had inculcated in him.

A few people in Granite Gulch outside his family had seen beyond the stigma he'd carried. Laura and Peg, of course. Peg's husband, Joe, who'd been Chris's best friend in high school. And when Chris had escaped Granite Gulch, when he'd gone to college in Arlington, no one had known who he was. No one had judged him except by his own actions. It had been a refreshing change, so refreshing he'd been tempted not to return to Granite Gulch after graduation.

But Laura had persuaded him to come back. Laura hadn't wanted to move to Fort Worth, even though that was where Chris had started his PI business, using connections he'd made in college. Laura had wanted to stay in Granite Gulch, near her parents and her sister. And because he'd loved her, Chris had compromised. He and Laura had lived in Granite Gulch and he'd commuted the forty miles each way to and from Fort Worth. But there'd been a price to pay for that compromise, a price Laura had increasingly resented. She'd never voiced that resentment to Chris…but deep down he'd known. He just hadn't been able to—

Chris stopped himself. He wasn't going there. Not tonight. Too many painful memories had already been dragged out into the light from the dark place Chris had stored them, and it was after midnight. He was going to have enough trouble sleeping without adding any more.

Holly woke to the smell of frying bacon. She hadn't had bacon in forever—it wasn't all that healthy for you, especially the kind sold in the United States—but she hadn't stopped Chris when he'd added a package to their grocery cart yesterday, because she secretly loved it. Bacon, eggs, toast and grits had been a Sunday-morning staple in her home growing up.

She glanced at the clock and realized it was early, just past six, which was why Ian and Jamie hadn't been what woke her up. If Holly slept past seven, the twins invariably woke her by banging on the sides of their cribs and calling "Ma-ma-ma-ma-ma!"

She dressed swiftly, brushed her teeth and washed her face, then decided to dispense with the wig. She wasn't planning to go anywhere, and besides, Chris had seen her without it. *And liked what he saw,* said a little voice in her head she tried to ignore.

Holly checked that the twins were still soundly sleeping before she headed for the kitchen, where she knew she'd find Chris. She'd thought about him last night as she'd drunk her tea, replaying that scene in the kitchen in her mind. Each time she'd thought of something different to say to him. Each time she'd wished she hadn't made it so obvious she was attracted to him. *But he was attracted to you, too,* her secret self reminded her now. And that gave her courage to face him without the shield of her twins.

"Good morning," she said as she walked into the sunny kitchen and saw the table set for two adults, with the two high chairs also set up.

Chris turned around from the stove. "Morning." He brought his attention back to his task and stirred something in a pot. "I should have asked you yesterday, but what do Ian and Jamie have for breakfast? I've got oatmeal here, do they eat that?"

Holly laughed. "They eat anything I'll let them eat, but they love oatmeal with a little milk."

"No sugar?"

She shook her head. "I'm trying to keep them from getting my sweet tooth," she confessed. "So no added sugar, no processed cereal except plain Cheerios."

"Good for you." He turned the stove off. "How do you feel about bacon and eggs?"

"I love them." She grimaced. "I shouldn't, I know. Nitrites and cholesterol."

Chris shook his head, his lips quirking into a grin as

he leaned one jeans-clad hip against the counter. "Guess you haven't read the latest studies. The cholesterol in eggs is the good kind of cholesterol, not the bad. As for nitrites in bacon being bad for you, that myth has been debunked. The vast majority of the scientific studies suggest that not only are nitrates and nitrites not bad for you, but they may even be beneficial to your health."

"Really?" Holly could hardly believe it.

"Yeah. Doesn't mean you should eat them every day, but a couple times a week won't hurt you." He took a carton of eggs out of the fridge as he said this. "Bacon's already cooked—it's in the oven keeping warm. So how do you like your eggs?"

"I prefer them over easy, but salmonella is an issue." Her eyes sought his. "Or am I wrong about that, too?"

"No, it's a concern. I'm like you—I prefer them over easy, but I fry them hard for that reason."

"Then fry mine hard, too."

Chris's smile deepened, and all at once Holly couldn't breathe. She couldn't tear her eyes away from his face, either. Just like last night, sexual attraction tugged at her. Chris was so uncompromisingly *male* standing there in jeans and a white T-shirt, with a day's scruff on his chin—he practically oozed testosterone. And yet, he was comfortable in his masculinity. He didn't need to thump his chest in the "me Tarzan, you Jane" approach so many men thought made them seem more macho. There was something particularly appealing about a Texan who didn't think cooking was women's work. Who didn't look on child rearing as women's work, too.

But it wasn't just that. What Holly couldn't reconcile in her mind was her reaction to him on a sexual level. Just like last night, he made her think of things she had no business thinking about. Of cool sheets and hot kisses. Very hot kisses.

A plaintive wail floated into the kitchen, breaking the spell. “That’s Jamie,” she managed from a throat that had gone uncustomarily dry.

“I’ll get breakfast on the table,” Chris told her, turning back to the stove. “You go take care of your boys.”

Evalinda McCay folded her lips together and stared at her husband over the breakfast table. “I don’t like it, Angus.”

“I told you what Mr. Colton said.”

“Yes, but I don’t like it. When we spoke with him last week, he didn’t think it would take very long. Now it sounds as if he’s not even *trying* to find Holly.”

“It’s not as if we’re paying him by the hour, Eva,” Angus McCay was quick to point out as he swallowed the last of his coffee. “He’s not even charging us at all, except for expenses, so what’s the complaint? Besides,” he said, “*you* were the one who was so sure he was the perfect PI for the job, what with his father being a serial killer. And he didn’t seem all that smart to me—he bought the story we told him.”

“Maybe,” Evalinda McCay said. “But now that I think of it, I wish we hadn’t mentioned the Alphabet Killer angle. Too far-fetched. That might have made him suspicious.”

“I don’t think so. If Mr. Colton believes the idea that Holly was ever in danger from the Alphabet Killer is ludicrous, I’m sure he’d chalk it down to us being loving in-laws, overly concerned about Holly’s safety.” He cleared his throat. “Either way, it’s no longer a concern now that the Alphabet Killer’s eighth victim has been found—Helena what’s-her-name.”

"That's good," Evalinda McCay said. "Just be sure you don't mention anything about the Alphabet Killer the next time you talk to Mr. Colton."

"Yes, dear. Of course." Angus McCay winced inwardly. He wasn't about to tell his wife he'd brought up the Alphabet Killer only the day before, when he'd discussed the progress in the investigation with Chris Colton. It wasn't important, and she didn't need to know.

He wiped his mouth on his napkin and rose from the table. "I'd better be getting to the bank. I'll call you if I hear from Mr. Colton."

Chris put out two fires at work via phone and made a judgment call to trim the bill on the case of a man who'd been desperately searching for his teenage daughter—*it'll barely cover expenses*, his office manager had protested, but the man had cried when his daughter had finally been located. *It's not always about money*, Chris thought as he dashed off an email to his office manager. Business was booming, especially since so many companies were implementing preemployment background checks on their new hires, and employing firms like Chris's to do the work rather than relying on in-house human resource departments. He could afford to take the hit financially. He could still remember the way the man had wrung his hands when Chris had escorted the onetime runaway through her father's front door. Could still see the heartfelt tears in the man's eyes.

Happy endings didn't always happen in his line of work. The joy on that father's face when he was reunited with his missing daughter was priceless.

Chris rose and stretched, then moved to the other end of his L-shaped office, to the window there. He stared out into the fenced yard, where Holly, her twins and Wally were playing Wiffle ball. The twins were—understandably—not very good yet. But Wally chased down every ball that got past the boys and herded it back to them or carried it back in his mouth. Then, his tail wagging cheerfully, did it again and again.

Chris smiled, remembering playing ball with his younger brothers and Bouncer the same way. For the first time in a long time, thinking about Bouncer didn't hurt. "I must have been eight," he thought out loud. "Yeah, because Sam was about two, which meant Ridge was six and Ethan four." Stair steps, his father had dubbed them. "Stair steps," he whispered now, wondering how he'd forgotten that nickname. Trevor had been three years older, and somehow hadn't been included—only Chris, Ridge, Ethan and Sam. Annabel hadn't counted in his father's eyes; neither had a soon-to-be-born Josie.

Thinking of his father reminded Chris that this was his month to visit Matthew Colton in prison. His month to obtain the next clue to his mother's resting place. He didn't want to go. Unlike his brother Trevor, an FBI profiler who'd visited their father in prison regularly as part of his job, Chris had never gone, despite Matthew's requests some years back. From the time Matthew had been arrested for murder twenty years ago, from the time a trembling and tearful seven-year-old Ethan had confessed to an eleven-year-old Chris how he'd found their mother lying in her own blood, he'd had no desire to see his father ever again. But he couldn't *not* go. Not when everyone was counting on him for that next clue.

Chapter 8

Fifteen minutes passed before Chris went back to his laptop. Fifteen minutes spent watching Holly, the twins and Wally, torn between getting back to work and going out to join in the innocent play. But then he remembered that moment in the kitchen this morning with Holly, and the similar instances last night, and he told himself discretion was the better part of valor. The more time he spent in her company, the more he would want her. The more he wanted her, the more difficult it would be not to touch, not to taste. Not to run his fingers through the spun gold that was her hair and drown in those soft brown eyes. Not to carry her to his bed that had been empty and lonely for so long.

Just thinking about doing those things to Holly made him hard. Made him ache the way he hadn't ached for a woman since Laura. Not just an ache. More like a hunger, really. And he wondered about that. What was it about Holly that pierced the iron shell he'd built around his body…not to mention his heart?

It wasn't just that she was a good mother, as his mother had been, although that played into it, sure. And it wasn't just that she was quietly lovely in a wholesome, All-American, girl-next-door way, although that was part of it, too. At first he couldn't figure it out. Then it hit him. Holly trusted him. What had she said late last night? *You're wrong if you think anything your father did is a reflection on you, or that you could turn out like him…*

Very few women who knew about Chris's serial-killer father had ever looked beyond that fact enough to trust him. Really trust him. Laura had. Peg, too. And now Holly. Somehow she'd sensed that he didn't have it in him to kill as his father had killed. That whatever had been missing in Matthew wasn't missing in his son. She'd known Chris just a little over a day, and yet she trusted him with herself and her sons. Implicitly.

Which was another reason to keep his distance from Holly. Because even if she trusted him, he didn't trust himself.

When Chris finally dragged himself away from the window, he sat down and began Googling for more information related to the article he'd read last night on Yahoo, the one he'd discussed with Annabel. As he'd told his sister, he didn't believe in coincidences. Six years ago Josie had disappeared. At first everyone thought she'd run away because her boyfriend had dumped her. Then there'd been that period of time when Chris had feared Josie had been murdered, her body hidden in a remote location. But after the supposed sightings of Josie, he'd reverted back to thinking she'd run away for some reason. But what if she hadn't just run away? Could her disappearance have anything to do with the death of the drug lord with the same last name as her foster parents?

But the more he dug, the more questions he had… because he couldn't find *anything* on the death of Desmond Carlton. Not a single story. Not even a reference to Desmond Carlton in a related story *before* his death six years ago. The only mention of the man Chris could find anywhere was in the article from the day before.

That could mean only one thing. Someone—or a group of someones—had gone to a lot of trouble to erase Desmond Carlton's existence.

Chris picked up his smartphone and hit speed dial. "Brad?" he said when a voice answered. "It's Chris. I need you to run a trace for me. And this one's not going to be easy. I need you to track down any references you can find to a Desmond Carlton." He spelled the name carefully. "Or to a couple who may be related, Roy and Rhonda Carlton… Yeah, same last name. All I know about Desmond Carlton is he was a drug lord who was killed six years ago. As for Roy and Rhonda, they used to be foster parents, so there's got to be some kind of record of them with the state—criminal background checks, home inspections, the works. Oh, yeah, and they died in a car crash about five years ago."

He listened for a minute, then said, "No, there's no case to charge this to, but I'll clear it with payroll. Oh, and, Brad, when I said this one wasn't going to be easy, I meant it. You're not going to find anything on Desmond Carlton on the internet—I already looked. You're going to have to hit the main libraries in Fort Worth and Dallas, see if you can turn something up the old-fashioned way. And if that doesn't work, try the offices of the *Star-Telegram* or the *Morning News*. I'm betting there will be articles in their morgues," he said, referring to the newspapers' private archives.

He listened for another minute, then laughed. "Yeah, that's why I called you. The younger guys wouldn't even know where to begin if they couldn't Google the name." His laugh trailed away. "Call me the minute you find out anything. And, Brad? Watch yourself, okay?…No, no, this isn't like the Winthrop case. But no one knows I'm looking for this info. Someone whitewashed the search engines, and until I know why…Yeah, exactly. Thanks, Brad."

Chris disconnected. His fingers flew over his laptop's keyboard and he pulled up the article he'd been reading the night before. He quickly skimmed through it again, noted the originating newspaper was the *Dallas Morning News* and jotted down the byline. "The guy must have dug deep to get as much as he got," he murmured to himself. "Good thing I told Brad to check those newspaper morgues—I'll bet a dollar to a doughnut that's where this guy found the link."

He thumbed through his smartphone's contacts until he found the number he wanted and hit the dial key. It rang three times before it was answered.

"Hey, Taylor, Chris Colton here…Yeah, long time." He shot the breeze with his old college buddy for a few minutes, then said, "I need to talk with one of your fellow reporters…No," he added drily at a question from the other end. "No, I'm not planning to give a scoop to a rival—any scoops I have go to you, you know that." Chris rolled his eyes, glad Taylor couldn't see him. "I just need to ask a few questions about an article this guy wrote, so I need his direct line." He gave Taylor the reporter's name and jotted down the phone number he was given. "Thanks, Taylor, I owe you one."

Never one to let grass grow under his feet, Chris had no sooner hung up than he was dialing the new number. But all he got was the reporter's voice mail. He thought about it for a few seconds, and before the recorded message finished Chris decided not to leave a callback number and disconnected.

He drummed his fingers on his desk for a moment, then called Taylor back. "Hey, buddy, it's Chris again. I need another favor. Can you set up a one-on-one for me with your colleague?…Yeah, him. ASAP." After a few seconds he said, "No, nothing like that." Realizing he'd need to reveal a few more details to convince Taylor, but not wanting to say anything about the possible connection to Josie, he dangled a carrot. "I might know something about a perp in a story your colleague wrote that he would find very interesting." *It's not a lie*, Chris reminded himself. *If the two cases are connected...*

"Okay, thanks. Call me when you set something up. You've got my number."

Chris checked his work email again while he waited to hear back from Taylor, scrolling through quickly, skimming and scanning as was normal for him. Three cases had been successfully resolved during his brief absence from the office, and he answered with "Attaboy!" messages, CCing the entire staff. It never hurt and cost him only a minute or two of his time. He paid all his staff well, especially his investigators—anyone who wasn't worth the salary Chris paid didn't last long at Colton Investigations. But money wasn't the best motivator—recognition was. Chris had learned that early on in his career. He'd just clicked Send on the last email when his cell phone rang.

"Hey, Taylor," he answered. After a minute he asked,

"Where?" followed by "When?" He wrote swiftly. "Okay," he agreed. "I'll be there."

As soon as he hung up he hit speed dial. "Bella?" he said when his sister answered. "You're off today, aren't you? I need a big favor."

"I don't need a babysitter," Holly said furiously when Chris told her he was going out but that Annabel was coming over to watch her. "If that's what you think, you'd better think again."

"Not a babysitter," Chris explained patiently. "A bodyguard."

"Same thing."

"No, it's not." There was something implacable in his face, in his voice, and Holly knew she wasn't going to win this argument…unless she took her boys and stormed out of the house. Which would be a stupid "cutting off your nose to spite your face" kind of thing to do.

"Look," she began, but Chris stopped her.

"No, *you* look. Do I think the McCays will find you here while I'm gone? No. But am I willing to take that chance? No." His blue eyes had gone cold, but there was something fierce in their depths that reminded Holly of an eagle's basilisk stare. "*No one* is dying on my watch ever again, you got that? I made myself responsible for you—and you agreed to it." He was breathing heavily now, as if he'd been running…or as if deep-rooted emotions were taking their toll on his body. "I've already lost—" He broke off, as if the rest of that sentence would reveal more than he wanted. "You agreed to let me protect you and your sons, Holly," he said after a minute, a little calmer now. "You have to let me do it my way."

"But—"

"No buts. My way, Holly."

She was going to keep arguing, but then she heard Peg's voice in her mind. *Chris needs to do this, Holly. I can't explain, but he needs to do this. So just let him take care of you and your boys.*

She breathed deeply once, then again, and pushed her independent spirit aside for now at the sudden reminder. She wouldn't always knuckle under to Chris—it wasn't her nature and it wouldn't be good for him anyway. But in this instance, maybe he was right. There was only a chance in a thousand something could happen to her or the boys while Chris was gone, but that was a risk he wasn't willing to take. She wasn't willing to risk it, either, not when it came to Ian and Jamie.

"Okay." She held up one hand before he could say anything. "Okay, this time. When are you going? And when will your sister arrive?"

Chris glanced at his wristwatch. "Annabel will be here in about fifteen minutes. I'm not leaving until she gets here."

Holly let the tension drain out of her muscles. "I'd better check on the boys—they've been quiet too long. Then I'll make lunch."

Chris was long gone. They'd eaten lunch, after which Chris had left and Holly had taken the twins to the master bedroom for their nap. Then, with Wally at her heels, she returned to the family room, where Annabel was reading a magazine she'd brought with her, *Law Enforcement Technology*. Holly had given Annabel the silent treatment during lunch but realized with a touch of remorse it wasn't fair—Annabel was just doing her brother a favor, and giving up her free time to do it.

Before she could speak, though, Annabel said, "Your kids are really cute."

"Oh. Thanks." Holly chuckled, taking a seat at the other end of the sofa. Wally plopped himself at Holly's feet, and she reached down to ruffle his fur before saying, "You've only seen them after they're worn-out playing ball with Wally. Wait until you see them after their nap, when they're reenergized. The word *rambunctious* was created with Ian and Jamie in mind."

Annabel laughed. "Kids are like that. All kids. But women still keep having them anyway." A wistful expression crossed her face. "I wouldn't mind..." She didn't finish that sentence, just tossed her magazine to one side and asked, "How old are Ian and Jamie?"

"Eighteen months."

"Identical twins? They look like it, but have they been tested to know for sure?"

Holly nodded. "Identical. Even so, Chris can already tell them apart."

"Really." There was something in the way Annabel said that one word, something meaningful. Not a question, just an acknowledgment of what that said about Chris.

Holly nodded again. "He's incredibly observant." She started to say "for a man" but realized that wasn't true. Chris was incredibly observant, period.

"That's what makes him such a good PI," Annabel stated. Then she laughed softly. "Of course, that wasn't always such a great thing when I was in high school."

"Chris admitted he scared away a few of your boyfriends."

"That's an understatement!" Annabel's laughter softened into a reminiscent smile. "I tease him, I know, but he's a great brother in most ways. When we finally reconnected in high school—"

"Reconnected?" Holly's eyebrows drew together. "What do you mean, reconnected?"

Annabel looked surprised. "Didn't you know? We were all sent to different—" Then she stopped. "You *do* know about our father…and our mother…don't you?"

Holly nodded. "Chris told me the first time we met."

"Hmm. Doesn't sound like Chris. He doesn't tell many people."

"He was trying to make a point," Holly said. "I think he wanted to shock me."

"Now, that *does* sound like Chris," Annabel replied. Her expression turned somber. "And it's not like it's a secret—just about everyone in Granite Gulch knows." She was silent for a moment. "Well, if you know what happened, then I would have thought you'd know when our mother was killed and our father went to prison, the whole family was split up. We were all sent to different foster homes."

"Oh, Annabel…" Holly tried to imagine someone doing that to Ian and Jamie, and could hardly fathom it.

Annabel sighed, then continued. "That's what I meant when I said Chris and I reconnected in high school. We were eleven when we were separated. We didn't meet again until then."

Holly didn't know any way of expressing the pain that speared through her for the brother and sister who'd been so ruthlessly torn apart. All she could say was "Oh, Annabel" again.

"Chris and I were close growing up. I was a bit of a tomboy—do they even use that word anymore? But we did nearly everything together. He was always protective—not just toward me, but toward our younger brothers and sister, too. Our mother's death and the separation only exaggerated that trait in Chris. So when we reconnected in high school…" She shrugged. "There were some bullies who tried to pick on me because of…well, because of our serial-killer father. Chris helped me put a stop to it."

"It sounds like him." After she said it Holly was struck with the realization that she'd known Chris less than two days, but she already knew this much about him. It didn't seem possible…but it was true.

Holly still had questions about Chris, however, questions she didn't really want to ask him, and this seemed like the golden opportunity. She looked at Annabel and blurted out, "What was Laura like?"

Chris's sister thought for a moment. "Sweet. Pretty. And she had a gentleness about her that was very appealing, especially to a man like Chris." She hesitated, then added, "Chris was her world, and whatever he did was right. Good in some ways, not so good in others." Annabel looked as if she could say more, but wouldn't.

Holly digested this, then asked, "How did she die?"

"Viral meningitis."

"Oh." Holly stared blankly at Annabel. "I thought that was treatable."

"It is…if you treat it in time. There was an outbreak in Fort Worth, and somehow Laura was exposed. She had all the classic symptoms—headache, stiff neck, fever. But she never mentioned it to Chris. By the time she called her sister, Peg—you know Peg, right?" Annabel said in an aside. "Isn't that what Chris said?" Holly nodded and Annabel continued. "By the time Peg rushed her to the doctor she was in a really bad way. She was airlifted to Baylor Medical Center in Fort Worth, but she didn't make it—she died en route."

A wave of empathy for Chris enveloped Holly, because she could relate. Grant had been airlifted from the scene of the traffic accident that had taken his life, but he hadn't made it to the hospital, either. "How horrible for Chris," she whispered.

"He took it hard," Annabel confirmed. "Especially since he blamed himself."

"What do you mean? How could he— If Laura didn't tell him she was feeling bad, how could he have known?"

"That's something you're going to have to ask him," Annabel said with a guilty expression. "I probably shouldn't have told you that much." She sighed suddenly. "But here's something maybe you should know, something Peg could tell you but probably didn't. Laura was four months pregnant when she died."

"Oh, my God." Holly covered her mouth with one hand. Suddenly the statement Peg had made about Chris the last time she'd seen her friend made complete sense. "Peg told me—she said she couldn't really explain, but she said Chris needed to take care of the twins and me. And I should let him. This must have been what she meant."

"Probably." Annabel's blue eyes—so like her brother's—held Holly's gaze. "You haven't known Chris very long, so you might not understand. Chris has a very stern conscience. He would never admit it, but he fervently believes in atonement. He knows you can't change the past, no matter how much you might want to. But he *does* believe you can make up for it—if you're willing to pay the price. And he is."

Chapter 9

Chris drove the roughly seventy miles to Dallas in just over fifty minutes, with his foot on the accelerator of his F-150 and one eye on the rearview mirror, watching for the highway patrol. He'd gotten a couple of speeding tickets in his lifetime, but nothing that appeared on his driving record, and he wanted to keep it that way. Not enough to slow down—this was Texas after all—but enough to be semicautious.

He was pretty sure he remembered where the sports bar he was heading to was located, but he had his GPS on anyway, and he followed the directions. His tires squealed only slightly when he pulled into the parking lot, stopped the truck and got out.

Chris was accosted by a wall of television sets, all tuned to different sports channels, when he walked into the otherwise dimly lit sports bar. He glanced around, looking for the clothing Taylor had described the reporter would be wearing, but realized he didn't need that help after all. Taylor was standing at the bar with the other man, both of them nursing beers and munching on bar snacks, when Taylor spotted Chris and waved him over.

The introductions were made swiftly, after which Chris murmured to his friend, "Afraid of being scooped?"

Taylor laughed. "No, but whatever you have to say to Roger, I want to know. Just in case."

Chris ordered a longneck and a plate of nachos—he'd yet to meet a reporter who wasn't hungry, literally as well as figuratively—then said, "Let's get a booth. More privacy."

Chris sipped his beer as the other two men dug into the nachos, then put the bottle down in front of him and abruptly said to Roger, "What do you know about Desmond Carlton?"

Roger swallowed. "Uh-uh. That's not how this works. Taylor said you might have information for me related to the article I wrote on the man who was captured, one of the FBI's Ten Most Wanted."

Chris shook his head and moved his beer bottle infinitesimally. "Quid pro quo," he said. "Give and take. You tell me what you know, and I'll tell you what I know. *That's* how this works."

Roger glanced at Taylor, who said, "I vouch for him, Roger. He's never lied to me yet."

Roger nodded thoughtfully. "Okay," he told Chris. "What do you want to know?"

"Desmond Carlton."

Roger shook his head. "I don't know all that much. I'd been working on a story for a while, gathering whatever bits and pieces I could find on *all* the men on the FBI's Ten Most Wanted list." He grimaced. "Okay, so the angle was how long each man had been on the list, and why the FBI wasn't making progress in catching them."

Chris pursed his lips. "And?" he prompted.

"And then, boom! The FBI arrests one, and that angle kinda sorta went out the window. But my supervising editor said we could salvage at least part of the work I'd done by publishing what I'd uncovered on the guy, including his past history, the creeps he ran with, everything."

Chris took another sip of his beer. "So how did Desmond Carlton's name come into it?"

"He was collaterally associated with the perp the FBI arrested. But Carlton's been dead for six years. Now that this guy's finally been arrested, everybody associated with Carlton is either dead or behind bars. End of story."

Chris mulled this over for a minute. "Not quite," he told Roger. "Are you aware there's not a single mention of Desmond Carlton on any search engine?"

Roger's face betrayed him. "Yeah," he said slowly, "I didn't really focus on it, but now that you mention it, you're right."

"How did you find out the facts about him you included in your story?"

"The morgue had a few articles on Desmond Carlton," Roger said, confirming Chris's hunch. "Including one on his death six years ago. But remember," he was quick to justify himself, "Carlton wasn't the main focus of the story. So it never occurred to me..."

Taylor spoke up finally. "Are you saying someone wiped Desmond Carlton's name out of every database?" He glanced at Roger. "Now, *that's* a story."

"I don't know who, and I don't know why," Chris admitted, "but yeah. Electronically Desmond Carlton is a ghost." He slid his beer bottle back and forth between his hands, considering what more—if anything—he should reveal. Finally he reached a decision.

"Deep background, guys," he said, his voice rough. His eyes met Roger's, then Taylor's. "Deal?"

Chris knew what he was asking. If Taylor and Roger agreed, they could never quote him on what he was about to disclose. They could only use his information if they could confirm it with other sources, sources willing to go on the record.

"Deal," said Taylor, and Roger echoed, "Deal."

Chris fixed his eyes on Roger. "In all your research, did the name Josie Colton ever come up in connection with Desmond Carlton in *any* way?"

Taylor blurted out, "Josie? You mean—" Chris kicked Taylor under the table, and his friend fell silent.

Roger thought a minute. "Josie Colton?" He shook his head regretfully. "Not that I recall, and I looked under every rock I could find." Then he made the connection. "Wait a sec. Josie Colton. Wasn't the FBI looking at her for the Alphabet Killer murders?"

Chris held back his sudden spurt of anger. "Not anymore." He didn't trust himself to say anything else at that moment.

Taylor, after one glance at Chris's suddenly closed face, said, "That's right. They've pretty much narrowed it down to Regina Willard, haven't they?"

Chris nodded, hoping that was the end of the questioning, but Roger said, "Colton, huh? Any relation of yours?"

"My youngest sister," he admitted reluctantly. But that was all he was going to say about Josie. No way was he going to mention her foster parents had the same last name as Desmond Carlton. No way was he going to reveal she'd been missing for six years, either—the same amount of time Desmond Carlton had been dead. If there was a connection…if Josie was somehow involved…

"You said you found an article in the morgue about Carlton's death," Chris said suddenly. "How did he die?"

"Shot to death. But there were no shell casings and someone even dug the bullets out of him, so there was very little to go on."

"Was anyone ever arrested for it?"

"Nope," Roger said. "The case is cold…not that anyone in the police department is losing sleep over it. Drug lord shot to death? A man who'd been a suspect in several murders but never arrested for any of them? The police probably figured whoever offed him was doing the public a favor taking him off the streets."

Taylor elbowed Roger in the ribs. "What?" Roger exclaimed. "I'm not saying anything other people haven't thought."

"Yeah," Taylor said. "But still…someone getting away with murder…it's not right. Whoever killed Desmond Carlton is probably still out there. And if he killed once, he could kill again. And the next time it might not be someone who deserved to die."

"Was there any mention of reprisals?" Chris asked. "Could Carlton's murder have been the result of some kind of rivalry between drug cartels?"

"I never uncovered anything about that. Doesn't mean it wasn't drug related, but there was no mention of any kind of drug war in the newspapers in the months following Carlton's death. I couldn't find anything indicating he'd been killed in a coup within his own organization, either."

Which brings me right back to Josie and her possible involvement, Chris thought but didn't voice. He couldn't imagine his baby sister killing anyone—he'd never really bought into the idea that Josie might be the Alphabet Killer, but he'd sure been glad when the finger of suspicion had finally pointed away from her. He also couldn't imagine what connection Josie could have to a slain drug lord...except the coincidences of the time frame of her disappearance and her foster parents' last name. Coincidences he didn't trust.

Chris rubbed a hand over his jaw, then asked Roger one last question. "Are you planning any follow-up articles?"

"Nothing about Desmond Carlton, if that's what you're asking."

He smiled briefly. "Yeah, that's what I'm asking. Just wondered if you were holding anything back." *The way I am*, he finished in his mind.

"Nope, not this time. But—" Roger held up one hand, palm outward "—if I find anything from other sources that ties Josie Colton to Desmond Carlton's murder...all deals are off."

"Understood." Chris finished the dregs of his beer and stood. "Thanks, Roger. I owe you one."

"Hey, what about me?" Taylor asked in a mock-serious tone.

"I bought you the nachos," Chris said with a sudden grin. "We're even."

Evalinda McCay hummed to herself as she ruthlessly pruned the hydrangea bushes on either side of her front door. But she wasn't really giving as much attention to her gardening as she usually did; she was thinking about Holly. *Snip!* went the shears, slicing effortlessly through the branches the way she could easily have sliced through her daughter-in-law's throat.

I should have taken care of Holly myself, she acknowledged privately. She could have done it, too—no qualms assailed her about the course of action she'd decided on to get custody of the twins…and their all-too-tempting trust fund. Angus had protested at first, but he hadn't been difficult to persuade—she'd been unilaterally making their major decisions for all the years they'd been married… and even before then.

If I had killed Holly, she'd be dead now, and all that money would already be mine.

But Angus had insisted they insulate themselves, make it appear to be an accident. Even more, he'd shrunk from having a direct hand in eliminating Holly, as if that made it less of a sin somehow.

Evalinda wasn't worried about sin any more than she was worried about divine retribution. All she cared about was the money that would preserve their standing in the community. The income from the trust fund would eliminate their debt, would remove the sword of Damocles hanging over their heads and allow them to continue to live lavishly…the way she deserved.

It wasn't just the income from the trust she intended to have, however—the principal was also in her long-range plans, although she hadn't mentioned that to Angus yet. But first things first. Custody of the twins was the primary step. Everything else would follow from that. Which meant one way or another, Holly had to die. And soon.

That night, after the twins were in bed, Holly sought out Chris in his office. She tapped on the open door and said, "Knock, knock," before she realized he was on the phone. Chris swung around in his chair, cell phone to his ear, and held up a finger to indicate his call was almost finished. “Thanks, Sam,” he said. “I appreciate it.” Then he disconnected.

“Hey,” he said to Holly. “What’s up?”

“I wanted to talk to you about the McCays,” she said, leaning against the doorjamb. “You said yesterday you wanted to set a trap for them, and I… Not that I’m not grateful for your hospitality,” she rushed to add. “I am. It’s a lovely house, and Ian and Jamie had a blast playing with Wally in the yard this morning.” One corner of her mouth quirked into a half smile. “Peg was right to insist we bring him. He has helped the boys adjust to this new place better than anything I could have thought of.”

“Boys and dogs,” Chris said softly. “Nothing like the bond that develops between boys and dogs.”

“Girls, too,” Holly was quick to point out. “I had a dog myself growing up, a cocker spaniel I named Chocolate Bar because she was such a rich brown color. I called her Chox for short. I got her for Christmas in first grade. She died when I was fifteen and I wept buckets.”

Chris’s eyes crinkled at the corners for just a moment, and though he didn’t say anything, Holly sensed there was a very sad story somewhere in Chris’s past about a dog. She hurried to get back to her original subject. “Anyway,” she said, “I wanted to discuss that trap you mentioned.”

He leaned back in his chair with a creak of leather and indicated the sofa. “Have a seat,” he said. “It just so happens I was talking with my brother about this when you walked in.”

Holly sat. “You were?”

“Mmm-hmm. Sam agrees you can’t keep running. He also agrees setting a trap for the McCays is the way to go, but we have to be careful about entrapment. Which means—”

"We can't entice them into committing an illegal act," Holly said before he could. "I understand."

A flash of admiration crossed Chris's face. "Exactly. We can do this, but we have to plan it carefully. And of course, Sam's concerned about using real bait."

"You mean me."

"Yeah. But I don't think we have a choice. You're the only way to draw them out into the open."

Holly nodded. "Makes sense."

"Sam's also worried about the twins. No matter what kind of trap we set, there's going to be some danger involved. He doesn't want the twins around when we spring the trap. I don't think you do, either."

"Of course not."

"So that means we need to stash them somewhere safe for the time being."

Holly stared blankly at Chris. "You mean…turn my children over to a stranger?"

Chris shook his head. "No," he said gently, and Holly realized despite his big, tough exterior, he really was a gentle man. "I'd never suggest that. But what about Peg? She'd do it for you, don't you think? The boys know her and her kids. And Peg told me you and she have traded off babysitting for the past three months."

"A few hours at a time," Holly said faintly as a sense of suffocation overwhelmed her. "And never overnight."

"If you've got a better idea, I'd like to hear it."

If she hadn't already been sitting down, she would have fallen, because her legs were suddenly weak and trembling. Leave her babies? Not just for a few hours, but for however long it took to set and spring a trap? She hadn't been able to go back to work after her maternity leave ended. How was she expected to spend nights away from them?

Holly's lips moved, but no words came out, and she forced herself to focus on Chris's face. "You want me to leave Ian and Jamie with Peg…indefinitely."

He shook his head again. "Not indefinitely. A few days, a week at the most."

Could she do it? She wasn't sure. But did she really have a choice? Chris and his brother were right—she couldn't keep on running. Not just because the McCays might eventually run her to ground, but also because the constant moving was too hard on Ian and Jamie, especially now that they were getting old enough to notice the change in their environment. She had to close that chapter in her life, and the only way to do it…the only *safe* way to do it…was to settle with the McCays once and for all. To get them arrested, tried and convicted. To get them locked away where they would no longer be a threat. Not to her, and not to her sons.

"Could I…could I at least talk to them every day?"

"Nobody's trying to stop you from being a good mother, Holly…except the McCays." That gentleness was back in Chris's voice. "But I don't want you to visit Ian and Jamie at Peg's, because once we set the trap the McCays will know where you are…and instead of going after the bait and trying to kill you, they could track you to Peg's house. Secretly. We'd have no way of knowing. And that would put the boys in danger. I know you don't want that."

"Of course not," Holly repeated.

"You can talk to Ian and Jamie several times a day, for however long you and they need. A week, max, I promise. Hard on you. Hard on them. But it'll be worth it if we catch the McCays in the act."

"Okay." She didn't want to do it, but Chris's points were irrefutable. She suddenly realized her palms were damp, and she rubbed them nervously on the sides of her jeans. "So when do we start?"

"As soon as I can coordinate things with Sam and Annabel—tomorrow or the next day. And I've got to get Jim Murray's blessing, too." She raised her brows in a question, and he added, "He's the Granite Gulch police chief. Sam and Annabel answer to him, so we can't do this without him giving it the green light. But I don't see Jim saying no."

"Can he be trusted?" Holly blurted out.

Chris smiled faintly. "He's honest as the day is long. I've known him since I was a kid, and I would trust him to do the right thing. Always."

"Okay," she said again. She didn't say anything more, but she didn't leave, either. She knew she should—that would be the safe thing. The smart thing. But suddenly all she could think of was the kiss in her dream yesterday. The kiss that had devastated her with how much she wanted this man she barely knew. And then there was the kiss that wasn't. The almost-kiss in the kitchen last night. She'd seen it in his eyes—he'd wanted to kiss her. Why hadn't he?

Then she realized he was looking at her the same way he had last night, as if he was a little boy standing on the sidewalk outside a store window gazing longingly at something he wanted but knew he couldn't have because he couldn't afford it. As if—

"Go to bed, Holly," he told her, his voice suddenly harsh. But she couldn't seem to make her feet move. "This isn't what you want." Oh, but it was, it *was*.

So when her feet finally did move it wasn't to leave. Six steps was all it took to bring her right up to Chris, right up to his rock-hard body that exuded unbelievable warmth, just like her dream. She reached up and brushed a lock of hair from his forehead, then let her fingers trail down his temple, his cheek. The slight scruff of his unshaven chin made her shiver with sudden longing, and her nipples tightened until they ached.

Then he pulled her flush against his body, and she wrapped her arms around his waist, holding on for dear life. She raised her face to his, her eyes mutely asking, and he kissed her.

Kissed? If she could think, she'd find a better word for what his lips were doing to hers, but every thought flew out of her head and all she could do was kiss him back. All she could do was match the hunger in him. The need. The frantic longing for something just out of reach, which they both knew could be theirs, if only…

She heard a whimper and realized it was coming from her throat. Heard a moan and realized that was hers, too. She couldn't seem to get close enough, even though he was holding her in his powerful embrace as if he would never let her go. *Don't let me go* reverberated in her brain, and if she'd had the breath she would have said the words out loud. But she couldn't, because he'd stolen her breath. Stolen her sanity.

He was hot and hard, but not where she wanted him to be—he was too tall…or she was too short. Then his hands grasped her hips and lifted her with unbelievable strength. She wrapped her arms around his neck and her legs around his hips, gasping with relief as she rocked up against the hardness she yearned for.

He was still kissing her and—oh, God!—just like her dream, she couldn't get enough of him. She was burning up from the inside out, and if he didn't make love to her in the next sixty seconds she would go crazy, she would—

A sudden wailing from the master bedroom brought everything to a crashing halt.

Chapter 10

Letting Holly go ranked right up there in the top ten most difficult things Chris had ever done, but he did it. He reluctantly let her slide down his body until her feet touched the floor. Compelled his lips to release hers. Forced his arms to set her free. Her breasts were rising and falling as if she was having the same difficulty he was having breathing, and there was a dazed expression in her eyes…one that quickly changed to mortification.

"I…I… That's Jamie," Holly stammered, practically running from the study.

Chris followed her, turning on the light in the hallway so she didn't have to feel her way in the darkness. She disappeared into the master bedroom before he could catch up, and when he turned the corner, she was already lifting a weeping Jamie from his crib.

"It's okay, sweetie," she soothed. "Mommy's here."

Ian, woken from a sound sleep by his brother's sobs,

started fussing, his face crumpling as if he was going to cry, too. But Chris wouldn't let him. He lifted the boy out of the crib and propped him up against his shoulder. "Hey, buddy, don't you start." He chucked the boy under the chin. "Come on now. You're okay."

He glanced over at Holly cuddling Jamie in her arms, his face pressed against her shoulder as she rocked him back and forth. "Bad dream, you think?"

"Probably."

Holly's eyes wouldn't meet his, and disappointment slashed through him as he figured she was already regretting what they'd done. The best thing that had happened to him since Laura died…and Holly was regretting it.

Should have known better, he berated himself. *Should never have touched her. You knew that, so why...?*

He didn't want to address that question, but the answer refused to be silenced. He'd touched Holly…kissed her…caressed her…damn near made love to her…because he had to. Because the yearning in her eyes had aroused an ache in him he hadn't been able to suppress. Because the need to hold her had swept everything aside like a force of nature, the way a river in flood swept away everything in its path.

And now she wouldn't even look at him. As if she was ashamed.

That was the most hurtful thing of all.

Chris sat in his study a half hour later. Staring at his laptop, but not really seeing the web page he'd opened. Work, which had been his saving grace after Laura's death, couldn't hold his interest. He kept reliving the scene of Holly and him in this very room tonight. Only this time when he told her to go to bed and she refused to go…this time when she walked toward him and touched his face…this time when she raised her face to his asking for his kiss…this time he didn't touch her.

Which was what he should have done in the first place.

"Chris?"

He whirled around in his chair when a hesitant voice from the doorway said his name. Then he stood, needing to be on his feet to offer Holly the apology she deserved. In one way he wasn't sorry—he'd wanted to kiss her since the first time he'd seen her walking up the driveway of Peg's house, and now he had. And it had been like nothing he'd ever experienced in his life. But in another way he regretted it…because now he *knew* what it would be like with Holly…and he couldn't have it. Couldn't have *her*.

"I'm sorry."

"I'm sorry."

Chris spoke first, but Holly's apology was only a half second behind his. He shook his head. "You don't have anything to apologize for," he told her. "I should never have touched you."

Holly blinked, then her eyes creased at the corners. "I started it," she said quietly. "I'm not one of those women who blame the man for losing control when—" She broke off and breathed deeply. "You didn't do anything I didn't want you to do."

"That doesn't absolve me of blame." Chris tucked his hands in his back pockets to keep himself from reaching for her. "You're under my protection, Holly. And you're feeling vulnerable—I knew that. I shouldn't have taken advantage."

A fierce expression swept over her face. "You shouldn't have taken *advantage*?" Her voice held that same fierceness. "What is this, the eighteen hundreds? If one of us took advantage of the other, it was me. *I* took advantage of *you*. I wanted you, and I—" She stopped, then continued bravely. "I wanted you, Chris. I've never wanted that way in my entire life, not even with Grant."

His brain tried to process her words, but they didn't jive with— "You ran out of the room," he grated. "You were mortified—no, don't deny it," he interjected when she tried to speak. "And in the bedroom you wouldn't even meet my eyes. You were *ashamed*."

"Not for the reason you apparently think," she said, a tinge of color in her cheeks. "When I heard Jamie crying, I…I didn't want to stop. Didn't want to go see what was wrong with him. *That's* why I was mortified," she explained. "Because I wanted you so much that for an instant I actually resented Jamie for interrupting." Her lips curved up slightly at the corners in a rueful smile. "I didn't want to be a mother at the moment, Chris. I just wanted to be a woman. A woman you wanted as much as I wanted you."

He could have sworn he didn't move, but suddenly he found himself standing right in front of Holly. "I wanted you," he said in his deepest voice. "I wanted you like I wanted my next breath." He raised a hand to her cheek and admitted, "I still do." He let that confession hang there for a couple of seconds before adding, "And when Jamie cried?" His rueful smile matched hers. "I wished him in perdition."

Suddenly they were both laughing softly, and Chris lowered his forehead to Holly's. "That doesn't make us bad people," he told her, unutterably relieved she hadn't been ashamed of what they'd done after all. "It just means we're human."

"So I'm not a bad mother because I didn't immediately switch off the woman gene and switch on the mother gene?" she whispered, but in a tone that told him she was teasing.

"Hell—I mean, heck no," he teased back.

Holly touched her lips to his. "Glad to hear it," she murmured.

Desire zinged through his veins, but this time he had enough self-control not to follow through on it. "Don't start something we can't finish," he warned lightly.

"We can't?"

"Holly…" he began, then realized she was teasing again.

"It's going to happen, Chris," she told him, all teasing aside. "Not tonight. Maybe not even tomorrow night. But it's going to happen." Despite her brazen words, the little flags of color in her cheeks, the not-so-sure-of-herself expression in her eyes and the almost defiant way she said it told Chris this wasn't normal behavior for Holly. *She's probably never made the first move in her life*, he thought. And that turned him on no end. The idea that Holly—sweet, innocent Holly—wanted him that much was incredibly arousing.

But he wasn't taking any chances. Not tonight. "Go to bed, Holly," he told her, gently this time. "But I won't be upset if you dream about me, 'cause I'll be dreaming about you." He laughed deep in his throat, and it felt good to laugh, even though he knew he'd go to bed hard and aching and wake up the same way. "Oh, yeah, I'll be dreaming about you."

Holly woke before the twins again and lay there for a moment, enjoying the peace and quiet. Then she remembered how she'd brazenly told Chris last night they would eventually become lovers. Just *thinking* about it made her cheeks warm—she'd never been that bold with a man.

Even when she'd made up her mind to do whatever she could to entice Grant into loving her, she'd never come right out and said it.

But then she'd never felt for Grant what she felt for Chris. Yes, she'd loved her husband, but…she'd never hungered for him. She'd never *craved.* And that was a revelation. She just wasn't sure what it meant.

She wasn't merely drawn to Chris physically, though. He tugged at her heart, too, now more than ever. Her conversation with Annabel yesterday afternoon had explained a lot about his behavior, and she believed she knew him better. But it wasn't just that. Watching him with her sons—could there exist a man more destined to be a father than Chris? He was a natural, his father instincts always on target. Like last night, for instance, when he'd stopped Ian from crying. How did he *know*? How did he unerringly know just what to do, what to say in every interaction with Ian and Jamie?

Holly turned over and tucked her hand beneath her cheek. Chris was a triple threat—hotter than sin, a perfect dad in the making and a man whose emotions ran so deep any woman would be drawn to him.

She sighed. Problem was…she was starting to fall for him. Which had epic disaster written all over it, because she wasn't the kind of woman men fell in love with. Okay, yes, Chris wanted her. She was pretty enough, sexy enough, and other men had wanted her before. Not Grant, though. Except for the night Ian and Jamie had been conceived—and it had taken a few drinks more than he normally allowed himself before he'd seen her as a sexy, desirable woman—Grant's lovemaking had been…restrained. Good enough in its way, but…restrained. They'd tried hard to make a go of their marriage for the twins' sake. But Grant had never been in love with her...because she wasn't the lovable kind.

Chris told Holly at breakfast, "I called Peg this morning. She agreed to take Ian and Jamie for as long as you need."

She stopped supervising Jamie's attempts to feed himself and darted a dismayed look at him. "So soon?"

"The sooner we start, the sooner it will be over," he said patiently. "But actually, I have something I need to get out of the way first." She raised her eyebrows in a question and he hesitated, then realized there really wasn't any reason not to tell her. "I have to visit my father in prison."

"Visit your father?" The faint way she asked told him he'd surprised her.

"He's dying," he said abruptly. "Back in January he promised Sam that if each of his children visited him, he'd give us clues as to where he buried our mother."

"I don't understand."

Chris glanced at Ian and Jamie, but they were completely occupied with eating and weren't paying the least bit of attention to the adult conversation. "I told you what he did to our mother," he explained, masking his words for the twins' benefit. "But I never said that when he did it he took her away and buried her somewhere. Law enforcement searched at the time, but they never found her." Chris couldn't keep the hard edge out of his tone. "My brothers and I, and Annabel, too—we've been searching for years."

"But no luck," Holly stated.

"No luck," he agreed. "We've all been taking turns visiting my father since January. Annabel went last month. Now it's my turn." He breathed deeply, trying to tamp down his emotions, then added in a low voice, "We just want to give her a decent burial, Holly. Is that too much to ask?" She shook her head. "I haven't seen him in nearly twenty years. I never wanted to. But I can't pass up the chance to find out where my mother is."

"Of course you can't," she said stoutly. Her lovely brown eyes were filled with empathy. "I understand. When my parents were killed in South America—they were missionaries," she explained, and Chris didn't bother to tell her he already knew. "I…I was only a teenager. But I knew I had to bring their bodies home. It was a nightmare of frustration and paperwork, but I finally did it. They're buried together in a cemetery not far from their old church, so their close friends can visit their graves." She paused, then added softly, "Grant's buried right next to them."

Chris saw the tears in her eyes she was struggling to hold back. "Grant's parents—they wanted him buried in a more fashionable cemetery, but…he loved my parents and they loved him. I wanted them all together, you know?"

He cleared his throat. "Yeah, I do." The silence was broken when Ian accidentally knocked his sippy cup off his high-chair tray. The lid was securely fastened, so only a small amount of milk leaked onto the floor. But Holly jumped up, retrieved the cup, then grabbed a paper towel to wipe up the spilled milk.

After she rinsed off the cup and gave it back to Ian, she resumed her seat, and Chris said, "Anyway, I have to visit the prison today. I was thinking…if you wouldn't mind…I could take you and the twins to Peg's this morning. You could stay there until I come back to pick you up. I think you'll be safe there."

Holly's mouth twitched into a faint smile. "Let me guess—you already suggested this to Peg, right?" Chris had the grace to look abashed, and she chuckled. "Why am I not surprised?"

The independent woman in Holly knew she should be insulted, the same way she'd been insulted yesterday when she'd told Chris she didn't need a babysitter. Nevertheless there was something appealing about Chris's protectiveness that spoke to a more primitive aspect of her nature. Grant had never been protective of her—not that way. They'd grown up together, so he knew Holly could take care of herself. Still…she couldn't really fault Chris for wanting to make sure she and the boys were safe in his absence. Especially since he'd told her, *No one is dying on my watch ever again...*

She needed to ask Chris what he meant by that statement. Based on what Annabel had recounted about Laura, she had a pretty good idea it had something to do with his dead wife…and their unborn child.

But before she could ask him, Chris rose and put his breakfast dishes in the dishwasher. "I'll load the cribs and high chairs in the back of my truck. You'd better pack enough clothes and things for the twins to last a week. And maybe their favorite books and toys. Susan and Bobby have plenty, but those little bunnies the boys sleep with? Don't want to leave them behind." Then he was gone.

Matthew Colton looked smaller than Chris remembered. *Only to be expected*, he thought after the first shock of seeing his father sitting at the table, behind the glass separating the prisoners from the visitors. Chris had been eleven back then—nearly twenty years had passed. And his father was sick…dying. Which would account for his frail appearance that made him seem…a pathetic old man. *He murdered your mother*, Chris had to remind himself, steeling against the sudden wave of good memories. *Not to mention all the others he killed.*

And yet…there were a lot of worse fathers than Matthew Colton had been. How to reconcile the two pictures of Matthew? *Remember the bad times*, he told himself. *Remember Ethan finding Mama's body with the bull's-eye on her forehead. Remember your family being torn apart. Remember Bouncer being sent to the pound. That's all on him. That's all Matthew's doing.*

Chris sat at the table across from his father, removed his Stetson and placed it on the table in front of him, then ran a hand through his hair, which the Stetson had flattened. Then and only then did he pick up the phone. He had no idea what he would say, but Matthew spoke first.

"You look like your mother." If Matthew had stabbed him, Chris couldn't have been more surprised, but Matthew wasn't done. "Not your coloring, of course. Saralee's hair was long and dark, not blond." There was a wistful intonation to his words. "But you and Annabel look like her in every other way."

Chris cleared his throat against the wave of emotion that rose in him. "Yeah," he agreed. "Everyone who remembers her says we look like Mama." He'd thought he could do this, but now that he was here… "So you wanted to see each of us. And you bribed us here by promising a clue to where Mama's buried. Piss-poor clues, but then you knew that, didn't you?" Matthew's eyes turned crafty, and Chris nodded. "Okay, I'm here. You've got your pound of flesh from me. So what's my clue?"

"No 'Hello, Daddy'? No 'How are you doing, Daddy'? Just 'What's my clue?'"

Chris drew a deep breath and held it, holding his anger in at the same time. "What do you want from me?" When

Matthew didn't respond, Chris reluctantly asked, "How are you doing?"

"I'm dying." The bald statement stood there while neither man spoke.

After a long, long time, Chris said the only thing that came to him. "I know."

Again there was silence between them, silence that was eventually broken by Matthew. "Twenty years, I've been locked away in this cage. Near twenty years, and the only one of you children to come see me was Trevor… and only because it was his job."

"What did you expect?" Chris couldn't keep the bitter edge out of his words. "You really think any of us wanted to see you ever again?"

"Don't you sass me, boy," Matthew retorted with a spurt of anger, his free hand forming a fist. "I can still tan your hide, and don't you forget it!"

All at once Chris was eleven again, facing his father over a broken window caused by an errant baseball Annabel had thrown. Matthew yanking his belt out of its loops and fiercely demanding of his children, *Who did it? Who threw that ball?*

Chris had stepped forward immediately. Matthew wouldn't have hesitated to use the belt on eleven-year-old Annabel, and Chris was too protective of her—of all the younger children—to let her take the imminent whipping. But Annabel had piped up bravely, *I did it, Daddy.* So Matthew had whipped them both—Annabel for breaking the window, Chris for lying. For trying to take the blame, for trying to shield Annabel from Matthew's wrath.

Chris and Annabel had hidden out in their secret hideaway afterward, lying on their stomachs in the shade of a catalpa tree so as not to further exacerbate the wounds on their smarting bottoms. Annabel trying so hard to be as tough as Chris, fighting back tears. But Chris hadn't cried. Not then…and not at their mother's memorial service a few months later. He hadn't cried until Bouncer…

Then Chris's mind jumped to Laura's funeral, and he realized he hadn't cried then, either. He hadn't cried at the loss of the two most important women in his life. But he'd cried over Bouncer. He'd never thought about it before, but now he realized maybe the reason he hadn't cried for his mother and his wife was because some things went too deep for tears. Heart wounds, both of them. And one of them had been caused by the man sitting across from him.

"Whatever happened to your dog, boy?" Matthew asked abruptly. "Whatever happened to that golden retriever I gave you when you were six?"

Cold anger shook Chris. "He's dead."

"Well, hell, boy, 'course he is." Matthew smirked. "Dogs don't live as long as humans. I just wondered how he died, that's all."

Suddenly it was all too much for Chris. Suddenly the years rolled back, and he wanted to wipe that smirk off Matthew's face. Not just for Bouncer, euthanized despite Chris's tearful pleas to his foster parents, but for his mother, too. And for his brothers and sisters, orphaned yet not orphaned. Fighting the stigma of being Matthew Colton's child—a serial killer's child—to this day. He gripped the phone in a death grip and rasped, "Tell me where Mama's body is buried, Daddy. I'm begging you, damn it! Tell me!"

Chapter 11

The crafty expression returned to Matthew's face, and he shook his head. "Can't do that, boy. You get your one clue, just like the others." He waited for Chris to say something, but when Chris didn't speak, he offered, "Biff."

"Biff? That's it? Biff?"

Matthew nodded, a secretive smile forming. As if he knew what Chris was thinking. As if he knew that if Chris could have reached through the glass he would have put his hands around his father's throat and—

No! A tiny corner of Chris's brain forced him back to sanity. *You are not a killer*, he reminded himself, the words becoming his mantra. *You are not a killer. He's your father, but you are not him. And you are not a killer.*

He settled his Stetson on his head, shielding his eyes from Matthew's searching gaze. "You are an evil man," Chris told his father evenly through the phone. "And yes, your blood flows through our veins. But Mama's blood flows through our veins, too. You killed her, but you can't kill her spirit—we're her legacy. She lives on in us."

He put the phone down and stood. Matthew was speaking—his lips were moving—but Chris didn't want to hear anything more his father had to say. He turned and walked toward the door…to freedom. Freedom his father would never know until the disease ravaging his body claimed him, and he left the prison in a hearse.

Chris would never return. Would never look on his father's face ever again, not even at his funeral…which Chris would not attend. But this visit had been necessary after all, and not just to receive his clue that was no more help than the clues the others had received. No, this visit brought closure. Chris hadn't realized he needed it, but now he finally acknowledged that the father he'd once known no longer existed. The stern father who—despite that sternness—had loved his wife and children had been a different man. This man—Matthew Colton, wife murderer and serial killer—wasn't the father of Chris's memory. Something had changed him. Twisted him. He was beyond the reach of even his children's pleading.

And knowing that, the shackles binding Chris to the past were finally broken. *I'm his son*, he acknowledged once again. *But I am not him.*

On the way back to town Chris passed the entrance to his brother Ethan's ranch. A sudden impulse to talk with Ethan made him brake sharply and swerve into the turn without signaling, earning him an angry honk from the truck behind him.

"Sorry," he muttered, glancing at his rearview mirror even though he knew the other driver couldn't hear him.

It wasn't just letting Ethan know the clue their father

had given him that had made Chris turn, but also the desire to share that he finally understood Ethan's complete rejection of Matthew all these years. Ethan had been only seven to Chris's eleven when their father had murdered their mother—he didn't have the memories Chris had of the good times with their father. But that was all gone now, erased by the knowledge that the father he remembered and the man dying in prison were two different people.

Chris pulled up in front of the ranch house, parked and got out, leaving his hat on the seat and not bothering to lock his truck. *Ethan's probably out on the ranch somewhere, but Lizzie can tell me where he is.* His boots thudded as he mounted the wooden stairs and crossed the front porch, thinking about the last time he'd been out here. Ethan's ranch—Ethan and *Lizzie's* ranch, he reminded himself with a smile—had quickly become the Colton family gathering place. And soon there'd be another celebration, when Lizzie gave birth.

His smile faded as the never-to-be-forgotten sadness came to the fore. The loss of his own baby when Laura died wasn't the constant heartache it had been at first, but the pain would never go away completely. *His* baby would have been the first Colton of the next generation, not Ethan's. But that wasn't Ethan or Lizzie's fault. And he would love their baby the way he loved Susan and Bobby. The way he loved Ian and Jamie.

He stood stock-still for a moment. The way he loved Ian and Jamie?

You do, his shocked mind acknowledged. *You love them as if you were their fath—*

He chopped that thought off before he could finish it. "Don't go there," he muttered. "Don't."

He forced himself to move, to knock on the screen

door. The front door was open, so he called through the screen, "Lizzie? Lizzie? It's Chris."

The only answer he got—a long, low moan—scared the hell out of him. "Lizzie!" He grabbed the handle on the screen door and pulled, but the latch was on and the door refused to budge. Another moan, and this time Chris wrenched at the screen door with all his might. With a creaking sound, the old wood gave way, the latch pulled free and Chris was inside. "Lizzie?" His gaze encompassed the neat living room, but he saw nothing, so he moved down the hallway, bellowing, "Lizzie, where the hell are you?"

"Kitchen— *Ohhh!*"

He found Lizzie there, her face drenched in sweat. She was bent over the back of a chair, gripping it tightly as the labor pain ebbed. His eyes took in everything, including the way her clothes were sopping wet and the panting sounds she was making as she breathed.

"Crap!" He lifted his sister-in-law gently into his arms and headed for the front door. *Hospital*, his frantic mind told him. "How far apart?"

"I…I couldn't time them," she gasped, "so I don't know. Four minutes maybe?"

"Your water broke already, so this didn't just start a few minutes ago. Where the hell's Ethan?" He was already outside, maneuvering his way to his F-150 as fast as he could.

"He went into town. I didn't tell him… I've had false labor pains twice before and…and I didn't want to worry him again."

"Where's Joyce?" he asked, referring to the wife of Ethan's foreman, Bill Peabody.

"Joyce and Bill went to visit their kids. I never expected…"

He listened to her explanation with only half his attention. The rest was laser-focused on what he had to do. "Open the door, Lizzie," he told her when they reached the passenger side, and when she did, he kicked it wide-open with one booted foot. He placed her as carefully as he could on the passenger seat and fastened the seat belt around her, but when he went to close the door, she grabbed his arm.

"My things. Suitcase by the front door. Please!"

"Okay," he told her. "I'll get them. Don't go anywhere."

Lizzie choked on a laugh. "Don't worry. Just hurry."

He found the suitcase right where she'd said it would be, then raced out, pulling the front door closed behind him. He wedged the suitcase behind his seat, sat down and belted himself in. As the engine roared to life he said, "Did you call Ethan?"

"I called him earlier, but…my water hadn't broken yet. He said he was on his way to get me."

Chris floored it, leaving a cloud of dust in their wake. The truck jounced and jolted until he got to the main road, and the minute he turned Lizzie clutched her stomach and started moaning again. "Crap!" he said again, glancing at his watch, then gave her his right hand, steering with the left. "Hold tight on to me," he said. "Scream if you want to—don't hold back. And aren't you supposed to be panting like a dog? Isn't that supposed to help?"

Between moans Lizzie laughed again the way he'd intended her to, but she didn't say anything, just gripped his hand in a death grip that—*holy crap!*—hurt.

When she finally let go, Chris surreptitiously wiggled his fingers to see if any bones were broken. When he figured they were still intact, he hit the Bluetooth button on his steering wheel as they barreled down the county highway.

He waded through the interminable questions the disembodied recorded voice asked him until he finally heard Ethan on the other end. “Ethan, it’s Chris,” he said, cutting his brother off. “I’ve got Lizzie and we’re heading to the hospital.” He darted a look at the clock on the dashboard. “I figure five to six minutes, tops.” It would take longer…if he wasn’t going ninety miles an hour. “Meet us there.”

“Got it,” Ethan replied. “Turning around now. Lizzie? Can you hear me?”

Chris glanced at Lizzie, then pointed to the speaker above his head. “Talk loud,” he advised.

Lizzie laughed again. “I can hear you, Ethan,” she shouted.

“Lizzie, honey, you hang in there, okay? I’ll be with you before you know it.”

“Okay.”

“And, Lizzie?” The hesitation, Chris knew, was because he could hear every word Ethan said to her. “I love you, honey. You and the baby are the best things that ever happened to me, and I—”

“Yeah, yeah, yeah,” Chris interrupted. “You love her, you need her, you can’t live without her. Forget that crap and *drive*!”

He hit the disconnect button and glanced over at his sister-in-law, who was sitting there with tears in her eyes. “Now, don’t *you* start,” he told her in bracing tones.

“I love you, Chris,” she blurted out as the tears overflowed. “I’m so lucky to have you as a brother-in-law.” Then she caught her breath as another labor pain snared her in its grasp, and Chris could actually see the ripples go through her.

"Crap!" he said again and depressed the pedal until the speedometer hovered around a hundred. He offered Lizzie his right hand again, mentally girding himself against the pain he knew was forthcoming, but also knowing that whatever pain Lizzie inflicted on him was nothing compared to what she was going through. "Hold on tight."

Two hours later Chris was still in the hospital waiting room. Ethan had met them at Emergency and had lifted his pregnant wife out of Chris's truck even more gently than Chris had placed her in it. Chris had parked in the visitor's lot, retrieved Ethan's truck from where he'd left it half on the driveway and half on the sidewalk—smooth talking a policeman out of a ticket in the process—then headed for the Emergency entrance with Lizzie's suitcase in hand. He'd turned the suitcase over to the admitting clerk and had followed her instructions on finding the waiting room. Where he'd waited. And waited.

He'd called Peg and told her what was happening, asking her to pass along the news to Holly and explain why he was delayed getting back. Then he'd called Annabel and Sam, who were on duty and couldn't talk for long. But they'd both spared him a moment to say Jim Murray had approved them working with Chris and Holly on setting the trap for the McCays.

Chris had forgotten about that. Well, not exactly forgotten, but Lizzie's crisis had driven everything else out of his head in the heat of the moment. He'd quickly called Ridge and Trevor after that, but both calls had gone right to voice mail. He'd left a message, though, both about Lizzie and the clue he'd obtained during his trip to the prison today—Biff. Then he'd turned his mind to the problem of how best to set a trap for the McCays.

Lost in thought, he didn't see Ethan walk into the waiting room. Not until his brother stood right in front of him did Chris realize he was there. Ethan looked wiped out. Pale beneath his tan. But happy. Ecstatically happy, and relieved.

Chris stood up. "Lizzie okay?" Ethan swallowed hard, as if he wanted to speak but couldn't. Then he nodded, and Chris asked, "And the baby? Everything okay there?"

"Yeah." The rasped word was accompanied by a sudden smile that split Ethan's face. "A boy. Eight pounds, eleven ounces. Twenty-one inches."

"Wow, big baby. Must take after his dad." Chris grinned and wrapped his brother in a bear hug. "Congratulations, little brother. You did good."

Ethan returned the hug, and when the two men finally separated, Ethan dashed a hand against his eyes, swiping away the moisture. "Got something in my eye," he muttered, turning away.

"Same here," Chris said, following suit.

But then the brothers faced each other again, smiling to beat the band. Ethan shook his head. "I can never thank you enough, Chris."

"It was nothing."

"Don't give me that BS. I should never have left Lizzie this close to her due date, especially since Joyce and Bill weren't there. But she swore to me she'd be okay, and I was only going into town." His eyes took on an expression Chris remembered from their childhood, when the two youngest boys—Sam and Ethan—had looked up to their older "stair steps" and wanted to emulate them. And all four of them had looked up to Trevor, the oldest. "If not for you," Ethan continued in a grateful voice, "I don't know what Lizzie would have done."

Chris flexed his right hand and joked, "That's some

woman you've got there. She almost broke my hand twice, so I figure she's tough enough to have worked out some other solution." Ethan laughed at that, and the emotional moment passed.

The brothers collapsed into two of the waiting-room chairs. Chris dug a hand into his pocket, pulled out Ethan's keys and handed them to him, saying, "Better give you these before I forget. Your truck's in the visitor's lot. Two rows down."

"Thanks."

After a moment Chris asked, "So you got a name picked out?"

"Lizzie and I had been toying with names ahead of time, but she and I talked just now and we're changing it. James Christopher Colton." Chris got that choked-up feeling again and couldn't have spoken even if he'd wanted to. "We figured a middle name would be okay. That way if you ever have a son and want to name him after yourself—" Ethan broke off as if he'd just remembered Chris's baby that never was, and a stricken look filled his eyes. "Sorry," he said quickly. "I didn't think… I didn't mean to…"

Chris tapped Ethan's jaw with his closed fist, but lightly. "Yeah, I know you didn't mean anything by it. Don't sweat it. And tell Lizzie I'm purely honored."

The two men were silent for a few moments, then Ethan said gravely, "You know, I never wanted to marry. Never wanted to have kids. With a serial killer for a father, I…I didn't want to pass on the Colton name, or—" repugnance was in his voice "—Matthew's blood."

"I understand." This wasn't the time to get into what he'd planned to tell Ethan earlier, that Chris had completely severed any emotional bond to the father he'd once known.

"But life doesn't always work out the way you plan," Ethan continued. "I never planned on Lizzie. I never planned on a baby. But Lizzie...well..."

"Yeah, yeah, yeah," Chris teased, trying to make light of another emotionally charged moment by using the same words he'd used in his truck on the way to the hospital. "You love her, you need her, you can't live without her."

"Yeah." The fervent way Ethan said the one word told Chris that—all joking aside—his brother adored his wife. And an ache speared through him. Not because he'd loved Laura and lost her, but because he hadn't loved her as much as Ethan loved Lizzie, as if all light and hope in life emanated from her.

"Lizzie and our baby—they're everything to me now. And I wouldn't change a thing even if I could. I thought I could cut myself off from life. Lizzie proved me wrong."

Simple words. Not particularly profound. Not even the kind of words that evoked a strong emotional reaction. And yet...there was something in those simple words that seemed to reverberate in Chris's mind. *I thought I could cut myself off from life.*

Wasn't that what he'd done? When Laura had died, and their baby with her, hadn't he tried to cut himself off from life, tried to build a fence around his heart? Hadn't he retreated—like Superman—into his fortress of solitude?

Those he already loved—his sisters and brothers, Peg and Joe and their kids—he couldn't stop loving *them*. But he'd walled himself off from loving another woman, because...

Because what you don't love you can't lose.

It sounded like a quotation from something. If it was, he couldn't place it, but it seemed singularly appropriate.

Only...he hadn't really been able to do it. Holly's boys

had crept into his heart in just three short days. Identical twins be damned—he could tell them apart, and not by their tiny physical disparities. Ian, the outgoing one, with his "damn the torpedoes" outlook on life. Jamie, the shy one, with that "don't hurt me" look in his eyes. Holly's eyes.

That was when it hit him. Ian and Jamie weren't the only ones who'd slipped beneath his emotional fences. Holly had, too.

Chris stayed to keep his brother company at the hospital until Ethan went up to visit Lizzie again, in her room this time with the baby, dragging Chris along. Lizzie looked a thousand times better than the last time Chris had seen her, and baby James looked so much like Ethan it was almost comical. Chris knew you couldn't tell what color a newborn's eyes were going to be, but between Lizzie's green eyes and Ethan's hazel ones, he figured the odds were good his nephew's eyes would at least be hazel.

He kissed his sister-in-law's cheek and told her he'd back her in an arm wrestling competition anytime—making both Lizzie and Ethan laugh. He admired the baby, marveling that something so tiny could have such powerful lungs. "Just like you, Lizzie," he said, again making them laugh. Then he left the three of them to have some family time alone together and headed out.

It was after dark by the time Chris finally reached the Merrill house. His stomach was rumbling—he'd skipped lunch, and breakfast was a distant memory, but even if Peg asked him to stay for dinner he couldn't. He'd left Wally at his house, not realizing he'd be gone all day. Although Wally was outside in the fenced yard with a food bowl and a water dish, the food was probably long gone, and maybe the water, too.

Peg answered the door, Susan at her heels, and the minute he walked in Susan grabbed his knee. "Pick me up, Unca Chris." He obliged, heading for the family room with her propped on his left shoulder.

"Everything okay?" Peg asked, trailing behind him.

Chris waited until he reached the family room to make the announcement. "A boy," he told Joe and Peg. "James Christopher Colton. Mother and baby are doing great. Ethan I'm not so sure about—he looked pretty shaky to me."

The Merrills laughed. "Yeah, Peg wanted me in the delivery room when that one was born," Joe said, pointing at his daughter cuddled in Chris's arms. "But I nearly passed out. Remember, Peg?"

She snorted. "Yes, but I wasn't about to let you off the hook when Bobby was born." She didn't say it—*little pitchers have big ears*, he thought with an inward smile—but he knew Peg well enough to know what she was thinking. *If you're there for the conception, you damn well better be there for the delivery.*

Joe said something in reply, but Chris wasn't really listening because just then Holly walked into the room and took a seat near the twins. This was the first time he'd seen her since that morning, and now, after his startling revelation in the hospital…now he couldn't seem to look away. Her long blond hair was clipped neatly away from her face on one side—she'd ditched the dark-haired wig, and Chris couldn't be sorry. Not when she looked like this. He remembered the corn-silk feel of her hair between his fingers last night when he'd—

He put a clamp on that memory. But then he heard Holly saying in his mind, *It's going to happen, Chris.*

Not tonight. Maybe not even tomorrow night. But it's going to happen.

Which was why he'd stopped off at the pharmacy in the hospital before he left. That package was hidden in the armrest of his truck, tucked there so Holly wouldn't see it and think he was assuming…well…what he was assuming.

"Staying for dinner?" Peg asked.

"What? Oh. No, we can't," Chris replied. "Wally's been home alone since this morning. Outside," he clarified. "But I'm sure he's as hungry as I am." He looked at Holly again. "You about ready to go?"

A stricken expression fleetingly crossed her face, then she pasted a smile in its place. She knelt between Ian and Jamie, who were arguing over who deserved the bigger truck, and tugged them into one last embrace. "Mommy has to go now. You be good for Ms. Peg and Mr. Joe, okay?"

"'Kay," Ian said, and Jamie echoed, "'Kay."

She kissed them both, then stood, stony-eyed, as if she refused to let herself cry in front of her sons. "Say goodbye to Uncle Chris."

Chris handed Susan to her father, then picked his way through the toys scattered across the rug. He leaned over, curled an arm around each boy and lifted them simultaneously, tickling their tummies with his fingers. "You be good for Ms. Peg and Mr. Joe," he reiterated and was rewarded with the same chorus of *'kays*, giggling ones this time.

He didn't know what made him do it—well, yes, he did—but he popped a kiss on Jamie's nose, then on Ian's, before he set them down. Then he grabbed Holly's hand and tugged her toward the doorway. "Come on," he muttered. "Let's get out of here before the waterworks begin."

They were already out the door before Holly gulped air and said, "I didn't think Ian and Jamie were going to cry. I've left them with Peg before, and they—"

"I wasn't talking about the twins. I was talking about you."

Chapter 12

"I wasn't going to cry," Holly insisted as Chris held the passenger door of his truck for her.

"Weren't you?" His voice held tenderness and understanding.

"Well..." She gave a little huff of semitearful laughter as she buckled her seat belt. "Not where the boys could see me anyway." Then she realized something. "Wait. My SUV is here."

"Yeah, I know. Give me the keys." When she did, he closed the door and left, but was back a minute later, climbing into the driver's seat. "I gave Joe your keys. I think it's best for now we leave your SUV here, rather than at my house."

He was already putting the truck into gear as he said it, and Holly asked, "Why?" Wanting an answer before they got too far away.

"Because I don't want the McCays to know you're at

my house, not until we're ready to spring the trap. Do I think they suspect anything yet? No. Am I willing to risk it? No. I told Joe to park your SUV in their garage so no one can see the license plates." He glanced at her. "We're not that far away. If we need it, we can get it. But I don't think we will."

She didn't know why a little dart of panic went through her. She was so used to having the freedom of her own wheels—was that it?

"Besides," Chris said drily, breaking into her thoughts, "this way you can't sneak off to visit the twins when my back is turned."

That made her laugh for some reason. "I wouldn't do that," she protested. "I already agreed it would be safer—"

He reached across the seat and clasped her hand for a moment. "I know you did. But this way you won't be tempted." Then he let her hand go so he could shift gears, saying softly, "You're a good mother, Holly."

"I try to be."

"You remind me of my own mother."

When he said that, she remembered Chris had been eleven when his mother died. Old enough to have vivid memories of her. "What was she like?"

He didn't answer right away. Then he said slowly, "Beautiful…to me. Now when I look at old photos, I realize she wasn't really beautiful. Not classically beautiful. But if ever a woman's heart reflected in her face, hers did."

She gathered her courage and asked, "Why did your father kill her?"

At first she thought he wasn't going to answer at all. Then he said, "No one can really answer that except him. She loved him through everything—the loss of his ranch, financial hardship, seven children. And for the longest time no one had a clue why he did it, because he refused to say. Not even when he was convicted of her murder. He finally told Ethan back in February—Ethan was the one who found her dead—that she figured out he was the bull's-eye serial killer.

"That's how my father used to mark all his victims," he explained, "with a red bull's-eye drawn on their foreheads." She heard him breathe deeply in the darkness. "She caught him in bloody clothes one day, which he tried to explain away. But then she found the permanent red marker in his pocket. And she saw something on the news the next day that made her put all the pieces together. She confronted him, told him what she knew and insisted he turn himself in. In a—I guess you could say a fit of rage…or fear…or both—he killed her. Before he knew what he was doing, he'd marked her forehead the way he'd marked his other victims."

"Oh, God," she whispered helplessly, her heart aching for him.

"Then he panicked," Chris continued, still in that deliberate way. "He realized he had to get rid of her body somehow, so he went to the garage…for a big trash bag."

She couldn't help her soft gasp of dismay. "Oh, Chris, no."

"Yeah…a trash bag. He killed her, and then he— Like she was garbage." This time she reached across the distance and touched his arm in empathy. He downshifted and turned a corner before adding, "He didn't know that in the few minutes he was gone, Ethan had come home from school—I told you Ethan found her. He was terrified. Imagine, you're seven years old and you find your mother's bloody, lifeless body."

"What did he do?"

"He ran to a neighbor's for help. But when they got back, the body was gone. Only the blood remained. But even though they never found Mama's body, Ethan's story of seeing her with the bull's-eye on her forehead led the police to finally arrest my—to finally arrest Matthew Colton, one of the most infamous serial killers in Texas history. Arrested. Tried. Convicted."

Holly hadn't missed the slight catch in Chris's voice or the way he'd changed *my father* to *Matthew Colton.* This morning he'd said he needed to visit his father in prison. *What happened between this morning and now?* she wondered. But she wasn't going to ask. If Chris wanted to tell her…that was a different story. If Chris *wanted* to tell her…he would.

Wally leaped to his feet and let out one bark of welcome when Chris pulled his truck into the driveway and parked. Chris grabbed the pharmacy bag from the armrest once Holly exited, and shoved it into his front pocket so she couldn't see it. Wally was eagerly wagging his tail and standing right by the front gate when Chris unlatched it and held the gate open for Holly, then closed it behind him so Wally couldn't escape. "Down, boy," he said when Wally threatened to jump on Holly in his exuberance at seeing them, but he wasn't surprised when Holly merely ruffled Wally's fur and let him shadow her footsteps to the front door.

Chris paused and picked up Wally's food bowl and water dish. "Empty. Just what I was afraid of." He unlocked the door, reached in and punched in the alarm code, then turned on the hall light before he let Holly enter.

"Are you really worried someone might have broken in?"

"No, but I couldn't take my gun to the prison with me today, so..." He caught the expression on her face. "I'm careful about gun safety, Holly," he said levelly. "I would never leave my gun where the twins could reach it, I promise. But in my line of work...a gun is practically a necessity." He flashed a grin at her. "Besides, this is Texas."

He didn't wait for her answer, just trod down the hallway toward the kitchen, flicking on the lights as he went. He filled the water dish, then he found the scoop in the dog food bag, filled the bowl and placed it beside the water Wally was already furiously lapping at. "Sorry, boy," he murmured, patting the dog's side. "Didn't expect to be gone this long."

Holly had followed Chris into the kitchen, and now she said, "You never explained what happened. What I mean is, Peg told me you were taking your sister-in-law to the hospital because she was having a baby, but..."

"Let me get dinner started," he replied, "and then I'll tell you."

A guilty expression crossed Holly's face. "No, it's my turn to make dinner," she said. "I can't let you do all the cooking—that wouldn't be fair." She bustled toward the fridge. "You talk while I cook."

"Whatever it is, make it quick, okay? I missed lunch and I'm starved."

Twenty-five minutes later Chris sat back at the kitchen table, replete. Holly's omelet and toast hadn't been fancy, but it had been good. Best of all it had been quick.

"I was terrified Lizzie was going to have that baby right there in the front seat of my truck," he confessed, finishing up his story. "But it all worked out."

Holly shook her head, a smile curving her lips. "I

doubt you were terrified." Her admiring eyes conveyed her conviction that whatever happened, Chris would deal with it competently. And his male ego responded. *So maybe you did okay,* his ego seemed to be saying, puffing out its chest a little. *Maybe you deserved to have baby James named for you after all.*

But his ego wasn't the only male part of him responding to Holly. And it wasn't only food he'd been hungering for. Now that one appetite had been satisfied…

But that wasn't fair to Holly, no matter what she'd told him last night. She deserved candlelight and romantic music, flowers and fine wine. She deserved gentle wooing. Not some guy with a box of condoms crammed into his pocket.

Which reminded him…he *did* have a box of condoms crammed into his pocket. A box he suddenly and desperately wanted to use.

Holly's smile faded. But before he could say anything, she jumped up from the table, cleared away the dishes, his included, and stacked them in the sink, saying, "Probably shouldn't use the dishwasher if it's only going to be the two of us, since it will take several days to fill, and—"

"Holly." That was all he said. Just her name. But she froze at the sink. He found himself standing behind her somehow. Just as last night he could have sworn he never moved, but there he was, sliding his hands down her arms, gently turning her unresisting body to face him. And he knew she could see the aching need in him he couldn't possibly hide.

"I want you," he admitted, as if it wasn't obvious. "God knows I want you. But not like this. Not if you're afraid of me."

"I'm not afraid of you," she said quickly. "It's me. I'm afraid of me." She must have read in his expression that he didn't follow her, because she added quietly, "I want you, too, Chris. In fact, that's pretty near all I can think about whenever you're around." Her voice dropped to little more than a whisper. "And even when you're not."

"Then why afraid?" he asked, one hand coming up to cup her cheek, to rub his thumb against her lips. This close he could feel the tremor that ran through her. "I won't hurt you, Holly, I promise. I'd never hurt you." Then it occurred to him maybe she was worried about—

"I haven't slept around, in case you're wondering." He brushed a strand of hair away from her face, tucking it behind her ear. "There hasn't been anyone since Laura." He hesitated, of two minds about revealing more. But then he figured she had a right to know. "And there wasn't anyone before her, either."

Something about the way his confession was made touched Holly so deeply she couldn't respond at first.

"Thank you for telling me," she whispered finally, cradling his face between her hands for a moment. She let her hands drop to her sides, wanting to be as honest with Chris as he'd been with her. "Grant was… I'd loved him all my life, so I never…" Her throat closed and she couldn't continue.

"Holly." The aching need embodied in that one word shook her to the core. Then he kissed her, and it was even better than it had been last night. Passion had exploded between them the night before, but tonight…tonight there was tenderness mixed in with the passion. And wonder. Chris kissed her as if he couldn't believe she was there in his arms, but at the same time as if he couldn't bear to let her go.

He whispered her name again, and Holly thought she'd never heard so many suppressed emotions in a man's voice. Want was there, and need. Overlaid with a cherishing tone that told her this would be more than just sex for Chris. If she hadn't already figured out from his confession that he only slept with women he cared for deeply, she would have known it by his voice.

And that made her decision easy. Here. Now. Tonight. It wasn't just that she wanted to know what it would be like with a man who hadn't grown up with her, who didn't see her as more of a friend than a lover. She wanted to know what it would be like with *Chris*, with this man who haunted her dreams and tugged at her heart in ways she'd never felt before. Ways she'd never realized she *could* feel. She wanted to know if the reality of making love with him came anywhere close to matching her dreams. Because if it did, that would reveal something about herself she was eager—and a little nervous—to learn.

Chris reluctantly withdrew his lips from Holly's and gazed down into her face. If she'd been wearing that "don't hurt me" expression, the one so like Jamie's, which appeared on occasion when she wasn't aware, he would have let her go. But she wasn't. Her expression said she wanted him…and she wasn't afraid anymore.

"I need a shower." He pulled away from her a little and coaxed. "Come with me."

"Okay." He loved the little catch in her voice, and the not-quite-shy way she agreed. Then she looked puzzled and reached down to his jeans pocket. "What's this?"

Crap. He'd forgotten. But he wasn't going to lie to her. "Condoms," he admitted. Then hurried to add, "I wasn't assuming… Okay, maybe I *was* assuming…but only if you… I wanted to be prepared, and I… Just in case…"

He was floundering—he knew that. But then Holly put her fingers over his lips to cut off his jumbled phrases and smiled. A womanly smile. "Thank you for thinking of it," she murmured, kissing the corner of his mouth. Then she took his hand and led him from the kitchen… down the long hallway…into the master bedroom.

They undressed in the master bathroom. Chris shucked off his clothes in no time. But after one moment staring at his naked body—a stare his body responded to noticeably—Holly stalled with only her jeans removed.

"Don't go shy on me now," he said, moving to stand in front of her and reaching for the buttons on her blouse.

"It's not that. Not exactly." She put her hands over his, stopping him from undoing the buttons. "It's just that… well…I've had a baby. *Two* babies. And…well…"

He got it. "You think I care about a few stretch marks?" He laughed softly. "Holly, Holly, Holly," he chided. "You must not have much of an opinion of me if you think that."

"I don't, but I…"

He was already undressing her. Parting the unbuttoned edges of her blouse, reaching back and unerringly unclasping her bra, then helping her out of them both. Caressing the skin he'd bared. Including the ever-so-slight protrusion that was a reminder of the babies she'd carried, and the silvery, barely there stretch marks.

He slid his fingers beneath the elastic on her hips and slipped her underwear free, then down. When she was as completely naked as he was, he knelt and placed his unshaven cheek against her stomach, grasping her hips so she couldn't escape, rubbing until she shivered and her nipples tightened for him.

Then he stood. "Do you have any idea how beautiful you are?" he told her in his deepest voice, meaning every word. So she was obviously a mother. So what? So her body wasn't model perfect. Did she really think he cared? He wanted her like hell burning, and she was worried about these little imperfections? “So beautiful,” he whispered, drawing her against his body and kissing her the way he’d dreamed of doing, with no barriers between them.

She was trembling all over when he finally let her go, and that turned him on big-time. But he needed that shower after the day he’d had. “Do you want to do something with your hair?” he asked. “So it doesn’t get wet?”

She twisted her hair up, then used a clip to hold her hair in place.

Without another word he tugged her into the shower with him. He soaped himself and rinsed off quickly but took his time washing her. Letting his fingers linger where he knew a woman loved to be touched. He’d made love to only one other woman in his life, but he knew the vulnerable places on a woman’s body. Knew how to fulfill her, too—a man didn’t have to be promiscuous to know that. All he needed was a little imagination and a strong desire to please.

He continued caressing her long after they were both clean, until she caught his hands and said, “Enough. I can’t… I don’t want…”

He captured her lips for a brief kiss. “Yeah,” he growled when he let her go. “I don’t want, either. I want to be inside you the first time. I want to feel you tight around me when you come.” Primal, maybe. Direct. But the God’s honest truth.

They barely managed to get the covers pulled down before they practically fell into bed together. Holly helped Chris roll on the condom—although *helped* wasn’t quite the word that came to mind when her fingers touched his erection. But he held his breath and let her because she obviously wanted to. Because he knew it gave her pleasure to touch him this way.

That was his last coherent thought. As soon as the condom was in place he lost any claim to rationality he'd ever had. He felt like a heat-seeking missile, with Holly his only target. Despite the urge to thrust hard and deep, he eased into the damp warmth between her legs and she welcomed him with a soft moan of pleasure. Then another when he withdrew and returned. Again and again. Faster and faster. He pulled her thighs up around his hips to delve deeper, and she arched beneath him, gasping his name.

His lips found her nipples, first one, then the other, and she arched again and cried out, her fingernails digging into his shoulders as if she couldn't bear it. But he knew she could. "Yes," he groaned when she involuntarily tightened around him, and he knew she was close. So close. "Come for me, Holly. Yes, like that," he managed when he felt her internal throbbing, though he could barely breathe. Barely speak. "Like that. Oh, God, Holly, like that." Then with a flurry of thrusts he came, too.

In the few seconds before he lost consciousness, Chris tightened his arms around Holly, wanting to never let her go. *Needing* it. Needing her.

Chapter 13

Oh, my was all Holly could think of as she lay beneath Chris, both of them breathing heavily, his body still embedded in hers. *Oh, my. Oh. My.*

Her dreams hadn't even come close, because she'd had no idea. None. She gave a little hiccup that was half laughter, half tears, as she realized she and Grant hadn't… They'd never… Not even once. Not like this. For just a moment she grieved for Grant, because she wasn't sure she'd ever satisfied him the way she was absolutely certain she'd satisfied Chris. And she grieved for herself, too, for all the times she'd wondered what was wrong with her.

Chris grunted suddenly, as if he had temporarily blacked out and had just resurfaced. He tried to separate himself from her, but Holly tightened her legs, not wanting to lose this euphoric feeling, as if she was floating above herself.

"I'm too heavy," Chris muttered, but Holly's hands grasped his hips.

"Don't make me hurt you," she warned, only half kidding. "Move and die."

He laughed, a rumbling sound, then swiftly rolled them over so she was on top. "That's better," he said. "But, Holly..." His eyes teased hers. "You can't keep me prisoner forever."

"That's what you think." She deliberately contracted and relaxed her inner muscles around him. Once. Twice. Three times. And each time she felt him respond. "Have you ever heard of Kegel exercises?"

"What's that?"

"Something they teach women after they've had a baby. It helps restore pelvic floor muscle tone."

"Oh, great." He laughed under his breath. "I guess I really *am* your prisoner, 'cause I'm not risking damage down there." That made her laugh, too. "But, Holly, much as I'm enjoying this, I have to do something about the condom."

She'd forgotten about that, but he hadn't. She stopped Kegeling him, then squirmed until he was free. Chris jackknifed off the bed and disappeared into the bathroom. She heard the shower running for a minute, then he returned, a towel wrapped around his hips. His narrow hips. Above which his abs and chest muscles rippled in masculine perfection that until a few minutes ago she'd touched up close and personal.

Holly's fingers itched to touch him again, but instead she grabbed the top sheet and pulled it up to hide herself and her imperfections from his view. "Oh, hell no," he told her, throwing the towel on a chair and diving across the king-size bed. He wrestled the sheet away from her, then playfully held her down while he looked his fill.

Warmth in her cheeks informed her she was blushing, although she couldn't see it. But still he looked. And when his eyes finally connected with hers, he said softly, "Beautiful, Holly. You have absolutely nothing to be ashamed of."

She caught her breath at the very male, very intent expression on his face, and almost believed him. "I couldn't lose those last five pounds after the twins were born," she said faintly. "I tried so hard, too!"

"Where?" He settled between her legs, bearing most of his weight on his elbows. "Here?" He cupped her breasts, breasts that had never quite returned to their original size and shape after she'd breast-fed Ian and Jamie. His thumbs played over her nipples until they tightened unbearably. "You'll get no complaints from me here, Holly," he bantered. His big hands slid down to her waist, his thumbs stroking back and forth over her belly until she quivered. "Here? No, I don't think so." His husky voice, the look in his eyes, told her he wasn't kidding. Then those firm masculine hands curved over her hips. "Must be here, then," he suggested, as if he were serious, his long fingers lightly squeezing. He shook his head after a moment. "Wrong again."

She was melting and he knew it. That was all she could think of as his wicked blue eyes held hers. She'd just had the most incredible orgasm of her entire life, and already she wanted him again. And impossible as it seemed, he wanted her again, too—he was already hot and hard at the crux of her thighs, and she wiggled a little until she could feel him pressed up against exactly where she wanted him.

"Again?" he teased, emphasizing the last syllable.

She smiled at his playful tone and tried to make her

tone just as light and playful. "Yes, please." She wasn't quite successful.

His eyes seemed to darken, and she shivered at the blatant desire that flared there. "Oh, I'm going to please you, Holly," he murmured, reaching for a condom on the nightstand, not waiting for her assistance. He fitted himself in place, then twined his fingers with hers. "I'm going to please you until you can't take any more," he whispered seductively. "And when I'm done, you'll know just how perfect you are." He smiled a very wolfish smile. "Hang on tight," he told her. "You may experience a little turbulence."

Holly's sudden laugh turned into a moan as he flexed his hips and thrust deep. Then withdrew and thrust again…slowly. Agonizingly slowly. Intense pleasure, sharp and urgent, knifed through her with each perfect thrust, until she clung to his hands and arched like a bow, crying his name.

"Still no word from Mr. Colton," Evalinda McCay reminded her husband as they dressed for bed…as if he needed the reminder.

"What do you expect me to do about it?"

The expression in her eyes bore no good for anyone. "How are we going to rid ourselves of Holly and get our hands on the twins and their trust fund if we can't locate her?"

"Mr. Colton promised us results," Angus protested weakly.

"One more day," she warned. "We'll give him one more day. Then I think we'll need to look for another detective."

"You really want to start all over? What if—"

"It was your idea to try to run her off the road the

first two times," Evalinda reminded him contemptuously. "You were so sure that would work…but it didn't. Either time."

"Yes," he was quick to defend himself, "but at least Holly didn't suspect anything. It wasn't until you suggested running her down in the parking lot that she—"

Evalinda wouldn't let him finish. "Don't try to shift the blame for that fiasco onto me. *You* were the one who hired the men to kill her. If they hadn't been so incompetent…"

"You think it was easy finding someone who—"

"One more day," she repeated implacably, cutting him off, and he knew further argument was useless. Just as he'd fallen in with Evalinda's plans to murder Holly in the first place, he knew he would cave on this, too.

Chris woke at two in the morning when moonlight crept through the bedroom window. He thought about getting up and completely closing the top-down, bottom-up blinds that were lowered at the top. The way the blinds were drawn now gave the room's occupants privacy but still allowed them to see the night sky. That also meant, unfortunately, it let the moonlight in, and he'd always been a "pitch-black" sleeper. The blinds were completely drawn in the bedroom he was occupying. He just hadn't thought about it here in the master bedroom because he'd been too focused on the other things he was doing.

But he wasn't about to get up to close the blinds at this moment. Holly was sleeping cradled against him, her head pillowed on his shoulder. And he'd be damned before he woke her.

He and Holly had worn each other out earlier, but a certain part of his anatomy twitched to life at the reminder of everything they'd done tonight. Two spent condoms now resided in the wastebasket in the bathroom, but he hadn't been satisfied to leave it at that. They'd dozed after the second time but had woken before midnight. And as they'd cuddled and lazily caressed beneath the comforter, he'd told her in all seriousness, "I want to watch you come. Will you let me?"

She'd been adorable in her confusion, and he'd had a strong hunch no one had ever done that for her before. Holly had told Chris her husband was the only man she'd ever slept with, but that didn't mean other avenues had been completely closed. Apparently that had been the case, though. Equally apparent was the fact that Holly's husband had never put her needs first, which didn't surprise Chris. There were still a lot of men out there who never worried about pleasing a woman. Who thought she was responsible for her own orgasms, and if it happened, fine. If it didn't, oh well. He wasn't one of those men, but he knew some who were.

It had taken a little coaxing but eventually Holly had conceded. And then—*holy crap!*—her response had been off the charts. Hearing her…watching her…tasting her… had turned him on so hard he'd been tempted to use a third condom, but she'd pretty much passed out by then, so he'd refrained. But he'd promised himself next time they made love he'd start with that and see where it took them.

Next time? What makes you think there'll be a next time, hot shot? The thought hit him out of the blue, and he stopped to consider it. He'd come up with some ideas for trapping the McCays when he was at the hospital this afternoon waiting for Ethan and Lizzie's baby to be born, and they had to get going on that pretty damn quick. Now that Jim Murray had given them the go-ahead, he needed to coordinate with Annabel and Sam, who were supposed to stop by for breakfast tomorrow. If they were successful, in less than a week Holly wouldn't need his protection anymore. Which meant she'd be free to…return to her old life. Her old life outside Houston, more than three hundred miles away.

Devastation sliced through him—another shock. He didn't want Holly to leave; he wanted her to stay. And Ian and Jamie, too. He'd realized this afternoon that all three had crept under his emotional fences. He just hadn't recognized how firmly entrenched they already were in his life.

Not even a week, the rational side of him protested. *You haven't even known her a week.*

That didn't seem to matter—somehow he and Holly just clicked. Not only in bed, although he couldn't believe how perfectly matched they were, as if she were made for his earthy brand of loving. He had no doubt he'd pleased her, too—no way could she fake her response, especially the last time. But their sexual chemistry had its roots in something deeper. He wasn't sure what to call it, but a connection existed between them. An emotional connection.

He examined that word—*emotional*—and acknowledged that somehow it fit. Problem was, he wasn't sure exactly what it meant to him. Even worse, he wasn't sure what it meant to Holly.

The pealing of the doorbell woke them. Holly unwrapped herself from where she'd migrated in the night—splayed across Chris's chest—and pushed her tousled hair out of her eyes. She clutched the top sheet, wrapping it firmly around her. When she was finally able to focus, she glanced at the clock on the nightstand and realized it was already close to seven thirty.

She nudged Chris's shoulder—the one she'd been using as her personal pillow—and said urgently, "Wake up, Chris! Someone's at the door."

He awoke with a start, looking from Holly to the clock, and groaned. "It's Annabel and Sam," he informed her. He was out of bed in a flash, retrieving his jeans and shirt from where he'd left them hanging on the back of the bathroom door. "I forgot to tell you they're coming to breakfast," he said as he pulled his jeans on commando and zipped them up. His shirt was halfway on before he realized it was inside out. The doorbell pealed again and he ripped his shirt off, turned it right side out and tugged it on.

He ran a hand through his shaggy hair—and oh, how she hated that it fell right into place as if he'd brushed it—then added, "They're coming to have breakfast with you and me so we can make plans for catching the McCays in the act. I'll go let them in and take them into the kitchen. You can come in after you're dressed."

He was almost out the door when he turned back, snatched Holly up from the bed into his arms and kissed her senseless. He took his time about it, too. "Good morning," he whispered when he finally raised his head. His eyes were an intense blue, and Holly couldn't think of anything to compare them to. "Thank you for last night." Then his expression morphed from romantic hero to hard-as-nails PI. "And for God's sake, don't let Annabel see that satisfied look in your eyes—she's a bloodhound. Sam, too, but Annabel's a woman—she'll know exactly what put that look there." Then he was gone.

"About time," Annabel said when Chris finally opened the door barefoot. "I thought I was going to have to use my key."

Chris stared at her, perplexed. "When did I give you a key?"

"You didn't. I asked Peg, and she gave me a copy. She gave me the alarm code, too."

"What the—" He started to say *hell* but remembered just in time he was trying to break the swearing habit. He shepherded Sam and Annabel toward the kitchen while his guilty conscience gave him hell for all the times he'd said "crap" yesterday. *You're supposed to be cleaning up your language*, his conscience reminded him. Not just for Susan and Bobby, but for Ian and Jamie, too.

Annabel was still explaining about the key. "I asked Peg what her cleaning schedule was, what days of the week she came out here, and I told her I'd swing by regularly to check on her. I also told her I'd stop by every few days when she wasn't here, just to keep an eye on the place for you."

Chris was touched. "Thanks, Bella."

Annabel said gruffly, "Just part of my job—serve and protect," as if pretending she hadn't done anything out of the ordinary. When they walked into the kitchen, she glanced around, then said drily, "Nice breakfast."

"Coming right up," Chris told her. "You and Sam have a seat. I kind of overslept this morning." He quickly dumped food in the dog's dish and checked there was still water. Then he grabbed bowls from the cabinet, spoons from the drawer, and slapped them on the table. The gallon of milk from the fridge was followed by boxes of Cap'n Crunch and Cheerios from the pantry.

"Are you frigging kidding me?" Sam asked. "Cap'n Crunch?"

"Hey," Chris said, feigning hurt. "It's one of the basic food groups."

"I thought we'd at least be treated to your signature French toast," Annabel said.

"I was planning on it, but I told you, I overslept." Chris turned back to the counter to grab a couple of paper towels for napkins when he sensed rather than heard Holly walk into the kitchen. He swung around and barely managed to keep the betraying smile off his face. She was dressed as she normally was, in jeans and a cotton blouse—a deep, rich yellow this time. But now that he knew what she looked like *without* her clothes…

"Good morning," Holly said, smiling at Annabel. Then she turned to Sam. "I've already met Annabel, but you must be…Sam, right? Sam Colton?" She held out her hand. "Chris said you're a detective with the Granite Gulch Police Department. I'm Holly McCay."

As soon as Sam let her hand go, Holly glanced at the table and said longingly, "Ooohhh, Cap'n Crunch. I haven't had Cap'n Crunch since I was little." Then she reached for the Cheerios box instead. "But I shouldn't."

Chris heard the regret in her voice. He poured Cap'n Crunch into a bowl and handed it to her. "Indulge. Once in a blue moon won't hurt you."

"Thanks." The smile she gave was one some women reserved for a gift of expensive jewelry, and Chris couldn't help returning her smile.

Out of the corner of Chris's eye he could see Annabel's head swivel from Holly to him and back again, and he could almost see her radar antenna quivering. *Crap!* He quickly amended the thought to *crud*, but it didn't come anywhere near expressing his fear that Annabel had somehow divined he and Holly had slept together. Just because he'd given her a bowl of Cap'n Crunch.

Chris tried to deflect Annabel's attention—and Sam's, too, for that matter, since Sam was giving him the once-over and doing the same to Holly—by saying, "Before I forget, I should tell you I went to the prison yesterday, and I got my clue." He snorted. "Biff."

"Biff?" Annabel measured Cheerios into a bowl and added milk. Then she handed the cereal box to Sam. "What's that supposed to mean?"

Chris turned the coffeemaker on, leaned back against the sink and crossed his arms. "Beats the heck out of me." He glanced at Sam. "Mean anything to you?"

His brother shook his head. "Doesn't seem to match the other clues. Texas. Hill. *B*. Peaches. Remember Trevor's theory that Matthew buried Mama on her parents' property in Bearson, Texas? That house sits on a hill, and there's a peach tree in the back yard. So all those clues fit. But Biff?"

"Sounds like a name," Holly volunteered.

"Yes, but…I can't think of anybody in the family by that name," Annabel replied. "Not even if it was a nickname." She turned to Chris. "Did you ask Trevor?"

He stiffened. He couldn't help it. "No," he said curtly. "Couldn't reach him yesterday. Left a message on his voice mail. And Ridge's, too." Annabel looked as if she were going to take him to task over his attitude toward Trevor, but he cut her off, warning, "Don't start, Bella. You can ask him if you want."

Which effectively ended that conversation. Chris's gaze moved from Annabel to Sam, who had his head down and his attention focused on his breakfast. Then Chris's gaze ended up on Holly. She was acting as if nothing was wrong, but she'd poured cereal into a bowl for him—his beloved Cap'n Crunch—and was adding milk. Just as if he were as young as her twins. Their eyes met, and for a moment they were alone in the room. "Eat your breakfast," she said eventually in a composed voice. Her "Mommy" voice, which she used with Ian and Jamie.

A smile tugged at the corners of his lips. "Yes, ma'am."

Sam and Annabel had left an hour ago, promising to start setting their end of things in motion. Holly was talking with her sons on the phone in the master bedroom. Wally at his feet, Chris was sitting in his office, brooding. Not over the plans they'd made about the McCays, but about his clue, Biff. And about Trevor.

A voice from the doorway said, "Want to tell me what that was all about?"

He swiveled around in his chair. He didn't ask "What do you mean?" because he knew. "Trevor and I have… issues."

"No! Really?" Holly said in a fake shocked tone. She moved into the room and took a seat on the sofa. Wally bounded over, tail wagging, and Holly scratched him behind his ears. "Want to talk about it?"

He did and he didn't. He knew what Holly would say. The same thing Annabel said—he wasn't being fair to Trevor. And he didn't want Holly to think he was holding on to a grudge like an eleven-year-old kid…although he was.

He sighed. "It's ancient history. And I know I should let it go. I *know* that. Annabel has told me often enough. But—"

"But you can't."

He shook his head.

"So what is it you can't let go?"

He didn't answer right away, tying to marshal his thoughts into some kind of order. Finally he said, "Trevor is three years older than me. I practically worshipped him as far back as I can remember. He could do anything in my eyes. And he was a great brother. I mean, he never seemed to mind when I tagged along after him, although three years is a pretty big gap in children's ages. He taught me to read when I was four. How to slide into second base when I was seven. How to throw a perfect spiral when I was nine, even though my hands weren't big enough to really hold the football right. He taught me so much..." The memories were all coming back to him, making his throat ache.

"So what happened?" The gentle, nonjudgmental way she asked the question told him she didn't want to know because she was curious. She wanted to give him the opportunity to talk about something he'd kept bottled up inside him for years.

"My father murdered my mother, that's what happened," he said flatly. "All seven of us were sent to separate foster homes. I was eleven. Trevor was fourteen." He swallowed the sudden lump in his throat that belonged to the eleven-year-old boy he'd been. "Trevor never made any attempt to stay in touch with me. I saw him a few times a year, but never at his instigation. Only during court-mandated visitation we all had with Josie at her foster parents' home. And when Josie decided she didn't want to see us anymore, that was it."

"Oh, Chris." Two little words that spoke volumes about Holly's tender heart.

"That's not all of it," he told her. "The story is that when Trevor turned eighteen he tried to get custody of Josie—the baby of our family. She was only seven at the time. But I always wondered just how hard he really tried before he headed off to college."

Holly's eyes closed as if she were holding back sudden tears, a conjecture that was confirmed when she opened her eyes again and they glistened. “What did Trevor say when you asked him?”

“I never asked him.”

There was a long silence. Then softly, “Why not?”

Why hadn’t he asked Trevor? When Chris had finally reconnected with all his brothers, why hadn’t he asked Trevor why he’d abandoned him? Why hadn’t he asked him about Josie?

“Because...” *Because why?* he asked himself. “Because a grown man doesn’t ask another grown man those questions.”

“Oh, Chris.” The same two words she’d said before but this time was slightly different. Even though the maternal tenderness was there, even though he could hear how she ached for the lost and bewildered eleven-year-old boy he’d been as well as the man he was, there was also a note of something he couldn’t quite put his finger on. Then it came to him. It was the same way all the women in his life had from time to time said, “Men!” As if the workings of the male mind were incomprehensible to women, and their feelings about it could be condensed down into one word that all other women automatically understood.

Despite the emotions churning inside him, something about it tickled his funny bone. “Stupid, huh?”

“Not stupid.” She looked down at Wally at her feet and scratched his head again. “But if you never ask, you’ll never know.” She raised her eyes to his. “And I think you need to know, Chris, one way or the other. You need closure. Just like you need to know where your mother is so you can bring her home. So you can give her a decent burial. Just like you need to find out what happened to Josie. Closure. You’ll never rest until you have it. One way or the other. Think about it.”

She stood and snapped her fingers at Wally, who immediately rose. "Come on, boy," she said. "I think it's time to let you outside."

Chris stared at the door through which Holly had just left, thinking about what she'd said, and realized she was right in one way. But she was wrong, too. Because there was another reason he'd never asked his brother why he'd abandoned him—he was afraid to know the answer. Because the answer might be…that Chris hadn't been worth the effort.

Chapter 14

After lunch Chris told Holly, "I need to take a ride out to my grandparents' place to check on something. It's about an hour from here, in Bearson. Come with me?"

It was worded as a question, but Holly knew it wasn't really. Chris didn't want to leave her alone in the house, not even with an alarm system and Wally to protect her. Thinking of the dog made her ask, "What about Wally?"

"We'll take him with us. He can run free to his heart's content out there—the house sits on a hill overlooking several acres."

"Okay."

"Need to call Ian and Jamie before we go?"

Holly was touched Chris had asked, but she shook her head. "I called them right before lunch. They're having a blast. And besides, Peg has my cell phone number. I hardly ever use it—"

"I know."

He knew because he'd been hired to find her. The reminder made her shiver, wondering what would have happened if the McCays had hired a different private investigator, one without the strong moral conscience that was such a large part of Chris's makeup. She sent up a little prayer of thanks that Chris *had* been the one who'd found her and the twins. And that he'd taken them under his protection.

"Well…anyway," she said, "Peg has my number if anything comes up, and she knows to call me."

"And we won't be that far away," he reminded her.

"Right." She smiled. "When did you want to leave? And is what I'm wearing okay?"

The wicked gleam in his eye as he looked her over sent warmth surging through every part of Holly's body, reminding her of last night. The way he wouldn't let her be shy with him. Especially the last time, when he'd coaxed her into letting him do unspeakable things to her body. Unspeakable things she wished he would do again. And again. But all he said was "If you've got boots, wear them. Otherwise you're fine. Five minutes okay?"

Chris had laid a blanket down in the back of his truck and had fastened Wally's leash to the side when Holly came out of the house, tugging the door closed behind her. "You want to lock this, Chris? And I don't know how to set the alarm."

He quickly hooked Wally's collar to the leash, then jumped down and headed to the house. "You should have reminded me to explain about the alarm the first day. All you do is this," he said, showing her, then making her repeat the six-digit code after him. He locked the door and resettled his black Stetson on his head. "You ready?"

They drove west, picking up US-380 and crossing over

the southern tip of Lake Bridgeport, then through Runaway Bay. At Jacksboro they switched to TX-114. The truck ate up the miles—Holly smiled a little to herself and didn't say a word about the speed-limit signs they passed. But she trusted Chris and his driving, so she wasn't unduly worried they were going a good ten miles per hour over the limit.

He slowed as they drove through the little town of Jermyn, then resumed his earlier speed. "You seem to know the way," she said for something to say.

"I've been here before. We visited my mother's parents every couple of months when I was a kid. But after Matthew mur—after we went into foster care, no. And my mother's death was the death knell for my grandparents. They went downhill quickly after that, is what I heard, and I never saw them again. I didn't even know they were ailing—but that's probably why we had to go into foster care permanently—they weren't able to take care of us. They passed away a month apart."

He was silent for a moment. "My brothers and sisters and me—we own the place now. No one wants to live there, but no one can bear to sell the place because it's where Mama grew up. We all chip in to pay the taxes and the upkeep—well, not Josie but the rest of us. And we rent out the acreage to the farmer across the road, who keeps an eye on the house for us—vacant houses are easy targets for vandals and migrants—we gave him a fair reduction on the rent to do that."

He drew a deep breath. "And I've been here a few times since I graduated from college. Not a lot, maybe once every two years, because—"

"Because what?" she asked when he didn't continue.

"Don't get me wrong, I don't believe in ghosts. But every time I go there, I feel…I don't know…sad, I guess.

Thinking about my mother as a little girl there. Remembering the whole family visiting my grandparents there. They were good people, Holly, and my mother was their only child. It killed them—literally killed them—when she was murdered. I don't know how anyone ever survives the loss of a—"

When he broke off this time Holly knew what he'd been going to say. *The loss of a child.* Chris had lost a child. Not a child he'd held in his arms, but still…

She tried to imagine losing Ian or Jamie, and couldn't. She just *couldn't.* Chris's baby had died unborn, but that didn't mean he hadn't already loved it. She remembered how she'd felt when she'd been four months pregnant, and how Grant had felt, too. They'd already loved their baby-to-be—before they'd known there were two—but that was nothing compared to now. So she knew how devastated Chris's grandparents had been at the loss of their only child.

She reached across and placed a comforting hand on Chris's arm, letting him know she understood. Not just how his grandparents had felt, but how he felt, too.

Just before Loving they turned south on TX-16—Loving Highway, the sign read. And Holly wondered where the name had come from. Loving Highway was obviously named after the town of Loving, but how had the town gotten its name? *Must have been named after someone*, she figured. She didn't imagine Texas cattle barons being the sentimental kind.

Her curiosity piqued, she asked Chris. "You're right," he said. "Nothing to do with loving." He glanced at her and all of a sudden she couldn't breathe. Couldn't think. Could only remember how Chris had made her body sing last night. Her nipples reacted as if he'd caressed them, tightening until they ached. She crossed one arm over her breasts to hide her reaction from Chris, because she didn't want him to know.

Then he turned his eyes back to the road and said, "The town was named Loving because it was built on part of the Lost Valley Loving Ranch. And *that* was founded by a famous north Texas cattle drover, Oliver Loving."

"Thanks." Her body still humming with need, Holly turned away and gazed out the window. Very, very sorry she'd asked.

Regina Willard surreptitiously slid the wallet she'd just stolen from a woman in the drugstore into her purse, then walked out as if she hadn't a care in the world. *Women are such fools*, she thought contemptuously. Carrying their wallets in purses so full they couldn't be zipped or snapped closed. Then placing their opened purses in the child seat of a shopping cart…and wandering away. *She deserves to have her wallet stolen*, Regina rationalized. She wasn't a thief. She would cut up and discard the credit cards. And she would drop the money in the wallet into the collection box of the first church she came to.

No, she wasn't a thief. But she needed the driver's license. Now that the FBI and the Granite Gulch Police Department had trumpeted her name and photo to the news media, she needed new identification so she could get a job. One middle-aged woman looked very like another in most people's minds. And besides, driver's license photos were notoriously bad, often looking nothing like the people they were supposed to represent. So she wasn't worried about bearing only a vague resemblance to the photo on the driver's license she'd just stolen. All she'd needed was new ID, so she was set now. Next step, finding a job…unless she spotted the woman who'd stolen her fiancé. Killing her would take precedence over anything else.

"This is it?" Holly asked as they drove up a long, winding drive to an older farmhouse perched on the top of a rise. "It's beautiful. Oh, I love those tall trees planted all around the house."

"Folks did that a lot in the old days. Windbreaks, they're called. Nowadays a lot of homeowners don't want to be bothered with trees—too many leaves to rake." He smiled as he parked the truck and they got out. "Back then the trees did more than act as windbreaks. They provided much-needed shade at a time when there was no air-conditioning. Which reminds me," he told her with a slight grimace. "There's no central air. My grandparents had window units installed, but…"

"I'll be fine. It's hot, but it's not that hot. When I was a little girl, before I started school, my parents used to take me on their missionary trips to South America. No AC in an Amazon rain-forest jungle hut. I think I'll survive."

They crossed the deep front porch, and Holly looked around curiously. Two wooden rockers resided on one side, a porch swing on the other. Chris saw where her attention was focused and said, "My grandparents called it a courting swing. But we kids didn't care about that." A reminiscent smile curved his lips. "We all tried to squeeze onto it when we younger—Trevor, me, Annabel, Ridge, Ethan and Sam. Five squirming boys and one long-legged girl with sharp elbows." He rubbed his ribs as if remembering all the times Annabel had dug her elbows into his ribs, but he was smiling, so Holly knew it was a good memory.

"No Josie?"

"She was just a baby." He laughed. "No way Mama would have trusted us with her on the porch swing." Then he seemed to recollect why he was here. He unlocked the door and pushed it open. "Come on. I want to see if I can find anything that might relate to Biff."

The curtains were drawn over all the windows in the front parlor, making the interior dim and gloomy even though the sun was shining brightly outside. So Chris flicked the switch, and the old-fashioned overhead light fixture came on. "We kept the electricity on," he explained. "The water, too. But we disconnected the propane and sold the stove and the refrigerator because we figured we didn't need them if no one was living here. Not that they were worth a lot—the fridge was almost twenty years old, and the stove was even older. But they were useful to someone, so…" He shrugged.

Holly looked around. "Who keeps the place clean?"

"The farmer who rents the land, his wife comes over once a month. She dusts—not that a lot of dust accumulates with no one living in the house—and she runs the vacuum over the floors. That's one of the reasons we kept the electricity on. We let her pick whatever she wants off the peach tree in the back, too, because otherwise it would just go to waste. She makes her own preserves and she bakes one heck of a peach cobbler."

He was silent for a moment. Then he admitted, "We probably should sell the place, but…as I told you, none of us can bear to let it go."

Holly was wandering around the room, picking up a knickknack here, a hand-crocheted doily there, then carefully replacing them. "I can understand in one way, but… someone put a lot of love into making this house a home with all these little personal touches. You shouldn't leave these things here where they can be stolen or vandalized."

Her eyes met his. "But it's not just that. You—I don't mean just you, but the rest of your family, too—should go through the furnishings and decide what you want for your own homes. These things should be used, Chris. Treasured…but used. Not left as some kind of shrine." She reverently touched the afghan folded and placed across the back of the sofa, crocheted in a lightning pattern of royal blue and grass green, with a thin stripe of orange to add pizzazz. "If this were mine…"

She sighed, remembering her home in Clear Lake City, which had contained similar handmade treasures she'd inherited from both her grandmothers. Including three patchwork quilts and a yo-yo quilt. Not to mention the old-fashioned foot-pedal sewing machine she'd never used but had proudly displayed, which had come to her from her great-grandmother. When she'd run, she'd called a moving company to pack up everything and put it in storage, because even though she'd been terrified, she couldn't just abandon her heritage. *Having money comes in handy*, she thought. What would she have done if she hadn't been able to afford to put her belongings in storage?

You still would have run, she acknowledged. *It might have broken your heart to abandon everything, but you still would have run.*

An hour later, while Chris was searching the bedrooms, Holly came across a stack of old photo albums on a bookshelf in the corner of what she insisted on calling the parlor. *Because that's what it is*, she'd stubbornly told Chris.

She knelt in front of the bookcase and pulled out a half-dozen velour-covered photo albums. The deep blue velour was faded, but the silver lettering was still visible, and she figured she'd just uncovered a gold mine. "Look at this, Chris," she called. When he joined her, she handed the photo albums to him and stood, wiping off the knees of her jeans even though the floor wasn't really dusty.

Chris was already sitting on the sofa, turning the leaves of the first album, when Holly sat next to him. "Look," she exclaimed. "There are captions on the photos!"

The books appeared to be in chronological order. They went through the first one, but it was mostly pictures of Chris's mother as a baby, then as a toddler, all of them neatly labeled. There were a few pictures of a man and a woman Chris identified as his grandparents—which matched the first names in the spidery handwriting beneath the pictures—and some of people he admitted he had no idea who they were. "Todd and Nora," he read. "Todd and Nora who?"

"Doesn't matter. Neither one is Biff."

Holly touched Chris's arm to get his attention. "Would you explain about the clues? You said your clue was Biff, and Sam mentioned other clues that seemed to point here to your grandparents' house. But why is your father doing this to you? Why won't he just come right out and say where he buried your mother?"

"Because he's a twisted son of a bitch," Chris said roughly. "I think he's getting a kick out of torturing us. Like 'Ha-ha-ha, you think you can find her?'" His right hand, the one he'd been using to turn the pages of the photo album, formed a fist.

She didn't know why she did it, but she curled her left hand around Chris's fist, her fingers stroking gently until he unclenched his hand and twined his fingers with hers.

"It hurts," he whispered. "Not just that we can't find her, but that he won't tell us. Won't tell me."

"Why does it hurt so much?"

Chris released her hand abruptly, stood and strode restlessly around the room. "All these years I never wanted to see my—to see Matthew. Never visited him in prison the way Trevor did, even when he asked to see us. Not that Trevor was visiting because he wanted to," he explained, "but because it was his job as an FBI profiler. He's the only one who ever visited Matthew until Matthew began this...blackmail scheme."

He drew a ragged breath. "Until I went to see him yesterday, though, I always believed... I don't know... I always believed that somewhere inside him was the father I remembered. Strict. Stern. Okay, yeah, harsh, too, sometimes. But a man who loved his children as best he could."

"But you don't believe that anymore."

He shook his head. "Yesterday I realized the father I remember no longer exists. If he ever did."

Holly tried to think of something to say, but all she came up with was "No one is all good or all bad. Do I think he's a twisted son of a bitch, as you called him? Maybe. And maybe he's using these clues to torture you, the way you think. But you said he's dying, and he knows it. You also said he asked to see you before—but that none of you did, except Trevor...and then only because it was his job. Isn't it possible Matthew wanted to see all his children one last time before he died? And in his sick, twisted mind, this was the only way he could think of to compel you all to visit him?"

She rose and walked to where Chris was, looking up at him, beseeching him to understand there was always another side to a story. "If he gave you halfway decent clues," she said softly, "you might solve the riddle before he provides the last clue. Which means the children who haven't yet visited him probably wouldn't have to."

The arrested expression on Chris's face told her he'd never considered this as a possibility. "You really think…?" he began.

"I don't know. But neither do you. Not for sure. Don't assume you know his motive. And don't erase what few good memories of him you have. Is he a serial killer? Yes. Did he murder your mother, who loved him? Yes. Am I glad he's in prison and can't do to anyone else what he did twenty years ago to all those other people? Of course. I despise what he did. But I also pity him from the bottom of my heart."

"You feel *sorry* for him?"

Holly nodded slowly, hoping she could make Chris understand. "Because he'll never know how wonderfully his children turned out. He'll never see the man I see when I look at you."

Chris didn't know what to say. He never knew what to say when someone gave him a personal compliment. *And why is that?* he wondered now. Insecurity left over from his childhood?

He was a damned good private investigator, he knew that. And he'd built Colton Investigations from nothing into the hugely successful business it was today with only his determination and willingness to work harder than anyone who worked for him—sometimes twelve- to fourteen-hour days. A thriving business with three—soon to be four—offices.

Self-confidence in the business arena didn't always

translate into self-confidence in the personal arena, however. And he'd never quite convinced himself that his older brother hadn't abandoned him…because he wasn't worth hanging on to.

Laura loved you, he reminded himself. But it had never erased that sliver of self-doubt from his psyche.

Not that he'd dwelled on it a lot—he wasn't the kind to waste time in fruitless self-analysis, as a general rule. But yesterday's meeting with his father, the heart-to-heart with Ethan at the hospital and the conversation with Holly this morning about his issues with Trevor had all forced him to consider how the man he was had been impacted by everything that had happened in his life. Losing his mother and his family, not to mention Bouncer, his constant companion for five years. Growing up in a town where he could never escape the notoriety of being a serial killer's son. Foster parents who'd never been invested in him, who'd taken him in not out of the goodness of their hearts but for the money. The deaths of his wife and unborn child.

Pity party, Colton? he jeered mentally. *Suck it up, old son, suck it up. Don't dump this crap on Holly—she's got enough to handle right now.*

So instead of (a) telling Holly how much it meant that she saw him as a wonderful man, (b) kissing her and telling her the same thing, (c) kissing her until the pleading expression in her eyes became a plea that he make love to her until neither of them could walk or (d) telling Holly what he was thinking, he settled for (e). "Let's finish going through those photo albums," he said curtly. "There's got to be a Biff in one of them."

It was in the second photo album, containing pictures of Chris's mother around the time she was starting kindergarten, with dark hair in two pigtails when she was wearing jeans, and hanging in loose curls when she was wearing her Sunday best, that they spotted it.

"'Saralee and Biff,'" Chris read, not quite believing what he was seeing. Then he said blankly, "Biff was her dog."

Chapter 15

"She looks to be about five, wouldn't you say?" Holly asked, a trace of excitement in her voice. "He's just a puppy, but he kind of looks like Wally. Biff must be a golden retriever, too."

Chris turned the page, and there were more photos of his mother as a child, and the dog—no longer a puppy—who appeared to be her best friend. There were photos of Saralee with other girls, too, but Biff seemed to feature in most of them. Chris flipped through all the way to the end, then quickly opened the third photo album. There were fewer photos of Saralee here, as if she'd become self-conscious about having her picture taken when she grew into her teens. But there were still photos of her with Biff, and Chris felt a sudden ache in the region of his heart, an unexpected kinship with his long-dead mother he'd never felt before. "I never realized…"

"Girls and dogs," Holly reminded him. "I told you a

strong bond can exist between a girl and her dog." She went through several pages, one by one, Saralee maturing with each page. They were almost to the end before they realized there were no more photos of Biff. Holly turned back to the previous page, and there was a photo of Saralee all dressed up, with a young man at her side, obviously her date for the evening. There were other teenagers in the background, and the caption read "Saralee and Jeff—Sweet Sixteen Birthday Party." Captured in the bottom right corner of the photo was Biff. Just one ear and his muzzle, but it was definitely him.

But on the following page and all the subsequent pages, Biff was noticeably absent. One picture caught Chris's attention, titled "Saralee and Luke—Junior Prom." He touched it, thinking how much Annabel resembled their mother when they were both that age. Annabel was a blonde and Saralee was a brunette, but their faces were nearly identical.

"Junior prom," Holly said softly. "She would have been seventeen." She was silent for a moment. "Biff must have died sometime between her sixteenth birthday and her junior prom. Seventeen."

"Yeah." Chris carefully went back through everything between the Sweet Sixteen and Junior Prom photos, but there was no picture indicating exactly when Biff had died, or where he might be buried. *Mama would have buried him in a special place*, he told himself, knowing it for the truth. Just as he would have buried Bouncer in a special place…if Bouncer hadn't been euthanized at the pound. If Chris had been allowed to bury his dog.

He couldn't help but wonder—if his mother really *was* buried somewhere here on her parents' land—if his father had buried her near her beloved dog. It didn't sound like the father who'd blackmailed his children into visiting him in prison. The father who'd grudgingly doled out meager clues to his wife's burial place. But it *did* sound like a man who'd once been in love with his wife. Who hadn't meant to kill her…and then felt remorse when he saw what he'd done. Who'd wanted to make amends in some way…even in something as simple as this.

Holly was right, he realized suddenly. *You can never really know another man's motivations. You might think you do, but...*

Chris didn't subscribe to the theory that to know all was to forgive all. His father had killed ten people. Not surprising he'd gotten the death penalty in a state where the death penalty was often imposed in capital murder cases, but behind the scenes political machinations had gotten those death sentences commuted to sentences of life in prison without the possibility of parole—to be served consecutively. Matthew would never get out of prison—except in a box. And Chris couldn't be sorry. Maybe his father had been sick, but if so, it was a sickness that could never be cured. No one else's loved one would ever die at Matthew's hand, and Chris was fine with that. Matthew was in prison—exactly where he belonged.

But…

Holly was right about that, too, he acknowledged. *No one is all good or all bad. Mama wouldn't have loved him if he was purely evil. And she* did *love him—I know she did.*

Which meant that Holly could be right and he could be wrong. Maybe his father *had* just wanted to see all his children one last time before he died. No matter what he had to do to make it happen.

Holly swung on the front porch swing while Chris strode around the outside of the house and the barn with an exuberant Wally at his heels. He'd told her he really didn't expect to find anything—it was twenty years ago, he'd stated flatly—but he had to look anyway.

Holly watched Chris from afar, her thoughts in turmoil. Every so often she pushed the swing with one booted foot to keep it moving. The hinges squeaked—*needs oiling*, she told herself—but it was still soothing to swing. And she needed something to soothe and calm her, because she realized she was in over her head.

Whatever this was with Chris had gone from zero to sixty in nothing flat. Last night—she couldn't get last night out of her mind. She'd never looked on sex as a recreational pastime. Sex with Grant had been an extension of her love for him, and even though it hadn't been…well…hadn't been anything like sex with Chris, she'd never in a million years have imagined she could react that way with a man she didn't love.

Three times in one night. The thought chased around and around in her mind, three orgasms that had shattered her image of herself. She'd almost convinced herself the first time had been a fluke…until the second time. Until Chris's fingers had intertwined with hers and he'd whispered in her ear, *I'm going to please you until you can't take any more. And when I'm done, you'll know just how perfect you are.*

Her response the second time had been as cataclysmic as the first, and she'd thought nothing could ever surpass either of them. She'd been wrong. Because the third time, when he'd said, *I want to watch you come. Will you let me?* she hadn't been able to refuse—she'd melted just *thinking* about it. She'd always been curious, but Grant had never wanted to do it, and she'd never pressed.

But Chris seemed to have no inhibitions. And he hadn't let her have them, either—that was what she couldn't get over, how utterly different she was when Chris was in her bed.

Best time ever, she acknowledged now. All because of a man who tugged at her heartstrings on so many levels. A solitary man who should never have been allowed to be such a loner—he was made for laughter and sweet loving. For children's hands trustingly clutching his, and a woman's tender smiles.

And sex. Holy cow, was he made for sex. All six foot two, hundred seventy-five pounds of solid muscle and bone, with an unerring knowledge of her body, as if she was made for him. As if he was made for her.

That thought brought her up short, and she dragged one foot on the ground to stop the swing. It wasn't possible. She'd known him for less than a week. "Not even a week," she muttered under her breath. But if she were honest with herself—something she tried very hard to be, always—it felt as if she'd known him forever, because she could usually tell what he was thinking, the way long-married couples seemed to be able to do.

Long-married couples? *What made you think of that?*

And sleeping with him? What was *that* all about? Not something she'd ever done before, sleep with a man she barely knew. Which begged the question—why *had* she slept with Chris?

She shied away from answering, because the question alone scared the hell out of her...much less the answer.

The drive home seemed to take longer than the drive out to the farm in Bearson, mainly because Chris and Holly didn't talk much. He glanced at her from time to time as she gazed out the window at the passing scenery—scrubland that wasn't much to look at.

Finally he couldn't take it any longer. "What are you thinking about?"

She turned and resettled herself against the truck door. "Last night."

"Before, during or after?"

She laughed as if she couldn't help it. "Why is it," she asked him, trying to look stern but failing miserably, "that you can always make me laugh, even when I don't want to?"

"Answer my question first." He cast her a wicked look before firmly fixing his gaze on the road. "Then I'll answer yours."

Laughter pealed out of her, and she shook her head. "Mine was a rhetorical question. I'm not expecting an answer."

"I am." And just like that he wanted her. His voice dropped, the husky sound taking on sexual overtones that at one time had come as natural to him as breathing. "Before, during or after?" He stole a sideways glance at her, and loved the way her cheeks betrayed what she was thinking, and guessed, "During."

"Yes." It was just a thread of a sound.

"If we hadn't been interrupted this morning…"

"Yes?"

His answer mattered to her. He didn't know how he knew, just that it did. So instead of teasing her—his first inclination because it was such fun to tease her—he confessed, "I wanted to see you in the light of day. Not with the sheets pulled up under your chin like they were this morning. But in all your glory."

"You…you shouldn't say things like that to me," she said faintly.

"Why not?" When she couldn't come up with an answer, he said, "Tell me you don't regret last night."

"Oh, no!" Those little flags of color were back in her cheeks, but she leaned over and placed a hand on his arm as if she thought he needed reassurance. He did…but he wasn't about to admit it. "I could never regret last night."

His ego liked hearing that. A lot. That was something else he wasn't going to admit, though, so all he said was "Me, neither." But he couldn't keep the sudden, lighthearted grin off his face.

The first thing Holly did when she got back to Chris's house was call Ian and Jamie, talking with them for almost half an hour while they babbled in their childish way about everything they'd done that day. Then Peg had gotten on the phone, filling her in on how the twins were doing. "They're fine today. No issues. And I wasn't going to tell you," Peg admitted, "but…"

"But what?" Sudden concern made her voice sharp.

"We did have a teensy scene at bedtime last night. Jamie wanted you, and when I told him you weren't there and weren't *going* to be there, he dissolved into tears and sobbed, 'Call-her-on-the-phone.'"

"Oh, Peg, why didn't you call me?" Guilt speared through Holly that she'd been having the time of her life with Chris while her baby needed her.

"I would have, Holly…if he'd continued crying. But Susan gave him her teddy bear to sleep with—you know the one that's bigger than she is?—in addition to his bunny, and he calmed down after that. It only took three bedtime stories and four lullabies and he was out like a light. We haven't had any issues today, although when I asked Ian and Jamie what they wanted for breakfast, they both said, 'Waffos!' So I—"

"You had toaster waffles in your freezer."

"Well, no, I didn't, but no big deal. I dragged out the

waffle iron, mixed up a batch of waffle batter, and they were happy as clams."

"Oh, Peg," Holly repeated, but this time it wasn't a reproach of her friend. This time it was said in gratitude that Peg was doing all this for her. "Thank you so much! I can never repay you for—"

Her response was typical Peg—she snorted a very unladylike snort. "Don't talk to me about repayment, missy," she told Holly. Then her tone changed. "Besides…"

"Besides what?"

"Our tenth wedding anniversary is coming up at the end of next month, Joe and me."

She didn't come right out and ask, but Holly quickly volunteered, "I'd love to keep Susan and Bobby for you and Joe. You could go somewhere nice and romantic."

Peg chuckled in a suggestive way. "Nice and romantic is how we ended up with two children barely a year apart."

Holly was forced to smile. "You know what I mean."

"Yes, and we'll be happy to take you up on your offer… as soon as your in-laws are in jail." That reminder drove the smile from Holly's face. "I know it's only the first day," Peg continued, "but are you making any progress?"

"Not on the McCays," she admitted. "Annabel and Sam have some things to do before we can get started on that. But we may have uncovered something more on where Chris's mother might be buried."

Chris was in his office. He considered calling Annabel and his brothers to tell them what he'd found out about Biff this afternoon, but then chose to shoot one email with the details to all of them instead, saving himself time.

He'd brought all the photo albums back with him, and now he pulled the fourth one out, wondering what else he might uncover. He and Holly hadn't reviewed the last two photo albums after they'd figured out Biff had died near the end of album number three.

But he regretted his decision to keep looking as soon as he opened the fourth album. Because there on the very first page was a professionally taken picture of his mother and father in their wedding finery. So young. So obviously in love.

Two pages later he came across another picture of his parents, both smiling, with an infant. The caption, in what by now he'd figured was his grandmother's handwriting, read "Saralee, Matthew and Trevor."

There were more pictures of Trevor—some with their parents and some by himself—from infant to toddler. Then Chris came upon another professionally shot photo, with three-year-old Trevor looking somewhat self-conscious in a tiny suit, propping up two babies—one in blue and one in pink. And underneath that photo it said "Trevor, Chris and Annabel—our first granddaughter."

Chris turned the pages slowly. Soon Ridge made an appearance, followed by Ethan, then Sam. Josie still hadn't shown up by the time Chris came to the end of album four, so he switched to number five. And there was Josie. Baby Josie as he vividly remembered her. He and Annabel had been closer than most brothers and sisters—that bond of twins—and he'd been protective of her…when she wasn't nudging him with those sharp elbows of hers or trying to wrestle him over something. But Josie had been his baby sister. So tiny, so beautiful, with dark, wispy hair and a baby smile that fascinated him. He'd been eight when Josie was born, and he and Annabel had tried to do whatever they could to help their mother—who'd never really seemed to recover completely after Josie's birth. "Why didn't I remember that?" he whispered as the memory came back to him now, crisp and sharp.

Pictures of all seven children now, some that Chris could have sworn were taken at his grandparents' farm, and— Yes! There was a picture of six of them wedged tightly in the front porch swing, with his parents standing behind them, Josie lying in the crook of his mother's arm.

Then all at once the photos stopped. Halfway down a page, two-thirds of the way through, the photos stopped. And Chris knew why.

Holly, with Wally at her heels, found Chris standing at the window in his office, staring out at nothing. She'd intended to pretend to knock, then ask him what he wanted for dinner. But when she saw him, silhouetted by the dying sun's angled rays through the window, it flashed across her mind that Chris could be alone even in a crowd.

"Chris?"

He swung around sharply, his right hand reaching for the gun in his shoulder holster in what she could tell was an instinctive move. "Holly," he acknowledged a heartbeat later, his hand dropping to his side. "Sorry. You took me by surprise."

Wally bounded across the room toward Chris, tail wagging, tongue hanging out. Sure of his reception in a way Holly envied. She would have liked to run to Chris, wrap her arms around him and let him know he wasn't alone. But she couldn't do that. Could she?

Chris squatted on his haunches, stroking Wally's head with both his hands. Scratching behind the ears where the dog couldn't reach, eliciting the doggy equivalent of a satisfied whimper. And in her mind Holly heard her own whimpers last night as Chris had caressed her body with those big hands of his—not once, not twice, but three times—then made her cry his name, a sound that still echoed in her consciousness.

Her heart kicked into overdrive, and in that instant she would have given anything to have Chris touch her that way again. Make love to her again. But instead of saying what she wanted to say, she glanced at the schoolhouse clock on the wall, drawing his attention to the fact that it was long past dinnertime. "It's getting late," she announced. "You must be hungry. Did you want me to make dinner for us?"

He raised his gaze from Wally and gave her his full attention. "I can cook," he said. His smile was a little crooked. "Pepper steak okay? You can help me chop the vegetables."

In the middle of slicing and dicing, Holly asked quietly, "You want to talk about it?"

Chris narrowly avoided slicing his own thumb when the knife he was using in a semiprofessional manner on the onions threatened to break free. "Not much to talk about."

He turned to the stove and dumped the contents of his chopping board into the cast-iron skillet he'd already used to sear the steak strips. As the onions began sizzling, he took Holly's neatly sliced bell peppers and dumped them into the skillet, too. "It's just…looking at old photos brought back…memories," he volunteered finally.

"Good memories?"

He nodded slowly. "And bad ones. They're a reminder—as if I really needed one—that we don't know where Josie is. But it's not just that. She was three when…

when she went into foster care, and we were only allowed to see her a few times a year. She turned Trevor down, she turned me down, when we tried to get custody of her."

"You mentioned that before."

He added a little water to the skillet using the lid, then stirred the onions and peppers, making sure they cooked evenly. "Yeah, but the hardest part is not knowing anything about *who* she is, not just where she is. I remember her when she was little—she was the happiest baby. And so precocious. She walked early. Talked early. She loved coloring and finger painting—" He chuckled suddenly at a memory. "And oh, how she loved to finger paint, but what a mess she always made. Mama used to say Josie got more paint on herself than on the paper."

"That's one of the good memories, then."

"Yeah." He smiled slowly at Holly. "I'd forgotten all about that. Guess sometimes it does pay to talk about what's on your mind."

They smiled at each other for a minute, until Chris suddenly realized the veggies for his pepper steak were in danger of scorching. He turned back to the stove and stirred furiously, then added in the steak strips he'd seared earlier. Finally he turned off the burner.

"Who taught you to cook?" Holly asked as she got the plates from the cabinet.

"Taught myself when I was in college. I lived off campus with three friends, none of whom could cook. I couldn't stand eating frozen cardboard-like food heated up in the microwave the way they did, and I certainly couldn't afford to eat out all the time. So I checked out a basic cookbook from the library and started messing around. I got to liking it—not just eating decent-tasting food, but the actual process of cooking from scratch. It's relaxing. Once I started Colton Investigations, though, I

rarely had time to cook except on the occasional weekend."

"This is really good," Holly said as she dug in. "Cooking must be like riding a bike. You never really forget how to do it."

Chris forked a bite and chewed thoughtfully. "Not too shabby, if I do say so myself. Meat could have used a little time to marinate—I should have planned ahead and done that."

Holly shook her head at him, smiling. "It's delicious and you know it."

"Well..." Once again he didn't know how to respond to a personal compliment. No one who knew him professionally would believe it, he acknowledged. He was supremely confident as a PI. Not so much in his personal life.

Holly changed the subject back to Josie. "So you've been searching for your baby sister for six years, that's what you said."

"Off and on. Whenever I can."

"But no luck."

He almost agreed, then realized that wasn't quite true. The whole Desmond Carlton thing was setting off alarm bells in his mind, telling him there *should* be a connection there...he just hadn't been able to figure it out. "There *is* something new on Josie—at least I think there is. Remember when I asked Annabel to look after you and the boys the other afternoon?" Holly nodded. "I needed to meet with a reporter in Dallas about an article he wrote."

He went on to give her all the details. If he'd stopped to think about it, he might not have. Holly wasn't a PI. She wasn't even family. But he suddenly wanted to share this with her, knowing instinctively she could be trusted to keep everything to herself. Including...

"So you're worried Josie might have killed Desmond Carlton," Holly stated, going right to the heart of the matter, "and that's why she disappeared."

Chapter 16

"I never said that," Chris was quick to point out.

"You didn't have to say it. But you *are* worried."

"Maybe. Okay, yeah. I am."

"If she did—and that's a big leap, Chris—but if she did, did it ever occur to you it was probably in self-defense?"

He took a deep breath, trying to dispel the tightness in his chest. "It occurred to me."

"Josie was seventeen," Holly said gently. "If she's anything like Annabel—I know Josie has dark hair and Annabel's hair is blond, so I'm not talking about that, I mean her features—but if she resembles Annabel, then she's extremely attractive. She wouldn't be the first seventeen-year-old to be accosted...possibly assaulted... by an older man. Especially if that man was a frequent visitor to her home. If Desmond Carlton was related to her foster parents..."

"Doesn't make it any easier for me to think she killed him in self-defense," he said grimly. "It just reminds me I failed to keep my baby sister safe."

"Oh, Chris…" The hint of gentle chiding in Holly's voice reminded him of the way she talked to the twins sometimes, when they did something she didn't approve of. "You can't blame yourself for *everything*."

"I'm not—" he began, then realized she was right. "Okay, maybe I am," he conceded. "But…"

"But nothing. You tried to get custody of her. You *tried*. She turned you down. You can't *make* other people do the things you want them to do, no matter how much you love them." A stricken expression slashed across Holly's face, and though they'd been discussing Josie, Chris knew instantly she wasn't talking about his sister anymore. "No," she whispered. "No matter how hard you try, you can't make someone choose you. You can't."

Regina Willard shuffled her way up the aisle with the rest of the crowd exiting the movie theater. Her prey was right behind her. Ingrid Iverson—the name the bitch went by these days—had no idea she was being stalked, of course. Inside Regina was cackling with glee. But outside she appeared no different from the other movie patrons who'd just spent an hour and fifty minutes in the darkened theater.

The bitch was with a friend, but Regina wasn't deterred. She slowly made her way to her car while the two women stood talking for a couple of minutes Then the women waved at each other, got into their own cars and pulled out of the parking lot, one turning left, the other turning right.

Regina turned right, following her prey from a safe distance. The woman drove a few miles over the limit.

Breaking the law, she thought self-righteously as her foot depressed the accelerator to keep pace. *But what do you expect from a loose woman like her?*

She'd first spotted Ingrid Iverson a few weeks back, at the Granite Gulch Bar and Saloon. Regina hadn't recognized her at the time, though. Hadn't realized Ingrid was the bitch in disguise. But she *had* seen what a loose woman Ingrid was. Flaunting herself to the men in the bar in a tight-fitting, low-cut blouse and jeans that appeared to be spray painted on. Accepting offers from three different men to buy her drinks. Then letting one of the men sweet-talk her into a booth, where the two sat canoodling until after midnight.

Disgusting, Regina had thought at the time. *No modesty. No morals.*

But she hadn't recognized Ingrid as the bitch who'd stolen her fiancé until she'd spotted her in the movie theater tonight just as the lights were dimming. Then she'd had an epiphany.

Regina had killed the bitch only three nights ago. What name had she been using then? Helena Tucker, that was it. But she was already back. The days between sightings of the bitch were getting fewer and fewer, forcing Regina to take shortcuts. Risks. But she didn't mind, because she was on a mission—making *sure* the bitch stayed dead.

So Ingrid Iverson had to die. And Regina could rest… for a few days, anyway.

Angus McCay propped the phone against his shoulder, writing furiously. Then he put the pen down and gripped the phone in his right hand. "Thank you *very* much, Mr. Colton," he said, waving the notepad on which he'd written an address and a phone number, trying to catch his wife's attention. "What's that?...Oh. Oh, yes, we'll see if we can get a flight up to DFW first thing tomorrow."

He listened intently to the man on the other end. "Hold on while I write that down. Bridgeport Municipal Airport, you said. Do I have that right?" He jotted the name down on his notepad. "Appreciate the suggestion, Mr. Colton. Not likely any plane out of Houston's international airport flies into there, but Houston Hobby might. We'll check."

He listened again, then said, "No, no, we don't need you to pick us up at the airport. We'll rent a car. We'll fly into whichever airport we can get the earliest flight to—we'll let you know. What's that?...Come to your office in Granite Gulch first?"

Angus glanced at his wife, who was nodding vigorously. "Of course, Mr. Colton. We'll call you once we have our flight, let you know when you can expect us tomorrow. And thank you for everything. My wife and I are thrilled we'll finally be able to see our grandsons after all this time."

He hung up. "Why did you say to tell him we'll go to his office?" His face displayed his surprise. "I don't think that's—"

"Of course we won't go to his office." Evalinda McCay's expression was the long-suffering one Angus had seen many times. "That was just a ruse. We aren't even going to book a flight. Call Leonard," she ordered, referring to Leonard Otis, the man who'd been behind the wheel during the last of the three attempts on Holly's life. "Tell him to drive up there tonight with his partner and take care of the problem. Permanently."

Holly was lying on top of the comforter on the king-size bed in her room, crying softly to herself because she didn't want Chris to hear her. She'd retreated to the bedroom after they'd done the dishes, and she'd been in here alone for the past two hours. Chris hadn't followed her. Hadn't sought her out. Had he sensed her need to be alone? Or was there another reason?

She'd almost blurted out her most closely guarded secret at the dinner table…but she hadn't. She'd managed to change the subject while they finished eating and had steadfastly refused to think about it until the kitchen was spotless. But then…then she'd escaped.

She'd called Ian and Jamie, needing to talk to them one last time before they went to bed. And when Peg had gotten on the phone, Holly had been secretly relieved the twins *were* missing her, although she would never have said that to Peg.

But that wasn't the only reason she'd called. She'd also needed to reassure herself she wasn't a bad person because of what she'd done. That the ends justified the means. And while she'd been talking with the twins, she'd believed it.

When she'd finally hung up, though, her thoughts had inevitably returned to her dinner conversation with Chris. She'd been trying so hard to convince him he shouldn't feel guilty over Josie…but she was just as bad. The guilt she was carrying…the guilt she would *always* carry… could never be forgotten. Pushed to the back of her mind much of the time, but…always there. Waiting to sabotage her happiness.

Her heart was breaking. Not for Chris and what he was going through—although she wished with all her heart she could take his pain and heal him. And not for herself—she'd long since acknowledged she couldn't undo what she'd done and she just had to live with it.

No matter how often her conscience gave her hell, she deserved it.

No, her heart was breaking for Grant…and her boys. Knowing she could never tell Ian and Jamie. She *couldn't.* Knowing, too, that wherever Grant was, he knew. Had he forgiven her? She would never know. Not in this lifetime.

A knock on the closed bedroom door startled her, and Chris's deep voice sounded on the other side. "Holly?"

She dashed the tears from her eyes and realized there was no way she could disguise the fact that she'd been crying. She darted toward the master bathroom, grabbed a clean washcloth from the shelf and ran it under cold water. She wrung the washcloth out and placed it like a cold compress against her red and swollen eyes.

"Holly?" he called again. "Are you awake?"

"Just a minute! I'm in the bathroom." Which she was, but not for the reason Chris would think.

She repeated her actions twice, then checked her appearance in the mirror. Passable. Maybe. She clutched the washcloth as she opened the door and pretended to be scrubbing her face, hoping the pink in her cheeks would make Chris think the remaining pink around her eyes was due to the same thing. "What's up?"

Chris stood in the doorway with a partially drunk bottle of beer in one hand, an unopened wine cooler in the other—the wine coolers he'd bought that first day over Holly's not-very-insistent protests. But the first words out of his mouth were "You've been crying."

And what do you say to that? she asked herself. "Yes," she finally admitted. "But nothing to do with you, so don't add it to the load of guilt you're already carrying." Her tone was wry. "That load is already stacked way too high."

The worry in Chris's face over Holly crying morphed

into something else, and for just a moment she couldn't figure it out. Then she recognized it—an expression she'd begun wearing herself shortly after she and Grant were married, whenever she forgot to disguise it. Remorse was a big part of it. And something else—a lack of forgiveness…for oneself.

"Why do you look that way?" she whispered, wanting desperately to know. Wanting Chris to confide in her. Wanting him to *trust* her…the way she already trusted him.

"I should never have touched you…" Holly barely suppressed a gasp, but then he continued, "Without telling you…"

"Telling me what?"

Chris glanced at the king-size bed behind her. "Not here," he said curtly. "Not where I…where we…"

"Then where?" She wasn't about to let him get this far without telling her everything.

"Let's go into the family room. I have something to tell you anyway." He handed her the wine cooler and smiled faintly. "And you might want Wally for moral support."

"I called Angus McCay," Chris said without preamble as soon as Holly settled on the sofa, with Wally at her feet, her wine cooler sitting unopened on a coaster on the end table beside her. Chris perched on the arm of the recliner, a few feet away, one booted foot swinging. He took a sip of his beer. "I told you I was going to, but I wanted you to be aware I actually spoke with him. Starting now we both need to be on high alert. Annabel and Sam will join us for breakfast again—and will stay with us all day tomorrow. So whatever the McCays intend to try, we'll have plenty of witnesses, and plenty of firepower."

"What about tonight?"

"In addition to Wally, this house is as safe as I could make it," Chris explained. "You know the little tinkling sound whenever the front and back doors are opened from the inside?" She nodded. "All the doors and windows are wired. Anything opened from the inside just warns you—that tinkling sound is the interior parent alarm, so parents know if a child is opening a window or a door. But the exterior alarm system is something completely different—it will give us ample warning in case someone tries to break in. I built the house knowing that Laura—" He broke off for a moment, and that remorseful expression returned.

He stared at the beer in his hand, then continued. "I knew Laura might be here alone at times, so I built in every fail-safe I possibly could. If the phone signal is lost, the alarm company calls the police. If someone cuts the electricity, the alarm has a battery backup it can run on for up to eight hours. And if the alarm switches to battery power, it goes off immediately—loud enough to wake anyone—and the alarm company is notified. You can override the alarm, in case the electricity goes out because of a storm or something like that, but you have to have the alarm code. Same thing for letting the alarm company know. There are special codes that tell them if something's wrong and you can't discuss it with them."

Holly started to ask when the battery had last been checked, but Chris forestalled her. "I checked it the day I brought you and the boys here, Holly." A muscle twitched in his cheek. "You think I would have let you stay here a single night without that safety feature?"

In her mind she heard Chris saying the other day, *No one is dying on my watch ever again, you got that? I made myself responsible for you...*

That was when she made the connection. Annabel telling her Chris blamed himself for Laura's death. Peg telling her Chris needed to take care of her and the twins.

"That's what you meant when you said you should never have touched me without telling me," she whispered. "It's something to do with Laura, isn't it?"

Chris stiffened, but he didn't look away. "Yes."

"Not that Laura was the only woman you ever slept with before me, because you told me that up front. It's something to do with her death."

His face could have been chiseled from granite. "Yes."

"Then..." Her throat closed as her heartbeat picked up. Whatever Chris told her was going to take their relationship to an entirely new level. One she wanted. But she would have to be as open with him as she was asking him to be with her. And that would take all the courage she had. "Then tell me whatever it is. Because I want you to touch me." She breathed deeply. "I want you to touch me again, and if you can't until you tell me...then tell me."

He contemplated his beer, then took a swig. And Holly knew whatever it was wasn't easy for Chris to talk about. He wasn't much of a drinker—this was the first beer she'd seen him with in all the time she'd spent in his company—but apparently he needed a little something to loosen his tongue.

Abruptly he said, "Do you know what it's like growing up in a town like Granite Gulch? Not many secrets remain secret for long. And of course, when something bad happens in your family, it's an albatross around your neck forever."

Holly nodded her understanding. "Your father was a serial killer *and* he murdered your mother. Granite Gulch never let any of you forget it."

"Yeah." His eyes met hers. "So I always felt I had

something to prove. From that time on I was driven—to excel. Not just to succeed, but to succeed spectacularly. Does that make sense?" She nodded again.

"I met Laura sophomore year in high school. I took one look at her and I knew I was going to marry her—it was that simple. Through the rest of high school and four years of college, I never really looked at another woman."

Envy unlike anything she'd ever known stabbed through her. Envy of a dead woman who'd had the unswerving love and devotion of a man like Chris, while she… "You loved her," Holly managed. "I know. And she loved you."

"Yes, Laura loved me, and I loved her. But not enough to temper my ambition. Not enough to make her my first priority…as I should have." He was silent for a moment, then dropped the bombshell. "And when she told me she wanted a baby, the first thing I thought of was that would at least give her something to do so she wouldn't always expect me to be home. She never complained, but I knew. I just never…" The expression of savage self-recrimination on his face tore a hole in Holly's heart.

"When she got sick, I wasn't here. I was at work. I was always at work. One office wasn't enough for me. Not even two. I was spreading myself too thin—I knew that—but I was driven to succeed…spectacularly. I was going to prove to everyone in Granite Gulch that I wasn't my father's son. Living here in Granite Gulch but having offices in Fort Worth and Dallas meant I had a hell of a commute every day. Something had to give…and that something was Laura. I loved her, but I didn't make time for her. I gave her *things*," he said bitterly, waving his free hand to encompass the beautiful house around them, "but not the one thing she wanted the most. Me."

He tilted the beer in his hand and drained the dregs,

setting the empty bottle on the chair behind him. Then he faced her again and said, "That's the kind of man I am, Holly. My father's son. A cold, uncaring bastard."

She couldn't bear it. She left the sofa and moved swiftly to stand in front of him, cradling his face in her hands. "You may be his son, but that's not the kind of man you are," she said softly. "You think you're the only one who makes mistakes? Mistakes you can't ever make up for, no matter how much you regret them?" She brushed her lips over his and blinked back tears.

"I never told Grant…never told anyone…but I…I trapped him into marriage." She swallowed hard. "The McCays were right. I trapped him. I loved him so much, I thought that made it right. I thought I could make him love me."

Chris shook his head. "I don't follow you."

"I…seduced him one night when he'd had too much to drink, but not so drunk he couldn't…couldn't perform. I just wanted him to *see* me for once. Not as his best friend since forever, but as a woman. I thought…"

She gulped air. "I didn't… I wasn't deliberately trying to get pregnant… We did take…precautions. But I was overjoyed when it happened. I thought…it's a sign this was meant to be. That we were meant to be together. I knew Grant would do the honorable thing when I told him—that's the kind of man he was."

Her tears spilled over, trickling down her cheeks. "Long before Ian and Jamie were born, I knew I'd made a mistake. But I couldn't undo it. I couldn't even tell Grant what I'd done. He went to his grave thinking it was *his* mistake, thinking *he'd* taken advantage of *me*."

She bent her head and covered her face with her hands, sobbing uncontrollably as remorse and regret swirled through her. Then strong arms closed around her, pulling her against a hard, male chest. "Every time I look at Ian and Jamie," she choked out, her tears staining Chris's shirt, "every time I see Grant in them…I think of how they were conceived. And I know I can never make it up to them. No matter how good a mother I am, I can never make it up to them."

"Shh," he soothed, his hand stroking her back in a comforting fashion. "It's okay, Holly. You're human. You made a mistake." She couldn't have spoken right then even if she'd wanted to. "You love those boys," Chris continued as his arms tightened around her. "Anyone can see that. That's all that matters."

Her fingers clutched his arm, needing something solid to hold on to. Needing the human connection as she cried out her grief over what she'd done to one man in another man's arms. When her tears finally abated, she raised her face to his. "I didn't tell you that for me," she whispered, catching her breath on a sob. "I just wanted you to know you're not alone. Just wanted you to know you're not a cold, uncaring bastard. It's not your fault you didn't love Laura the way she wanted. The way she needed. Just as it wasn't Grant's fault he wasn't in love with me the way I was in love with him." Her eyes squeezed shut for a moment, then opened to face him honestly. "You're human, too, Chris. You made a mistake, just like me. But that doesn't mean you need to live in purgatory the rest of your life to atone for it."

They ended up back in the master bedroom. A part of Chris knew he'd kissed Holly as if his life depended on it, and she'd kissed him back. Then he'd swung her into his arms and carried her in here. But another part of him was taken completely by surprise. He wasn't the romantic kind. He was earthy. Direct. And his lovemaking had always reflected it. But somehow, Holly brought out the romantic in him, and at the moment he'd done it, carrying her into the bedroom had seemed like a good idea.

But he wasn't the only one having romantic ideas, and Holly surprised him. She dragged him into the master bathroom but prevented him from stepping into the shower when he stripped. "Uh-uh," she said, tugging his hand. "Whirlpool tub. When I was giving Ian and Jamie a bath in this tub, I couldn't help thinking it's big enough for two adults." She was already running the water, and when it was six inches deep, she asked, "How do you turn the jets on?"

He showed her, and with the water still running Holly put his hands on the top button of her blouse. Her suggestive "Help me" sent blood pulsing through his body—and one body part in particular.

When she was as naked as he was, he turned the water off, climbed into the whirlpool and helped her in after him. But when Chris would have sat down with his back to the tub, Holly stopped him. "I have this fantasy," she told him, a tiny smile on her lips. "Do you mind?"

Mind? He had no mind when she looked at him that way, when her voice curled through him as tangible as a caress. And the fantasies that came to Chris made his voice husky when he asked, "What did you have in mind?"

Chapter 17

Chris lay half-submerged in the whirlpool, his head pillowed on Holly's breasts, the water swirling around him. Holly's fantasy hadn't involved kinky sex—but then, neither had his. Her fantasy had turned out to be relatively tame compared to some he'd thought of. But how could he complain about fulfilling a fantasy that had him cradled in Holly's arms? A fantasy that involved breasts as tantalizing soft and smooth as hers beneath his head?

And oh, yeah, let's not forget what her hands are doing, he reminded himself blissfully. *Not to mention her legs*. Holly was amazingly limber.

Eventually, though, he couldn't take any more. "Holly," he warned.

"Me, too," she whispered.

They dried themselves quickly, and Chris was glad to note Holly no longer seemed shy about letting him see her body. He looked his fill, which took his body from low gear to full throttle in less than a minute.

He knocked the box of condoms off the nightstand next to the bed in his haste. “Leave them,” he told Holly when she made a move to retrieve the spilled contents. “I have enough for now.” He opened his fist and let the handful he’d grabbed fall onto the nightstand. All except for one.

She gasped and he sucked in his breath when his fingers stroked over her tender flesh and found her ready. His voice was guttural when he said, “So damned ready for me, Holly. Do you know how much that turns me on?”

He captured her right hand and wrapped her fingers around his erection. “Take what you want.” He almost went ballistic when she squeezed, then seated him in place, raising her hips as if to envelop him. She couldn’t quite accomplish it—but he wasn’t going to deny her or himself. His lips found hers as he slid into her tight sheath, swallowing her moan of pleasure. Her hips rose to meet his, taking him so deep he again experienced that sense of coming home he’d felt last night.

He soon found a rhythm that pleased Holly—if her little gasps meant anything. As for him, he loved riding her soft and slow, holding back and building her excitement to fever pitch. “Wait for it,” he panted when her breathing quickened too soon. “Wait for it.”

“Can’t.”

“Yes, you can.” He slowed and she whimpered in frustration. He knew she’d been close, but that orgasm would have been a prairie grass fire—easily started, quickly over. He was aiming for an all-out conflagration, and he wouldn’t be satisfied until she achieved it.

Deep and slow, deep and slow. Her fingernails digging into his shoulders, urging him to go faster. Sharp little fingernails that would have hurt—if he could feel anything other than Holly tight and wet around him, and oh so perfect. *Made for you*, he thought with that fraction of his brain that could still think.

But eventually his control cracked. His thrusts quickened. And Holly's body arched as she cried out his name and came. And came. And came. Her orgasm triggered his, and he let go with one last thrust and her name on his lips.

Wally's howl woke them both from a profound sleep. Holly was dazed and disoriented for a moment, but Chris wasn't. He was in and out of the bathroom before she knew it, tugging on his jeans and zipping them carefully. Wally's howls changed into urgent yips, as if he was trying to get at something. Chris's hands clasped Holly's arms and he pulled her close in the darkness to whisper in her ear, "Get dressed, but stay here. I'm going to check it out." Then he was gone.

"Oh, heck no," she muttered, scrambling into her clothes and tugging her boots on. "What kind of a wuss do you think I am?" She grabbed the first thing she could find that was big and could be used as a weapon. Then she ran after Chris.

She made it into the living room just in time to hear an engine roar as a car or truck accelerated away from the house down the long, winding driveway. A bare-chested Chris was crouched at one of the front windows, peering through the curtains. One hand was tightly clutching Wally's collar, holding him back. The other hand held a gun.

"Chris?" she hissed, and he whirled around.

"Damn it, I told you to stay in the bedroom."

"You're not the boss of me," she shot back without

thinking. Then could have smacked herself for the less-than-adult response. She and Grant had used that phrase when they were kids, and it had become something of an inside joke when they were older. But Chris wasn't to know that.

The tense, worried expression on Chris's face rapidly changed to amusement. "I'm not the boss of you? What are we, in grade school?"

"Okay, that came out wrong. What I meant to say is you can't expect me to just obey you blindly."

"And what's that in your hand?"

Holly glanced down. "Oh. Well. I thought I might need a weapon."

"You were going to take on intruders with a Wiffle bat?"

"It belongs to the boys. I couldn't find anything else." She quickly put it down. "Forget about that." She pointed to the front door. "Was someone trying to break in? Is that why Wally was barking?"

Chris's expression went from amused to grim in a heartbeat. "Apparently so." He opened the front door, then turned on the porch light to see better before stepping outside. But there was nothing to see; whoever had been there was long gone.

"Burglars? Or do you think the McCays…?"

"Could have been your garden-variety burglar, but I doubt it. Too coincidental. But the two figures I saw moved way too quickly to be the McCays—late twenties, early thirties, I'd say." He turned to look at her, his face half in light, half in shadow. "You said the McCays tried to have you killed. Could have been the same goons. If it was them, they probably drove up from Houston—they had enough time."

"It probably *was* them." Holly shivered even though

the evening was warm. "I know this is going to sound funny coming from their intended victim, but…they didn't seem all that competent when they tried to kill me before. What I mean is—"

"If they were halfway good, you'd already be dead?"

She laughed a little. "Something like that." Then another thought occurred to her. "The alarm didn't go off."

Chris came inside, closed the door and locked it with the two dead bolts. "They never got close enough to try the door or attempt to pick the lock. They took off as soon as Wally started howling."

He did something with his gun—*putting the safety on?* Holly wondered—then slid the weapon into the shoulder holster she hadn't noticed before was sitting on the floor by the window. He must have drawn his gun right away, as soon as he retrieved it from his bedroom, she reasoned, but he needed the other hand to hold on to Wally.

"Be right back," Chris told her, disappearing down the hallway. When he returned, his hands were empty.

He crouched down and scratched Wally's ears. "Good boy!" He praised the dog for several more seconds, getting his face washed in the process by an adoring Wally, then stood. "Let's continue this discussion in the kitchen. I want to give Wally a treat."

The clock in the kitchen said it was a quarter to four. Holly watched Wally gobble down the treat Chris gave him in one gulp, then plead for another. "Oh, hell, why not?" Chris said, suiting his actions to his words. "You deserve it." Then he glanced up sharply at Holly and stood. "Sorry."

"Sorry?" She wrinkled her brow in a question.

"I shouldn't have said *hell*. I should have said *heck*."

A smile slowly dawned along with understanding.

"You're trying to clean up your language." Chris looked abashed, and she knew she was right. "I noticed it before, but I didn't really focus on it, if you know what I mean."

"Yeah." He put the bag of doggy treats back into the cabinet. "Peg mentioned the other day that Susan understands a lot of what she hears now. Peg also said she told Joe he needed to watch his language. She didn't say *I* did, too, but..."

The backs of Holly's eyes prickled suddenly, and she knew tears weren't far away. "You're such a good man, Chris," she whispered, moved by his attempt to do the right thing, to set a good example for the children around him, even in something as simple as this. "*Such* a good man."

That was the moment she fell in love with him.

No, that's not true, her inner self argued. *You've been falling in love with him since the first day. You're just now acknowledging it, that's all.*

She walked toward him, then placed her hands on his bare chest. She didn't realize her tears had overflowed their banks until Chris said, "You're crying again." Bewildered. His right hand came up to cup her cheek, his thumb brushing her tears away. "And this time I think it *does* have something to do with me. I just don't know why."

Holly choked back her tears as the laughter Chris could always evoke came to the fore. "Because..." She wasn't about to tell him her sudden revelation that she was in love with him, so she settled for "Because you're such a good man. The kind of man I want Ian and Jamie to grow to be someday."

Chris shook his head. "I'm no role model, Holly."

She cradled his hand against her cheek, smiling through the tears. "Think again."

* * *

Chris and Holly decided to try for a couple more hours of sleep before morning, although Holly made a sound of dismay when Chris brought his gun into the bedroom with them. "Just to be on the safe side," he assured her. "I don't think those men will be back. Not without a better plan." He placed the holstered gun on the nightstand… right next to the box of condoms she'd picked up and returned there last night.

He drew her into the curve of his shoulder. "You're safe here, Holly. I won't let anything happen to you."

"But what if the McCays don't fall for the trap we've set? What then?"

He smiled in the darkness. A grim smile he didn't let Holly see. "Those goons they sent? I'll call Angus McCay first thing in the morning, let him know they failed to kill you."

"How will you do that? You're not supposed to be staying here with me—at least that's what the McCays believe—so how would you know? And besides," she added, "you're not supposed to know the McCays want me dead, remember? So even if you know someone tried to break in, you wouldn't know they were anything other than burglars."

"Trust me, I'll come up with something believable." He laughed, but the humor was missing. "The McCays thought I was stupid enough to fall for their original story and not do a little digging on them. I won't do anything to disabuse their minds of that belief. But I'll get them up here in person." He kissed her temple, his voice softening. "See if I don't."

This time when Annabel and Sam arrived, Holly and Chris were dressed and ready for them. Chris was in the kitchen, putting together the fixings for his "signature French toast," as Annabel called it, and Holly was setting the table.

"I'll get it," she said when the doorbell rang.

Chris glanced at the clock as he whisked eggs in a bowl. "They're late." He looked at Holly. "Make sure it's them before you open the door."

Holly cast him an "are you kidding me, you think I need to be told that?" expression, but didn't say anything.

She glanced through the peephole and saw Chris's sister and brother on the porch. She swung the door open. "Hi, Annabel. Hi, Sam." Sam was in plainclothes; Annabel was in uniform. But they both looked…exhausted. Neither returned her cheerful greeting. And there was no answering smile on either face. "What's wrong?"

"Where's Chris?" Sam asked.

"He's in the kitchen making breakfast for you. French toast?" she faltered.

Sam headed straight for the kitchen, Annabel right behind him. Holly clutched at Annabel's arm. "What's wrong?"

Annabel didn't stop, but she did say over her shoulder, "We found another woman murdered last night. Another copycat serial killing, with the red bull's-eye on her forehead."

"Oh, my God!" Holly covered her mouth with her hand, then quickly followed Chris's twin into the kitchen.

Sam was already telling Chris, "…and her name was Ingrid Iverson. Did you know her?"

Chris put down the bowl he was holding, turned off the fire beneath the skillet and shook his head. "Name doesn't ring a bell. But then the last few years new people have been moving into Granite Gulch. It's not like when we were kids."

Annabel said bluntly, "We're here, Chris, because we promised we would be. But we've been up all night." She glanced at her younger brother. "Sam won't admit it, but he's dead on his feet. I am, too."

"I'm okay," Sam insisted, but Holly saw the smudge-like circles of total exhaustion beneath his eyes. Beneath Annabel's, too.

"No, you're not." Chris's voice had that big-brother quality to it, mixed in with concern. And love. The kind of emotions most men hated to admit they felt toward a brother…even if they did.

Holly would have smiled if this wasn't so serious. Annabel and Sam were supposed to help them spring the trap for the McCays today. That was why they were here. And Chris had already set the plan in motion last night—the attempted break-in early this morning was proof the McCays were already taking the bait.

"I'm not letting either of you participate in this sting in the condition you're in now," Chris said unequivocally. "You're practically weaving on your feet." He thought for a moment. "The McCays sent men to kill Holly early this morning. Yeah," he confirmed when his siblings cast him alert looks that contradicted their exhausted faces.

Chris gave them a brief rundown of what had happened. "Their goons were here, but the McCays are still in Houston, so—"

Annabel interrupted him. "How do you know that?"

Chris smiled faintly. "Trust me, I have my sources. If they're coming in person—and I have a plan to get them here—they can't possibly arrive for a few hours. If they fly, we're talking three to four with all the hassle of flying nowadays. If they drive, at least four hours, maybe five or six even, depending on traffic. Either way, there's time for the two of you to get a few hours of shut-eye."

He gestured toward the stove. "How about I make breakfast, then you can sack out." Chris was already heading out of the kitchen and down the hallway toward the bedrooms, Sam and Annabel following him. Holly brought up the rear.

"You can take my bedroom," Chris told Sam, opening a door. "And, Bella, you can have the other bedroom." Thinking she was being helpful, Holly opened the door to the bedroom across from the master bedroom. "Not that room!" Chris warned…too late.

A baby's room confronted Holly's eyes. Pale green with yellow-and-white trim, colorful decals decorating the walls. A baby crib held pride of place in the center of the room, a darling mobile of butterflies and flowers dangling above it. Exactly the kind of bedroom she'd decorated for the twins—times two—back in Clear Lake City.

Tears sprang to Holly's eyes as she realized this room had been lovingly created by Laura in joyous anticipation of her baby…her baby and Chris's. How much Laura had wanted her baby was clearly evident, even though she'd been only four months pregnant when she…

Holly blinked rapidly to hold back her tears and closed the door as quickly as she could. She turned, and when her eyes met Chris's across the hallway, she mouthed, *I'm sorry.* He shook his head slightly, as if telling her it was okay, he didn't want her to feel bad about her honest mistake. And though she knew he meant it, she hated seeing the shadow of sorrow cross his face.

"Must be this one," Annabel said in her calm voice, as if she hadn't witnessed the interchange between her brother and Holly—something Holly was sure Annabel had seen. "And you're right, Chris. I'm wiped out. A good breakfast and a couple hours of sleep, though, and I'll be good."

"Okay, okay," Sam finally conceded. "You've made your point. But I want a hot breakfast and a warm shower before I hit the hay."

Angus McCay hadn't had a decent night's sleep in months, and last night had been no exception. He'd managed to stave off his creditors, but robbing Peter to pay Paul only worked in the short run, and now the vultures were circling. If he and Evalinda didn't get their hands on the income from the trust Grant had set up for Ian and Jamie—and soon—the house of cards Angus had built would come crashing down. The fallout from that would be disastrous. Not to mention Evalinda would hold him personally responsible.

He and Evalinda had tried to overturn Grant's will legally…to no avail. They'd tried to gain custody of the twins legally, by painting Holly as an abusive mother… but that had gone nowhere. Angus hadn't wanted to resort to murder, he really hadn't. But Evalinda had convinced him it was the only way.

The problem was, as Evalinda had been quick to point out at four this morning, the men he could afford to hire weren't all that bright. Thugs willing to commit murder, yes. But easily stymied. They'd called him shortly after they'd been scared away—by a damn dog—from the house where Chris Colton had told him Holly was staying. But instead of lying in wait for Holly to come out of the house in the daytime and killing her then, they'd been spooked. They hadn't turned tail and run all the way back to Houston—not yet—but they'd called Angus in a panic, looking for direction.

"Lie low," he'd instructed them. "I'll come up there."

He didn't want to. As Evalinda had stated last night, it was far better for the two of them to stay in Houston, establish an alibi there, than to head to Granite Gulch to take care of Holly themselves. But it was beginning to look as if they had no other choice.

And that was another thing. He wasn't sure he could actually pull the trigger. *Squeamish*, Evalinda had called him in that despising way she had when he'd balked at killing Holly, back when Evalinda had first raised the possibility. Eventually he'd caved…as he always caved when Evalinda had her heart set on something. This huge house in the best neighborhood, which they really couldn't afford. The luxury cars that screamed "money," money they didn't really have. The expensive jewelry Evalinda just had to have, *because I deserve it*, she'd insisted.

This time, though, he wasn't going to cave. If Evalinda wanted Holly dead, she was going to have to do it herself. Sure, he'd help. But he wouldn't pull the trigger, and that was that.

Chapter 18

"Give me your keys," Chris told Sam as soon as breakfast was over. "I'll park your truck in the garage—make it look as if Holly's alone in the house." He glanced at Holly. "And as soon as I make one phone call, I'm driving over to the Merrills' to swap my truck for your SUV, so we can set the stage. I'll park your SUV right out front, so anyone who knows what you drive will know you're here."

Holly looked hopeful. "I can go with you and see Ian and Jamie?"

He shook his head and said gently, "Probably not a good idea. You wouldn't be able to stay long, and it might upset your sons more to have you come and go quickly than if you don't show up at all."

At her crestfallen expression he said even more gently, "Why don't you go call them now? I'll clean up in here."

He could tell she was disappointed, but she was putting a good face on it. "You cooked, I'll clean," she insisted. "Besides, it's still early. They might not be awake yet."

Chris was going to argue but thought better of it, since he was anxious to call Angus McCay. So while Sam and Annabel went to get some much-needed sleep, he moved Sam's truck, then headed for his office.

He hooked a recording device to his phone and dialed Angus McCay's home phone number. It rang five times before it was answered, and by the third ring he was saying, "Come on, be home!" under his breath.

"Hello?" A man answered and Chris had no difficulty recognizing Angus McCay's gruff voice.

"Mr. McCay? Chris Colton here."

"Oh. Oh, yes, Mr. Colton. I…I haven't had a chance to book a flight yet, so I can't tell you when my wife and I will be there. But soon, as soon as we can, because we can't wait to see our grandsons now that you've found them for us."

"About that," Chris said, smiling to himself. "I thought you should know your daughter-in-law called the police early this morning. Apparently someone tried to break into the house where she's staying. The police took her report, of course, but they have more important things to worry about than a break-in that never actually happened. You've probably seen the news by now—the Alphabet Killer claimed another victim last night. The FBI and the Granite Gulch police are all focused on that investigation."

"Sorry to hear—another victim, you say? No, I haven't read my newspaper yet this morning, so I didn't know." Angus cleared his throat. "Of course, it's terrible two men tried to break into Holly's house. Good thing her dog scared them off."

Bingo, Chris exulted inside. *Got you on tape, too.*

Angus kept talking. "If Holly was back home where she belonged, and Ian and Jamie, too, she wouldn't be alone at a time like this."

Chris rolled his eyes at the fake concern, but all he said was "Yes, sir. I totally agree with you. Holly and her sons need the kind of protection and support only a family can give." Spreading it on thick. "So when do you think you might get here? The thing is, an emergency cropped up in my Dallas office, and I'm going to have to drive over there—it'll probably take me all day to resolve. So I won't be able to meet you at my office in Granite Gulch today after all."

"Don't worry about a thing," Angus McCay reassured Chris. "You gave us the address last night. If we can get a flight, I'm sure we can find the place. As for your bill—"

"Not an issue. I can mail the bill to you after your daughter-in-law and your grandsons are safely back in Houston. Good luck convincing her that's where she belongs."

Chris hung up, laughing softly to himself. He disconnected the recording device and played back the conversation, nodding to himself as Angus McCay revealed three things that could be crucial at trial. First, Chris had never mentioned any details about the attempted break-in. But Angus McCay had revealed without prompting he knew it was two men. Second, he knew the men had been scared off by a dog. A dog he had no idea Holly had. Third, Angus McCay had admitted Chris had given him Holly's address last night. So he couldn't claim he didn't know where she was staying.

"What's so funny?" Holly asked from the doorway.

"Your father-in-law makes a lousy criminal," Chris joked. "Almost as bad as you."

Holly's face turned solemn, and Chris realized too late

it wasn't a joke to her. "I had more difficulty accepting he was trying to kill me than I did about my mother-in-law," she said quietly. "She never liked me. Not when Grant and I were little, and not when we got married. But I never got that impression from my father-in-law. He… he's weak, though. His wife rules him. So if she decided I had to die, he'd go along."

She breathed deeply, letting the air out long and slow. "My parents were so different. Theirs was an equal partnership as far back as I can remember. Neither tried to dominate the other. Doesn't mean they didn't have their ups and downs. Doesn't mean they never argued. But the few times they couldn't reach an agreement, they agreed to disagree and left it at that. I promised myself that when I grew up I'd have a marriage like theirs."

He had to ask. "And did you? Was that what your marriage to Grant was like?"

She nodded slowly. "In a way. It wasn't like my parents' marriage, because Grant never— I mean, he loved me, but he was never *in* love with me. And that made things difficult at times."

She sighed softly. "But it wasn't like Grant's parents' marriage, either, thank God. I'm not a doormat kind of woman," she said, as if she were revealing a closely held secret. "Maybe you can't see that in me because you've only known me on the run. Terrified something will happen to me, but more because if something did, Ian and Jamie wouldn't have a mother. They've already lost their father. I can't let them lose their mother, too. If I didn't have them, I don't think I would have run. I would have stayed and fought it out with the McCays."

One corner of his mouth turned up in a half smile. "I know you're not a doormat kind of woman. Would a doormat have told me I'm not the boss of her?"

She smiled, but there was a touch of sadness to it. "That was an inside joke between Grant and me. If one of us tried to—oh, you know what I mean—the other would say that as a joking reminder. Then we'd laugh and things would be okay between us. But that was before we were married. When we were just friends."

More than anything in the world, he wanted to erase that sadness from her face. Wanted to banish it forever. Wanted to tell her how sweet she was, without being *too* sweet. Wanted to confess what a difference she and her sons had made in his life. Wanted her to know he couldn't imagine a more responsive lover—not just in the heat of passion, but the before and after, too. The way she fit so perfectly in his arms. The way she touched him so tenderly. The way she looked at him at times as if all light and hope in life emanated from him.

The way she loved him.

The realization hit him and knocked him for a loop. *She loves you.*

Hard on the heels of that thought came another, just as much of a body blow as the first. *And you love her.*

He opened his mouth to tell her, but the words wouldn't come. And before he could stop her, she turned away, saying, "I'm going to call Peg, see if Ian and Jamie are awake now." Then she was gone.

Chris stared at the doorway where Holly had stood, calling himself all kinds of a fool for not grabbing the chance to tell her how much he loved her. He started after her and was halfway across the office when his cell phone rang. He was going to ignore it at first, but when he glanced at the touch screen, he recognized the caller and cursed softly because he knew he had to take the call.

"Hey, Brad," he said when he answered his phone. "What's up?"

"Hey yourself. Just wanted to touch base with you about those names you asked me to track down. Desmond Carlton and Roy and Rhonda Carlton."

Chris quickly sat at his desk and pulled a pen and a pad of paper in front of him. "Okay, yeah, what have you got?"

"You were right. There's no mention of Desmond Carlton on any search engine I could find. Not that I didn't trust you, Chris, but it never hurts to double-check, you know? Desmond Carlton is a zero in cyberspace. A cipher. You'd think the guy didn't exist, unless..."

"Unless what?"

"Unless you peruse old police blotters and dig out old copies of newspapers. That's where I hit pay dirt. Desmond Carlton *was* a drug lord who was murdered six years ago—I located an article from that time. And get this—the obit on the guy lists he was survived by his brother and sister-in-law—"

"Roy and Rhonda Carlton?"

"Give the man a cigar. Also mentioned was a daughter, Julia. I haven't been able to track her down, but what I *could* find is that she was eighteen when her father bought the big one."

"She could have moved away. Gotten married. Changed her name some other way."

"Gee, thanks, why didn't I think of that?" Brad asked drily.

Chris chuckled. "Sorry. What else have you got?"

"Roy and Rhonda died five years ago in a car crash, just as you said."

"Was it really an accident?"

"Sure looks that way. Particularly gruesome one, but there never seemed to be a question it was anything other than an accident." Brad hesitated. "You know, when I dug into Roy and Rhonda, I came across a couple of names that—"

"Let me guess," Chris said laconically. "Josie Colton and Lizzie Connor, now Lizzie Colton. Right?"

"Yeah." Brad seemed relieved this wasn't news to Chris. "Lizzie's older than Josie, but both fostered with the Carltons from an early age. Josie until she was seventeen—when she up and vanished—Lizzie until the car accident. Apparently the Carltons considered her like their own daughter, and she was still with them even after the state was no longer paying for her foster care."

"Anything tying Desmond and Roy together other than they were brothers?"

"Nada. Roy was a straight arrow, and so was his wife. But Desmond?" Brad snorted his disgust. "Desmond had a rap sheet as long as my arm," he said. "But get this, Chris—no convictions. A dozen arrests, not a single conviction."

"That's got to be a mistake. A major drug dealer with no convictions?"

"No mistake. Not even a misdemeanor." Brad's voice took on a cynical tone. "One thing after another. Problem with the chain of custody of the evidence? Case tossed out. Witness against him fails to show up at trial? Case tossed out. Oh, and I love this one. Evidence mysteriously disappears from the police lockup? Cased tossed out. The prosecutors were fit to be tied."

Chris cursed under his breath. "Either this guy was the luckiest SOB on the planet, or—"

"Or someone on the police force—maybe more than one—was helping him out."

"Right." Chris thought for a moment, trying to put all the puzzle pieces together. "Anything else?"

"Desmond Carlton's name came up in a murder investigation eleven years ago. He was never arrested, but he was brought in for questioning. A small-time drug dealer was murdered and word on the street was that Carlton had something to do with it. You know how that goes. But the police could never pin it conclusively on him, and the case went cold."

Eleven years ago. Something about that niggled at the corners of Chris's memory, as if it should mean something. *I was twenty*, he mused. *I'd just finished my sophomore year in college, but Laura and I weren't engaged yet. That was in the fall. So what happened eleven years ago?*

Try as he might he couldn't pull a thread loose, so he shelved the question, knowing that forcing your brain to remember rarely worked. But if you put it aside, the answer usually came when you least expected it.

"Is that all?" Chris asked.

"Pretty much."

"This is terrific stuff, Brad. No kidding. I knew you were the right guy to put on this case, and you really came through for me. I won't forget it."

Chris took a moment to ask about Brad's wife and his three daughters, who were all in college and grad school. Then he disconnected and sat there, staring at the notes he'd jotted down on the pad of paper. "Eleven years," he'd written near the bottom, and circled it twice. It meant something. He didn't know what, but he knew it did.

The more he stared, the more convinced he became. Then he did something he would never have done a week ago…before Holly entered his life. He picked up his cell phone and hit speed dial. When the phone was answered, he said, "Trev? It's Chris. I know you're busy, but I need to ask you a quick question."

* * *

The urge to see her sons was so strong when Holly hung up the phone, she acknowledged Chris had been right. If she'd had her SUV, she wouldn't have been able to resist driving over to Peg's, even if only for a few minutes. And that could have been fatal. Not just for her, but for Ian and Jamie, too. Whoever had tried to break in during the wee hours of the morning could be lying in wait somewhere, watching for her SUV. She could be followed to Peg's house, and…

Chris had also been right about not going with him when he went to pick up her SUV. Ian and Jamie were doing okay. They missed her, but they were okay because Peg was making sure of it. It wouldn't be fair to Peg to flit in and out, getting the twins all wound up when their mother left.

One more day, she reminded herself. *Only one more day away from my babies.*

Holly wandered into the bathroom to brush her teeth, which she'd forgotten to do after breakfast. Her gaze fell on the whirlpool tub, and her memories of last night came rushing back. Not just what she and Chris had done in the tub. Not even what they'd done in the bed, although that qualified as one of those "just once in my life I want to" occasions she'd never forget. No, it was the moment they'd stood together in the kitchen, when she'd fallen in love with Chris, that she was thinking of now.

She stared at the mirror, but she wasn't seeing herself, she was seeing Chris in her mind's eye. So many different aspects of his character, but none more lovable than the "born to be a father" persona that came so naturally to him.

She wasn't looking for a father for her sons. She could never fall in love with a man who *wouldn't* be a good father, but that wasn't why she loved Chris. She loved him for the gentle, caring way he had, for the tenderness not far beneath the surface. She loved him for his straightforward approach to sex, and how he made her believe physical perfection was highly overrated. She loved him for the protectiveness he displayed, not just to her and her sons, but toward his sister and brother—his love for them ran so deep, but she wasn't sure he knew how deep it ran. She even loved him for his insecurities, for his self-doubt.

But most of all she loved Chris because he made her laugh. Despite the threat hanging over her head, despite her fear for herself and the twins, he made her laugh—she'd forgotten how much *fun* life could be. Nothing could ever be so bad that Chris couldn't find some humor in it, and she loved that about him. Gallows humor, maybe, but humor nevertheless.

"Now all you have to do is make Chris fall in love with you," she murmured to her reflection, "and you'll be in high cotton."

That was the problem in a nutshell. Holly had tried to make a man love her once and had failed spectacularly—she wasn't going down that road ever again. She'd even done something of which she would forever be ashamed in her quest for her love to be returned. Never again would she marry a man who didn't love her, heart and soul, unreservedly. No matter how much she loved him. No matter how tempted she might be.

"But if Chris *grows* to love you," Holly whispered to herself, "then…"

He was attracted to her. Okay, *more* than attracted. She was the first person he'd made love to since Laura, and that said a lot about how much he wanted her for herself. The question was, did he want her permanently? With all the baggage she brought with her?

"Not that Ian and Jamie are baggage," she corrected. "But we *are* a package deal."

She wouldn't use her sons, though. She wouldn't hold them out as an inducement to Chris to replace the child he'd lost—Chris had to love her for herself alone.

But if he did…she and the twins could make him so happy. Ian and Jamie were already attached to Chris—they could easily grow to love him, just as she did. They could be a family here. So much love had gone into this house—Holly could feel it. Not just the love Laura had for Chris, wanting to make a happy home for him and their baby. But the love Chris had for Laura, too. All the safety features he'd built in, to make his wife and child as safe as he could when he wasn't there.

Holly wouldn't be taking anything away from Laura—a part of Chris would always love Laura, just as a part of Holly would always love Grant. Holly didn't want to *replace* Laura in Chris's heart, she wanted to build her own place there…if he wanted it, too.

Love wasn't linear, it was exponential. And there was room in Holly's heart for the man she'd once loved…and the man she loved now.

She just prayed Chris would come to feel the same way.

"Eleven years ago?" Trevor asked Chris. "All I can think of is Josie telling the social worker she didn't want to see us anymore. I was a year out of college, just starting my career with the FBI. It was a knife to the gut, but Josie was adamant."

Chris snapped his fingers. "That's right. I'd forgotten exactly when that happened, but you're right."

"Is there anything else you needed?" Chris heard the exhaustion in Trevor's voice and figured he'd been up all night with the latest Alphabet Killer murder, same as Annabel and Sam. He'd been tempted to do as Holly had suggested—ask Trevor point-blank why he'd abandoned him when they all went into foster care. But his brother had enough to deal with right now. "Nothing urgent," Chris said. "Thanks for reminding me about Josie. Good luck on the case."

"Same to you."

"How'd you know I—"

Trevor cut him off. "I hadn't seen you around for a few days, so I asked Annabel. If anyone knew what was going on with you, it'd be her. She mentioned she and Sam were helping you set a trap to catch a couple of attempted murderers in the act. I wish *we* were that fortunate—catching our serial killer in the act," he added drily. "So good luck."

"Thanks." Chris disconnected, then sat there for a moment, mulling over what Trevor had said, carefully fitting one more puzzle piece in place. Then he saw it, the whole picture. And he could have kicked himself it had taken him this long.

Chapter 19

"You had it all wrong," Chris murmured to himself. "Josie didn't kill Desmond Carlton, not even in self-defense. That's not what this was all about." Pieces of the puzzle were still missing—pieces only Josie could fill in—but he was pretty sure he knew the basic outline of what had happened.

Josie's strange behavior eleven years ago…at the same time that small-time drug dealer was murdered. She'd only been twelve—she couldn't possibly have had anything to do with it. And word on the street was that Desmond Carlton had killed the other man. What if Josie had witnessed the murder? Carlton had probably been a visitor in his brother's house—heck, the murder could even have taken place there for all he knew. And what if Carlton had threatened Josie somehow? Carlton could have killed her, but…he had a daughter himself, just a year older than Josie. What if he couldn't bring himself to kill Josie because of that, but had threatened her instead? *Keep quiet or I'll kill everyone you love.*

That made a heck of a lot of sense. Lizzie had given them all a clue back in February, when Josie had still been a suspect in the Alphabet Killer murders, but none of them had made the connection because they hadn't known about Desmond Carlton. Chris couldn't recall Lizzie's exact words, but the gist was that Lizzie and Josie had been extremely close, like sisters. Right up until Josie suddenly became distant and guarded at age twelve…eleven years ago.

Josie had never given Lizzie an explanation, Lizzie had told them, no matter how hard Lizzie had pressed Josie to open up to her. But Lizzie had also been adamant back in February that Josie wasn't the serial killer, long before there was concrete proof. That Josie didn't have it in her to kill at all.

Someone had killed Desmond Carlton six years ago, but not Josie. And someone—or some *organization*—had done their best to erase Carlton's name from existence. "Should have focused on that before," he berated himself. "Only one entity has that kind of power. That kind of clout." Conspiracy theories be damned, in this case there was only one answer—the federal government. That led directly to federal agencies that might have reason for secrecy of this nature, and only one came to mind. Witness Security, run by the US Marshals Service.

Which would mean Josie was in Witness Security, commonly known as Witness Protection by the general public. Which would also mean she hadn't run six years ago because she was guilty of something. And she hadn't cut off communication with her family when she was twelve because she no longer loved them, either. She'd been *afraid* for them...*because* she loved them. Carlton's threat wouldn't have worked otherwise.

Now Chris's mind was flowing freely from one conjecture to another, but conjectures that fit all the facts. What if six years ago Josie decided she was tired of living in fear, tired of living under Desmond Carlton's threats? What if she went to the police and told them what she'd witnessed? And what if they'd set up a sting to trap Carlton...a sting that went horribly wrong?

That matched what the reporter had said about Carlton's death. *There were no shell casings and someone even dug the bullets out of him, so there was very little to go on...* A botched sting would explain it. Or even a *deliberately* botched sting. Either way, they'd whisk Josie away into Witness Security afterward. Give her a new identity, just in case any of Desmond Carlton's associates decided they wanted revenge.

The more he thought about it, the stronger Chris's hunch became that Carlton's death might somehow be connected to why he had no convictions after twelve arrests. Why his murder had never been solved. Because someone didn't *want* it solved?

Maybe. But that wasn't the most important thing right now. Because all of Desmond Carlton's known associates were either dead or in prison. And if Chris's conjectures were true, Josie no longer needed to fear reprisals. Which meant...if she really *was* in Witness Security...she could finally come home to her family.

Annabel had told Chris where the man from the FBI's Ten Most Wanted list was currently incarcerated—the man who'd once run with Carlton. After this whole thing with the McCays was wrapped up, Chris was going to rope Trevor into paying the guy a visit with him. And get some answers.

* * *

Chris left, but not without telling Holly he was leaving. "I already took Wally outside, so he's good," Chris told her. "I'll be back long before the McCays can get here, but don't answer the door, just in case last night's goons return. Sam and Annabel are here—if Wally starts barking or the alarm goes off, they'll know what to do—so you don't need to worry about that. If the phone rings—"

"Don't answer it. Got it."

He shook his head. "*Do* answer it. We *want* the McCays to know you're here because we want to draw them here." He grinned suddenly. "Gotta bait the trap with something irresistible, and..." He looked her up and down, sending her pulse racing when he waggled his eyebrows at her and said in his most suggestive voice, "I can't think of anything more irresistible than you."

Then he kissed her as if he meant it, and her racing pulse went into overdrive. He muttered something Holly couldn't catch and reluctantly let her go, then grabbed his black Stetson from the hook by the front door and settled it firmly on his head. He turned with his hand on the door handle and said, "And stay away from the windows. I mean it, Holly," he added implacably when she started to speak. "You trusted me to keep you safe, and I will. I'm not chancing a marksman taking you out with a high-powered rifle."

He grinned again. "And before you say it, I *am* the boss of you when it comes to this."

The morning dragged for Holly. "Stay away from the windows," she grumbled under her breath. Problem was, there wasn't a single room in the house that didn't have at least one window, not even the bathrooms. She made the rounds of the house, Wally at her heels, and confirmed she was right.

The drapes were drawn in the living room and formal dining room—neither had been used since she'd been here—but could someone see her shadow if she got too near those large windows? The kitchen windows only had café curtains—they let in the sunlight beautifully, but she would be a sitting duck if someone took aim at her while she was in there. The family room wasn't any better than the living room, unless she crouched in the corner—something she wasn't about to do.

There were no drapes in the master bedroom, only those top-down, bottom-up shades, with a valance across the top and floor-length swags on either side. But those swags were decorative only—they wouldn't close. They looked pretty, but they wouldn't provide any additional coverage. The two guest bedrooms were occupied. And no way was she going into the baby's room, not for any money—she'd probably start crying for Chris and everything he'd lost.

Which left Chris's office. It had a window, but only one. And it was L-shaped. If she sat at his desk, no one would be able to see her.

She fetched a book from her bedroom, then settled down in Chris's desk chair to read. But for some reason the book couldn't hold her interest, so she glanced around the room. For the first time she realized that of all the rooms in the house, this was the only room that reflected Chris's personality. The rest of the house—even the master bedroom—had been furnished to a woman's taste. Laura's taste.

But this room was different. There were none of the little decorative touches here that were in the other rooms. Chris's office was beautifully furnished—desk, bookcases and credenza were all honey oak—but there was a solidity to the furniture and a lack of feminine knick-knacks that bespoke a man's occupancy.

Holly nodded to herself, smiling a little. If she never saw Chris again after this was all over, if she returned to her life in Clear Lake City with Ian and Jamie, she would always remember Chris in this room. Sitting on the floor with Wally draped across his legs, Ian on one side, Jamie on the other, as he read them their bedtime stories. Sitting at this very desk, concentrating on his work. Standing in front of this desk and kissing her as if his life depended on it—their first kiss that had devastated her with how much she wanted him, and—oh, God—how much he'd wanted her. *Go to bed, Holly*, he'd told her in that deep rasp his voice made when he was hurting. *This isn't what you want.* Thinking of what was best for her and the hell with what he wanted.

"How could I not love him?" she asked herself.

Still smiling, but just a tad misty-eyed, Holly glanced down at the notepad sitting in the center of the desk. Cryptic notes jotted down in a distinctive scrawl that had to be Chris's—who else could it be? But she couldn't make heads or tails of it, although she was sure it meant something to Chris. Especially the two words circled near the bottom—*eleven years*.

She realized with a sudden start of guilt she had no business reading anything on Chris's desk, and she hurriedly put the notepad down. She turned away, and that was when she saw the silver-framed photograph standing in a secluded corner of the desk. Not large—four by six, maybe—but the face, surrounded by wavy light brown hair parted on one side, was immediately recognizable. The resemblance to Peg was obvious, but even if it wasn't Holly would have known who this woman had to be. Annabel had described Laura to a T—sweet, pretty, with a gentle, almost shy smile.

Curious, even though Holly told herself not to be, she reached over and picked up the photograph, studying it minutely. Peg's features were here, but nowhere did she see what Peg had an abundance of. Grit. Determination. Character. Not Wonder Woman, but a woman who did what she had to do without complaint. Her love for those around her flowed from strength.

What had Annabel said about Laura? *Chris was her world, and whatever he did was right. Good in some ways, not so good in others.*

If this photograph was anything to go by, Laura wasn't much like her older sister. Not that sweetness and gentleness were traits to scoff at. And Laura was far prettier than Holly could ever hope to be. But there was something lacking in Laura's face Holly couldn't quite make out. Then it dawned on her—Laura wasn't a fighter. In Holly's place she could never have stood up to the McCays.

Maybe that was what Annabel had been trying to tell Holly the other day, that what Chris really needed was a strong woman. An independent woman. A woman who wouldn't always agree with him, who wouldn't let him immerse himself in his work, body and soul. Who would force him to have some balance in his life.

A woman like me.

The phone shrilled suddenly, and Holly almost dropped the framed photograph. Remembering that Chris had said to answer the phone if it rang, she snatched up the receiver. "Hello?" Nothing but dead air answered her. "Hello?"

Whoever it was disconnected without saying a word,

and Holly shivered. Could it have been one of her in-laws? One of their henchmen? Or just a wrong number?

She hung up and carefully replaced the photo of Laura exactly where she'd found it. Then whirled and caught her breath when the bell-like alarm went off, indicating a door or window had been opened somewhere in the house.

"Holly?"

She breathed sharply when Chris called her name, only then realizing she'd been holding her breath until she knew who it was. She shook her head, impatient with herself because she should have known by the tinkling sound it wasn't someone trying to break into the house. "In here," she called back. "Your office."

Chris appeared in the doorway, so reassuringly big and male. "Hey," he said, juggling her keys in one hand. "Anything happen when I was gone?"

"Someone called just now. I answered, but they didn't say anything."

He smiled and nodded with satisfaction, as if this was just what he expected. "The McCays checking to make sure you're here."

"It could have been a wrong number, but—"

"But probably not," he finished for her. "I parked your SUV out front. They can't possibly miss it."

"So what do we do now?" she asked.

"We wait."

"What if they don't show up?"

He leaned his weight on one hip, his eyes narrowing as if debating whether or not to tell her something. Then he said, "They're already on their way. Driving, not flying."

"How do you know that?"

A faint smile touched his lips. "Because I sent a couple of men down there yesterday to shadow them."

She stared at him. “You did?”

“You think I’d have told the McCays yesterday where you were if I didn’t have eyes on them? You think I’d have left you here today—even with Annabel and Sam—if I didn’t know exactly where the McCays were at all times?” He laughed under his breath. “What kind of PI do you take me for, Holly?” He held up one hand when she started to speak, and joked, “No, don’t answer that.”

Holly’s lips curved in a smile as she walked toward Chris. “But I want to answer the question,” she said when she was close enough to touch him. Her fingers brushed a lock of hair from his forehead, then trailed lightly down, coming to rest on his shoulder. “I think you’re incredible. Amazing. There aren’t words to describe you. I thank my lucky stars the McCays hired you to find me, because I’d be in a world of hurt if it had been anyone else.”

His slow smile rewarded her. “You’d have managed somehow,” he said. “You’re a fighter—no way would you ever surrender. I knew that from the minute I entered your room in the rooming house. That’s what I lo—”

Chris stopped midsentence when the sound of bedroom doors opening down the hallway and questions asked and answered between Sam and Annabel suddenly intruded on their conversation.

Holly rarely cursed—it hadn’t been acceptable in her home growing up as the daughter of missionaries. But if she *did* curse, she would have just then. She would have given anything to know what Chris had intended to say. Love? As in, “that’s what I love most about you”?

But she couldn’t bring herself to ask, especially since Chris had already turned toward his sister and brother. “Well, if it isn’t Beauty and the Beast, finally awake,” he drawled.

"Bite me." Sam obviously wasn't of a sunny disposition when he first woke up.

Annabel elbowed Sam. "What makes you think *you're* the Beast?"

Chris turned his head and his eyes met Holly's, a glint of humor in them. "And there you see why Ridge is a better choice than 'don't you dare call me beautiful' Annabel and 'don't call me a beast even though I am' Sam."

"I think I'm missing something here," Sam growled.

Holly laughed. "Let's have lunch and I'll explain."

Holly went to her bedroom after lunch to call her sons—"Keep away from the windows," Chris told her in no uncertain terms.

"I will."

Chris watched her go. Part of him wished they hadn't been interrupted earlier, but another part was glad. He hadn't intended to say anything to Holly yet—not while she still needed his protection. He'd already had one tussle with his conscience over making love to Holly while he was guarding her—he didn't want her to think there was some kind of quid pro quo going on, that he expected sex in exchange for looking after her and her sons. And he'd had no intention of telling her how much he loved her until she was free to make a decision without the threat of murder hanging over her head.

But somehow, when Holly had smiled at him, when she'd touched him and told him he was incredible and, oh yeah, amazing, the words of love had almost come tumbling out despite his best efforts.

Annabel jabbed Chris in the ribs to get his attention, her tone caustic. "Wake up there."

"Ouch!" Chris rubbed his ribs. "Darn it, Bella," he complained. "You still have the sharpest elbows of anyone I've ever known, even if you *are* my favorite sister over thirty."

"I'm your *only* sister over thirty," she retorted.

"*Darn* it?" Sam raised his eyebrows in a question Chris wasn't about to answer.

He headed for his office, with Annabel and Sam right behind him. "Before we get caught up in the sting," he said as soon as they sat down, "I want to run something by you two."

He recounted his conversations with Trevor, Brad and the reporter for the *Dallas Morning News*. He reminded them of what Lizzie had said about Josie back in February. Then he gave them the conclusions he'd drawn. "Am I way off base here?" he asked. "Or does my theory fit all the facts as we know them?"

Sam glanced at Annabel, who nodded. "Your logic is sound," he told Chris. "But the only way to know for certain is to track Josie down and see what she says."

"Trevor might be able to help there," Annabel said. "If Josie really *is* in the Witness Security Program, the FBI is in a better position to approach the US Marshals Service. Let's see what he can shake loose."

Chris ruthlessly suppressed the tiny flare of jealousy triggered by Trevor's name. Annabel was right—Trevor was in a better position than Chris to take the investigation into Josie's disappearance to the next level. Yeah, Chris had been searching for his baby sister for years, but it really didn't matter who ultimately solved the mystery. Bringing Josie safely home was more important than his ego. "You're right," he told Annabel. "As soon as we wrap up this case, I'll talk to Trevor."

Holly walked into the office with a smile on her face, and Chris couldn't help it—his eyes softened at the sight of her. Then he caught Annabel watching him, and he quickly schooled his expression into one of pure professionalism. "Everything okay with the twins?"

"Fine, but Peg says they're starting to fret over the least little thing. Which means—"

"They're missing you something fierce." He and Holly shared a private smile.

"I shouldn't want them to," she confessed. "But I do. I want them to miss me." She glanced at Annabel. "Does that make me a bad mother?"

Annabel chuckled. "No, it makes you a perfectly normal mother."

Chris brought his mind back with an effort to the reason they were all here, and said, "Let's get everything nailed down—who's going to do what. Planning ahead is half the battle."

Fifteen minutes later Chris had laid out his plan in detail. "Any questions?"

He glanced from Sam, who shook his head, to Annabel, who did the same, and finally to Holly. "Got it," she said.

"My men tracking the McCays already called from the road. We'll know in advance almost to the minute when they'll arrive, so no worries there. My men will turn off before they get here—we don't want to spook the McCays, let them know they're being followed. I'll have them double back afterward, although I don't think we'll need them. But just in case…"

Just like the morning had, the afternoon dragged. Holly just wanted it *over*—she was unexpectedly calm about the upcoming confrontation with her in-laws, but she wanted it to be past tense.

Everyone, it seemed, had something to keep their minds distracted—except her. Sam read the morning newspaper he'd brought with him. Annabel had another police procedural textbook she soon became engrossed in. And Chris worked on his computer, answering a string of emails. Holly felt a twinge of guilt. Chris had a business to run after all. He'd made her case his top priority, but that didn't mean everything else came to a screeching halt. She wanted to ask him about the notes he'd left in the middle of the desk, but she didn't—for two reasons. She didn't want to interrupt him, and she didn't want him to think she'd been snooping. She wasn't sure which reason reigned supreme.

Holly sat on the floor stroking Wally, who lay in a contented heap at her side. And she wondered if Chris would let her take Wally back with her to Clear Lake City…assuming she went back. Assuming something didn't go wrong this afternoon. Assuming Chris didn't love her.

Chapter 20

At six minutes past three, Chris's cell phone rang, and he closed his laptop. He answered his cell phone, listened for several seconds, then said, "Thanks, Matt. Tell Andy the same from me…No, I think we've got it covered, but just in case, have Andy double back and park about a quarter mile before the driveway leading to the house. You can't see that part of the road from the house, so the McCays won't know you're there. If you don't hear from me in…oh…fifteen minutes, assume the worst and come to our rescue. But be careful—"

He broke off sharply, and Holly knew he could hear the same thing she did—the sound of a car pulling up in front of the house. "They're here. Gotta go."

Holly scrambled to her feet and wiped her suddenly sweaty palms on the sides of her jeans. Annabel and Sam were already moving purposefully to their assigned places—Sam to the coat closet near the front door and Annabel secreted behind the door in the kitchen.

The doorbell rang a minute later. Chris grabbed Holly's arm, pulling her back as she started to leave the office to answer the door. "We're right here," he reminded her." But worry etched furrows in his face. "If there was any other way, I—"

She put her fingers on his lips to stop him from completing that sentence. "I know," she said, her earlier calm returning. "But there isn't another way. And I won't let them get away with it this time."

The doorbell rang again, sounding somehow impatient, and Holly looked Chris directly in the face. "I love you," she said quietly. "If anything happens— I know you'll do your best, but… Anyway, I wanted you to know." She turned and walked out without waiting for a response, Wally at her heels.

Chris swore under his breath. Damn Holly for choosing that moment to tell him she loved him, when he couldn't do a thing about it. And damn her for walking out before he could tell her he loved her, too. That he couldn't imagine life without her. That there was no way—*no way*—she was dying on his watch.

Gun drawn, he double-checked the switches on the two hidden cameras in the living room, making sure the cameras were rolling—the different angles would ensure at least one would capture whatever the McCays tried to do. Then he did the same for the voice-activated recorder. The wireless microphones were already set up, just waiting to record every word the McCays said.

He pulled the door to the office nearly shut, listening intently. Time seemed to stretch out, and he could hear Holly clearly as she opened the door and exclaimed,

"Angus! Evalinda! How did you find— I mean, how lovely to see you."

Chris smiled grimly. Holly was playing it perfectly—acting surprised to see the McCays, but also acting as if she had no idea they were there to kill her. If the McCays were innocent, the first thing they'd ask was why Holly had run away with her sons six months ago. But they never asked…because they already knew the answer.

"Come into the living room," Holly invited.

This was the most dangerous moment, Chris knew. He'd theorized earlier that the McCays wouldn't just open fire the minute they saw Holly. That they'd make *sure* she was alone in the house before they started blasting. But theories were one thing. The woman he loved turning her back on her murderous in-laws as she led them into the living room was another thing entirely. He took comfort in the fact that Sam should be able to see everything from his vantage point in the closet, which was cracked open. And if one or both of the McCays reached for a gun…

"Where are the boys?" Angus asked.

Chris shifted slightly for a better viewing angle. *Nice job!* he told Holly in his mind as she seated the McCays on the living room sofa, directly in his line of sight—and right in the field of vision of each camera. She disappeared from his view, and he knew she was sitting in one of the armchairs across from her in-laws, exactly as planned.

"They're not here right now," Holly replied. "They have a playdate with friends—Susan and Bobby. Their mom and I take turns having playdates for the children." She laughed easily, as if she didn't have a care in the world. "It gives both of us a little free time to ourselves. And you know how it is with small children, Evalinda.

Much as you love your children, sometimes you just need to be alone."

"So you're alone in the house?" Evalinda McCay asked sharply. Chris saw Mrs. McCay's hand reaching into her capacious purse, and he readied himself to launch.

"Yes, I'm alone. Except for Wally here." Chris couldn't see Holly, but he imagined she was patting the dog's head. "Why do you ask?"

Even if Chris hadn't seen the gun come out, Wally's sudden growl would have warned him.

"You should never have opposed us," Evalinda McCay said, as matter-of-factly as if she were discussing the weather.

"What are you— No, Wally," Holly said when Wally's growls deepened. "What do you think you're doing, Evalinda? I'm your daughter-in-law. The mother of your grandchildren. Why are you—"

Regret was evident in Angus McCay's voice when he explained, "I'm sorry, Holly. We didn't want to do this, but you left us no choice."

"Is it money? Do you need money?" Holly's voice held just the right panicked note. "I have Grant's insurance money. I'll be happy to share it with you, if you—"

Evalinda McCay laughed, but it was an ugly sound. "That pittance?"

"Not a pittance," Holly insisted. "Half a million dollars. If you had told me, I—"

"We want the money Grant put into a trust for Ian and Jamie," Evalinda McCay stated viciously. "That damned unbreakable trust. The only way to get our hands on that money is to get custody of the twins. And the only way *that's* going to happen is if you're out of the picture."

"You'd kill me for money?" Holly's disbelief sounded like the real thing.

"You turned Grant against us. You convinced him to leave us out of his will." Chris saw the evil smile that tugged at the corners of Mrs. McCay's mouth. "So killing you will be a pleasure, not just a necessity."

"I didn't!" Holly insisted. "Grant did that all on his own, I swear!"

Wally's growls were nearly ferocious now, and Chris imagined Holly was having difficulty holding the dog back. *Good boy!* he thought. *Protect Holly!*

"It doesn't matter either way," Evalinda McCay said. "But don't worry. We'll take good care of Ian and Jamie… for now. Everyone will be convinced—just as that stupid private investigator was convinced—that we're loving grandparents who only have our grandsons' best interests at heart." She sighed with mock regret. "You'll be the victim of a terrible home invasion. Thank goodness the twins weren't here when it happened! We'll play the grieving grandparents to the hilt, stepping in to care for our orphaned grandchildren." Evalinda McCay was obviously already getting into the role.

She stood suddenly. "Now get up. Slowly. I can make this easy, or hard. If you try to run…I'll have to shoot you quickly. The first bullet might not be fatal." The evil smile was back. "But I'll make sure you're dead before I leave, Holly. Count on it."

"Police! Freeze!" Annabel and Sam's voices rang out almost simultaneously, using the exact same words.

Chris burst through the library door, his one thought to get to Holly before Evalinda McCay fired. But Wally was there before him. With one last growl the dog pulled away from Holly's restraining hold and leaped for the hand holding the gun. His jaws closed on Evalinda McCay's wrist and jerked, so the bullet went wide.

"On the ground!" Sam ordered, wrestling a shocked

Angus McCay down, then cuffing him with his hands behind his back.

Annabel was doing the same to Evalinda McCay, who was moaning in agony. She'd already dropped the gun and was holding her bleeding wrist, where Wally's teeth had broken the skin and nearly broken her bones.

"You're under arrest for attempted murder," Annabel intoned, then began reciting the Miranda warning to both McCays. "You have the right to remain silent. Anything you say can and will be used against you in a court of law..."

She reached the end and said, "Do you wish to talk to us now?"

"Go to hell!" snapped Evalinda McCay. "This is entrapment! And police brutality. My wrist is broken, and these cuffs are making it worse."

Annabel listened politely, then said, "We'll stop off at the hospital to have your wrist x-rayed. But you're still under arrest."

Long before the McCays had been cuffed, Chris had enfolded Holly in his arms, his gun still drawn. She was trembling—aftereffect, he knew—and his arms tightened. "It's okay," he told her.

"She was really going to kill me," Holly whispered as Annabel and Sam led the McCays away in handcuffs.

"Yeah, but you already knew that." Chris pulled back just long enough to holster his weapon, then his arms closed around her again.

Wally was bounding around the room in excitement, following the prisoners and, when the front door closed behind them, snuffling enthusiastically around Holly's and Chris's legs.

Holly extricated herself from Chris's arms and knelt

to embrace the dog. "Good boy, Wally!" she praised. "I knew I could count on you."

Chris crouched down to ruffle Wally's fur in silent affirmation of the dog's heroic actions. "What about me?" he asked Holly.

Her unexpected smile warmed his heart. "I knew I could count on you, too."

He could have stayed like that forever, except he suddenly remembered something. "Oh, cra—crud," he amended, rising to his feet and whipping out his cell phone. He clicked quickly between screens and hit the callback button. "Matt? We're good here. Sam and Annabel put the McCays under arrest for attempted murder and are taking them to jail with a short detour to the hospital. You and Andy are done for the day, and there'll be a special bonus in your next paycheck—you've earned it. I'll talk to you both tomorrow."

Holly was still kneeling beside Wally, and after Chris disconnected, he helped her to her feet. "You and I have some talking to do," he told her.

"I still can't believe she was really going to kill me herself. I mean…it's one thing to want someone dead. Hiring someone to do it—that's worse. But killing someone yourself…looking them in the face and pulling the trigger…" She shivered. "That's so cold. I can't imagine hating someone enough to do that."

Chris drew Holly into his arms again, staring down into her face. "Forget that," he told her dismissively. "I have a bone to pick with you, and I'm not deferring this conversation until you have time to come to terms with what Mrs. McCay was going to do to you."

Holly shook her head, puzzled for a minute. Then her eyes widened in understanding. "You mean…?"

"Yes, I mean…" he replied. "You sure can pick your

times, Miss Holly," he teased. "Dropping a bombshell on me, then walking out cool as you please to face down murderers."

Warm color rose in her cheeks. "I didn't mean to tell you— Well, yes, I did, but not— And anyway… You see, the thing is…"

"The thing is you love me."

It wasn't a question, but she answered it anyway. "Yes."

"If you'd waited half a second instead of rushing out, you'd have heard me say the same thing."

If anything her eyes grew even bigger. "You mean it?" she whispered. She clutched his arms. "Don't say it if you don't mean it. Please don't."

He tightened his hold on her. "I never say what I don't mean, Holly." He drew a deep breath. "I don't know how it happened, honest to God I don't, because I was determined it wouldn't. But it *did* happen. And now…"

A hint of a smile appeared in her eyes. "Is this where I say I love you and you say 'ditto'?" she teased, referring to an incredibly romantic movie more than twenty-five years old she'd seen on cable. "Because if that's the best you can do…" Her smile melted away, replaced by a touch of uncertainty. "I need the words, Chris—I think you understand why. So please…*please…*"

He tilted her face up to his with one hand and, with heartfelt conviction, said, "I love you. I need you. I can't live without you." He'd mocked Ethan—not once, but twice—with those same words the day Ethan and Lizzie's baby was born. But he'd never been more serious in his life. "If any of those statements match how you feel, Holly…please tell me. Because I'm dying here."

"I can't believe you even need to ask." She touched his lips. "I already told you in the office earlier."

"Tell me again."

She smiled tenderly. "I love you, Chris. I need you in my life. And I don't think I can live without you anymore, either."

He grinned as a weight lifted from his shoulders… and his heart. Even though he'd already figured it out on his own, even though she'd told him right before the McCays had arrived, he'd needed those words from her, too, and not uttered in the heat of the moment.

Then his grin faded and he said, "I don't just want you, Holly. I want Ian and Jamie, too. I want to be their father. Not that I want to replace their real father. From everything you've told me about Grant, he was a decent man and the twins are his legacy—I would never want them to forget him. But I love your sons, and I want the chance to be the kind of father I never had."

How was it possible to love Chris even more than she already loved him? Holly didn't know, but when he said things like this, she didn't have much choice. "The other day you said you were no role model. And I told you to think again. I knew then that I loved you. And I knew there couldn't possibly be a better role model for Ian and Jamie than you. You want to be their father? You can't want that more than I do—I would be honored to share them with you."

They kissed then. Not a passionate kiss, but a sacred pledge for the future.

"You don't read poetry, do you?" Holly asked when their lips finally parted.

"Not unless country-and-western lyrics count."

She laughed softly. "That wasn't exactly what I was referring to, but I'll keep it in mind." She cupped his cheek and said, "Robert Herrick wrote a sonnet hundreds of years ago that begins, 'How Love came in, I do not know.' That's how I feel. I don't know how it happened, just that it did. And I wouldn't change it for anything."

He chuckled. "Okay, so *now's* the time I say *ditto*."

"Chris…" she warned, but in teasing fashion so he'd know she wasn't serious. Much.

He shook his head at her. "I already told you I have no idea how it happened for me, but I wouldn't change it for anything, either." He drew a deep breath. "So, Miss Holly. If I were to get down on one knee and ask you to marry me, what would you say?"

Her heart sped up, then slowed down, but not back to normal. Not by a long shot. "Ask me and see," she murmured.

She thought he'd been joking, but when he gently pushed her into the armchair and knelt on one knee, she realized he was dead serious. *Yes, yes, yes!* her heart was already answering, but she waited.

"I know you loved Grant," he began. "But I also know you love me. I don't want to replace him in your heart, Holly. But I *do* want to build my own place there. Will you marry me?"

She was barely able to contain her gasp, because Chris was saying almost exactly the same thing she'd told herself yesterday. She didn't want to *replace* Laura, she just wanted to be the woman he loved *now*. Now…and in the future.

"I would be honored," she answered softly. She framed his face with her hands, the face that had become so incredibly dear to her in such a short time. "I would be honored to be your wife."

Chapter 21

Two weeks later the doorbell of Holly's Clear Lake City house rang at a quarter past six in the morning, waking her from a not-very-sound sleep. A jumble of dreams centering around Chris had woken her every few hours, and she was just dozing off again when she heard the chime.

She grabbed her robe and scrambled into it as she hurried to the front door, her only thought being *Please don't wake the twins!* Ian and Jamie had been fractious ever since the three of them had returned to Clear Lake City—apparently they were missing their life in Granite Gulch as much as she was—and she didn't want them to start off the day short of sleep.

The chime sounded again just as she reached the door, and she glanced through the peephole, intending to give whoever it was a piece of her mind for ringing the bell this early. Then she gasped and fumbled with the locks in her haste.

"Chris!" Holly threw herself at him, and his arms closed around her. "Oh, my God, what are you *doing* here?"

"I couldn't bear it without you a minute longer," he said when his lips finally let hers go. "I couldn't sleep because I was thinking of you, so I threw a few things in a bag, jumped in my truck and hit the road. Made good time, too."

"No speeding tickets?"

He grinned at her. "Not even one." His eyes softened as he gazed at her. "But if I *had* gotten one, it would have been worth it."

Two weeks' worth of yearning was obliterated in less than fifteen minutes. They snuggled in the aftermath, their hearts racing, both still having difficulty breathing.

"Wow," Holly said. Then, "Do that again."

Chris started laughing so hard he wheezed. "Give me five minutes—ten max—to recover, and you've got yourself a deal."

She joined Chris laughing helplessly. "I didn't mean *now*. Just *sometime*. Sometime soon."

He rolled her beneath him before she could protest. Then stroked his fingers over her still-hypersensitized flesh, making her breath catch in her throat. "Sometime soon can be now, Holly," he whispered seductively. "Just wait. I'll prove it to you."

And he did. All she could think of as her body took flight was that Chris was a man of his word. Then she couldn't think at all.

"When are you coming back to Granite Gulch?" Chris asked over the breakfast table an hour later. "I'm not trying to rush you—okay, yes, I am. The house just isn't the same without you and the twins."

"You're living in the house?"

He nodded. "I moved all my things out of my apartment the day you left. I also talked to Annabel and my brothers about the farmhouse in Bearson—what you said about not leaving it as some sort of shrine. So whenever you're ready, you can go through the farmhouse and pick out what you want for our home." A slow smile spread over her face, and Chris asked again, "So when are you moving back?"

"I've already listed this house for sale," she temporized.

"Yeah, I saw the sign on the front lawn."

"But I can't just move in with you," she began.

"The heck you can't." His voice was pure steel, his expression obdurate, but then he grinned suddenly. "Hey, did you hear that? I didn't even have to think about it, I just said *heck* instead of—" He broke off suddenly, glancing at Ian and Jamie, who weren't paying the least bit of attention to the conversation—they were eating their Cheerios with complete unconcern.

A lump came into Holly's throat. *How* she loved this man, especially at moments like this. But… "I can't just move in with you," she repeated. She tore her gaze away from Chris and looked at her boys, then back at him, praying he'd see what the problem was. "I don't want people to think—"

"That you're living in sin?" Chris waggled his eyebrows at her.

She flushed. "I know it's old-fashioned. And if it was just me, I wouldn't care, honest. But I don't want anything said that the twins might hear. They understand a lot more about what's going on around them, and I—"

Chris put his hand on hers. "You don't have to justify it to me, Holly. I told you two weeks ago, I love you. I need you. I can't live without you. I wasn't kidding. I asked you to marry me, and you said you would. So in my mind we were officially engaged the minute you consented to be my wife."

"Mine, too," Holly said softly.

"If it was up to me, we'd find a justice of the peace and make 'engagement' a thing of the past." She started to speak but he stopped her. "No, let me finish. I know weddings mean a lot to women. And I know you were denied a fancy wedding when you married Grant. I intend for this to be the last chance you have for the kind of wedding women dream of—so we'll do it right. Formal engagement party, formal wedding, and everything that entails."

Holly smiled at Chris through sudden tears. "Thank you for understanding."

"But once we're formally engaged, you're moving back to Granite Gulch, right?" The eagerness in his voice touched something deep inside her. She'd sworn she'd never again marry a man who didn't love her, heart and soul, but that would never be an issue with Chris. "I need you, Holly," he added in a low tone. "These past two weeks without you—life's too short. We both know that. So please don't—"

"I won't," she assured him. "They say suffering is good for the soul. I don't know about you, but my soul has suffered enough."

He laughed softly. "Mine, too."

They stared at each other for endless seconds, then Holly cleared her throat. "So regarding an engagement party—would you believe I was going to call you about this today?—I was thinking next week would be good."

"We always go to Ethan and Lizzie's ranch for family celebrations now. I'd have to check with them."

Holly gave Chris her best "are you kidding me?" look.

"What?" he asked, obviously clueless.

"Lizzie just had a baby. Do you have any idea of the kind of work involved in a party like this? Even if it's potluck, the hostess—and the host, too—have a mountain of work both before and after. No way are we having our engagement party at their ranch."

"Then what do you suggest?"

"Peg offered to have it at her house, but I don't want to put that responsibility on her, either, any more than I want to do it to Lizzie. What about renting out the Granite Gulch Bar and Saloon for the afternoon? It's plenty big enough, it's right there on Main Street in the center of town and everyone would be free to enjoy themselves—no one would have to worry about the food or drinks or anything. And before you ask," she told him, "I already inquired. It wouldn't cost an arm and a leg, and besides, I have the money." She flushed a little. "My money, not money from the twins' trust."

Chris shook his head, a stubborn expression on his face. "We haven't talked about money, Holly, but I guess now's as good a time as any. I'm not a millionaire—not yet—but I'm not hurting, either. Your money is yours. Whatever our family needs I'll provide. You want to be a stay-at-home mom until the twins are in school? Fine. I can afford it, no problem. I can afford to pay for our engagement party, too."

Holly lifted her chin, her eyes narrowing as she prepared to do battle. While she understood Chris's desire to provide for his family, to feel that he was taking care of them, there were a few things he needed to get straight before they went any further. She loved him with all her heart, but she couldn't be anything other than the independent woman she was. Not even for him.

She almost retorted that their marriage was going to be an equal partnership, with each of them pulling their own weight and all decisions made jointly, or else no deal. But then an idea occurred to her. "You're not the boss of me," she said softly. Hoping Chris would get the message.

The stubborn expression vanished and a lighthearted grin replaced it, followed by a reluctant chuckle. "Okay," he said after a minute. "We'll split the cost of the party fifty-fifty. But *I'm* buying the engagement ring. That's *not* up for negotiation."

In that moment Holly knew everything was going to be all right. Chris could always make her laugh…but she could always make him laugh, too. And that was just as important as love in building a relationship that would last a lifetime. There would be arguments in the future—of course there would be—but neither of them would ever go to bed angry with the other, because one of them would always make sure of it…with humor.

Epilogue

The engagement party was in full swing when Chris wandered over to one of the large coolers packed with ice and cold bottles of beer and cans of soft drinks. He helped himself, removed the bottle cap and let the ice-cold brew slide down his throat. It was only the end of May, but the day was hot and humid—typical north Texas weather—and even though the room was air-conditioned, the beer hit the spot.

Chris turned and watched Holly for a moment, the center of a small gaggle of women across the room, Annabel and Peg among them. Holly's dress was golden yellow—God, he loved her in yellow. Loved her in anything, really. But he loved her best when she was wearing nothing at all except the tender look of love she reserved for him alone. Their eyes met across the room, and there it was again—the expression that melted his heart every time he saw it.

"How did I ever get so lucky?" he asked himself quietly.

The rowdy song the band was playing came to an end, and the strains of a popular ballad soon filled the air. As Chris watched, Jesse Willard, Annabel's fiancé, walked up to her and touched her on the shoulder. The loving face Annabel turned to him was matched by the expression on Jesse's face, and a wave of happiness for his twin washed through him as the couple began to slow dance. All he and his brothers had ever wanted for Annabel was for her to find a good man to love her. She had that in Jesse. But Annabel was her own woman, the consummate professional police officer, finally doing the work she loved. Chris could understand that—he loved his work, too.

Peg was soon claimed by Joe for a dance, and Chris smiled. Peg and Joe were the best friends a man could ever have. Peg could have resented Holly on her sister's behalf—and he wouldn't have blamed her. But there was too much love in Peg for her to wish unhappiness on someone else. She deserved a steady-as-a-rock man like Joe to make her happy. And Joe, Chris knew, was counting his blessings, too.

Chris glanced away, and his gaze fell on his younger brothers. Ridge dancing with his high school sweetheart, Darcy, whom he'd finally reconnected with after all these years. Sam with Zoe, who was the best thing that had ever happened to him. And Ethan, with his arms wrapped tight around Lizzie, not really dancing, but swaying back and forth to the music.

"How did we all get so lucky?" Chris asked himself now.

Only Trevor was alone, and Chris's heart went out to

his older brother. At the same time he promised himself, *Soon. Holly's right. I have to ask Trevor why.*

Suddenly Holly was standing right in front of him. "Howdy, cowboy," she murmured. "You look familiar. Do I know you?"

Conscious that eyes were on them, Chris tamped down the urgent desire to kiss her until she was too dazed to tease him. Instead, he raised her left hand to his lips—the hand wearing the engagement ring that was his pledge to her—and kissed it. A romantic gesture he would have felt foolish making a few weeks ago. Before he'd known Holly.

"Okay, cowboy," she drawled, "you've made your point. I don't know who you are after all."

Chris laughed and feigned hurt. "And here I thought you'd be impressed with how romantic I could be."

Holly's soft brown eyes turned misty, and she whispered, "You're romantic enough for me, Chris, just the way you are. Every single day."

That deserved a kiss, and he didn't care how many people saw him do it. When he finally raised his head and took in the dazed expression in Holly's eyes, he couldn't help it—primitive masculine pride surged through him… particularly a certain body part.

"Don't you dare move," he warned Holly.

She laughed deep in her throat, but she knew what he was talking about so she stayed right where she was for a minute. Eventually he was able to release her without being too embarrassed, but he tugged her hand. "Come on," he told her roughly. "Let's go outside where no one can—"

That was when he spotted the dark-haired woman standing in the shadows across the room from them, near the door to the bar. A stranger, yet not a stranger. Incredulous, he whispered, "Josie?"

He dropped Holly's hand as if in a dream and took two steps toward the woman he instinctively knew was his baby sister. But when the woman saw him move toward her, she darted from the room like a frightened colt.

Chris gave chase. "Josie!" he called to the fleeing woman, who had already escaped through the front door. "Josie, wait! Don't run, Josie. You're safe, damn it! You're safe! It's all over!"

She must have heard him, because she stopped suddenly on the sidewalk, turned around and stared at him. But she was still poised to run. "It's over?"

Chris didn't stop running until he reached his sister, until he was sure he could prevent her from fleeing if she tried to take off again. "Josie," he whispered, still not quite believing she was really here. Then she was in his arms. "My God, it's really you."

Brother and sister finally stepped back, and all at once Holly was at Chris's side, her breath coming quickly. Then the rest of the family appeared—all crowding around Josie, hugging her repeatedly, exclaiming over her—their joy at finally being reunited with their baby sister mirroring Chris's.

Questions peppered the air. "Oh, Josie, we've been searching for you ever since you vanished."

"Where have you been? We've been worried sick."

"Why didn't you let us know you were alive?"

Chris held up his hands. "Hold it, everybody! One at a time."

Before anyone could ask a question, Josie looked at Chris, regret in her eyes. "I heard about Laura," she blurted out. "I wanted to call you when it happened and tell you how sorry I was. I really did, Chris. But I couldn't. I just *couldn't*. 'No phone calls,' they said. 'Let them think you're dead,' they said."

"Who said?" Trevor asked, getting his question in first. "Where have you been?"

"Witness Security. Six years. Ever since—"

"Desmond Carlton was killed," Chris said, cutting Josie off. When her eyes widened that he knew, he nodded, saying, "Yeah, I think I have most everything figured out." For the benefit of the rest of the family, he said, "Here's what I think happened. Correct me if I'm wrong, Josie." He laid out his theory of what had occurred eleven years ago, and then six years ago.

Josie interrupted him a couple of times to clarify a point, but when he was done, she said, "I can't believe you pieced that all together from what little you knew." Her eyes held admiration.

"Thank Lizzie and Trevor," he told Josie. "They're the ones who gave me the clues I needed." His gaze met Lizzie's, then Trevor's. Lizzie's eyes held nothing but joy, because she finally knew what had caused Josie to turn away from her friendship; Trevor's eyes held joy that Josie was found, tinged with...redemption? *Thanks, Trev*, Chris mouthed and knew Trevor had seen it by the slight nod he gave. Chris still didn't know why Trevor had abandoned him. But he no longer believed Trevor hadn't tried his damnedest to get custody of Josie when he turned eighteen. And that was a tremendous load off Chris's mind.

He turned back to Josie. "The most important thing in all of this is, everyone who was associated with Carlton six years ago is either dead or in prison—and will stay in prison for a long time. Which means it's all over as far as you're concerned. You don't have to hide anymore."

"You really mean it?" Josie couldn't seem to take it in at first.

Chris nodded. "And you're just in time. Holly and I are celebrating our engagement." He caught Holly's hand and raised it so Josie could see the ring.

"I know. That's why I came, because I…I wanted to be here with the family, even if I couldn't join in the celebration. Even if it meant risking being seen."

"You were spotted before," Chris told her. He glanced around the circle of his family. "Ridge saw you. So did Lizzie. And Annabel—"

"You left a gold heart charm in my house, didn't you?" Annabel interjected. "The one Mama gave you that's just like mine." When Josie nodded, Annabel asked, "Did you leave it on purpose?"

Josie nodded again. "I couldn't bear having you all think I was dead. No matter what my handlers in Witness Security told me."

Another flurry of questions ensued, and this time Holly intervened. "Let's take this back inside." She smiled at Josie and held out her hand, saying softly, "I'm Holly McCay, Chris's fiancée. I'm so glad you came to our engagement party. I can't think of anything that would make Chris happier than having you here. It's been tearing him up not knowing where you were. Not knowing if you were safe. Now he can really celebrate."

Chris disconnected and slid his smartphone into his pocket. He jumped guiltily, then whirled around when Holly said behind him, "How are the boys doing with the babysitter?"

"How'd you know I was checking on them?"

She smiled the tender smile he loved. "Because I know *you*. Because that's the kind of man you are." She came to stand right in front of him and deliberately placed her hand on his heart, which immediately kicked up a notch at her touch. "You made yourself responsible for us that very first day," she said. "And thank God you did, because if you hadn't I never would have known you. Never would have loved you." Her voice dropped to a whisper. "And I never would have known what it was like to be loved the way you love me."

A lump came into his throat, and he wished he had Holly's way with words. Wished he could express what her love meant to him. But all he could do was touch her cheek with a hand that wasn't quite steady and say, "I don't want to lose you, Holly. Tell me that will never happen."

What you don't love you can't lose. He'd told himself that in the hospital right after Ethan and Lizzie's baby had been born. He'd lost so much in his life—Mama, Trevor, Josie, Laura, their baby—he hadn't wanted to risk loving again. Mama was dead, and so were Laura and their baby—he wouldn't see them again in this lifetime. But Josie had been miraculously restored to them. And if Chris ever got up the courage to ask Trevor one all-important question, maybe he'd finally find the older brother he'd once loved unreservedly—the brother who could do no wrong—in the man Trevor was now. Which meant it was still possible to find his mother and lay her to rest, the one remaining thing he desperately wanted to accomplish.

Holly seemed to understand what he meant when he said he didn't want to lose her, seemed to understand the lurking fear he refused to name but couldn't completely banish. "I can't promise not to die," she told him solemnly. "No one can promise that. But I *can* promise I'll love you, now and forever. Because love...enduring love…is a choice. And I choose you, Chris. I will always choose you."

The lump in his throat was back, but all he could think of to say was "Does this mean I get to be the boss of you sometimes?"

Her gurgle of laughter warmed the lonely place in his heart the way it had from the first time he'd heard it. The way it always would. "If I get to be the boss of you sometimes, too," she told him, her soft brown eyes alight with the laughter they would always bring to each other.

"Then I have nothing to worry about," he assured her, "because you already are that. Sometimes," he hastened to add, needing to be completely honest with her.

She laughed again, her twinkling eyes telling him she knew exactly the kind of man he was, flaws and all… and she loved him anyway. Then she kissed him, and in that instant he knew he was going to be all right. *They* were going to be all right.

Ethan had said it best. *I thought I could cut myself off from life.* Chris had thought that, too, but Holly had proved him wrong. You couldn't play it safe where life was concerned. Where love was concerned. You had to risk it all. You had to put your heart out there where it could get trampled, hoping and praying it wouldn't.

His heart *had* been trampled. There was no denying that. But Holly had healed him. She'd seen something in him worth loving, so she'd somehow mended the cracks. His heart wasn't good as new, it was *better*—because loving and losing and loving again had taught him never to take anything for granted, and he never would again. The really important things in life didn't entail proving a darn thing to anyone—except proving his love to those he cared about. It was a long list—something he finally acknowledged—and getting longer every day. Heading that list was Holly.

"Life is good," he murmured, drawing Holly back against him so they could look out at all his brothers and sisters together again...finally. And all his and Holly's friends also in attendance at their engagement party. Family. Good friends. Almost everything a man needed to make life worth living. Almost. Only one thing was missing from the picture—the one thing that was no longer missing from his life.

He curved his arms around Holly's waist, holding his future securely. "Life is good."

* * * * *

SPECIAL EXCERPT FROM

HARLEQUIN®

INTRIGUE

One night, when Mary Cardwell Savage is lonely, she sends a letter to Chase Steele, her first love. Little does she know that this action will bring both Chase and his psychotic ex-girlfriend into her life…

Read on for a sneak preview of Steel Resolve *by* New York Times *and* USA TODAY *bestselling author B.J. Daniels.*

The moment Fiona found the letter in the bottom of Chase's sock drawer, she knew it was bad news. Fear squeezed the breath from her as her heart beat so hard against her rib cage that she thought she would pass out. Grabbing the bureau for support, she told herself it might not be what she thought it was.

But the envelope was a pale lavender, and the handwriting was distinctly female. Worse, Chase had kept the letter a secret. Why else would it be hidden under his socks? He hadn't wanted her to see it because it was from that other woman.

Now she wished she hadn't been snooping around. She'd let herself into his house with the extra key she'd had made. She'd felt him pulling away from her the past few weeks. Having been here so many times before, she was determined that this one wasn't going to break her heart. Nor was she going to let another woman take him from her. That's why she had to find out why he hadn't called, why he wasn't returning her messages, why he was avoiding her.

HIEXP0619

They'd had fun the night they were together. She'd felt as if they had something special, although she knew the next morning that he was feeling guilty. He'd said he didn't want to lead her on. He'd told her that there was some woman back home he was still in love with. He'd said their night together was a mistake. But he was wrong, and she was determined to convince him of it.

What made it so hard was that Chase was a genuinely nice guy. You didn't let a man like that get away. The other woman had. Fiona wasn't going to make that mistake, even though he'd been trying to push her away since that night. But he had no idea how determined she could be, determined enough for both of them that this wasn't over by a long shot.

It wasn't the first time she'd let herself into his apartment when he was at work. The other time, he'd caught her and she'd had to make up some story about the building manager letting her in so she could look for her lost earring.

She'd snooped around his house the first night they'd met—the same night she'd found his extra apartment key and had taken it to have her own key made in case she ever needed to come back when Chase wasn't home.

The letter hadn't been in his sock drawer that time.

That meant he'd received it since then. Hadn't she known he was hiding something from her? Why else would he put this letter in a drawer instead of leaving it out along with the bills he'd casually dropped on the table by the front door?

Because the letter was important to him, which meant that she had no choice but to read it.